The
KEEPER
of
LONELY
SPIRITS

The
KEEPER
of
LONELY
SPIRITS

E.M. ANDERSON

/||MIRA

/// MIRA™

ISBN-13: 978-0-7783-6852-6

The Keeper of Lonely Spirits

Recycling programs
for this product may
not exist in your area.

For questions and comments about the quality of this book, please contact us at CustomerService@Harlequin.com.

TM is a trademark of Harlequin Enterprises ULC.

Mira
22 Adelaide St. West, 41st Floor
Toronto, Ontario M5H 4E3, Canada
MIRABooks.com

Printed in U.S.A.

Author's Note

This is a cozy book. There are plants. There are birds. There's a cast whose collective love language is feeding people, because I can't write a book *without* feeding-people-is-love.

That said, this is also a sad book. On purpose. Sorry about that. While cozy, the story deals heavily with grief and loss. The main character has anxiety and experiences panic attacks on the page. Another character has depression. Several characters experience dissociation and flashbacks on the page, discuss or remember past suicide attempts, and think back to or experience the death of close family members. Additionally, parts of the story involve bodily injury, and there are brief mentions of physical abuse, homophobia and alcoholism.

If any of these topics might be triggering for you, you may want to proceed with caution or even set the book aside. Of course, I hope you'll read it. But it's more important to me that you be well.

If you do set the book aside, I hope that, should you pick it up again someday, it'll be as much of a comfort to you as it is to me.

to grandpa

1

A spirit was lurking in the stairwell of the historic steps on Savannah's waterfront.

For months, the steps had been even more treacherous than usual. Not only tourists but folks who had lived in Savannah all their lives had slipped going up or down—skinned knees, scraped hands, laughed nervously and said they must have missed a stair or misjudged the height. A few accused friends of pushing them, but said friends vehemently denied it, accusing the accusers of clumsiness in turn.

At last, a tourist had broken a leg and threatened to sue the city. Never mind the signs at either end, warning users the steps were historical and therefore not up to code. The signs probably would have prevented the success of such a lawsuit, but the city, tired of complaints, hung caution tape across the stairwell, and closure signs for good measure, and turned their attention to other things.

Unbeknownst to them, the unassuming old white man standing before the steps in the wee hours of a mild April morning hoped to solve their problem before the sun rose.

He didn't look like a ghost-hunter. He was tall and thin, with blue eyes, a hawkish nose, and thin lips that rarely smiled. Just now, a messenger bag was slung over his shoulder. Dressed in flannel, jeans, and work boots, he looked like a farmer—which he wasn't but had been in his boyhood some two centuries ago.

Now he was a groundskeeper. At Colonial Park Cemetery for the present, but not for much longer if all went well this morning.

He thumbed up the brim of his flat cap, contemplating the stairwell and the spirit therein. No corporeal form, but a haze of color and smell and emotion, a rotted greenish brown that smelled like Georgia's coastal salt marshes but *more*. The whole stairwell was mucky with fear. Windows rattled in the buildings on either side.

The groundskeeper glanced down the street, saw no one, lifted the caution tape, and stepped under it.

A cloud of fear enveloped him. Rot oozed on his tongue, a phantom feeling of sludge. When he'd been young and freshly cursed, the spirits' swell of emotion had overwhelmed him. He'd drowned in it, unable to separate the feelings of the dead from his own. They'd scared him, the feelings. The voices, not that they were precisely voices. For decades, he'd avoided them when he could, ignored them when he couldn't. Even Jack had never known about them.

These days, the dead comforted him: company he didn't fear losing and never got to know too well. The closest to death he ever came. A reason for him to live, if there were a reason when life had been too long already.

Of course, there was the curse. But the curse wasn't a reason to live so much as the thing keeping him alive.

The windows rattled harder. The rusting metal handrail in the center of the steps groaned.

The groundskeeper sucked in his cheeks, hoping he at last had good information. He'd spotted the spirit right off, soon as he'd visited the east end of River Street, but he'd had a devilish time finding anything out about it. When his usual hunt through libraries and newspapers failed him, he'd resorted to riding around with the tourists on three of Savannah's many ghost tours. The last had set him on the right track, after two hours on a cramped trolley beside an Ohio teen who never once let up complaining.

This ghost tour was nothing, the teen had said. He'd spent loads of time in the cemetery back home, and it was *way* scarier. He'd *seen* ghosts at home. He'd thought they were going to see one on the tour, too, and didn't their guide have any better ghost stories?

The groundskeeper, of course, had actually seen several spirits on the tour. But in the absence of anyone under age twelve, he was the only one. As the trolley bumped over the cobbles, tilting alarmingly on the steep ramp down to River Street, the tourists saw the still water, the three-story riverboat *Georgia Queen* docked alongside the quay, the dark windows of the nineteenth-century storefronts lining the near side of the street. The groundskeeper saw the dead.

Most ghost tours—most ghost stories—were largely hogwash, but they often contained nuggets of truth. In this case, the guide had told the tragic tale of two tween girls who had disappeared less than a year ago. The police had barely bothered looking for them; the disappearance had never been solved. Their ghosts had allegedly been spotted over a dozen times in the last six months, always on the waterfront: they'd ask strangers for help, only to vanish when people tried to take a closer look.

Hogwash—partly. The spirit in the stairwell was a newer one, young and scared, so the groundskeeper had investigated any disappearances reported in Savannah in the past year. In a newspaper article dated nine months back, he'd found a small paragraph mentioning the disappearance of two tween girls and instructing anyone with information to go to the police. Less than a week later, one girl had been found, traumatized but alive, at which point all information about the incident had dried up.

The other girl, the groundskeeper reckoned, had never been found and was likely dead.

What there were of the spirit's memories fit such a story. It remembered neither life nor death, only the confused terror of its last moments. The clearest glimpse the groundskeeper had gotten was the frightened face of a girl: the one who'd been found. This, then, might well be the girl who hadn't.

He'd returned to the waterfront this morning to find out. To send her on, if he could, into whatever awaited in the hereafter, before she did something worse than break a tourist's leg.

"Layla Brown," he said.

The spirit twisted toward him. He let out a soft breath. Finally. The right name. A name alone often wasn't enough to calm a spirit, but names had power, his mam had always said. This spirit's name had been buried nearly as deep as his own: Peter Shaughnessy, a name no one now living knew and the last connection he had—aside from an old pocket watch—to his family and the place he'd been born and raised and cursed.

"Layla Brown," he repeated more forcefully.

The spirit shuddered. The nearest window splintered.

"Sure, there's no need for that. Ain't here to bother you none. Here to help, is all."

She hung over him like a storm cloud. His heart stuttered, but he reassured himself that she couldn't touch him. His messenger bag was filled with iron, salt, yellow flowers, various herbs.

She could bust a window over his head, though. If she was stronger than he thought, she could whip up a wind that'd send him tumbling down the steps, same as if she'd pushed him herself.

"Died bad, it seems," he said softly. "Never found. That right?"

The rot soured, her fear tinged with regret. She wasn't strong enough to take form, but a faint whisper echoed in his ears. Even that much took more power than most ghosts had, but speech took less than corporeality.

Keisha.

And he knew what she wanted.

"They found Keisha," he said. "Whatever happened to you, she didn't share in it."

The spirit wheeled and shifted. Wind moaned, ruffling his shirt and the caution tape behind him. Images flashed before his eyes like a slideshow. That same frightened face he'd seen before: Keisha. A rough hand gripping a thin wrist. The steps, slick with rain. A sudden burst of pain in her temple, a scream, sneakers squeaking. Then, nothing.

She was remembering her death.

The wind howled in the stairwell. The groundskeeper slipped, gripped the shaking handrail. Shivered, blinked the images away before they could overwhelm him.

"Layla!" he shouted. "Layla Brown!"

A window shattered. The groundskeeper ducked, hoping the building was empty at this hour. Glass rained on his cap. She'd gripped onto his words about what had happened to her, same as she'd held tight to her fear the past nine months. If he didn't remind her of something else soon, there'd be no calming her.

He dug into his messenger bag, searching for the beaded bracelet he'd stashed there yesterday afternoon. He hadn't wanted to use it, if he didn't have to, aware of its importance and concerned so small a thing might be destroyed or lost in the confrontation.

"Layla Brown," he repeated, more forcefully than ever as the wind threatened to swallow his voice. The caution tape fluttered, ripped itself from its fastenings, and blew away. "Look here."

He thrust the bracelet out.

The wind died. The windows stopped rattling. The handrail stilled. A thin, butter-yellow strand of affection threaded through the greenish brown of the spirit's fear.

A new memory emerged. Two girls, younger, maybe ten or so, singing loudly and off-key to a pop song as they braided embroidery floss into friendship bracelets. They shouted out the chorus and fell giggling to the ground, pelting each other with lettered beads.

The bracelet in the groundskeeper's hand was grubbier now. The embroidery floss was fraying; the lettering on one of the beads had worn away. But it was still legible.

Best friends 4ever.

Keisha Adeyemi had tied it to a fence post during the candlelight vigil for Layla Brown held outside their middle school not two days ago.

"Keisha's all right," the groundskeeper said. "Newspaper didn't say much but that she'd been found, but she left that for you."

The spirit softened. The rotten fearful smell lessened, the feeling of sludge on his tongue with it. He breathed deep. Used to it, he was, after dealing with the dead for so long, but it was a relief nonetheless when they calmed down.

"She's all right," he repeated. "But you been scaring people—hurt some of 'em, too. Aye, you have."

She rattled a window, not as vigorously as before, annoyed with the accusation. She'd never hurt anyone in her life, she insisted.

"In life, maybe not. Now you have. Best for you and everyone else if you let go of all that fear and move on, now you know Keisha's all right."

The handrail groaned, swaying back and forth. The nearest support rattled, then ripped out of the ground, bending the rail and leaving a crack behind. For a moment, he thought he was losing her again.

Then the shaking stopped.

Eyeing the ghost, the groundskeeper bent to examine the crack. Wedged into the stone was a friendship bracelet matching the one in his hand. More of the lettering was worn away; the braiding was frayed and broken. The groundskeeper plucked it carefully from the stone with a handkerchief, like it was made of diamonds and pearls instead of embroidery floss and plastic beads. The spirit sighed around him.

"This one's yours, is it?"

She confirmed it. He hesitated.

"You understand," he said, "likely they won't find who done this to you even if I send it along."

She agreed, going gray like the Spanish moss draping Savannah's many live oaks. Not scared, now. Just sad and regretful, wishing she weren't dead.

The groundskeeper ignored that particular wish. His own wants, to the extent he allowed himself any, tended the opposite way. He empathized with the dead, understood them. But he envied them, too.

"No helping that, now. I'll make sure whoever you want to have it gets it. Promise. But you got to let go. All right?"

She twisted over the twin bracelets in his hands, faintly yellow again. Glad to know her friend was okay, if nothing else.

He wished he could do more for her. Spirits of children were among his least favorites. Not because of the spirits themselves—they were no worse, nor better, than any others. He just didn't like knowing how young they'd died, and so often terribly.

"Tell me about Keisha," he said.

She didn't speak, of course. Instead, she shared memories. Two girls on the swing set, daring each other to jump off the higher they flew. Painting each other's nails in a bright purple bedroom. Holding hands, skipping home from school in the rain. In every memory, both of them, together.

The groundskeeper's insides twisted. It'd been a long time since he'd been that close with anyone. He said nothing, did nothing, merely stood as silent witness to the ghost's memories of the friend she was leaving behind.

The spirit glowed softly gold, shimmering like morning mist.

As the memories faded, she faded alongside them, until at last she winked out.

The stairwell was dark and empty, the air clear. Layla Brown's fear had gone along with her.

The groundskeeper breathed deep, feeling like a weight had lifted off him. For a moment, he was satisfied. Another spirit sent on, at peace now, he hoped. Living folks saved further trouble, even if none of them realized it.

Then he looked at the bent handrail, the busted support, the shattered glass, and he sighed. Easier to deal with a haunting's aftermath when the spirit was confined to a cemetery, where there was less to destroy and destruction could more easily be explained by natural phenomenon.

He stuck the support back in the stone and reattached the rail, swept the glass to the side. He found the caution tape a ways down the street. Best he could, he hung it back across the stairwell's entrance before trudging uphill and uptown to tie the two friendship bracelets back on the fence by the school.

II

Few people noticed the groundskeeper. Those who did could not have told anyone anything significant about him. They knew nothing of his mother, brother, or sister; of Jack; of the tragedy that had exiled him from Ireland and the fey creature whose curse ensured he could never return, even as it stretched his life long past its expiration. To wander eternally far from home—that was his curse, the full focus of his life, but no one who met him knew of it.

The young waitress at his usual hole-in-the-wall diner, for example, a white SCAD student with a multicolored undercut who'd served him breakfast twice a week for the past six months. Molly. If asked about him, she would've shrugged and said, *Always orders eggs and grits with his coffee. Doesn't say much.* If further asked whether she liked him, she would've said, *Sure. He tips well.*

As he entered this morning, Molly sang out a greeting, calling him Stretch instead of Peter because—like everyone else—she didn't know his name. He nodded at her, sat at the counter like always, and opened an abandoned newspaper, more so no one would talk to him than because he was looking for anything. Now that Layla Brown was gone, all he was looking for was his next hunt.

Savannah had been warm and pleasant through the winter

months. With its dearth of spirits, a shocking number even for a city this age and size, it had kept him busy. It was old, and he always felt more at home in old cities. Easier to be two centuries old in a city still older; new cities, new streets, new buildings chafed him like a woolen sweater.

But he'd sent four different spirits onward in the last six months. Dangerous, staying in one place so long. He came to like it. He came to know people, despite his efforts not to, like the bright-haired waitress whose name and major and favorite menu items he knew.

It was time to move on.

Smiling, Molly topped off his coffee. "Something on your mind there, Stretch? You're taking an awful long time with your breakfast."

The groundskeeper dimpled at her, as close as he ever came to smiling himself. "Heading out soon enough. Work to do."

"I won't tell your boss you're running late if you don't." She moved on.

Draining his coffee, the groundskeeper left some crumpled bills, the newspaper, and his half-eaten breakfast on the counter and left. He wouldn't see her again.

The sun was rising now, throwing long shadows across Savannah's streets. Dawn light limned the buildings' edges, same as the memories only the groundskeeper could see wafting faintly from stones and bricks and planks. Errant spirits dripped from live oaks. The sidewalk shone hazily.

The live oaks grumbled as the groundskeeper passed. As he did the dead, the groundskeeper understood plants. He heard their speech in the rustling of leaves or the groaning of a tree, knew their deepest fears and desires and all the secrets of their restless green hearts.

The live oaks were his favorites. They were quiet and gruff but not unfriendly. Reminded him of himself, except that they grew toward each other. Their gnarled branches arced over streets to embrace the oaks on the other side. As they spoke, their voices tangled together. It made the groundskeeper's insides ache.

When he arrived at Colonial Park Cemetery, the usual early-morning visitors were waiting. He unlocked the gate. Joggers flooded inside, followed by dog walkers. Last came a widow named Madge Wilkins, an octogenarian Black lady who dressed unfailingly in bright red, from her kitten heels to her pillbox hat. She patted the groundskeeper's arm.

"Leaving it a little late this morning, aren't you?" she said cheerfully.

Grunting noncommittally, he gave her his arm. Sometimes she brought her cane (also red), but not always. He'd noticed she had some trouble walking without it.

She said nothing as he deposited her at her habitual bench, for which he was grateful. He had a terrible suspicion they might almost become friends if she spoke to him more.

As if she'd heard his thoughts, she patted the bench beside her. The groundskeeper hesitated.

"Got work to do."

Madge scoffed. "You're late already. Might as well let it go a little longer and humor an old woman."

He sat, twisting his flat cap in his hands.

They watched the sun climb higher. It gilded the tips of the cemetery's wrought iron fence, the trees inside, the historical markers scattered among tombstones and vaults. Spanish moss danced in the breeze. Spirits wavered across the grounds, so numerous the cemetery looked like it was underwater.

Older, these ghosts. Barely present, mists colored only faintly with emotion. Since none were causing trouble, the groundskeeper had left them alone, same as he left the green flickers drifting in the treetops. Will-o'-the-wisps. All spirits eventually faded to wisps, if they didn't move on first, and so many didn't.

"Do you know why I come here so often?" Madge asked.

The groundskeeper cleared his throat. "Ain't because your husband's buried here, that's certain."

She chuckled. Colonial Park had ceased new burials in the 1860s. "I may be old, but I'm not that old. No. Eddie and I used to walk here every morning before he went to work. It's funny, you know. He's over in Greenwich, and I do visit him there sometimes. But I feel him more here, sitting on this bench like we used to."

The groundskeeper said nothing. He didn't know whether Edward Wilkins had left a spirit. One thing was certain, however. If Edward Wilkins had lingered after death, he hadn't done so at Colonial Park. The groundskeeper would've seen him by now. Likely he was at Greenwich with his remains, although if he'd been cremated he could've been anywhere. The Wilkinses' house, or their pew at church, or his office at work, even clinging to Madge herself. Anywhere important to him in life.

"I don't know why I asked you to sit." Madge fiddled with her wedding ring. "I wanted to sit *with* someone for once, I suppose. It's not the same sitting alone, you know."

He knew. He still remembered with aching clarity the morning long ago when he'd awoken alone for the first time in the bed he'd shared for so many years with Jack.

A spirit sighed through the nearest tree. The groundskeeper rubbed his knees, already feeling it had been a mistake to humor her by sitting at all. He was about to point out, again, that he had work to do when Madge said blithely, "Well, anyway."

Her eyes were a little too bright, but the groundskeeper merely nodded. "Nice seeing you, Mrs. Wilkins."

"Yes, of course, honey. You, too."

Still blithe, like she hadn't said anything about the husband she'd lost only months ago, but her hands were scrunched in her skirt and her eyes were too bright and turned determinedly on a distant grave. The groundskeeper's heart clenched, but he went to his work without another word. Except where they were threatened by spirits, the living weren't his problem. His business began and ended with the dead.

At lunchtime, the groundskeeper returned to the cramped studio he'd been living in, over a hundred-year-old brick garage on Perry Lane. Upon first moving in, he'd caught a glimpse of the memories the building held: a pair of horses snorting and stamping, back when it had been a stable; a little girl sneaking in to see them; the faint fondness whoever had left the memories had felt for her.

Most times, memories were so faint the groundskeeper could ignore them. Buildings' walls shone softly with them, but he didn't see details unless he focused. The garage's memories had been clearer but easy to blink away without resorting to the tricks the groundskeeper had used before to keep buildings' memories at bay. He'd been more concerned that these memories heralded a spirit: the people who left the strongest memories were also most likely to leave spirits, especially powerful ones. But whatever long-dead inhabitant had left them here had either left no ghost—at least not on the property—or already moved on.

As he entered now, the potted plants on every surface greeted him with a chorus of questions; he'd been gone all night.

"Aye, it's time," he said, opening the steamer trunk at the foot of his bed. "Going back north for the summer."

Sometimes it took an effort to decide on a new place to go. Not so this time. On the last ghost tour, when he'd been stuck beside that Ohio teen, he'd noted the details of the teen's claim that he'd seen a ghost in his hometown.

Harrington, Ohio. A small town not far from Toledo, with a ghost—if the teen was to be believed—strong enough to take corporeal form. Razzed by the Savannah cousins on the ghost tour with him, the young Ohioan had insisted the ghost had appeared before him, whispered a threat, and chased him from the property.

What property was unclear, but since the teenager had mentioned spending time in the cemetery, the groundskeeper would start there. As they often were, the story was likely less true than claimed. But despite his cousins' teasing, the teen had not backed down. If the apparition had indeed been corporeal and seen as recently as the teen had said, it might mean trouble. Few spirits were strong enough to take corporeal form; those that could were most often angry or fearful. And while small children could see spirits, same as the groundskeeper could, half of them lost the ability by age eight. By age twelve, the number was down to zero, with fair few exceptions. A ghost who'd taken form, visible even to someone maybe fifteen years old, was a ghost liable to cause trouble.

By eight that evening, the groundskeeper was on a train, watching coastal Georgia slide away out the window. Despite himself, he thought of Madge Wilkins. Something faintly like regret tugged at him, but he shoved it away. Regret was nothing new to him after all. Better regret than the ache of losing mortal friends.

He busied himself with his notepad, writing down every detail of the Ohio teen's ghost story. He'd be in Harrington in two days.

Harrington was not quite sure where the new groundskeeper had come from.

The mayor assumed the cemetery director had hired him. The director assumed the board of trustees had hired him. The board assumed the mayor had hired him, considered an action to discourage such overreaches, and decided they were too busy to bother.

As Savannah had before it—as so many towns and cities had before that—Harrington, Ohio, collectively shrugged and accepted his presence.

The first person who met him was the cemetery director. Nevaeh Key-Flores was a tall Black woman in her early thirties, with wide, dark eyes, sepia skin, and black hair usually braided and hidden in a satin wrap. For the six months since taking this position, she'd biked the five blocks from her studio apartment to Harrington Public Cemetery every morning to unlock the gates: 8 a.m. in winter, 7 a.m. in summer.

When she arrived one chilly, late-April morning, the gates were already open. They thrust wrought iron points into the blue-gray dawn, the one break in the cemetery's moss-furred stone wall.

Nevaeh wheeled toward them cautiously, but they were

thrown wide. Not cracked as if college kids had busted in to drink and smash empty bottles on the headstones.

The groundskeeper thumbed up the brim of his flat cap as she entered. He was a white man in his seventies, shorter than she was—of course; most people were. He might've been her height when he was younger, but now he stooped a little, as old men did. He wore her father's go-to outfit, flat cap aside: long-sleeved flannel, aged jeans, and work boots, the uniform of Harrington's farmers.

His blue eyes were abundant with crow's feet and startling bright in his sun-bronzed face. A shovel was stuck in the ground beside him.

"Morning," he said, but Nevaeh didn't immediately realize he'd spoken. His voice felt as much a part of the dawn as the robins singing.

"Who unlocked the gates?"

"I did. Found a spare key in the caretaker's cottage."

Nevaeh gripped her handlebars. "What were you doing in the caretaker's cottage?"

He extended a hand. "I'm your new groundskeeper."

She smiled tightly. She wasn't sure what the board of trustees did, but it wasn't anything along the lines of caring for the cemetery. They'd hemmed and hawed when she'd asked to hire someone two months ago. After appointing the cemetery's first Black director, they'd sat back, congratulated themselves, and ignored her.

It figured they'd finally hire someone without telling her.

She supposed she ought to be glad they'd bothered. She needed the help.

Her smile relaxed as the groundskeeper shook her hand. His fingers were rough and calloused, but his grip was gentle.

It wasn't his fault the board were assholes.

"Nevaeh Key-Flores," she said. Soil crescented his fingernails. "You're not wearing gloves."

"Wear 'em when I need to. Like feeling the dirt."

He turned back to the headstone. Weeds crowded its engraving, as they did most. The old director had neglected the place, same as the board did.

Nevaeh adjusted her hair wrap, amethyst-colored today. She didn't need the engraving to identify this headstone. It was why she'd moved back to Harrington, even though the town's changes deepened her depression. Why she'd fought for this job. Why her mother had called her crying, multiple times, and her granny had begged her to come home. Her granny never begged.

But she hadn't been able to face cleaning the headstone up yet.

The groundskeeper cleared the weeds. She wasn't sure how. He didn't pluck them; he prodded them, saying, "Budge up, now," and—she blinked—were they weeds? Overgrown, sure, but in bloom and awfully pretty: blue phlox, violet, wild geranium.

"Figured coreopsis by this one." The groundskeeper trailed his finger along the headstone. "What d'you think?"

Nevaeh's eyes prickled. Harrington's negative spaces, spaces in the shape of her father, were the freshest and worst change. "Coreopsis was my dad's favorite."

The groundskeeper nodded but said nothing.

Nevaeh blinked her tears away. "I have paperwork to do. If you don't need anything?"

"I'll be fine." The groundskeeper nodded at the headstone. "We're good friends already."

She laughed, or maybe sniffled. "I'll check in at lunchtime."

She bent her head over her handlebars and wheeled toward the office.

The groundskeeper leaned on his shovel. The spirit at his side formed itself into a question. Sweet but tart, like an early peach.

"Oh, she does," the groundskeeper said. "She absolutely does."

He lingered by Elijah Key-Flores's headstone. A sense of love as strong and yellow as a dandelion had flared up when Nevaeh appeared. Now it stretched toward the office, reminding the groundskeeper of things he'd rather leave buried. Winter nights in Ballygar, when the livestock was bedded down and he and Eoin and Catherine gathered around the hearth to listen to Mam's stories while she darned socks. Chilly mornings in Melbourne, wrapped up warm in bed with Jack's arms around him. Savannah hadn't reminded him so much of all that, with its subtropical climate, its live oaks and cabbage palms.

Maybe he should've stayed south, and never mind the miserable summers.

He focused on the wildflowers around Elijah's grave, shutting out that dandelion-yellow love, and coaxed the geranium into being coreopsis instead.

A minty note of curiosity permeated the yellow. The air hummed with questions felt more than heard: what he was doing, how he was doing it. Whether it was magic.

"Mmm?"

A clump of coreopsis bloomed bright yellow. Elijah flinched, a jolt disrupting the mint of his questions.

The groundskeeper persuaded the yellow blooms to turn pink. The ghost relaxed.

"Magic?" the groundskeeper said absently. "Sure, if you want to call it that. I say I'm just a man who knows his plants."

IV

At lunchtime, the groundskeeper was nowhere to be found. Nevaeh sighed, hoping he wasn't in the creepy, wooded back lot.

If she ignored the neglect, Harrington Public Cemetery was beautiful. Honeysuckle draped the front walls, not yet blooming. Pines and redbuds sprinkled the lawn. Forsythia burst into golden sprays along the eastern wall. A magnolia spread its branches in the northeast corner, and lilacs that hadn't bloomed in years clumped in the northwest; maybe the groundskeeper could revive them. With Nevaeh in charge, the grass was mowed, though she kept it longer than at most cemeteries: she'd read that would decrease weeds.

The back lot, however, was the original cemetery's site and as creepy as expected of a centuries-old graveyard. Trees, so dark and hoary they starred in local ghost stories, shrouded crumbling headstones with engravings weathered to nothing. Ashmead Creek ran east to west through the trees before widening and cutting northwestward, slicing Harrington in two. A stone bridge—old as the headstones and crumbling worse—arced over its narrowest point, the only crossing within cemetery walls.

Nevaeh had spent one hour back there so far, to see whether it was worth salvaging for historical reasons. Her skin had prickled the whole time, like something was watching her.

Smoke coiled from the caretaker's cottage; the groundskeeper must have moved in. Nevaeh eyed the building suspiciously. She hadn't bothered repairing the cottage, since demolishing it would've taken less work. The roof needed reshingling. Time had worn the exterior smooth. A stone wall hugged the house, enclosing an overgrown garden. Snarled wisteria half hid the door, a family of swifts had claimed the chimney, and leggy vines clung to the decaying chicken coop out back.

If the groundskeeper found charm in the crumbling cottage, he could have it. Nevaeh didn't need anything from it. The riding mower and pickup truck were in a storage shed and driveway nearby; her office was in the small but modern building to its west.

The cottage door stood open. Nevaeh stepped past the half-rotted gate, into the tangled garden, and peered inside.

Plants on every surface. Monstera, orchids, pothos, jade, widow's-thrill. Plants Nevaeh didn't consider houseplants, like the Saint-John's-wort in the terra-cotta pot on the floor. Plants she didn't recognize.

Only the faded love seat under the window to her right and the austere little bed and steamer trunk in the back of the room were plant-free. And even the love seat's upholstery was floral-patterned. It reminded her of her grandmother's couch.

"Hello?"

A muffled voice greeted her from the back. "Come on in. I was just having a bite."

"Yeah, me, too. After." Nevaeh ducked to avoid the ceiling and picked through trailing leaves. "Should I shut the door?"

"Nay, leave it. The greenlings like their air."

Nevaeh frowned, mouthing *greenlings* to herself, but she joined the groundskeeper in the cramped kitchen. There was a bit of counter on either side of the sink, an ancient icebox, a corded phone on the wall, and a round table tucked into the corner with two chairs. Sunlight streamed through the window over the sink. The top half of the Dutch door in the back corner was open, affording a view of the garden, the slope, and the forest beyond.

The trees stood silent and dark. Nevaeh rubbed her arms.

"What're you having?" the groundskeeper asked.

"Mmm?" Plants abounded here, too. Various herbs, mostly. Lemon balm. Sage. Spearmint. Basil. Sharp-scented and earthy. "Oh. It's one of those frozen dinners."

The groundskeeper stirred an oniony stew simmering on the stove. He wore a faded pink apron spotted with tomato paste. A smile tugged at Nevaeh's lips, but she suppressed it.

"Sure, a frozen dinner." The groundskeeper tasted a fingerful of stew and added a pinch of salt. "I had one once. Don't remember much about it."

"They're not very memorable," Nevaeh said, "but they're cheap and they're fast."

She lingered in the doorway. The plumbing and electricity worked, but the icebox hummed worryingly.

Unsurprising. It looked older than the groundskeeper.

He paused in his stirring. "Welcome to some of mine, if you'd rather."

Nevaeh gave the tiny space another glance. The only chair, aside from his own, was already occupied by a pot of bulbs.

"I wouldn't want to impose," she said uncertainly.

The groundskeeper glanced at her. Not at her: at the space beside her, she thought, though there was nothing there.

"No bother."

He shifted the bulbs onto the table, rearranging herbs to make room.

"I know that's your spot," he said, like the bulbs had spoken, "but we have company. Sit down, lass."

Nevaeh perched on the chair with her hands folded. The bulbs nodded at her, ruffled by the breeze. She repressed an urge to apologize to them.

The groundskeeper ladled stew into two bowls. He set one before her, alongside a crusty hunk of bread. Steam wafted from the bowl.

He joined her. "Tuck in."

She scalded her tongue on the first bite. He paused in blowing on his bowl.

"It's hot," he said, helpfully. He pointed his spoon toward the cottage's front. "Weeded by the gates this morning. Figured you'd want me to start up yonder so's we make a good first impression. But there's a couple headstones need repairing."

Nevaeh swallowed a spoonful of stew, not sure why he was telling her.

"I can take care of 'em, if you want," he said. "Done a fair bit of headstone repair in my day."

Right. She'd come to check in, not eat. She'd forgotten, thrown by the plants, the stew, and the offer of lunch.

After far too long a pause, she said, "That'd be great. I don't suppose you know how to repair historic headstones? I've been considering preserving the original cemetery. There's actually a historian coming in to catalog the graves. David Schwertner. Old family friend."

She shredded her bread.

"To be honest," she continued, "I'm out of my depth. I have three degrees in public administration, but my background is in urban parks. I've never handled a cemetery. I wouldn't be back here at all if I hadn't lost my—"

She clamped her lips. A tractor's wreckage loomed before her, eclipsing everything else.

Her chest caved in. Panic coiled around her stomach and heart and lungs. She squeezed crumbled bread in her fist.

A hand on her shoulder anchored her like tree roots. The tractor dissolved.

She shuddered. The sunlight faded like an old photograph. As if in concern, the bulbs dipped toward her.

"Sorry," Nevaeh whispered.

The groundskeeper squeezed her shoulder. "Happens sometimes."

The Dutch door slammed.

Nevaeh jumped, her spoon clattering to the floor. She dragged a hand over her face.

The groundskeeper latched the door.

"Hsst," he said under his breath. His smile, when he turned to her, was strained. "Beg pardon for the scare. Work to do on this old place yet. All right now?"

She nodded, shoving her bowl aside. Her heart pounded so hard she felt sick.

He retrieved her spoon and wiped stew off the floor. She felt silly: for panicking in the middle of a normal conversation, for flinching because a door had slammed, for not grabbing the spoon herself.

"It was my dad," she blurted.

He got to his feet, frowning at her. Her cheeks burned. She looked away.

His expression cleared as he took her meaning. "Sure, that's hard. A boy, I was, when my pa died."

Nevaeh hugged herself. "I hate being back here. Nothing's the same anymore."

The groundskeeper washed her spoon. "Feels that way, when someone passes."

It was more than that. True, those negative spaces glared in her mind. The kitchen table where her father and his friends had played poker on Thursday nights, empty now unless her mother had a night off from the hospital or her grandmother stayed home from bingo. The hardware store her father had frequented on weekends whether he needed anything or not. The diner they'd gone to for Saturday-morning breakfasts when she was a kid, just the two of them.

But even before, she hadn't liked coming home. When she was ten, the diner's entire waitstaff had known her name. The last time they'd gone for breakfast, over a year ago, she hadn't recognized the servers, and they hadn't recognized her. It was like that everywhere: old stores had closed; old houses had been condemned; old schoolmates had married or had children or moved away. Harrington changed with each visit, like it had grown up without her. She felt out of place in her own hometown.

Feeling out of place in Cleveland had been easier: she could tell herself she hadn't settled in yet.

She couldn't explain that to a stranger, however. Never mind that he'd made her lunch.

She sniffed, hard. "They say it gets better."

The therapist she'd seen exactly once did, anyway. Her hand strayed to her pocket, where an appointment card shamed her for canceling that morning. Again.

The groundskeeper sagged against the sink. "Do they, now?"

Creases scored his forehead. Nevaeh might've misjudged his age; he looked much older, suddenly.

He straightened, clearing his throat. "Historic headstones. Sure, I can fix those. You tell your historian friend to make a list of which ones need repairing, and I'll take care of 'em."

Maybe she'd guessed his age right after all. Just her panic attack and out-of-placeness and the faded sunlight making him look as gray as his cottage.

He hustled her out, all strained smiles and promises to get back to work after cleaning up. Nevaeh returned to her office, fridged her Salisbury steak, and worked on a report for the board.

She couldn't stop replaying the conversation, wondering if she'd upset him. If she'd overshared. If her panic attack had discomfited him. If, if, if.

What had really worried him, of course, was the Dutch door.

But Nevaeh didn't think of that.

V

The groundskeeper watched until Nevaeh reached her office. Then he spoke into the empty cottage.

"Elijah Key-Flores."

So brilliantly warm and yellow when the spirit entered, the air had, at his daughter's panic, rotted to the same greenish brown that had colored the stairwell in Savannah. Now, the greenlings shuddered like their roots had sprouted mold. The doors rattled at their hinges.

The groundskeeper sucked in his cheeks. He should've warded everything when he arrived. He should've sent Nevaeh away when the spirit followed her inside, giving the Saint-John's-wort a wide berth.

But while the groundskeeper avoided friendship, he couldn't stand to see a living thing hurt. She'd been sad this morning, no less so by lunchtime. She'd been unenthusiastic about her frozen dinner.

And he hadn't expected danger from her father.

In the kitchen, the pot rattled off the stove and flipped onto the floor. Herbs shrieked as hot stew splashed them. The groundskeeper flinched.

"Elijah Key-Flores." Likely the ghost's name alone wouldn't stop its tomfoolery, but it was what he had. "Your little girl's fine.

She misses you something fierce, but she's a grown woman. She'll get by. You scaring her didn't help none."

The doors rattled again, not as angrily. The rotted air grew tart. The greenlings fretted.

"You did, sure. Didn't you see her jump when the door slammed? You scared me, too, that's a fact."

The tartness soured to rue, swallowed up the rot. The greenlings relaxed in a rustling of leaves.

The groundskeeper expelled a long breath. "She'll be fine. But she'd be better if you wouldn't go scaring her when she's already ate up with worriment."

The scent of faded flowers engulfed the groundskeeper.

"Sure, therapy could help her plenty. But these things take time. She'll go when she's ready."

A draft blasted his bones to ice.

Memories ripped through him. Not his.

Elijah's.

A living room phone ringing on a quiet Tuesday night. Elijah's wife, a curvy woman with Nevaeh's sepia skin and rounded chin, laying aside her knitting to answer. She stiffened, turning with panic on her face.

A hospital in another state, clinical and white. A nurse leading them down a hallway.

Nevaeh, much younger, comatose in a cot. Looking so much like she had as a child—head bent into the crook of her shoulder, tight black curls loose and uncovered—but hooked to an IV to flush sleeping pills from her system, eyes ringed with dark circles. Crying when she awoke.

One question haunting Elijah even in death: *Why?*

The groundskeeper collapsed under the memories' weight. No blinking them away this time. In Savannah, Layla Brown's death memories had been just that: her remembering. Now, in the caretaker's cottage in Harrington, Elijah was *pushing* the memories onto him, trying to make him understand.

"Stop," the groundskeeper gasped. *"Stop."*

The memories left him.

He was on his hands and knees in his front room, sweating, shivering despite the afternoon's warmth. The creeping fig curling over the wall clock reached down to stroke his cheek.

The groundskeeper staggered to his feet. His shoulders bowed, burdened by memories.

"You shouldn't've shown me that. It weren't my business."

The air twisted.

"Aye, I see why you fret for her. But that's private, so it is. It weren't yours to tell. It's hers and no one else's." He rubbed his inner arm. His flannel shrouded three long, jagged scars from the last time he'd tried to die. Some thirty years after Jack's death. "I should know."

The spirit huffed, ruffling the greenlings. It slipped from the cottage in a mopey, slate-gray haze.

Slumping against the wall, the groundskeeper listened to the greenlings murmuring amongst themselves. The cottage was dim, smelled of soil and unfurling flowers.

With shaking hands, the groundskeeper cleaned the kitchen. His mind was stuck on that younger Nevaeh unconscious in a hospital bed.

His anger flared. Her father had had no right to show him that, no matter how worried he was.

The groundskeeper paused in drying a bowl. Elijah's *why* rang in his head.

No one understood why. Not even if you explained. Not even if you understood it yourself.

The groundskeeper left the dishes and carved a Marian symbol into the Dutch door's frame with a penknife. Two overlapping *V*s, forming a triangle where their branches met. Not his preferred warding. Too thin and simple. Too easily disrupted.

But it kept ghosts in or out, provided no one destroyed it, and putting it up was quick work.

He carved another into each windowsill and the front door's frame. It would do until he warded everything properly. The cottage. The office and storage shed. Any space on cemetery grounds meant for the living.

He'd dealt with plenty ghosts in his day, ghosts far angrier and more powerful than Elijah. But never in his own house.

At least Elijah had gone back outside. The spirit wouldn't be able to harm anyone once things were warded. And if Nevaeh talked to a therapist about his death—not once, not superficially, but if she stuck with it and truly dealt with the loss—her father would move on to whatever waited beyond. The heaven and hell and in-between the groundskeeper had been raised on back in Ballygar, or reincarnation, or nothing—though he thought "nothing" unlikely.

He carved a final Marian symbol. It might've been a record: less than twenty-four hours in Harrington, and the groundskeeper had already found a ghost scaring folks. More importantly, he knew how to get it to leave. Figuring a ghost out was usually the hard part.

Something niggled at him as he returned to his work, however. The groundskeeper had been dispelling ghosts for over a century. He'd become adept at sussing a spirit's nature right off. Spirits weren't like the living, with a range of moods. Whatever kept them from moving on after death only intensified, subsuming the rest of the emotional spectrum.

Elijah Key-Flores had been all love and concern for his daughter, until he hadn't.

The ghosts the groundskeeper normally dealt with were fear, anger, despair. Powerful spirits for whom slamming doors was another Tuesday. Spirits who destroyed buildings, possessed people, killed livestock, stormed through cities in the guise of strange weather patterns. Who acted out because they were scared or angry or heartbroken and didn't know what else to do.

Maybe Elijah was such a spirit. Maybe even the one the

groundskeeper had come looking for. But if the teen whose tale had sent him to Ohio had been talking about Elijah, the spirit should've been much more powerful. Enough to take corporeal form. Based on what the groundskeeper had seen so far, he thought that doubtful.

As he staked around a killdeer's nest so it wouldn't get mown over, love again stretched toward the office. Bitter, knowing its object had been frightened by its subject. That love made the place feel familiar like nowhere had felt since the groundskeeper left Melbourne in 1905. He wasn't sure why. It wasn't as if he hadn't come across affectionate ghosts before.

He rubbed his inner arm again, unconsciously.

The spirit's unexpected behavior, the memories it had shared without consent—his or Nevaeh's—had rattled him. He'd ward everything tonight. As soon as the cemetery closed.

VI

The kids broke into the cemetery that night. One suggested it, the others teased, the first rebutted, on and on, until all three had to go or admit they were scared.

Thirteen-year-old Sayid al-Masri hesitated, watching his friends clamber down from the al-Masris' tree house. "I told Mama and Baba I'd watch Samira."

Chloe Wu jumped the last few rungs of the tree house ladder. "She's in bed, right? She probably won't even notice we're gone."

In bed, sure, but Samira rarely stayed in bed even when her parents had sent her there. Sayid doing so had resulted in arguing, complaints, and rude names, until he'd persuaded her to go to bed on time in exchange for his doing the dishes next time it was her turn.

Chloe gazed up at him, her hands on her hips. "Are you coming or what?"

Sayid bit his lip. He didn't want Chloe, of all people, to think he was chickening out of something, even though Chloe had known him since they were little and likely expected it. Their other friend, Jess Halowachko, shrugged at him.

"We're coming right back," he said decisively, joining them on the ground.

"Of course," Chloe said. "We're not *doing* anything. We're just getting inside. That's all."

They grabbed their bikes and went.

Night had fallen cool and misty. The string lights over Main Street swayed, flickering as the kids crossed and headed south down Thompson. Long, thin shadows reaching from the spindly Victorians on the east side of the street clutched at the damp grass in the park opposite. Ashmead Creek burbled past the park, a welcome respite from the silence of the sleeping town.

A sedan trundled up the street, ghostly in the mist. Its headlights flashed in the kids' faces. Then it was gone.

They were halfway there when Sayid's eight-year-old sister shouted behind them.

"Wait for me!"

They braked, exasperated. She pedaled hell-for-leather until she caught up.

"You're supposed to be asleep," Sayid said. "I'm not doing the dishes for you if you're not staying in bed."

Samira put her hands on her hips, which would've been more impressive if she weren't a skinny kid in a tank top, shorts, and flip-flops.

"You're supposed to be watching me, so there."

Sayid ignored his friends' giggles. "We're going to the cemetery, Samira. It's going to be really scary. Ghosts and everything."

His sister stuck out her skinny chest. "I'm not scared."

Chloe swallowed her laughter. "Should've known *that* wouldn't work."

"I know," Sayid moaned. Samira hated to be thought scared. Nothing short of carrying her home, locking her inside, and throwing away the key would keep her from following them now.

Probably not even that, given her recent interest in lock picking. He *was* supposed to be watching her.

"Fine. But you better keep up."

She scowled. "I pedal faster than you anyhow."

She beat them to the cemetery to prove it. Hopping off her bike, she rattled the gates. The hinges groaned.

"Don't do that," Sayid hissed.

The stone wall frowned over them.

"It's locked," Samira announced, like the padlock on the gate hadn't clued them in.

"Yeah, I see that." Sayid swatted her hands. "Stop that."

His friends stifled their giggles.

"What now?" Chloe picked at a thumbnail in defiance of her mother's constant adjuration not to. "Are we going in, or...?"

"We can't." Jess fiddled with her braid, her new nervous habit since a boy she'd liked had taunted her for the old habit of chewing on it. "It's locked."

A train moaned in the distance. The three older kids scuffed the sidewalk, relieved not to enter. Sayid, in particular, was relieved at the thought of being home again before anyone noticed they'd left.

"We did come here," Jess said. "We said we'd come, and we did."

"We would've gone in if we could," Chloe added.

"I could pick the lock," Samira said helpfully.

Sayid choked. "Could not!"

Too late. Samira produced a pair of unbent paper clips.

Chloe snorted. Sayid took the paper clips more seriously.

"Samira, don't."

"Why?" Samira struggled with the lock. "Are you scared?"

"We'll get in trouble."

"So you are scared."

"It's illegal!"

Chloe stopped laughing. Jess forgot herself and chewed the tail of her braid.

Chloe picked at her thumbnail. "I don't like this."

"Yeah," Jess said. "Maybe we shouldn't..."

The lock clicked. Samira whooped. The others hushed her.

She slipped the paper clips into her pocket. "You guys are no fun."

She tugged at the gate. It scraped open.

"What are you doing?" Sayid squeaked.

"You *said* you wanted to break in."

"We didn't mean it!"

Samira dumped her bike under the lilac trees and raced up the cemetery lawn, her flip-flops squelching on damp grass. Headstones slept around her.

"Samira," Sayid said in a strangled whisper.

Jess bit her lip. Chloe glanced at her. Throwing down their bikes, they sprinted after Samira.

"Wait," Sayid choked.

The three girls disappeared over the knoll.

Sayid oscillated on the sidewalk, wanting *not* to enter the cemetery but horribly aware of the trouble he'd be in if Samira were missing when his parents returned from dinner.

"Ya Allah," he muttered.

Scared someone would lock up if they saw the gate open after hours, he pulled it closed and placed his bike against the wall. The moonlight threw elongated shadows onto the grass.

Slinking up the knoll, he whacked his shin on a headstone. He blurted a curse, glanced around, and muttered a hasty prayer. Touched the headstone with trembling fingers. Flinched—not at the headstone, but at the sleepy sort of *mintiness* emanating from it.

Curiosity, like someone wanted to know who he was and what he was doing here.

Sayid didn't like it.

He rubbed his fingertips on his jeans, shying away from the small Muslim section of the cemetery around a nearby redbud. Whatever that minty feeling was, he didn't want to know whether he'd feel it bumping into his uncle's headstone, too.

"Samira?" His whisper came out louder than he'd intended. "Chloe? Jess?"

A screech owl whinnied. Sayid's mother had liked to tell tales about owls and death and spirits and omens, back when she had time for such things. His father had scoffed, claiming omens, good or ill, were mere superstition. But an owl screeching in a moonlit graveyard is alarming no matter what you believe.

And while Sayid didn't believe in omens, he didn't *not* believe in them.

"Samira?"

He scrunched his T-shirt in his fists, skittering past headstones. From the crest of the knoll, he could see the caretaker's cottage and the dark trees beyond. He swallowed and trekked downhill.

As he approached, the cottage huddled in its garden. Sayid patted the garden wall like it was a frightened dog.

Something moved in the doorway. Sayid's mouth went dry. "Samira?"

Silence.

Definitely not Samira.

"Chloe? Jess?"

In the garden, an owl hooted. Sayid jerked away as if scalded, heart hammering.

"Guys, this isn't funny!"

A figure detached from the dark maw of the doorway. Sayid screamed.

"Hsst! Hsst, lad, stop your caterwauling. I'm no ghost or ghoul, here, look—look!"

The groundskeeper fumbled for the light switch just inside the door. His hands shook so badly he kept missing it. At last he hit the switch, flooding the front garden with light.

Sayid shied like a spooked horse but didn't run off. His eyes darted toward the groundskeeper, the paintbrush he'd dropped, the paint can on the ground, the symbol half-completed over the doorframe.

Breathing deeply, the groundskeeper peered into the boy's thin brown face. He was slight for his age, with anxious dark eyes and a mop of curly hair.

"See, lad?" the groundskeeper said. "Naught to fear."

"Have you seen my sister?" Sayid blurted.

Footsteps squelched. Sayid tensed, but he relaxed as Chloe and Jess emerged from the darkness.

Then Chloe cried, "We lost her, she went into the woods," and his hands balled up in his T-shirt. So much for getting home quickly. The girls skidded to a halt at the sight of the groundskeeper. Recovering—grateful for an adult to take over the situation—they swarmed around, speaking over each other and Sayid.

"We weren't *really* going to break in—"

"It was Samira—"

"You lost her?"

"It's not *our* fault—"

The groundskeeper shepherded them into the kitchen, flicking more switches. Warm yellow light spilled over everything. The teenagers' words tripped over each other. The greenlings clamored, awoken by the flood of light and noise.

"Hsst!"

The bulbs grumbled as the groundskeeper lifted them onto the table, but Sayid's voice broke through the rumpus.

"Please, sir, she's lost, she could get hurt—"

"Sit," the groundskeeper said. "You, lad, calm down and start over."

The girls perched on the kitchen chairs, glancing around like they expected a ghost to pop out of a cupboard. Chloe picked her thumbnail until the skin cracked and bled. Jess mangled her braid.

Stumbling over hiccups, Sayid explained what had happened. Jess giggled nervously.

Sayid turned overlarge eyes on her. "It's not funny! She's probably—hic—she's probably—hic—she's—hic—hic—"

The groundskeeper plunked hot chocolate before them, shoved water into Sayid's hands, and rummaged the cupboards. Sayid hiccupped through his water.

The groundskeeper reached into the cupboard over the stove. "Drink it upside down."

"Upside—hic—down?"

"Aye." The groundskeeper's fingers brushed an iron cross. He grabbed it. "That's what Mam always said."

Sayid stared, hoping the groundskeeper would elaborate, but he was still rooting around his cupboards. Sayid put his mouth to the cup's far lip, bent forward, and spilled water down his front. He jerked upright, sputtering.

"Are you okay?" Jess asked.

"Yeah." Sayid put the cup in the sink. His T-shirt was damp.

"Your hiccups are gone," Chloe offered.

Sayid twisted his shirt. "Yeah. I guess."

A cupboard banged closed. The teenagers jumped. Slipping salt, herbs, candles, and iron into his messenger bag, the groundskeeper slung the bag over his neck. Out the window, the forest was silent and black, but the warm, bright cottage promised safety.

"Right," the groundskeeper said. "You three stay here. Don't open the doors or windows. Don't leave the house. I'll find— what's her name, lad? Your sister."

"Samira." Sayid made a decision, one he didn't like at all. His voice cracked. "I'm coming with you."

"No," the groundskeeper said, predictably.

Sayid puffed his chest out the way Samira did when confronted with *no*.

"Yes." His voice trembled. "She's my responsibility."

The groundskeeper thought of his siblings. Both younger. He'd never learned when or where Eoin had died. Last Jack had known, he'd emigrated.

Catherine had died on a night like tonight, cool and misty. Midsummer.

He remembered well; he'd been there.

He grasped Sayid's shoulder. His hand was heavy, rough with calluses, but gentle.

"You're a brave lad. But I can't let you come. Could be dangerous."

"It's just a cemetery," Sayid whispered.

However old the groundskeeper was, he suddenly looked far older. He squeezed Sayid's shoulder.

"Stay here."

He slipped outside and was gone.

Sayid clenched and unclenched his fists. He took a deep breath and raced after the groundskeeper, ignoring the calls of his friends.

Like Samira would.

VII

"Wait!"

The groundskeeper kept walking. "Go back, lad."

"Please, sir." Sayid jogged alongside him. "She wouldn't have come here if it weren't for me."

Old, old, *old* memories of Catherine toddling through the market on Midsummer Eve flashed through the groundskeeper's mind, so sudden and painful he faltered.

"Sir?"

The groundskeeper shut the memories away. "Keep close, then. No knowing what might be back in these woods."

He slowed so Sayid could keep pace. The boy clung to him like a cocklebur, bumping into him as they went.

The groundskeeper didn't mind. The closer Sayid stuck, the less likely something would snatch him away, or worse. Thinking of the creature that had cursed him, the groundskeeper clenched his fists. *Them folk* might not be about, but that didn't mean nothing else was. Until he'd explored back here himself—alone, by daylight—he couldn't be sure whether or not angry spirits haunted the forest.

They stopped at the tree line. Moonlight fell silver behind them, but no light penetrated the woods. Oak, sweetgum, buckeye, black walnut, the sycamores whose white trunks gleamed in the sun, all loomed black in the night. Mist twisted through the undergrowth like ghosts.

Sayid moaned, pressing close.

The groundskeeper pulled a braid of Saint-John's-wort from his bag. "Sling this round your neck."

"Why?" Sayid asked, knotting the braid into a circlet.

"Protection. Come on."

The groundskeeper strode onward. Sayid pulled the circlet over his head, deciding he didn't want to know from what he needed protecting. His hand stayed glued to the flowers.

Peepers and chorus frogs sang deep in the woods. Green lights flickered.

Sayid whimpered. "There are eyes in the trees."

"Fireflies, lad." It wasn't the season for fireflies yet. "You're scared, is all."

Keeping an eye on the green flickers, the groundskeeper pulled the iron cross from his bag. Its sharp angles comforted him. The wisps avoided him.

His ears strained. He felt watched.

Something snaked over their shoulders. Sayid yelped, slapping it away.

"Hsst!" The cross dug into the groundskeeper's fist. "S'all right, lad. Here, look."

He held out a trailing branch dotted with yellow catkins. Sayid swallowed.

"Oh." He patted the branch gingerly. "It's a willow tree." He fiddled with the Saint-John's-wort, his voice small. "How are we going to find her?"

"Come on."

More willow branches trailed over them. Sayid whimpered.

The ground turned from dirt to mud to rock. A stone bridge arced over Ashmead Creek, bathed in moonlight where the canopy broke open.

The groundskeeper tested each step as he crossed.

"Step where I step." He paused. One side was crumbling. "Don't touch the sides."

The Ashmead rushed white below. A pair of great horned owls hooted back and forth. Wisps drifted along the creek without crossing.

As they should. The groundskeeper relaxed.

"Samira!" Sayid shouted.

The groundskeeper's heart skipped a beat.

The nocturnal chorus broke off.

Silence pressed in, relieved only by the unconcerned rush of the creek.

The trees were not unconcerned. Their unease crept into the groundskeeper's lungs like a parasitic vine.

The chorus resumed.

Sayid gave a strangled cry, ran back down the bridge, and splashed into the creek.

The groundskeeper followed, mouth dry. "What're you doing?"

Sayid held something up. A little pink flip-flop.

"Your sister's?"

Sayid nodded.

Lighting a candle, the groundskeeper waded to the far bank. A trail of small footprints vanished where the mud hardened to dirt.

He held the candle higher, but the slim flame couldn't penetrate the darkness.

"Stay here."

Sayid's voice quavered. "No way."

"I ain't asking." The groundskeeper softened. "I know you're scared. But trust me when I tell you it's safer out here in the creek than it is in those trees. You keep that Saint-John's-wort round your neck and stay on that bridge, you'll be all right."

"What if you get lost?"

"That's why I need you here, ain't it? If I get lost, I'll yell out, and you yell on back so's I can follow your voice. You'll give a holler when you hear me, won't you? You can do that for me, aye?"

"Okay," Sayid whispered.

"Good lad."

Sayid splashed to shore and scuttled back up the bridge.

The groundskeeper hoped the flowers and stream would be enough to protect the boy. Mam had always said spirits couldn't cross moving water. In the groundskeeper's experience, it was usually true. Moving water, yellow flowers, salt, iron, various shapes and symbols—things ghosts couldn't withstand. Things with which the groundskeeper had protected himself and others over the last century and which had kept Layla Brown's spirit from touching him, that last dark, early morning in Savannah.

But powerful spirits didn't always play by the rules.

The groundskeeper ducked into the trees, the iron cross in one hand and the candle in the other. He liked these sea-salt candles. Hard to find them in manageable sizes, but a candle made from salt was a godsend. The more mischievous spirits snuffed wax candles and deadened flashlights, but they left salt candles alone.

Not that this candle did much good. It threw light barely six inches in front of him. Darkness clawed at the flame like a living thing.

On the other side of the stream, the frogs had been deafening; here, they were silent. Leaves crunched. Twigs snapped underfoot. Trees twisted out of the darkness, muttering at the groundskeeper's intrusion.

He tripped over a headstone so sunken he could decipher only the word MOTHER. A stone beside it read DAUGHTER. The groundskeeper skirted both, his eyes peeled for more. MOTHER and DAUGHTER weren't around anymore, but spirits slumbering nearby might waken if he smacked into their headstones.

"Samira?"

He knew how it sounded, a stranger, a grown man, calling

her name. But he couldn't bring Sayid back here when he didn't yet know what, if anything, lurked in the shadows.

"If you can hear me, your brother's looking for you."

Branches clattered, then fell silent. The groundskeeper shivered. The silence pressed in on him.

He hummed a hymn as he walked, stopping occasionally to call for Samira.

The wisps were absent on this side of the creek, but it felt as if something were watching him.

He hummed louder and walked on.

VIII

Alone on the bridge, Sayid tried to believe the green flickers back on the bank really were fireflies. But they didn't blink like fireflies. They drifted without crossing the water.

The mist thickened to fog, vanishing the creekbanks. Sayid's shorts and sneakers were damp. He clenched the pink flip-flop, shivering.

For a second, he considered how scared Samira must be, wherever she was.

But Samira was never scared. She ruffled at the idea. She was certainly nowhere near as scared as he was, *if* she was scared.

He wished he were like her.

What a horrible prank the universe had played, mandating him, Sayid al-Masri, the older sibling. How could he keep Samira safe when she never listened? When she did things just to prove she could?

He wished he'd stayed in the cottage with Chloe and Jess. He wished he could return, but he didn't know the way.

Even if he did, no way could he run through the woods *alone*.

His only comfort was that his parents must not have returned from dinner yet. If they'd come home and found their children gone, they would've called him immediately.

The comfort was short-lived. Checking his pockets, Sayid realized he'd forgotten his phone in the tree house. If his parents tried to call, no one would answer.

He worried the Saint-John's-wort. He wanted to pick at it but resisted, since the flowers were, apparently, protecting him from…something. The circlet reminded him of the ta'weedh his grandmother had both worn and made for him and Samira: little leather pouches, filled with slips of paper covered in verses of the Quran, that they'd worn like necklaces until the bands had frayed and given way. His mother still had them somewhere.

If only he had one on him right now.

"I wish there were more of you," he mumbled to the flowers. "I wish I had a whole jacket of flowers. Or a blanket. Or a fort. And I could hide in it until he found Samira."

The Saint-John's-wort was scared, too. It might have been protecting the boy from spirits, but it was itself unprotected. Protecting someone else made it braver.

So, quietly and without fuss, without Sayid noticing, the braid of Saint-John's-wort grew a little bit thicker.

IX

The groundskeeper reached the cemetery's southern boundary. Moss furred the wall, which had worn so low in places that an eight-year-old with a mind to could clamber over it. She might twist an ankle on crumbled stones, but based on what Sayid had said, that wouldn't stop her. If Samira had gone over the wall, she could be anywhere.

"Samira?"

The groundskeeper returned to his hymns, quieter. The silence seethed.

Farther west, a pine grove even darker and denser than the woods grew where the wall crumbled away to nothing, filling the gap with trunks and boughs. The pines were spicy with the scent of resin.

Needles shifted.

"Samira?"

A small silhouette twisted around the nearest pine, a black shape on a black shape on a black background. The groundskeeper's candle guttered.

"Samira, is that you?"

"Who wants to know?" a ferocious voice said.

The groundskeeper let out a breath. Ferocious, yes, but young.

"If you're Samira," he said, "your brother sent me to find you."

The skinny shape of a girl detached from the pine.

"Prove it," she demanded. "What's his name?"

"Sayid, was it? Weren't much time for names aside from yours. Skinny lad, he is. Not real tall yet, thin face, twists his shirt in his hands when he's nervous—which, beg pardon, seems near constant."

A delighted laugh. "It is. He's a scaredy-cat."

"He's right to be scared. You shouldn't've run off, child."

She stepped close enough for the candle to cast dim orange light on her if it tried hard, as it did now.

The family resemblance was striking. Samira had the same thin face and pointed chin as her brother. The same dark, curly hair, trailing over her shoulder in a wayward ponytail. The same eyes, too. But while Sayid's were anxious, Samira's were fierce and gleaming and, just now, faintly cautious.

"They *said* they wanted to break in," she said. "It's not my fault they were scared."

"Never mind that. Your brother's waiting."

"I lost my shoe."

"I know. We found it."

"Okay."

Samira winced, limping over needles, cones, and sweetgum pods.

"Here." The groundskeeper crouched. "Climb on my back."

"I'm not a baby."

She clambered aboard anyway. Holding the candle away from her, the groundskeeper hooked his other arm under her leg. The iron cross clenched in his fist hurt his fingers, but he wasn't about to put either cross or candle down.

"Hold tight."

He stood with a groan; his knees ached. Samira laughed, ducking a sweetgum branch.

Her laughter calmed him. At this age, it was fifty-fifty Samira could still sense ghosts. Even if she'd outgrown the ability, surely she'd be on edge if something powerful were back here, no matter how brave she was. Sayid was on edge, and folks over twelve generally only saw spirits when powerful spirits wanted to be seen—though likely it wouldn't take a ghost to unnerve the boy.

Eyes watched as the groundskeeper limped through the woods. No nightjars, frogs, or crickets sang. The forest's unease slithered after him like a rat snake.

But with Samira laughing on his back, he wondered if he were imagining things. The wisps had behaved exactly as expected. He'd had no mishaps. No cold spots had startled him, no footsteps but his own crackled in the leaves, no spectral faces had appeared. The few spirits clinging to the earthly plane, their graves long neglected, were indolent and hazy.

The silence was the only sign anything was amiss, and the explanation might not be supernatural. He'd come looking for a spirit, yes, but it might well be elsewhere in the cemetery—even elsewhere in town. Sometimes a cemetery really was just a cemetery.

The fog thickened by the creek. A bullfrog's bassoon bellow broke the silence. Peepers piped; wood frogs clucked; chorus frogs chirruped. After the silence, their amphibian chorus was deafening.

Still clutching the flip-flop, Sayid was safe on the bridge. The groundskeeper relaxed, fingers unclenching from the cross. Rare, the people he was trying to protect listening to him. It made a nice change.

Sayid sagged in relief at the sight of them. Something about him seemed different, but the groundskeeper set Samira down without puzzling over it. He flexed his aching fingers, listening to Sayid admonish his sister.

"What were you thinking? What if you'd gotten lost?"

Samira tugged her flip-flop from his grasp. "I did get lost. It was fun."

"We are so dead if Mama and Baba get home before us," Sayid moaned.

"They won't care."

Samira marched across the bridge. Sayid danced backward before her, worrying at the Saint-John's-wort. The grounds-keeper strode on ahead, since he had the only light and Samira was going the wrong direction.

"They will so," Sayid said. "We'll be in so much trouble. Don't you care?"

Samira faltered.

"They won't," she said sadly, then jutted her chin and walked faster. "And no, I don't."

Sayid mussed his hair, muttering about the uselessness of little sisters. The groundskeeper grabbed him by the shirt as he tripped over a headstone.

"Best pay attention. Lots of old stones back here."

"I know." Sayid rubbed his shin, eyes trained on the ground. "All those, um—"

"Sick people," Samira said helpfully, looking every which way but the ground.

The groundskeeper raised an eyebrow.

"Col...ic?" Sayid said. "Everyone got real sick a hundred years ago or something."

"Cholera?"

"Yeah, that's it. Mr. David told us on our field trip. So I know there are, like—" he pressed closer to the groundskeeper "—graves around, I've just...never been back here."

"It's cool," Samira said. Sayid shook his head.

They emerged from the trees. Sayid exhaled shakily. Samira sighed in a manner suggesting the rest of the cemetery was a bore compared to what they'd left.

Chloe was in the garden, fingers hooked over her arms. Her grip loosened when she saw them. "They're back."

Jess joined her, tugging at her braid. The girls fussed over Samira as they went inside. Best get them home, the groundskeeper thought, and he could finish his warding later. The Marian symbols he'd carved at lunchtime would do for now.

But shepherding the children into the front garden, he found he didn't need to finish the warding. His paint can sat beside the love seat, loosely closed, the brush placed neatly so it wouldn't drip paint onto the floor. The symbol he'd left half-painted above the door was complete. Wobblier than it would've been had he done it but in the proper shape and form.

He cocked his head at the girls. Jess tugged her braid.

Chloe shrugged. "Jess noticed you weren't done. I did the painting."

He raised an eyebrow. Jess blushed.

"It's not like we had anything to do," Chloe said, "except worry. And it looked like you were painting that symbol on the windows again."

"I was." The groundskeeper hesitated. People didn't often notice what he was doing. "Thanks."

From the hook by the door, he grabbed the spare keys to the cemetery's rust-bucket of a pickup.

Jess hugged herself. "What are they for? The symbols."

The groundskeeper's eyes bored into the top of Samira's head. She probably wouldn't run off with a grown-up right there, but he wasn't taking chances. "Keeps the ghosts out."

Sayid shivered. The girls exchanged glances but said nothing. Samira nodded like it made perfect sense the symbols repelled ghosts.

A handful of graves clustered around the storage shed, but no spirits awoke as the groundskeeper unlocked the pickup parked beside it. Everyone piled inside. They stopped by the gates to retrieve the children's bicycles, then drove to the al-Masris' house a block north of Main Street.

Samira was in front despite her brother's half-hearted protests. Sayid sat between his friends, knees drawn up to his chest and head in his hands.

They pulled up to the house, a two-story brick-and-vinyl affair with a porch swing and tidy landscaping. Sayid curled up tighter. More cars than usual were in the driveway. Every light in the house was on.

Their parents were home.

The front door burst open as the children tumbled from the truck. Yafa and Khalid al-Masri raced down the steps in their dinner clothes, followed by Chloe's mother and Jess's older brother.

"There you are!"

"Hi, Mama," Sayid mumbled. Chloe and Jess skulked by the truck as their guardians rushed over.

Yafa hugged her children, then held them at arm's length. "Where have you been? You were supposed to stay here! If Leslie hadn't called—"

"If Mr. Taylor hadn't called me first," Leslie Wu said from beside the truck. "It's a good thing he recognized Chloe on her bike. What were you thinking?"

"We weren't supposed to be gone long," Sayid said shrilly. "If Samira hadn't run off—"

Samira scowled. "You left first."

Sayid faltered, but their father intervened. "Inside. Both of you. Now."

Sayid slunk up the steps. Samira stomped after him, muttering.

"I heard that, young lady," Yafa said.

The muttering lowered in volume but didn't subside until Samira disappeared indoors. The screen door slammed.

Khalid pinched the bridge of his nose.

"Thanks for calling, Leslie," he said to Chloe's mother.

She waved it aside. "You would've done the same. I'll see you at the PTA meeting, Yafa."

Chloe's bike was strapped to her mother's car, Jess's to her brother's, and the girls were driven away. The groundskeeper lifted Sayid's and Samira's bicycles out of the truck and wheeled them up the drive.

"Mr. and Mrs. al-Masri?" The al-Masris looked at him blankly. Yafa was short and plump, with the same pointed chin as her children; her husband was tall, thin, and bespectacled, and shared their eyes. "These are yours. Or your weens', I s'pose I should say."

Yafa fiddled with the sleeves of her tunic. "Where did you find them? The children."

"They found me. I'm the new groundskeeper over at the cemetery. They thought they'd come see the place after dark and had a right scare. Place'll give you the collywobbles if you're not used to it."

"The cemetery?" Khalid worried his hairline with a thumb. "Why would they...?"

"Was it really Sayid's idea?" Yafa's face was strained. "Lately Samira's been...well... But I didn't think we had to worry about Sayid."

Khalid reached for her hand.

"Couldn't say," the groundskeeper said. "Didn't get up to any mischief, though."

Khalid raked a hand through his hair. "How did they get in? The cemetery's not open this late, is it?"

Yafa sagged. "Samira's paper clips."

"Nay, that was me. My first day on the job and I plumb forget to lock up."

Khalid rubbed his forehead. The groundskeeper gave a quiet smile. He wasn't sure he ought to lie, but he didn't want to get the children into trouble.

Well, not *more* trouble.

Their parents' eyes were crescented with exhaustion. No need to make things worse by confirming their children had broken in.

"Well...I'm sorry if they were any bother," Yafa said.

"No bother. It's good wee ones you've got, Mrs. al-Masri."

"Yafa, please. And my husband is Khalid." Her smile faded. "We just wanted to have dinner…"

Khalid squeezed her pinky with his. "Sayid said he and his friends had a group project to finish. We thought they'd be fine. We were only gone a couple of hours."

The groundskeeper's heart clenched. He remembered Catherine rumpled in the leaf litter. His mother saying in tones too bewildered to be hurt, *She was in bed. I put her to bed not an hour past.*

He tugged at his flat cap. "You know how weens are. Wanted some excitement, I'm guessing."

Yafa laughed thinly. "I suppose. Thank you so much for bringing them home."

The groundskeeper slipped into the pickup. "Happy to do it. They're welcome anytime, provided it's open hours. They end up at the cemetery again, I'll look after 'em for you."

He trundled back to the cemetery alone, wondering what had gotten into him to say such a thing.

X

It rained all weekend. Never deterred by weather, the grounds-keeper slogged downhill to the back lot on Saturday morning. He had a troublesome ghost to find.

He used to think it would break his curse, hunting ghosts. If he sent the right spirit packing, or enough of them, he'd finally die. After all, he hadn't seen ghosts until he was cursed. Afterward, he saw them everywhere.

After a century of hunting ghosts, he was no nearer to death. The curse was playing tricks on him, that was all. Letting him see the dead without joining them.

The groundskeeper kept at it anyway. It was something to do. A way to help the living without becoming involved.

He still had Elijah in mind. Elijah had scared his daughter, rotted the air, upset the greenlings. And the groundskeeper could send him on if he convinced Nevaeh to go to therapy and stick with it—a new one for the groundskeeper, but straight-forward, if not easy.

But he wanted to reexamine the back lot. Determine whether last night's unease was real or imagined. Whether the spirit he'd come here to find might be back there.

No sooner had the groundskeeper reached the woods, how-ever, than he turned back. The rain drove down in sheets, soak-ing through his flat cap. Wet leaves slicked the ground. Mud sucked at his boots. He sloshed through ankle-deep puddles. At last he could go no farther: the creek had burst its banks, swirling with thigh-deep water.

The trees muttered about root rot and uprooted seedlings. More than one thought *such* April showers unnecessary to bring May flowers.

Ignoring them, the groundskeeper felt for nearby spirits. If there were any, they were dormant, though extreme weather often woke dormant spirits.

He trudged home. He'd investigate when everything dried.

In the meantime, he had plenty to do. The cottage roof leaked, filling the pots he put in the front room so quickly he resigned himself to repairing it in the rain. He was already soaked through anyhow.

He fixed the roof, then replaced water-damaged floorboards and electrical outlets. He drove to the farmers market on North River Road to stock his icebox. The vendors asked if he'd swum there. A stout woman selling rhubarb in colorful bunches gave him directions to the farm supply co-op west of Ashmead Creek, where he bought chicken feed, a coop, and six pullets he allowed to stalk through the kitchen while he tore down the old coop and assembled the new one.

It was still raining when he finished, so he fed the pullets in the kitchen instead of moving them into the coop. He squeezed out his flat cap and hung it on a peg, toweled his hair, and changed into fresh clothes. Sitting in the kitchen to keep the chickens company, he recorded what he'd found so far in his notepad.

He always started a ghost hunt this way, after a day or two spent settling in: noting his initial impressions and thinking through the research he'd need to do to learn more about a place's spirits.

The pullets snuggled into a feathery mass at his feet and clucked themselves to sleep. The groundskeeper scratched at his notepad, expanding his notes on Elijah Key-Flores and the few other spirits he'd met so far.

Elijah's behavior at lunchtime yesterday bore looking into; he might've been affected by another ghost on the knoll. A powerful spirit's fears and anxieties could infect others with ill will and mischief, no matter how pleasant they normally were. If any ghosts in Elijah's vicinity had an overflow of negative emotion, that could explain his sudden shift in mood. The groundskeeper hadn't noticed any such emotion his first day of work, however—until he'd entered the forest.

The back lot. So silent. So watchful.

It might've been nothing. But with the cholera victims buried there, agitated spirits were bound to be about. Perhaps one of them was the one that had chased that teen back in Savannah off the property.

As he always did, the groundskeeper would also look into local history. It could point him toward people who had died scared or angry and might've left spirits behind.

When he finished with his notepad, he had several pages of observations and questions and a brief to-do list.

- *Search knoll*
- *Search back lot, esp. south of creek*
- *Research—library*
- *Research—cemetery archives*
- *Research—local history museum? Schwertner?*

He stretched, made supper, and settled into bed to read poetry as rain drummed on the roof.

XI

Monday dawned chilly and misty and golden, the kind of morning the groundskeeper liked best. Robins chorused the sunrise. Red-winged blackbirds trilled. A pair of mourning doves strutted down the garden path as the groundskeeper emerged. He chirruped at them, grinning. They fled to the roof in a whistling of wings.

The damp grass gleamed; the pullets explored their coop; the weekend's toils had improved the cottage. The groundskeeper's icebox was full, as was his belly, and his to-do list was in his pocket. He whistled as he worked on the knoll. When Nevaeh waved on her way into the office, her hair wrap a bright spot of purple among the cemetery's greens and grays, he waved back.

Elijah flared yellow at her entrance. Since he couldn't follow her into the office, with the building warded now, he moped by his headstone. The groundskeeper spent far too long trying to cheer him, but at last he moved on. He weeded around the headstones, acquainting himself with every ghost on the knoll.

Not every grave had a spirit; not all the dead remained. If whatever had made them cling to the living plane in the first place wasn't resolved, those who did remain sometimes tarried so long they forgot what that was. They lingered for decades, centuries, fading away to wisps before finally winking out of existence.

The graves by the entrance were too recent for that. From

north to south, the cemetery was a reverse timeline of Harrington's deaths: graves from the past fifty years by the gates; earlier twentieth-century graves where the knoll crested and dipped downhill; late-nineteenth-century graves clustered by the cottage and garden, the office and storage shed; and, in the woods, the earliest graves, dating back nearly two hundred years. Hence the wisps. The longer it had been since death, the less powerful a spirit was to begin with, the more likely they were to be a wisp.

There were no wisps by the gates, but there were about two dozen spirits of varying moods and strength. The groundskeeper already had notes on some, but now he made his way through them all, spending enough time with each to glimpse its reasons for staying.

An Italian woman dead in the 1980s was annoyed she could no longer cook and worried her grandchildren weren't eating enough. The groundskeeper's stomach rumbled at the whiff of basil and oregano at her grave.

A little girl found dead in a cornfield in the 1950s was looking for a stuffed dog she'd lost. Ghosts who didn't know they were dead were the groundskeeper's least favorite. Worse when they were children. At least Layla Brown had been aware of her state.

Luckily, *this* spirit had no memory of her death, which had surely been violent, and she was a cheerful little ghost. The groundskeeper planted daffodils, listening to her memories of her stuffed dog, her parents, and her grandmother's garden. Not knowing she was dead, she didn't realize she was sharing memories; she thought she was speaking.

A young couple recently killed in a car crash had stayed for each other. The groundskeeper was pleasantly surprised they were affectionate rather than fearful spirits, given how they'd died, but he was glad they weren't powerful enough to take form. Otherwise, they would've been necking right by their headstone.

The groundskeeper wasn't opposed to a little necking, theoretically, but mostly it made him uncomfortable. In two hundred years, he hadn't wanted to do such things with anyone but Jack.

He'd come close, once. In the 1940s, he'd gotten to know a man in Brooklyn pretty well. They'd gotten coffee at the same diner every morning, each sitting at the counter alone, and they started talking, and it became a habit.

They didn't say much. Talked gardening, mostly. And the war, because you couldn't help talking about the war.

Nothing happened, but they held each other's gazes too long when they said goodbye each day. The groundskeeper had hoped something might happen, even as he convinced himself he hoped no such thing.

Then, one day, he was drinking his coffee, listening to the rain. Charlie hadn't arrived yet. A quarter hour later he still hadn't arrived, and another quarter hour after that, and another. The groundskeeper couldn't stop watching the clock, couldn't stop imagining all the terrible things that might've happened, and then Charlie walked in, sopping wet but fine.

His train had broken down. He'd waited half an hour before walking the fifteen blocks in the rain.

They'd had their coffee and said goodbye, and the grounds-keeper had skipped town that night. A rare ghost hunt left un-finished.

New Yorkers were used to danger anyhow.

He buried the unwanted memory and hurried away before the couple could recall their canoodling.

While most of the knoll's two dozen ghosts had stayed for surviving friends or relatives, a handful had other reasons. A woman dead of a brain tumor had been too terrified of death to move on. A businessman was certain his accountant had been cheating him but had never proved it. The accountant, buried across the knoll and indeed a habitual cheat, sulked over the wealth left behind in death. There was a spirit whose murderer had never been found; a spirit who'd burned to death smoking in his sleep; a spirit whose unfaithful spouse had since married his mistress; and a spirit angry about an unjust civil suit, though the groundskeeper thought, based on the spirit's memories, that the case had been decided correctly.

Upset as these spirits were, none was any more powerful than Elijah. Certainly not enough for their negativity to have infected him, let alone for them to take corporeal form themselves.

At midmorning, the groundskeeper plopped down on a bench by Elijah's grave. He recorded the names and birth and death dates of every spirit, along with their moods and memories, in his notepad. He crossed "search knoll" off his to-do list and slipped it into his pocket, then stretched with a soft groan.

He jerked upright.

Something was moving in the woods.

He narrowed his eyes, wishing he'd looked up sooner. He couldn't tell whether it was a deer or something less innocent. No bird or squirrel, that was certain. Too big.

Creaking to his feet, he hastened into the woods.

Sunlight fell greenly through the canopy. The trees stood silent as he passed.

"Ain't here to bother you none. Taking a look, is all."

Several saplings whispered together about him. He pretended he didn't hear.

The water had receded, but mud sucked at his boots. Still high from the weekend's rain, the creek glittered in the sunlight, hurting his eyes.

"Hello?"

A pewee called back. The groundskeeper headed deeper into the trees.

More of the headstones he'd tripped over Friday night reared crookedly from last year's leaves. Most needed resetting, sunken into the ground like MOTHER and DAUGHTER . Those dated from the 1840s and 1850s, victims of three different cholera epidemics, were hastily erected and minimally engraved. Older stones scattered among them, better set if no less simplistic. Newer stones, even dated as far back as the late 1850s, were few.

Evidently, Harrington had abandoned the back lot after the last bout of cholera.

South of the creek, unseen birds flitted through the branches. No wisps drifted. The younger trees were uneasy, drawn in as if holding their breath; the older trees were disinterestedly curious. A few spirits shimmered, wistful and indolent.

Usually, the groundskeeper blocked out the dead's feelings. If they weren't trying to communicate, he could ignore them.

Now, as he had on the knoll, he tuned in.

Unlike then, he didn't get much. These spirits no longer remembered why they'd lingered. One radiated images of its home and family, but they were hazy. The others didn't emit even that much. Soon, most would fade away to wisps.

He moved on.

These spirits might not have felt much, but something did.

The woods were quiet. The air weighed more than it did on the knoll.

The groundskeeper glanced around, nape prickling. Nothing was there.

Sunlight flooded a break in the trees. He stepped into the clearing, blinking; his eyes smarted. Red maples flowered all around, less recalcitrant than the sweetgums nearby. He breathed in deeply.

A figure emerged from the dimness ahead.

He stumbled back. His heart pounded. How careless he'd been, coming here without salt, a candle, iron, anything—

"Whoa!" the figure said. "I'm so sorry, I didn't mean to startle you—are you all right?"

The groundskeeper gripped a tree trunk, blinking wildly as his eyes adjusted. He breathed hard through his nose.

Not a ghost. Not with a voice like that. He'd lost his head because he'd expected to find something nasty back here.

The tree, a sturdy buckeye, fluttered its leaves. His fingers dug into its bark.

"Are you all right?" the figure repeated.

It was a little old white man in galoshes, a rainbow-striped waistcoat, and a button-down with the sleeves rolled up, with a sky blue backpack over his shoulders and a pencil behind his ear. He was about seventy, with thick white hair, once golden like his lashes, and gray eyes creased with laugh lines. He shone as the groundskeeper's eyes worked to balance out images in the brightness.

The man's brow puckered. "Can you say anything? I don't mean to push, but a scare like that, at our age——"

"I'm fine," the groundskeeper managed. "Startled, is all."

The man squinted at the sky, which was pearly blue; the morning mist had burned away.

"I imagine you couldn't see me coming." He smiled apologetically. "I could see you fine, standing in the sun like you were. Otherwise I guess you would've startled me, too. It's spooky back here, isn't it?"

The buckeye's leaves, pale green with spring newness, curled in agreement. The groundskeeper nodded, heartbeat calming.

"You must be the new groundskeeper Nevaeh told me about." The man offered a hand. The groundskeeper peeled away from the buckeye to shake it. "David Schwertner. I run the museum."

His hand was warm and firm. The groundskeeper's brain felt like a stream dammed by a log. Instead of a ghost, there was this little man with his smile, his galoshes, and his colorful waistcoat. The appearance of a unicorn couldn't have flummoxed him more.

"You're cataloging the cholera graves," the groundskeeper said at last. He'd forgotten all about it.

"Starting to." David jerked a thumb over his shoulder at the tangle of late-April greenery. "I thought I'd see how far back this goes first, map out the edges. I still need to decide how to divvy it up, but this seemed like a start. I've never done this sort of thing." He grinned. "Sounded like fun, though, when Nevaeh asked."

He released the groundskeeper's hand, which was when the groundskeeper realized he'd still been holding it. Without their fingers linked, the groundskeeper's felt strangely empty. He cleared his throat.

"Do you—" he faltered, his thoughts slipping like a deer on ice "—need any help?"

"If Nevaeh can spare you, I'd love some," David said. "It's a lot of ground to cover, and I'm not sure how many sites there are. I have death certificates and cemetery records at the museum, of course, and Nevaeh has more extensive records in her office, but mine are incomplete, and hers are... I don't know how much she's told you about the old director, but—well, the point is, I can't be sure every stone is accounted for. Recordkeeping got shoddy during the epidemics anyway, especially the first one, people were running scared and, well, sorry, I'm rambling."

He ran a hand through his hair.

"I love this stuff." He laughed. "That sounded grim. Not cholera. Or death. Or graves. I meant—history! And research. I realize that sounds boring, but I promise you it's not. It's fascinating, the things people have thought worth documenting throughout time."

"It don't sound boring to me," the groundskeeper said, intelligently. "Done a fair bit of research in my day."

He neglected the reasons for his research: the futile years investigating ways to break his curse, and the more fruitful time researching ghosts both general and specific.

He rubbed his neck, feeling wrong-footed. "Should be back to work."

David nodded. "Of course. I'm so sorry, I shouldn't have kept you. If it's all right, I might find you at lunchtime. I have some questions I think you could answer."

"All right," the groundskeeper said uncertainly.

David waved and headed into the trees. The forest swallowed him up, even more silent in his wake.

The groundskeeper might've imagined the whole thing except for the clearing's flattened grass. He blinked, like he'd stumbled across some fey creature who had vanished in a twinkling of the light.

Something was still watching him.

XII

Putting David Schwertner from his mind, the groundskeeper trawled the woods for whatever spirit or spirits had made them so uneasy. The air weighed on him, like gravity had increased on this stretch of earth. The trees' boughs drooped.

A sycamore shivered. The groundskeeper patted its trunk.

"S'all right," he murmured. "I feel it, too."

The sycamore's leaves curled inward. It leaned toward him, groaning.

He found several more spirits, but they were no different from the others. Faint, with few memories. The clearest belonged to one John Kowalczyk, according to his headstone, dead in eighteen-something-or-other. The date had weathered away.

The groundskeeper concentrated on John Kowalczyk's memories. A hazy street, Harrington in its early days: horses, carriages, and pedestrians crowding a dirt road lined with the wooden frames of new buildings. A stark bedroom, clouded as a reflection in a tarnished looking glass. A packet of letters, their lines unreadable. A face, more vivid than the other images—an old woman hovering near with worry etched into her brow.

The sweet scent of violets engulfed the groundskeeper as John remembered the woman, but her face slipped out of focus.

The groundskeeper reached for her; his fingers brushed stone instead of skin. He shook his head, but the violets persisted.

Surfacing from memories was easier when he entered them intentionally than when a spirit forced them on him as Elijah Key-Flores had. But he still had to reorient to the present when he entered rather than simply viewing them.

It was harder when the memories were, like John Kowalczyk's, from a period near his own.

It might've been Ohio, not County Galway, but memories from small, nineteenth-century farm towns disoriented the groundskeeper. Like he was a boy back in Ballygar, uncursed, with a life ahead of him spanning decades instead of centuries.

The memories were faded enough that, this time, it was easier. But the groundskeeper frowned in momentary confusion. The forest was right, the trees wrong: buckeye, maple, walnut instead of Scots pine, beech, ash. What was he doing out here anyway? Surely Mam needed him home, surely the sheep needed tending—

Then he saw John Kowalczyk's vague, formless shimmering, and he remembered.

Something cracked inside him. New memories flooded him—not John Kowalczyk's, but his own. Mam darning shirts by the fire, telling tales of wisps and selkies and *them folk* and the ancient heroes of Ireland. Feeling his forehead when he took sick. Eoin's initials chipped into the plaster beside the bed. Catherine's ragged old cloth doll.

The groundskeeper didn't know what it was about Harrington. The familiarity of Elijah's love for Nevaeh. The history from a period he knew so well, when time had gone the way it should and life was full of the normal joys and griefs. He wasn't sure.

Whatever it was made him *feel* things.

At lunchtime, he returned to the bench by Elijah's headstone and ate a cheese sandwich, ignoring the memories thorning at him like briars.

The back lot nettled him. The quietness. The watchfulness. The weighty air pressing on him. Could be a spirit, maybe. Could even be the one he'd come here to find. Someone ate up with misery at their own memories, making him remember his.

But not a one he'd found could cast such a pall.

Perhaps the back lot's disquiet wasn't due to a single spirit. They'd all died bad, sick and racked with pain. Surely other cholera victims had lingered there once, too, before whittling away to nothing. The weight in the air could be nothing more than the collective grief and fear and anger of every ghost that had ever haunted the place. He'd seen it before.

It couldn't have affected Elijah, though. That had to be a single spirit's work. None of those in back were powerful enough for that.

Even if they had been, why Elijah? His grave was clear across the cemetery, with other spirits in between. If another ghost's influence had spread this far—a possibility, if it were upset enough, and certainly if it were powerful enough to take form as the spirit in that teen's story had—more of them should've been affected. So far, Elijah was the only one.

This suggested a ghost in his vicinity was the problem instead, but the groundskeeper had met every one of them this morning. The angriest, most fearful spirits weren't the ones closest to Elijah, nor were they strong enough to take form or infect others with their rage.

The groundskeeper wasn't worried about such ghosts. He never was. There were far too many, for one thing, and they rarely hurt anyone unless a vase went flying in the wrong direction.

Hearing that teenager's story back in Savannah, the groundskeeper had assumed he'd be looking for bigger fish. A spirit whose rage or regret broke like water through a dam, sometimes at random, sometimes with purpose, hurting everyone and everything in their path.

A spirit who needed to be expelled before it destroyed a town and everyone in it.

"Are you okay?"

Nevaeh was scrunching her hair wrap in her fist, her brow furrowed. She'd undone her braids; her hair was a burst of black curls. Elijah hung around her, faintly blue.

The groundskeeper roused himself. He'd been glaring, willing the lawn to reveal its secrets.

He dimpled with difficulty, stuck on the back lot's memories. "Thinking, is all."

Her fingers loosened on her wrap. "Okay. You looked… That's the worst case of resting bitch face I've ever seen."

She recoiled, her expression horrified. Her fingers tightened again.

"Shit—I mean, shoot—oh my god, I'm sorry, I shouldn't've said—"

He chuckled despite himself. "S'all right, lass."

"I wasn't thinking, it popped out—"

"S'all right. No harm done. You headed out?"

She relaxed at the change in subject, but she touched her hair self-consciously. "Uh, yeah, I'm meeting a friend for lunch."

Her voice dipped on *friend*. In addition to redoing her hair, she'd applied deep plum lipstick that was beautiful on her sepia skin. She avoided his gaze, but they'd just met. It wasn't his business, her having a lunch date.

He dimpled again. This time, it came easier. "You go on have fun. I'll hold down the fort."

She exhaled, giving a small smile. Relieved he hadn't commented, then.

"Do you want anything? A coffee?"

He shook his head. "Fine with my sandwich."

"Okay. See you in a bit."

She paused at Elijah's headstone, running a finger along its top. Elijah brightened, buttery yellow. The groundskeeper pretended not to notice.

His thoughts turned back to ghosts as Nevaeh biked away. Elijah nosed at him, minty with curiosity.

"You could help. Tell me if you've seen anything odd."

The mint sharpened at his tone. Elijah had only been dead these nine months, thank you; he wasn't an expert on ghosts just because he'd become one. Ghosthood was nothing like he would've expected, if he'd considered it—which he had not. He'd been a faithful Pentecostal.

"What about before?" the groundskeeper asked patiently. "Surely you heard some good tall tales when you were alive."

Still sharp. Of course Elijah had heard the local kids talking about ghosts, but he hadn't paid them any mind. He'd known they liked sneaking into the cemetery after hours. Before Nevaeh had taken over, teenagers routinely broke in with illicit beer to flirt and drink and smash bottles against the headstones. Elijah shifted from minty to a sour copper. He had disapproved and was glad the cemetery's new upkeep had sent the teenagers in search of more neglected properties to use for their gatherings—although if *he* had any say, they wouldn't be gathering so close to curfew (and drinking! imagine!) at all.

The groundskeeper sighed. It wasn't much, but at least Elijah had confirmed that Harrington's teens had spent time in the cemetery after hours. Might be on the right track, then, searching the back lot for something nasty. But he'd have to expand the search if he didn't find a stronger ghost soon.

Elijah was still complaining about the teens' past parties. The groundskeeper banged his heel against the bench. "Away with you, now."

Elijah retreated with a huff. A napkin fluttered off the bench.

The groundskeeper retrieved it. He was considering apologizing when a shadow fell over him.

"Is this seat taken?"

David Schwertner, in his galoshes and waistcoat. The groundskeeper plucked his flat cap off the seat beside him and tugged it on.

"Is now," he grunted.

David shrugged off his backpack, smiling. "Great. Thanks."

The groundskeeper kept eating, squashing the memory of a diner in Brooklyn and a daily cup of joe that had started this way. This was nothing like that.

Elijah stretched toward them, buttery yellow again. For David, this time.

The groundskeeper expected an earful like he'd gotten this morning, but David ate a sandwich and applesauce in silence. Except for his small smiles, the groundskeeper might as well have been alone. But David was a splash of color among the headstones, golden and rainbow and sky blue.

The groundskeeper checked his pocket watch, the only thing he had of his father's and the only thing he'd had on him when he fled Ireland. Barely visible in the polished bronze case were thin Marian symbols. At present, however, he wanted it for the time.

Twenty minutes left of lunch yet. He wasn't one to waste his personal time by returning to work early.

David worked on a chocolate chip cookie, breaking off one piece at a time.

"Feeling quiet this afternoon, I ken," the groundskeeper said.

David laughed. "I talked your ear off enough this morning. You looked like you were thinking anyway. I didn't want to disturb you."

"Why'd you ask to sit, then?"

David crumbled a piece of cookie, scuffing his galoshes in the grass. The groundskeeper could've bitten off his own tongue.

"Forget I said that," he said gruffly, but David shook his head.

"It's all right." He trashed the remaining cookie in a brown paper lunch bag. "The museum gets lonely at lunchtime."

He ran his hands through his hair, mussing it up. The groundskeeper tracked the path of his fingers.

"My husband died last year. Pancreatic cancer. By the time I convinced him to go to the doctor..." David spoke to his lap. "I keep myself pretty well distracted when I'm working, but when it's time for a break... I'm not used to the silence. Not being alone in it. Not reading in my office and hearing nothing but the museum settling. I used to hear Isaiah moving around in his office or going through files upstairs. We used to sit in the living room at home together on Sunday evenings, and he'd work on his sudoku, and I'd watch a movie, and we wouldn't say a thing for hours. But it wasn't the same. It's different, the silence when I'm alone."

Grief etched every line of his face. Smiles suited him better, the groundskeeper thought.

He hesitated. "You do get used to it, eventually."

David glanced at him. "Who was it for you?"

The groundskeeper faltered. The thorns were back, needling his insides.

"It was a long time ago."

"I'm sorry for your loss."

"Yours, too."

David crumpled his bag, scratched his forehead with a thumb.

"So," he said, "how long are we talking? I'd love to get a time-line on this whole 'getting used to the silence' thing."

The groundskeeper snorted.

David giggled. "Sorry. Things were getting depressing there. Truth be told, I hope I never get used to being alone."

"Why not?" the groundskeeper asked. "It's easier."

"Maybe," David said, "but it's sad."

They lapsed into silence. The groundskeeper picked at his shirt. It wasn't sad, getting used to loneliness. Better than the alternative.

He rubbed his inner arm. "You had questions?"

"Oh—hang on." David pulled a smartphone from his back-pack, smiling at the groundskeeper's raised eyebrows. "Yes, yes, I know. I may be an old man and a historian, but there's no need to be a dinosaur. This thing's awfully good for taking notes and keeping appointments. Eli used to razz me about it."

He nodded at Elijah's headstone. The spirit perked up. He drifted around David, nearly as brightly yellow as he was every time Nevaeh appeared.

"Nevaeh's father," David said, "and a dear friend. We used

to play cards on Thursday nights, Eli and Isaiah and Noah Rosten and me. When Nevaeh was little, she used to sit on my lap, and Eli would spend the whole game trying to get her to tell him what my hand was. He died six months after Isaiah. Tractor flipped on him."

The buttery yellow soured to mustard brown. Elijah twisted, but he settled when the groundskeeper said softly, "Hsst."

"It's just me and Noah now. And he's talking about moving into a home like his kids want." David opened his notes app. "There's a home not far from here. Nice place. I visited with him when he first considered it. It'd be good for him, I think. He's older than the rest of us. And it'd be easy for me to visit."

He scrolled through his notes. "Okay, here we go."

He was businesslike, suddenly. The groundskeeper almost missed the ragged edges to his cheer.

"I'm interested in recording names and dates, but some of the stones—*if* they haven't sunk into the ground, *if* they're not mossed over—some of them are so weathered they're impossible to make out. I found tons online—" David held up his phone "—ways to make stones easier to read, but I'm not sure about some of them. Like here, this is a link to a YouTube video that shows how to rub flour on a headstone so you can—"

"No."

David chuckled. "All right, see, this is why I'm asking you. What about—this one says shaving cream?"

"Best figure they're wrong if they're saying to put anything direct on the stone. You'll damage it."

"Okay, let's delete that entire section." David amended the note. "What about rubbings? I found conflicting information."

"If the headstone's safe to be cleaned and you know what you're doing, fine."

The lunch hour was over long before their discussion about methods for reading worn headstones. Nevaeh stopped by on her way back, hugged David, and disappeared into her office.

Elijah pined after her. The groundskeeper didn't notice, too caught up in David's questions.

The sun shifted. The spirits wavered, thin in the golden light.

David checked the time, put his phone away, and stood. "I'd better get going. I still have things to do at the office. Things to do here, too, but—well, it's all right, I'll be back tomorrow."

The groundskeeper stretched lazily. "Time's it?"

"Nearly two. I can't believe I kept you from your work for so long, I'm so sorry. I'll make sure Nevaeh knows it was my fault."

The groundskeeper narrowly avoided telling him it was fine. That he'd liked it.

David shouldered his backpack.

"Oh—you know what—all that time gabbing at you, and I never asked for an introduction." He laughed, rubbing the back of his neck. "That's how it goes. I get talking and forget all about social niceties. What was your name?"

The world ground to a halt. Everything stretched away until the cemetery felt empty except for them. The groundskeeper was so muddled from the two hours in which he'd forgotten the tragedy of his own life that his name escaped before he could keep it caged.

"Peter," he said. "Peter Shaughnessy."

A slow smile spread across David's face.

"Peter. I'll remember that." He hitched his backpack higher. "It was nice meeting you, Peter. See you tomorrow."

He walked off.

The groundskeeper didn't say goodbye. He felt like static before a lightning storm, water falling down a mountainside. Like himself, three thousand miles away and two hundred years back, young and uncursed.

He swallowed, eyes prickling, chest heaving, unaware of the concern emanating from the nearest graves. His ears rang over and over with the sound of his name on someone's tongue for the first time in almost one hundred years.

XIII

David had been in Nevaeh's office for an hour. Not that the groundskeeper was keeping track. He was working.

David's voice hadn't stopped echoing in his head.

Peter. Peter, I'll remember that.

Since Jack had died and he'd distanced himself from their neighbors—since he'd started hunting ghosts to keep himself distracted, useful, unattached—the groundskeeper had meant nothing to anyone.

He'd made sure of it. Each time he helped a spirit move on—helping, without their knowledge, the people whose lives were destroyed when such spirits stayed—he moved on himself. Names had power, Mam had always said so, and he'd always believed it. When he left, he left no name behind. No friends to miss him or by whom he might be drawn back. He never passed through the same town twice. He didn't like how they changed without him.

It got powerful lonesome, but he preferred it that way. If no one knew his name, he was nothing to them, nor they to him; he'd never know the pain of their passing. If loneliness meant to hunt him forever, better he should meet it on his own terms than wait for its jaws to close around him.

Now someone did know his name.

He wasn't sure he liked that.

He mulched a redbud near the gate. Not because David would come this way when he left. It wasn't that the groundskeeper wanted to see him again. Or say goodbye properly. Or hear his own name once more.

Wanting such things was out of the question. The groundskeeper never allowed himself to want anything. All he wanted, these days, was to die.

His eyes flickered toward the office. Elijah brushed against him, mildly minty.

The groundskeeper flushed, returning to the redbud. "I don't know what they're talking about, and I don't much care. S'none of my business anyway. Yours, neither."

Elijah gentled into something sweeter and subtler than mint. The groundskeeper ignored him. The dead didn't need to care for him any more than the living.

The office door opened. The groundskeeper cricked his neck, glancing over his shoulder so fast, but returned to mulching. He did not track the approaching footsteps (two sets, he might've thought, were he paying attention), nor did he listen for anyone calling goodbye on their way out.

"...says you canceled your appointment again," David was saying.

The groundskeeper piled still more mulch around the redbud. The tree fluttered new spring leaves, but he ignored it.

Nevaeh's voice was strained. "Ma talks too much."

"I just want you to know you can talk to me about it if you want. It doesn't have to be a therapist if you're not comfortable with that."

"I know."

The mulch was six inches deep. Faded pink flowers showered the groundskeeper's head.

"Hey—"

The redbud fluttered again, reproachfully.

"Well, sorry," he muttered. "Didn't mean to pile it on so thick."

He nudged mulch away from the trunk. The footsteps drew closer and stopped.

David's laugh went through the groundskeeper like music. "You must have irritated that tree something awful."

The groundskeeper said nothing, because David thought he was joking. He turned, brushing petals from his flannel.

David smiled. The groundskeeper avoided his gaze, feeling it dangerous to attend too much to that smile. Nevaeh offered a smile, too, the merest lift at the corners of her mouth. Her brow was drawn.

"All right?" the groundskeeper asked.

She nodded, shoving her hands in her pockets. Her lips and hair were still done up, but she was as faded as the dwindling crocuses in the office garden.

David's smile dimmed. He hugged her with one arm. She leaned into him briefly—then straightened, giving that same small lift of her lips. Something tugged at the groundskeeper's insides.

"I have to get back to work," she said. "Are you coming for dinner Sunday? Uncle Noah's going to be there."

"I'll think about it." David patted her arm. "Take care, kiddo."

She returned to the office. Elijah followed, the soft, yearning orange of a winter sunrise, until the building's warding stopped him.

David sighed. The groundskeeper cleared his throat.

David caught his eye. "She's having a tough time."

"So I've noticed."

David gazed at the office a moment longer, then turned away.

"Well, anyway," he said, in a voice of forced cheer. That tug came again, a pang of sympathy for these people who were trying so hard not to show their hurts. "I'll leave you to your work. Really, this time."

The groundskeeper hefted the bag of mulch over his shoulder, to the redbud's relief. "Right."

They tried to move past each other, bumped into each other instead. Several times. David laughed, the sound less forced now. He put a hand on the groundskeeper's chest and maneuvered around him.

"There. Much better. See you tomorrow, Peter."

"Tomorrow," the groundskeeper echoed. His skin twitched at the pressure of David's fingers on his chest. He trudged down the knoll with the mulch, resisting the urge to look over his shoulder and wondering whether David had done the same.

XIV

On the first of May, a cold snap broke the late-April warmth. Clouds scudded across the sky. Phlox and violet, already blooming, curled in on themselves. The spirits shivered, faintly aquamarine.

Nevaeh emerged from her office at midmorning. Her wide, dark eyes slid over her father's headstone, settling on the groundskeeper.

His crow's feet deepened. Although she didn't know it, her father had, as usual, flared buttery yellow when she'd stepped outside.

"Uncle Dave called." She flushed. "David Schwertner, I mean. He'll be here in twenty minutes. I don't need you for anything in particular, so if you don't mind helping him out today—"

"Be happy to."

Her shoulders hunched. She seemed small despite her height, dull despite her amethyst hair wrap and yellow cardigan, the same soft shade as her father's affection.

The groundskeeper thumbed up the brim of his cap. "All right?"

Her appointment card was in her pocket, but she hadn't called her therapist to reschedule. Even though she'd only met with him once, she felt weirdly like she was letting him down by canceling her subsequent appointments—and like she was letting down Yafa al-Masri, who had referred her to him. "I'm fine."

The groundskeeper had used that tone himself on any number of occasions. "You sure?"

She fiddled with her hem.

"Yeah. It's nothing. I'm fine." Nevaeh pulled the cardigan tighter. Elijah enveloped her like a blanket. "Glad he wants your help instead of mine."

The groundskeeper paused in his work. "Been in back already, have you?"

"A few days ago. Just for an hour or so. I thought I'd check it out before calling him, but the place gives me the creeps." Her words echoed in her ears. She laughed. "Sorry. I'm sure you'll be fine. It's just...spooky. People have been saying it's haunted for longer than I've been alive."

"Mmm."

Nevaeh fussed with her hem again, waiting, but he was lost in thought and said nothing more. Shrugging, she headed back inside.

Elijah returned to his grave with a sigh. It ruffled the groundskeeper's shirt.

"Went back there with her, did you?" the groundskeeper murmured.

Elijah shuddered. Though he was limited by the cemetery boundaries, not powerful enough to travel farther without a vessel, he was determined to follow his daughter about as much as possible. But he hadn't liked the back lot any better than she had.

"I see."

The groundskeeper abandoned his work, retrieved his messenger bag, and strode into the woods. Twenty minutes didn't give him much time, but he wanted to revisit the back lot without any distractions. Maybe he'd missed something.

Elijah followed Nevaeh everywhere within the cemetery

walls. He was likely the only spirit on the knoll who'd ventured into the back lot, the only one with any reason to do so.

No wonder he'd been the only one affected. No wonder there'd been no repeat incident. Once he'd slammed the Dutch door, working off the anger that wasn't his, he'd shaken off the other spirit's influence.

Said other spirit might be in the back lot after all.

The groundskeeper buzzed with excitement. He whistled, pleased at the prospect of finishing the job soon. The chill breeze invigorated him, though the trees shivered and rattled. New leaves curled inward to escape the cold.

The air was heavier today, faintly crimson. Vibrating like a nest of yellow jackets.

The groundskeeper paused midwhistle, the hair on his nape standing up. The crimson weight hung over him.

An oak groaned. One of its branches cracked and crashed through the undergrowth. The groundskeeper flinched.

Whatever was back here wasn't merely watchful: it was angry.

He hoped the anger would deepen as he walked farther, but it was uniform. He couldn't feel his way to its source. That didn't bode well.

He gripped the strap of his bag. "Hello?"

The air twisted briefly. A nearby spirit vibrated with resentment not its own. It flung a pebble at him.

"Hsst. Don't mean no bother."

The spirit's ire didn't abate, but it didn't fling anything else.

The groundskeeper walked on, calling softly as he went. No response, not that he expected one; angry spirits weren't much for polite conversation. The trees were too nervous even to hush him.

But each time he spoke, the air twisted, as if someone disliked the attention.

"Hello?"

To his astonishment, a voice behind him responded. He jumped.

"Over here, Peter!"

David Schwertner. Of course. The groundskeeper had forgotten. He squeezed his bag's strap, grounding himself against the unexpected meeting of his name.

David was in a fawn trench coat with its collar turned up, his sky blue backpack on his shoulders. A gasp of calm and color. He smiled at the groundskeeper through the trees.

He must not have sensed the anger. The living's reactions to a spirit was one way the groundskeeper determined how strong it was. The stronger the spirit, the more likely the living could sense it—although in this case, the crimson weight of the air, the unease of the trees and the other spirits, had already been decent indicators.

"I thought that was you," David said. "Nevaeh said you'd agreed to help me."

The groundskeeper nodded. Now that David had come, he was glad he'd agreed. A living person back here alone wasn't a good idea with an angry spirit about.

"Not so wet today," he said, feeling the need to say something.

"Happens. It'll rain so much everything floods, and a day later it's so dry you'd never know. The ground soaks it right up. Northwest Ohio used to be a swamp, and it's never forgotten."

"Mmm," the groundskeeper said, intelligently. "What're we up to this morning?"

"We're sectioning things off." David gestured at the forest. A bittersweet vine clung tighter to the sycamore it was strangling like it didn't want David to draw attention to it. "I mapped out the edges, so I know how much ground we have to cover. Now we'll split everything into grid squares so I can log each grave's location and make sure I don't miss any. I think that's the best way. But it's a big job, and I expect it'll be tedious, so I thought it'd go faster with two people."

The groundskeeper raised his eyebrows, impressed. Decades of ghost-hunting, and he'd never once gone about it this methodically. Maybe it would help his investigation. In the meantime, he could protect David from whoever was so angry.

More than once as they worked, the groundskeeper caught himself paying more attention to David than the spirits. His brow creasing. His tongue poking out. The numbers he mumbled as they blocked out grid squares.

Each time it happened, the groundskeeper told himself off. David wasn't his concern, so long as he wasn't beset by a spirit.

But he couldn't help it. David distracted him from the air's weight, and he needed distracting. The weight stole his breath, slowed his steps.

When they broke for lunch, the studiousness fell away. David sat on a log and shared his sandwich, laughing as damp seeped into his pants when he sat.

The groundskeeper responded when necessary but trained his eyes on the forest. If he hadn't already, he now would have rejected the idea the unease was an amalgam of the lingering hurts of every spirit who'd ever haunted these woods. If it had been, it wouldn't have been anything more than yesterday's faint weight, a despair the living would never feel. No more noticeable now than then.

Instead, there was the buzzing. The crimson haze. The weight bowing his shoulders like a yoke.

When David declared them done, everything south of the creek had been sectioned off. The groundskeeper rolled his shoulders as they headed north, muscles tense from fighting the air.

With a glance at him, David slowed.

"It's been hard on you today, hasn't it?" he said. "All this walking and bending and carrying... I'm so sorry, I should've asked if you were okay to do this kind of work."

The groundskeeper shook his head, well aware his winded

voice would negate what he was about to say. "Ain't that. It's... Ain't been sleeping too well of late, is all."

David's brow furrowed. The groundskeeper gazed at him evenly, but it was hard. David looked concerned, like the groundskeeper might be hiding a health problem.

David looked away first. The groundskeeper exhaled, feeling like a powerful spotlight had shifted off him.

"Okay. I just wanted to make sure."

They kept walking.

"Anyway," David said, "you can get your sleep again starting tomorrow. We got everything done I needed to today, and the rest I can do alone."

The groundskeeper looked up in alarm. "Be happy to keep helping. Anything you need."

David smiled, but he shook his head. The groundskeeper's heart sank.

"I appreciate it, truly. But I shouldn't keep you from your day job. Nevaeh needs the help more than I do. This was the hard part, I promise."

"All right," the groundskeeper said, but his mind whirred as they approached the creek.

He did have his own work to do. He couldn't be back here every day, keeping an eye on David.

But he didn't want to risk David working alone, unprotected. If he could've sent David off with iron or salt or a braid of Saint-John's-wort, if he had a good excuse for giving him some... Somehow, he didn't think a grown man would take such protections like Sayid al-Masri had, simply because the groundskeeper told him to.

The creek glinted in the intermittent sunlight. The groundskeeper followed David over the bridge, grateful to cross the slate-gray water.

Wind gusted through the trees. It carried a bright burst of crimson with it, writhing and angry. Branches rattled.

David stumbled. He caught himself on the bridge's side. A stone dislodged, splashing into the water.

The groundskeeper reached for him. "You all right?"

David laughed, but the sound was weak. "That was some wind, huh?"

"Some wind," the groundskeeper echoed, his eyes trained on the canopy. The air twisted. "Are you all right?"

"Peter."

His eyes snapped to David's face.

The historian was pale, but he wore a small smile. "Are *you* all right?"

The groundskeeper's eyes flickered toward the trees, but David patted his arm.

"It scared the bejeezus out of me, I'll admit," he continued, "but I'm fine. I didn't break a knee or a hip, still in one piece— no need to worry."

"Let's get out of here."

David plodded along the bridge's side without touching it. The groundskeeper kept close. The trees rustled, whispering about anger and intruders and death.

XV

Away from the back lot, the air was clear and light, but the groundskeeper was too busy thinking to appreciate it. He couldn't let David work alone unprotected. Surely something could keep him safe in case a ghost played another nasty trick like the one at the bridge.

Nevaeh stepped outside as they crested the knoll. Another person was with her, a head shorter than she was, with dark brown skin, an undercut, and inky lashes, wearing stylishly ripped jeans and a bomber jacket. David eyed them, but Nevaeh didn't introduce them.

"How'd things go today?"

"Excellent, thanks to my helper." David grinned at the groundskeeper. He seemed to have forgotten the incident at the bridge.

The groundskeeper tugged his cap over his pinkening ears. He wasn't about to forget.

"We got the whole area squared off." David's gaze returned to the person in the bomber jacket. "Tomorrow I'll start recording grave sites. I can do that on my own."

"Great." Nevaeh fiddled with her cardigan. "The board's coming for a visit next week, so I'd love to get this place looking nice. Not that it doesn't look nicer already," she added.

The groundskeeper tore his thoughts from the back lot long enough to dimple at her. No need for her to think anything was wrong; she didn't like the back lot anyway. Likely he didn't have to worry about *her* going there unprotected.

The person in the bomber jacket touched Nevaeh's back. She smiled at them—no bigger a smile than the groundskeeper had yet seen on her, but her whole face lit up. David swallowed his own smile.

"Sorry," Nevaeh said. "I know you have to go."

Their hand was still at her back. "A few of us are going to Creekside Park tonight for a bonfire. Come with?"

Her smile brittled.

"It's cool if not," the person said.

Nevaeh flushed. "Next time."

The person flashed a smile. "Next time."

They started for their car, a beat-up, jellybean-purple Neon in the office lot, but Nevaeh plucked their sleeve, her eyes even wider than usual.

"Lunch tomorrow, though?"

If the person noticed the strain in her voice, they didn't show it. They smiled again, their inky eyes flickering over her. "Definitely."

She relaxed and let go.

The moment the car door shut behind them, David asked, "Who was that?"

"No one." Nevaeh rubbed her arms. "A friend. Nothing."

David bit back another smile. "What's their name?"

"Nothing."

"That's an unusual name."

Nevaeh punched him gently in the shoulder. "It's Benji, okay? Benji Huang. Anyway," she said loudly, turning to the groundskeeper, "the board's visit."

David rubbed his shoulder, smile fading. "It might do you good to go out with people your own age, kiddo. Margo, or Yafa, or—"

Nevaeh ignored him. "They'll be here next Wednesday. The board."

David tried again. "I know everything's different, but—"

"This place looks a thousand times better than it did, but—"

"—it's okay to make new memories in old places."

"—I don't want to give them anything to complain about."

Nevaeh's nostrils flared. David worried his hairline with a thumb.

The groundskeeper's fingers twitched, but he decided to pretend he hadn't witnessed any of that. "They won't have anything to complain about by the time I'm done. Don't worry 'bout a thing."

Nevaeh sighed. "Thanks, but I always worry when the board visits. I'll see you guys later."

David touched her arm. "Nea—"

"Later." Nevaeh avoided his gaze. "Drop it, okay? Please?"

She was closed off again. Shrunken, arms around herself defensively. She caught the groundskeeper's eye, looked away too quickly.

David's lips quirked, but his eyes were sad. "Of course. I'm sorry."

Nevaeh's phone buzzed.

"I have to take this," she said, but she paused with the phone halfway to her ear. Her expression was strained again, her voice, too. "You're coming to dinner Sunday, right?"

David gave a small smile. "Wouldn't miss it."

She nodded and walked away, answering the phone.

David sighed softly. "I didn't mean to push. It's just been so long since I've seen her smile like that."

"I've never seen her smile like that," the groundskeeper said.

"She used to. When she was a kid." They paused at Elijah's grave. "It's a shame she didn't come home more. Eli missed her terribly."

Elijah's yearning for his daughter was cranberry-tart. It made the groundskeeper ache. He'd never returned home, once he'd left. Even his letters hadn't made it. Until Jack told him no one had received a single one, he thought they'd refused to write back, too angry and ashamed over what they believed he'd done.

"I know she missed him, too." David scratched his forehead. "And the rest of us. But every time she visited, she was just like this—tense and uncomfortable and in a hurry to leave."

The groundskeeper said nothing. He'd never returned home because he couldn't. Because the curse wouldn't let him. If he could have—if he could've seen his family again—he would've stayed forever.

"Leta's trying to get her to stay. Her mother," David said. "But I think she's fighting a losing battle. With Eli gone…" He touched Elijah's headstone. "I miss you, you old grump."

The spirit's affection for his friend spun upward like a flurry of autumn leaves. David couldn't feel it, but the groundskeeper could, and he let himself bask in it. It soothed his aching muscles, draining the tension from his body.

If Nevaeh could feel this, he thought, surely she'd never leave.

David fiddled with the placket of his coat. "That was silly, wasn't it? Talking to a headstone like that."

The groundskeeper's fingers twitched again, but he didn't touch David's shoulder. That brief pat at the bridge had been more than enough. "Not at all."

David rubbed his neck.

"I never talk to Isaiah like that. Well—he's not here anyway. Cremated. I have an urn at the museum. Thought people might want to pay their respects. And they do." He dropped his backpack in the grass and plopped down. The groundskeeper sat beside him. "The kids talk to him all the time. It's funny. They say he haunts the place. But I never talk to him like that."

He drew his knees up to his chest. "Maybe I should."

The groundskeeper almost asked what exactly the kids said about Isaiah haunting the museum, but he changed his mind.

He made a mental note in case he needed to know more about Isaiah later—if the cemetery's back lot yielded nothing and he needed a new place to look for the ghost story that had sent him here. He could ask the al-Masri children about it, if he saw them again.

Anyway, David sounded so soft and sad that the groundskeeper didn't want to press.

Instead he said, "I never talked to Jack like that, neither."

He didn't mention never visiting Jack's grave. He'd avoided cemeteries for decades after realizing he could sense the dead. After Jack's death, he'd avoided one cemetery in particular, scared he'd find Jack lingering among the throng of spirits.

Scared he wouldn't.

David rested his cheek on his knees. "Jack, that was your husband?"

Officially, it hadn't been possible. They'd shared a life for fifty years. Their neighbors in Melbourne had understood the nature of their relationship. But in those days, everyone discreetly referred to them as confirmed bachelors and accepted that, were one of them invited to a wedding or barbecue or dinner party, the other would tag along.

He sank his fingers into the grass. "We were boys together. Heard nary a word from him for years after I left home. Years and years. But when we met again, it was like we'd never been apart."

He buried memories of his homeland and family as best he could, but Jack was on his mind more often than not. Yet he rarely remembered him like this: their earliest days in Ballygar, the trajectory of their history. The hope, the disbelief, when, after eighteen years, that familiar voice had murmured his name in his ear in a crowded Melbourne pub.

The memories illuminated his face. David, looking at him, forgot about the headstones, the cemetery, and how their conversation had started. His breath caught at the sight of the groundskeeper wearing that quiet joy.

Then the groundskeeper's face grayed and slackened. Thinking of Jack inescapably meant thinking of him old and frail, withering like cut flowers until the morning Peter had awoken with him dead in his arms.

Fifty years snuffed out in an instant. So many intervening decades of loneliness.

He sighed. The grass was cool under his fingers.

David smiled crookedly, the way Jack always had. The groundskeeper looked away. Whatever was lurking in the back lot, he needed to find it and get gone. The sooner, the better.

"I'm grateful for the time I had with Isaiah," David said. "If I had that back, even knowing how it would end—the time we had was worth it."

The groundskeeper said nothing. He didn't regret the time he'd had with Jack, but the loss wasn't worth repeating. He had a feeling Nevaeh might understand that better than David did.

David lay back and linked his hands behind his head, squinting up at the clouds. His trench coat pooled around him.

"Sure you'll be able to get up from there?"

"I absolutely will not," David said, "but it doesn't matter. I was a goner the second I made the mistake of sitting on the ground."

The groundskeeper stroked the grass, watched the clouds' shadows pass over David's face, and told himself he was watching no such thing.

David pushed back into a sit with a groan. "Good gracious. I'm getting too old for this."

"On your own head be it. Said you wouldn't be able to get up."

"I'm getting up. I'm just getting up more slowly than I used to."

The groundskeeper stood, shaking his head. He, too, felt all the aches common to people in their seventies. Immortality guaranteed he wouldn't die, not that he wouldn't feel the effects of age.

He wasn't sure why he'd stopped aging at seventy, instead

of five decades earlier, when he'd been cursed. He had the un-comfortable feeling it was because he would've died at seventy had he not been cursed.

"Mr. David!"

The al-Masri children stood on the sidewalk with their bi-cycles, backpacks over their shoulders. Samira waved madly. Sayid waved once, twice, three times, then stopped as if it might bother them. He was wearing his circlet of Saint-John's-wort. The groundskeeper's mouth twitched.

David waved back. "Hey, kids. How's school going?"

Samira dumped her bike by the entrance. "We're done for today."

She tackled David with a hug. His laughter punched out of him. "I should hope so, since you're here."

"Mama said we could." Sayid leaned his bike against the cem-etery wall, propping his sister's beside it. "I asked. She called Auntie Nevaeh to make sure it was okay and everything."

Samira flung herself at the groundskeeper next, to his con-sternation. He patted her head gingerly.

David grinned. "I see you've met. Samira and I are well ac-quainted. Her father brings her to the museum at least once a month, if he's not out of town on business."

Samira sagged against the groundskeeper. "Not this weekend."

"We were *grounded,* Samira," Sayid said in a long-suffering voice. "Thanks to you."

Samira stuck her tongue out and let go of the groundskeeper. He hastened out of range of her hugs, tripping over David's legs. David stifled his laughter.

The spirits were less subtle. Elijah's giggles gusted through the cemetery like wind. Sayid shivered, hugging himself.

"Hey, I have to get going." David plucked at the groundskeeper's jeans. "Help me up, would you?"

The groundskeeper hauled David to his feet. David stumbled; Peter steadied him with a hand on his waist.

David smiled. "Thanks."

"Sure," Peter said, not entirely sure what the thanks was for. His brain had frozen like a pond in winter.

He let go, stepped back.

David grabbed his backpack. "See you tomorrow. Bye, kids. Say hi to your parents for me."

The groundskeeper pulled his cap over his eyes and turned to the children to keep his gaze from following David up the street.

"So," he said gruffly, "you've permission to be here this time, have you?"

Sayid blushed. Samira rolled her eyes.

"Sayid wouldn't let me come unless we called Mama first."

The groundskeeper worried his hairline. "You hungry?"

Sayid scrunched the hem of his T-shirt. "Mmm-hmm."

"Starving," Samira said.

The groundskeeper nodded toward his cottage. "Come on, then."

Samira slipped her hand into his. His heart stuttered. He pulled away, with the pretense of picking lint from his shirt, and shoved his hands in his pockets so she couldn't do it again. The spirits shivered with laughter behind him.

XVI

Samira kept up a steady stream of chatter as the groundskeeper made potato cakes. He grunted now and then to show he was listening, until she mentioned an upcoming field trip to the museum.

That caught his interest. The children's unexpected arrival had distracted him from ghosts, but now he remembered that David's deceased husband supposedly haunted the museum. The groundskeeper loaded a plate with potato cakes and set it on the table. Samira immediately grabbed a cake and chomped on it.

"Hear tell it's haunted," the groundskeeper said. "The museum."

"Ghosts aren't real," Sayid said at once.

Samira snorted, spraying him with potato. "They are, too."

"Don't talk with your mouth full," the groundskeeper said, handing a kitchen towel to her brother so he could wipe himself off. "Tell me after you swallow."

Samira rolled her eyes but obeyed. "Mr. Isaiah haunts the museum."

"Mr. Isaiah?"

"Mr. David's husband," Sayid said.

"We see him all the time," Samira added.

"We do *not*."

"Do so," Samira said, taking a second potato cake.

The groundskeeper ate his own supper at the stove, if you could call it supper at three thirty in the afternoon. Their disagreement didn't bother him: Samira was still young enough to likely see ghosts; Sayid wasn't, unless they wanted him to.

"Scares you, does he?"

Samira shook her head. "He's a nice ghost. He only scares people for fun."

The groundskeeper's lips twitched. "That so?"

"Mmm-hmm." Samira took another bite of potato cake, forgetting his earlier request for her to swallow before speaking. "All the kids want him to scare them."

"Do not," Sayid mumbled, but he said nothing more.

No matter. He and Samira had said enough. Probably true that Isaiah haunted the museum, with that kind of detail about his ghostly doings rather than questionable stories about a tragic death. If Sayid hadn't seen him, he might not be powerful enough to take form; if he were, it sounded as if he were far too friendly a ghost to be the type the groundskeeper had come here for.

Eating a third potato cake, Samira asked, "When can we go exploring?"

Sayid choked on potato. "It's a cemetery, not a playground!"

"Why did you think I wanted to come?"

"You'll not be doing anything 'til you've finished your supper," the groundskeeper said mildly, not planning to let her explore at all if he could help it. Like as not, she'd disappear in back, and he'd have to find her again. "What about homework, then?"

"I did mine at school," Samira said.

Sayid snorted, opening his backpack.

The groundskeeper chuckled. "Did you, now? P'rhaps you won't mind showing me. Loved school, I did."

She hesitated. "I did most of it."

"Most?"

"Well…some of it."

"Some. I see."

She scarfed down her remaining food, opened her backpack and flopped on the floor on her stomach with it. "I'll just finish the rest real quick."

The groundskeeper tended the pullets as the children worked, with the Dutch door open so he could keep an ear on them. The scent of potatoes lingered, mingling with the resident herbs. Sayid worked silently. Samira sighed and complained and (when she really was working) mumbled to herself a great deal. Upon completing a math worksheet, she announced herself done, but her brother, without looking up from his essay, reminded her of her daily ten-minute read-aloud.

"I don't have my book." Samira stuffed her folder into her backpack. "I left it in my desk."

"Again?"

"I got books," the groundskeeper said from outside. "Not many, mind. There on the crate in the other room."

Samira slunk away, reappearing with a tattered book. A finger of sunlight lanced through the window.

She squinted. "Mama's not here for me to read to."

The groundskeeper closed the coop. The pullets pecked at their food, peeping. "Read to me, child."

She bit her lip, settling back onto the floor. "Okay."

She didn't read; she fidgeted. Cleared her throat. Fidgeted some more. The groundskeeper had been examining his hydrangeas, but he peered inside when she sniffled.

To his astonishment, her face was twisted up against tears.

"Samira?"

She swallowed. Her voice trembled. "I can't read this."

Sayid looked up from his work for the first time. "Did you forget your slider? I can tear out a piece of paper for you."

His voice was encouraging, understanding, and the groundskeeper's heart clenched. He'd calmed Catherine with that voice long ago, when she had a fit and no one else could mollify her for love or money, not Eoin, not even Mam.

"No." Fat tears rolled down Samira's cheeks. "I can't read it at all."

"Yes, you can." Sayid slipped the book from her limp grasp, then frowned. "Wait. I can't read it, either."

Ah. The groundskeeper had forgotten.

Samira sniffled. "You can't?"

"Nope." Sayid held the book out. Joining them at the table, the groundskeeper took it. "What language is this?"

"Irish." The book was the groundskeeper's oldest one, a volume of Irish poetry Jack had brought from home when he'd emigrated. He'd given it to the groundskeeper not long after they'd found each other in Melbourne. It was the first piece of home, aside from his father's watch, that Peter had had since he fled. "I'm sorry, child, I wasn't thinking."

"Can *you* read it?" she asked.

"Sure, I can read it."

He opened it at random, fell upon the last stanzas of "The Lament for Art O'Leary." It had been a long time since he'd read it, far longer since he'd read it aloud.

"Ní scaipfidh ar mo chumha," he read, "atá i lár mo chroí á bhrú…"

The words on his tongue were like coming home. Sweet and aching and familiar.

Like Ballygar.

Like Harrington, strange as that was.

"…dúnta suas go dlúth mar a bheadh glas a bheadh ar thrúnc 's go raghadh an eochair amú."

He ran a finger down the page, the sounds echoing softly in his own ears, then abruptly shut the book. Lár mo chroí á bhrú, indeed. He ought to have chosen something less tragic.

Samira wiped her eyes on her arm. "Oh. It's like Jeddo's books."

The groundskeeper raised his eyebrows.

"Our grandpa," Sayid said. "He reads to us in Arabic. Used to." He returned to his essay. "He lives at the hospital now."

The groundskeeper handed the book to Samira. "Grab me the red one with the gold lettering on the front. That one's in English."

Samira disappeared again.

"Didn't mean to confuse her." The groundskeeper pulled up a chair and sat backward in it. "Forgot I had books in Irish and she wouldn't know which ones."

"It wasn't you." Sayid frowned, checking something in his textbook. "She has a hard time reading. Mama thinks she's dyslexic, but the school won't test her."

Samira returned and sat cross-legged on the floor, repeating her earlier fidgeting and throat-clearing like a ritual. When she opened the requested book, she frowned.

"This book should get an F. The writer didn't capitalize his sentences."

Sayid peered over her shoulder with interest until he saw it. "Oh. E. E. Cummings. That's kind of his thing."

"Mrs. Albright says you have to capitalize every sentence." Samira flipped further through the book as if to determine how low a percentage grade E. E. Cummings should get for failing to follow grammar conventions.

The groundskeeper chuckled. "Poetry has but a passing acquaintance with the rules, near as I can tell. There, child. Read that one to me."

Sayid tore a piece of paper from his notebook. Samira folded it over to cover up every line but the one she was reading. The poem was "anyone lived in a pretty how town," a favorite of the groundskeeper's since he'd found this book in a four-story Detroit bookstore in the 1980s.

Samira read the poem hesitantly but fine. The groundskeeper knew it by heart and helped when a word tripped her up. He'd always had a head for memorizing poetry, if not for analyzing it.

When it was over, they sat in silence. Sayid was wrapping up his essay. Samira frowned at the page.

"What's it mean?"

The groundskeeper rested his chin on his arms like an old hound snoozing in the sun. "Don't rightly know. I catch bits of it, I reckon. But I like it because it sounds so nice."

"That's why I don't like poetry," Sayid said. "What's the point of something if you can't understand it?"

"That's why I do like it," the groundskeeper responded. "I don't understand poetry, and I don't understand life, neither. The poetry at least is beautiful."

Sayid frowned, but he put his essay away without answering. The sky had cleared; late-afternoon sunlight slanted inside. The kitchen glowed. The herbs hummed.

"'With up so floating many bells down,'" Samira quoted softly. She thumbed through the book. "Are there any more like this?"

Sayid abandoned the kitchen for the garden, poking his fingers into the chicken run and mumbling to both pullets and plants. When she tired of poetry, Samira drew in Sayid's notebook. Nevaeh poked her head in to say hi to the kids and ended up sitting on the kitchen floor for almost an hour, drawing with Samira.

The sun was setting by the time Yafa called Sayid to say she was coming home and ask if they'd finished their homework. Nevaeh saw them to the front gate, locked up, and biked away.

The groundskeeper drove the children home. Yafa waved as she herded them inside. He drove off in the twilight alone, humming old jazz tunes and marveling at the sky streaked orange and purple. The first stars had emerged by the time he made it back.

One of Samira's drawings sat on the table, a monstrosity of pencil, blue and black pen, and various shades of highlighter because Sayid hadn't had crayons in his pencil case. It was, best the groundskeeper could tell, his kitchen. There was the Dutch door. The sink, with its window and checkered curtain. The table, with a smiling stick-figure Samira and a frowning stick-figure Sayid, and a stick-figure Peter standing nearby.

He chuckled. Warmth bloomed inside him like a dandelion growing through a crack in the pavement. He stuck the picture on the icebox.

He should've realized then the danger he was in.

XVII

A couple days later, the cold spell broke. The May sky was deep blue. The groundskeeper cut flowers from the Saint-John's-wort in his front room and the rue and lavender in his garden. He twirled the sprig of flowers between thumb and forefinger, humming as he arranged them and tied them with twine.

It wasn't much, the sprig, but David could keep it in his pocket to repel spirits without knowing its purpose. It would do until the groundskeeper thought up an excuse to provide him better protection.

The groundskeeper stuck the sprig in his breast pocket and puttered around, awaiting David's arrival. With his intern out of state, finishing up her semester, David was alone at the museum; he didn't want it closed *all* day. He planned to spend mornings at the museum and join the groundskeeper for lunch before cataloging graves in the back lot.

When he arrived at noon, David wore a white-and-silver pin-striped bow tie and a royal blue waistcoat patterned with silver fish. He smiled and said, "Hey, Peter," and the groundskeeper's heart stuttered. He presented the sprig.

David took it even as he asked, "What's this for?"

The groundskeeper tugged at his flat cap. He'd hoped it wouldn't come up.

He held out a hand. "I'll take 'em back if you don't want 'em."

David tucked the flowers into his pocket. "Oh, no, I want them. They're beautiful. Thank you."

The groundskeeper blushed.

"Lunch?" he said gruffly.

When David headed into the trees alone after lunch, the groundskeeper swallowed his worry. David had his flowers. If the groundskeeper wanted to keep Harrington safe, best find whatever angry spirit was back there and be rid of it. Since he couldn't suss it out, he abandoned his work and headed for the office.

The building glinted in the sunlight, a utilitarian frame of windows. Its newness prickled like a woolen sweater. The groundskeeper removed his cap as he crossed the threshold.

He knocked at Nevaeh's open door. She hunched in her swivel chair, turning an appointment card over in her fingers. Her curls were uncovered today.

"Heading out," he said. "So's you know."

Her eyes were glued to the card. "What?"

He repeated himself, and again. She looked up blankly.

He twisted his cap. It was none of his concern.

He asked anyway.

"All right, lass?"

Her expression cleared. She gave the smallest imaginable smile.

"I'm fine. Yeah. Sorry. I'm…" She hadn't stopped fiddling with the card. "Sorry, what were you saying?"

He told her where he was going. She nodded. He still wasn't sure she'd heard.

He walked to the library, enjoying the warmth. Clover and violets bloomed in Harrington's lawns. Birds sang in trees and shrubs: wood thrushes, house finches, bluebirds, various warblers. His walk took longer than it should've; he kept stopping to listen.

The library was slammed. RVs with out-of-state plates crowded the parking lot alongside locals' cars. Inside, people in cargo pants, vests, and sneakers milled about, holding massive cameras. Several gathered in the nonfiction section, comparing the photos on their cameras to the pictures in field guides. More had crowded into a small side room, where a naturalist was giving a presentation called "Waterfowl of the Maumee River Watershed."

Four more such people were at the library's four computers, which was going to spoil the groundskeeper's afternoon plans if they didn't log off soon.

He joined the line stretching from the information desk to the door, cap in hand. Someone tapped his shoulder.

"Hi," Sayid said shyly.

The groundskeeper dimpled. "Hello, lad. No school today?"

"It was a half day." Sayid fidgeted with his T-shirt but smiled back. "What are you doing here?"

"Hoping to do some research, but I don't figure I'll get much done less'n one of those computers frees up." The groundskeeper nodded at the group arguing in the nonfiction section. "Where'd all these people come from?"

"They're here for the birding," Sayid said. "Early May is peak season. Mama likes to take a weekend at the state park for it. We camp out and she goes birdwatching with Auntie Leslie, and Baba takes us to the beach and we eat lots of s'mores. But I don't think we're going this year." He bit his lip. "If you need a computer, you can borrow my Chromebook."

The groundskeeper smiled at him. "Might take you up on that."

"Okay." Sayid pointed, looking pleased and trying not to. "We're over there."

Books and papers cluttered their table. Samira waved so hard she seemed liable to wave her arm off. The groundskeeper waved back.

He joined them after he'd gotten his new library card. Every one he'd ever had was in a little box at the bottom of his steamer trunk, with the few other precious things he owned.

Samira was drawing with crayons this time, on computer paper from a librarian.

"I'm glad you joined us," she said, as if they'd had a meeting scheduled. "Sayid wouldn't let me go to the cemetery."

Sayid sighed, digging his Chromebook from his backpack. "I *told* you, Mama will be here after work. She wants to sit in on that talk about warblers."

Samira huffed. "Bet she'll forget."

"Will not. She's been looking forward to it all week."

The groundskeeper sat between them so they wouldn't argue.

Sayid connected to the library's internet and handed his Chromebook to the groundskeeper. He hesitated. "Please be careful with it. It's just that I have to give it back to the school at the end of the year."

With his notepad beside him, the groundskeeper dug into the library's database on Ohio history. He doubted he'd get much more today than avenues for further research. He preferred spirits considerate enough to be obvious; feeling his way to a well-marked grave was faster than researching suspects likely to become vengeful spirits. If he found the thing, at worst he could trap it until he figured out why it had stayed and how to send it on.

He had time, however. It was only the first week of May. Like as not, he'd have the ghost found and expelled in a couple weeks. By month's end at most. Well in time for him to leave, to hide away for Midsummer, before moving on to the next town.

He never chased ghosts at Midsummer.

He searched for local ghost stories first. Unless a local historian, paranormal investigator, or anthropologist had collected them, ghost stories were scant in databases; usually, he found mere whispers. Flyers advertising haunted locales. News reports of strange occurrences, victims blaming ghosts. Local kids scared witless by something they hadn't initially believed in. Samira's insights into Isaiah Schwertner had been much more straightforward than the things he usually heard. Helpful to know someone around town. Usually, the best he could hope for was an inaccurate claim containing nuggets of truth that might eventually lead him to whatever ghost he was looking for.

Research into Harrington's local legends yielded nothing. An old woman interviewed in a newscast about gas prices in 2008 had said, "It's the ghost, always is," but the correspondent, with a steely smile, had abruptly returned the story to the studio. With nothing to go on but "the ghost," the groundskeeper couldn't find anything more about the allegedly price-hiking spirit.

Perhaps he didn't need a database.

He set the Chromebook aside. "You two tell me anything more about ghosts?"

Sayid's brow furrowed. "Ghosts aren't real."

"They are so," Samira sang, drawing a flower.

"So you said." The groundskeeper rubbed his chin. "Maybe you disagree on the ghosts themselves, but what about the stories? Local legends. Hauntings."

Sayid fiddled with his book. "Why do you want to know?"

"Call it a personal interest."

Samira swapped her crayon for a pencil and practiced writing encoded messages in the flower's petals.

"Well..." Sayid paged through his book like he'd find Harrington's ghost stories written there. "There's the one on Morrow Road. This woman. Her son disappeared there, and they never found him. She's still looking for him. They say." He closed the book with a snap. "And, um, there's this ghost Chloe blames whenever she does bad on a test."

"Chloeeeeeeeee," Samira singsonged, working on her code.

Sayid's ears pinkened. "It's not *just* Chloe. The grown-ups around town talk about him, too. Like last year...it was really bad. A bunch of people lost work when this factory closed, and Mr. Isaiah died, and so did Uncle Qasim, and we had this gross, hot summer, and everyone got eaten alive by mosquitoes or sunburnt or both...and all our neighbors blamed the ghost."

Samira's brows puckered.

"Where's he s'posed to be, this ghost?" The groundskeeper scratched a note in his pad. "The other's on Morrow Road, but what about this one?"

Sayid raised and lowered one shoulder. "Bobby Sawyer says he haunts the old general store, but I've never seen him."

The groundskeeper huffed a laugh. "But you seen the other one, huh?"

Sayid blushed, reopening his book. "No."

"Either of these ghosts have names?"

"Marie-Louise Delacour. That's the one on Morrow Road." Sayid buried his nose in his book, sinking low in his chair. "I don't know about the other one."

It was a start. The groundskeeper added *Morrow Road* and *general store?* to his to-do list. Even if Sayid's friend was wrong, and no spirits haunted the old general store, the groundskeeper could dig into the building's memories—if it held any—to see what he could find out about its past inhabitants. The memories buildings held weren't always helpful, but sometimes they told him things research couldn't.

Beside him, Sayid popped up from his book. A family of five had just walked in; one of the children was a Black boy around his own age. Sayid sank down again as the family drew closer, but his eyes followed the boy over the top of his book.

The corner of the groundskeeper's mouth turned up. He'd once looked at Jack that way, hoping and fearing in equal measure that Jack would look back.

"We can't get books yet," the boy explained to one of his younger siblings as they passed. "We have to get library cards first. Then we get books."

The family joined the line at the desk, which was shorter than it had been when the groundskeeper arrived. Birders were still everywhere, but they had abandoned the desk for the shelves or formed into groups to debate the identification of birds they'd seen that morning.

Samira went to talk to a librarian. Sayid twisted around to make sure she was out of earshot.

"Can I ask you something?" he said in a low voice.

"Course."

Sayid thumbed through his book. "How do you know if you like boys?"

His ears were pink. The groundskeeper considered him. *You know because you look at them the way you just looked at that one there* seemed like a bad answer.

"The same way you know you like girls, I reckon."

Sayid twisted around again, but Samira was now helping the librarian reshelve books. He kept thumbing through his book, turning pinker and pinker and glancing occasionally at the boy and his family, but said nothing more.

"Thinking you like boys, are you?" Peter asked, not unkindly.

Sayid sank so low in his chair he almost slid out of it. "Maybe."

"No shame in it."

"I know." Sayid fidgeted with his shirt. "Can I tell you a secret?"

"All right."

Sayid was pinker than ever. "I like Chloe."

Peter bit back a laugh. "Ain't much of a secret."

"That's not the secret." Sayid's voice cracked. His eyes flickered back toward the boy, whose family had acquired their library cards and were now heading for the children's books. "The secret is, I like Chloe, but there's this new boy in our class who's… He's… I think I might sort of like him, too." His voice grew mumblier and mumblier. "He just. He has. Really pretty eyes."

He had all but disappeared under the table. Peter arranged his face so he wouldn't be laughing when the boy reemerged.

"Anyway," Sayid mumbled, "I was wondering if that was, like…a normal thing to think. About another boy."

"Normal to think if you like boys. Couldn't tell you if it's normal if you don't."

Sayid nodded without sitting up.

Peter rubbed his neck. "S'all right, that. My Jack was that way. Liked boys and girls both."

Sayid chanced a glance up. His blush faded. "He did?"

"Sure, he did." Peter's expression softened. He caught himself, cleared his throat. "Any more questions?"

Sayid shook his head and scooted upright. "Thanks. For talking with me about it."

Peter had worried over it himself, when he was young. How much he'd liked other boys. As much as he'd longed for Jack to notice him, he'd been scared when it had finally happened. "Anytime."

Sayid bit his lip. "You won't tell anyone, will you?"

"Ain't mine to tell."

Sayid relaxed.

"I know they won't care. My friends, I mean. Mama and Baba…" His brow furrowed. "I don't know. Baba's friends with Mr. David, and everyone knows he's gay. And Auntie Maryam is queer. She even brought her girlfriend over to celebrate Eid with us, but… I don't know. They never really talk about it."

Peter squeezed his shoulder, not sure what to say. It hadn't been talked about in general, in his day; he'd been almost as afraid of his mam finding out about him and Jack as anyone else.

"They'd still love me, anyway," Sayid concluded, looking a little less uncertain. "I just…don't want to say anything until I figure it out, I guess."

"I never liked saying anything much about it at all." Dangerous, in Peter's day. Dangerous still, depending on a number of things including where you were and who was with you, but far better overall than when he'd been young. "Good you know you've got folks you can talk to about it if you want."

Sayid bit his lip again, hands fisting in his shirt.

"Like you?" he said softly. "Can I talk to you about it again sometime, if I need to?"

The corner of Peter's mouth turned up. "If you need to, sure."

Samira returned with the librarian in tow, eager to show off her drawings. Sayid hastily pretended to be engrossed in his book.

Peter resumed his research with a chuckle.

He spent the afternoon studying Morrow Road, Marie-Louise Delacour, and Harrington's old general store. The birders persisted, but he forgot them as he dug deeper into the library databases.

He found little on Morrow Road. An announcement of the marriage of Marie-Louise Arnaud to André Delacour in 1887. A newspaper clipping, barely a paragraph, noting the disappearance of the Delacour boy in 1893. Various maps marking the location of Morrow Road back to its days as a cow path. It ran along the cemetery's southern end, separated by nothing but a cornfield, which was the only promising thing about it.

He found considerably more information on the general store, most of it connected with the original owner—a ghost he'd met. John Kowalczyk had built the place, when Harrington was little more than a work camp on the Ashmead's banks, and died of cholera in 1849.

The groundskeeper added John Kowalczyk to his notes with grim satisfaction. He'd found John Kowalczyk's grave once and could find it again. John's memories hadn't been terribly clear, but they'd been clearer than any others in the back lot. He had an important connection to the general store. His grave was in the back lot. Maybe he was stronger than he'd seemed.

The groundskeeper stretched, rubbing his eyes. The internet made his research easier than it had once been, but sitting at a computer for hours on end did a number on him.

Yafa al-Masri arrived as he shut down Sayid's Chromebook. She had bags under her eyes, but the sight of her children softened the crease in her brow. She kissed their foreheads, dropping into the last empty chair with a sigh.

"How was work?" Sayid asked.

"Well, it's over now." Yafa grimaced. "I want to hear this talk and go home." She smiled at the groundskeeper. "Hi. Sorry. It's been a long day."

"S'all right. Been a long day all around."

A laugh escaped her. Her eyes were red and puffy. Sayid squeezed her hand.

Samira's brows puckered again. She picked at her crayon's paper label.

Yafa watched her.

"You know," she said to the groundskeeper, "I didn't catch your name when you drove the children home. I don't know how I didn't realize."

His skin prickled. Sayid frowned. No doubt he'd realized he didn't know the groundskeeper's name, either.

The groundskeeper recovered, clearing his throat.

"Peter," he said. "Shaughnessy."

"Yafa," Yafa said.

"I remember."

Her smile deepened briefly.

The librarian at the desk rang a bell. The crowd in the library, smaller now, fell silent.

"'Who's Singing: Identifying Warblers by Call' starts in fifteen minutes," the librarian said. "Naturalist Matt Perry will be presenting. We have limited seating, so I recommend making your way to the conference room now. Thank you."

Yafa's face lit up. She waved to a small clump of birders heading into the conference room. They waved back, promising to save her a seat.

"That's me," she said to the children. "Do you want to come, or would you rather wait here?"

Samira shredded the paper she'd peeled off the crayon. "I'm coloring."

Yafa's smile faltered, but she hitched it back into place. "Okay, habibti. Sayid?"

He shook his head, his eyes boring into his sister. "I'll stay here."

"Okay." Yafa pinched the bridge of her nose. When she smiled again, her lips were too wide, pressed tight, her eyes too crinkled. "Peter," she said, and his heart stuttered, "would you like to join us for dinner after? I thought we'd go for pizza, since Khalid's out of town."

His breath caught. He had lunch with David every day, but it was always on cemetery grounds. David had never asked, really; he'd come and sat and had done so every day since.

An invitation felt different.

Likely they'd appreciate the company. Yafa looked so tired. He hadn't missed the catch in her voice when she mentioned her husband's absence.

But he couldn't.

"Thank you kindly," he said, "but I'm previously engaged."

"Another time, perhaps."

"P'rhaps." The groundskeeper flipped his notepad closed and gave Sayid's Chromebook back. "Thanks for the help, lad."

Samira glanced up. "You're leaving?"

"Aye. Things to do at home yet." He hesitated. "Be here round about the same time tomorrow, and maybe a few days after. If you're looking for me."

"Okay." She scrambled to her feet for a hug, her arms tight around his waist. She shoved her drawing at him. "This is for you."

He made his escape with the drawing crumpled in his hand, feeling he'd been right to decline dinner.

XVIII

He'd expected the next few days to go the same, but he hadn't counted on the birders.

Each morning, they flocked to the cemetery like they flocked to parks across Northwest Ohio every May. The groundskeeper's blood pressure rose as dozens of people traipsed the woods with binoculars, field guides, and telephoto lenses. He couldn't offer every one of *them* a daily sprig of flowers.

Nevaeh worried, too, for different reasons.

"That bridge is going to collapse on someone," she said to him one morning. "The thing's older than dirt. With all this extra foot traffic… The last thing I need is someone suing the cemetery because they break a leg or something. And what if they damage the headstones?"

"Could put up signs."

Nevaeh laughed hollowly. "I grew up here. I know how they are. But it's better than nothing, I guess."

They spent an hour erecting signs warning people to cross the bridge at their own risk and not to touch, stand on, sit on, put anything on, or otherwise damage the headstones. Nevaeh shouted at a middle-aged white woman who was balanced on a stone, snapping a picture of the Tennessee warbler above. The groundskeeper shouted at the same woman a moment later, when she muttered some unflattering things about Nevaeh. The woman stalked off in a huff.

Nevaeh blinked. "Whoa. You *yelled* at her."

He tugged on his cap. Elijah had followed them, despite the groundskeeper's whispered warnings. Now he was a bright, vicious orange, pleased the groundskeeper had shouted at the woman since he couldn't. "So did you."

"Yeah, I know *I* did. But you're…you know—" she gestured at him "—like that."

"She deserved it," he said mildly. "I won't stand for such language."

Nevaeh scratched her forehead. "Well…thanks, I guess."

They headed out of the back lot. The groundskeeper breathed easier. The signs wouldn't protect the birders from ghosts unless they kept the birders clear out of the back lot, but Nevaeh, at least, would be safe in her office. And Elijah was fine so far.

But he'd been fine that first morning, too, until he hadn't. Best keep an eye on him, the groundskeeper thought.

Nevaeh chewed the inside of her cheek. "Thanks for your help today."

"S'what I'm here for. Not that I wouldn't've wanted to help you anyhow," the groundskeeper amended. "You're a nice lass. Pleasure working with you."

She ducked in embarrassment. "You, too. It's nice not being here by myself all the time."

Elijah flowed around them like water, soft and yellow, but he blued at her words. She was never alone here; she just didn't know it. His sigh ruffled her hair wrap, which was different today, though equally bright: she'd swapped the amethyst for lime green.

"Hsst," the groundskeeper said softly. Elijah moped alongside them.

"Did you say something?"

"Thinking, is all."

"What about?"

The groundskeeper glanced at Elijah, who was still tinged blue.

"Family." He scratched his cheek, considering the spirit. The yearning and care, that warm yellow love, all the things Elijah felt that the groundskeeper had gone so long without. "Can I ask you something?"

She eyed him. "That depends on what it is."

"Don't have to answer, if you don't want."

Nevaeh smiled unwillingly. "I'm holding you to that."

He dimpled, but it faded.

"Love your family, don't you?" he said. "That's clear enough. But David says you never did like coming back."

She looked away. "Did he put you up to this? I'm moving back to Cleveland once things are set here. He knows that."

"Asking, is all. On no one's account but my own." The groundskeeper glanced at her. "My folks been gone a long time. If I could go home again—if they were there—figure I'd never leave. Don't understand why you're so eager to keep away, I guess."

Nevaeh didn't answer. Fair was fair; she didn't have to. He trained his eyes on the ground as they crested the knoll, pretending he hadn't said anything.

At last she said, in a strained voice, "They're not all here, though. Pops died, god, fifteen years ago. And Dad…"

Her voice cracked.

"Sure, that's hard," the groundskeeper said softly.

They stopped near his cottage. She hugged herself. Elijah hugged her, too, wrapped her in that blue-tinged yellow she couldn't feel.

"It's *different*," she said. "It's always so different. Every time I come home, something's changed. I always think, when I come back, it'll be here waiting for me just the same, but instead…"

"It moves on without you. I know. Nothing's how you left it."

She hadn't expected him to understand. Her posture loosened. "Yeah."

She scuffed her feet in the grass. The groundskeeper averted his eyes, waiting for her to ask how he knew. He hadn't meant to show her that the same things that bothered her bothered him; he didn't want to explain his lonesome, itinerant life. He'd only wanted to make her feel better.

She picked nonexistent lint from her shirt.

"Well," she said, "hopefully those signs will keep people in line for the board's visit. Not that the board members will want to go back there, but just in case. If you get the time, maybe you can make the office garden look nice, too, now that everything else is ready for them."

His insides twinged at her suddenly businesslike attitude. But it wasn't as if they were friends.

"Sure, I'll take care of it." Determined to make her smile again, despite himself, he added, "And if that board has a word to say to you about this place not being shipshape, I ain't above yelling again."

She huffed a laugh, relaxing. Elijah brightened.

"Thanks, but yelling at them probably won't do either of us any favors."

They returned to their respective work. The groundskeeper hummed as he went about his weeding, never wondering why making her laugh, however slightly, should please him so.

XIX

The birders were relentless. They spent hours looking for birds who refused to appear because *they* knew something was wrong. Since the lack of birds didn't deter the birders, the groundskeeper spent his mornings watching over them. Already the birders complained of chills and unseen creatures pelting them with twigs, acorns, walnuts, and buckeyes.

He'd been pelted, too, with pebbles and sweetgum pods, and had thrown them right back, in no mood for such nonsense. So many living people back here hindered his work. The air's weight, its vibrations, the crimson snaking through the trees—darker each day—increased his irritation.

A volley of leaves, twigs, and dirt assaulted him. He dropped to his knees by the nearest headstone.

John Kowalczyk.

His irritation evaporated. He'd been so worried about the birders that he'd forgotten his plan to revisit John's grave.

Leaves rustled. The light shone green and gold through the canopy. Several yards away, birders hidden by trees whispered about an indigo bunting overhead.

"John Kowalczyk?" the groundskeeper said softly, so they wouldn't hear.

A pebble hit his shoulder. He laughed.

"You after all, is it? If we figure out what your problem is and send you packing, I can be on my way. Dead of cholera, I gather."

A jolt of fear, pus yellow. Another volley showered him, less volatile. The spirit's anger fizzled.

Doubt set in. If the spirit were strong enough to affect others, it ought not to tire so quickly.

But it was the most promising spirit he'd found. As it had some energy left to hurl things, he wasn't willing to give up on it.

"John Kowalczyk." Anger hung heavy in the air, even as John's faded. "Show yourself."

Most ghosts never took corporeal form, but a ghost powerful enough to affect others certainly could if it wanted to.

The air twisted. The groundskeeper waited.

Nothing more happened. His heart sank.

"John Kowalczyk," he repeated forcefully.

Nothing.

He gripped the headstone, pushing into it with all the presence-sensing in him.

The spirit was there, angry and fearful. But quiet. Worn from throwing things. Not permanently, but such tricks wearied your run-of-the-mill ghost.

The groundskeeper sat back with a sigh. Despite John's exhaustion, the air pressed on him. He'd dig deeper into John's history, but odds were this wasn't the ghost he was looking for.

He returned to his rounds. Someone yelped. He came running, but a cold spot had merely startled a teenager birding with her father.

"Can't we go yet?" The girl rubbed her arms. "It's freezing."

"I told you to wear long sleeves."

"It's *May*."

A screech, from a different direction. An acorn had hit someone in the arm.

"Was that a squirrel?"

"I've never known squirrels to throw things."

Two birders nearby were arguing over an expensive field guide one of them was certain the other had lost.

"I *didn't*. I swear it was right here. I put it down for a second to switch lenses..."

Long after they'd gone, the groundskeeper found their field guide in the crevice of a black walnut. Though the anger's source was hidden, it had now spread across the creek and delighted in whipping the lesser spirits into a frenzy. It enjoyed the birders' unease.

The groundskeeper brought the field guide home with him at lunchtime. His shoulders untensed, the anger's weight lessening with each step farther from the back lot.

"Taking an interest in birding?"

The groundskeeper cricked his neck. David grinned at him from the cottage garden, wearing a turquoise waistcoat patterned with flamingos.

Peter chuckled over the flamingos, relieved to escape the anger. "Not s'much as you are, I reckon."

David laughed. "It's the Biggest Week in American Birding. I'm contractually obligated to wear my best bird-themed clothing. Lunch?"

"In a minute. Figure if I drop this at the office, they might come looking. Door's unlocked if you want to wait."

"That's all right," David said. "I've been making friends with your chickens."

A pullet pressed against the chicken wire so he could stroke her back. The others nosed at him as if expecting a treat.

Peter chortled. "Might need your help soon, so's you know. With some research."

"Sure thing. Come by the museum sometime. What are we researching?"

"Ghosts," Peter said.

XX

Lenses, books, Fitbits, and journals filled a box in the corner of Nevaeh's office.

Nevaeh rubbed her temples at the sight of the field guide in the groundskeeper's hand. "Maybe we should close for a few days. I'm not loving our new lost and found. This is a cemetery, for god's sake."

That night, they hung a sign reading ENTRANCE BY APPOINT-MENT ONLY, along with another directing birders with missing items to the museum. David had taken the lost and found off their hands.

"Maybe I'll get more traffic this week if I hold their belongings hostage," he'd said.

He, of course, had a standing appointment and ate lunch with the groundskeeper daily before disappearing into the now-deserted back lot. He didn't wear his sprig of flowers—of course he didn't; he didn't know what it was for. The groundskeeper had prepared for this, however, and presented a new one every afternoon. David put it in his pocket without fail, and the groundskeeper resisted worrying overmuch as he headed to the library.

Until the day David didn't come.

With no birders to fuss over, the groundskeeper returned to the cottage well before noon, cheerful today without that weight burdening him. He left the door open for David and timed his shepherd's pie so it'd be ready for their lunch hour.

The cottage was bright, the plants humming snatches of secret song. He sat at the table and waited.

And waited.

And waited.

And got up, and fed and watered the pullets, and peered toward the cemetery gates, and went back in, and sat back down.

And waited.

His lunch hour ended.

He kept waiting.

The cottage shrank. It crowded him, small and warm and dizzying. He hadn't eaten, but his stomach twisted into knots.

He went to the office.

"David's not here."

Nevaeh was responding to an email. "The board canceled their visit. Not that I'm not glad to put off dealing with them awhile longer, but... Sorry, what did you say?"

"David's not here."

"Isn't he?"

"Did he call you?"

She looked at him for the first time, brows knitting together. "No. Should he have?"

"He's not here," the groundskeeper repeated desperately.

"Yeah, you said that." She took his hand. He looked at her like he was drowning and she had the only life ring. "Are you okay?"

He wrestled his panic, swallowed it best he could. His mouth was so dry his tongue stuck in his throat. "Fine. It's lunchtime, is all."

She squeezed his hand and let go. "Lunchtime. Gotcha. I'm sure he got caught up doing things at the museum."

"Where is the museum?"

XXI

The groundskeeper hurtled up Washington, his heart hammering. Shabby Victorians loomed. A utilitarian apartment building squatted between them. In a bedraggled dog park, an old beagle waddled along the chain-link fence, howling as the groundskeeper passed. The howling continued long after he left the dog park behind.

A funeral home full of death and spirits made his palms itch. He avoided looking at it, avoided looking, too, at the Catholic church beside it, a narrow brick structure clawing at the sky.

He hadn't stepped into a church in decades. The last time, he'd crept in in the evening, intending to light a votive for Jack even though he wasn't sure he believed in all that anymore. He'd felt like a criminal. A thief trying to steal some grace.

Then a voice had said, "Can I help you?" and he'd fled.

Now, in Harrington, the church's stained-glass windows glinted at him like eyes. He strode past with his head bent.

The Hodinka-Kopczyk Boarding House Museum was a massive Greek Revival house at the corner of Washington and Main, where the speed limit increased and Main turned into a highway barreling through corn and soy. David's Civic sat in the gravel parking lot, the lights in the building were on, and a tent sign stood at the bottom of the porch steps, reading COME ON IN!

The museum was open.

David was here.

Of course he was here.

The groundskeeper was a fool.

He stood by the historical marker at the roadside, chest heaving. He ought to leave, but he did have more research to do. Pulling his cap off, he dragged a hand through his hair and read the marker's inscription.

OHIO HISTORICAL MARKER
HODINKA-KOPCZYK BOARDING HOUSE MUSEUM

BUILT IN 1836 BY JOHN HODINKA FOR ANNE HARRINGTON AS A WEDDING GIFT, THIS GREEK REVIVAL BUILDING SOON BECAME HOME TO MORE THAN THE NEWLYWEDS. IN RESPONSE TO THE PANIC OF 1837, THE HODINKAS SUPPLEMENTED THEIR INCOME BY RENTING ROOMS, CONTINUING THIS PRACTICE LONG AFTER THE FINANCIAL HARDSHIP HAD PASSED. UPON THE DEATHS OF JOHN AND ANNE HODINKA, THEIR DAUGHTER, NINA, WITH HUSBAND, KASIMIR KOPCZYK, TOOK OVER THE BUSINESS.

THE HOME OPERATED CONTINUALLY AS A BOARDING HOUSE FROM THE TIME IT FIRST OPENED UNTIL THE LAST DESCENDANT OF NINA HODINKA KOPCZYK DIED IN 1998. UPON MARGARET ANNE KOPCZYK'S DEATH, THE HOUSE WAS GIFTED TO THE CITY OF HARRINGTON. THE MUSEUM OPENED TO THE PUBLIC IN 2002 AND HAS BEEN IN OPERATION EVER SINCE.

The groundskeeper hadn't made it past the porch when he sensed the ghost. He stopped in his tracks, staggered by its love.

The spirit's love permeated every molecule of air, every grain of wood, the glazing of the windows, everything, everything. The ghost—Isaiah Schwertner, if the children were any authority—loved this place with every fiber of his nonbeing. Loved it so much it fair glowed.

The groundskeeper had never seen such a powerful spirit

formed from love. But no mistake: it was no mere memory, no imprint from someone long gone. The spirit was here, infusing this place with all he felt.

The love washed through the groundskeeper, reminding him, despite his efforts to forget, of how much he loved everyone he'd ever lost. Of the affection he'd had for various people throughout the last century despite his attempts to feel none, the times he'd fled when he'd cared too much. How little affection anyone had had for him in that time, because he'd made sure they hadn't. The love wrapped him up warm and tight, put tears in his eyes and a lump in his throat.

It was wonderful and terrible, and it was several minutes before the groundskeeper felt equal to going inside. But at last the love settled under his skin, warm and pleasant, quelling his earlier panic.

He entered. A bell jingled.

David called from the back of the building, his voice muffled, "Be with you in a moment."

The groundskeeper's frantic heart calmed. David was fine. "Take your time."

He peered around the entryway, fiddling with his cap. To his left was the entrance to a dining room; to his right, a drawing room. A mahogany staircase was before him, with a hall tree beside it and the building's single, tiny bathroom beyond. In a small display case in the center of the entryway, a leather diary lay open. Anne Harrington Hodinka's, according to the plaque. The groundskeeper peered at it, but Anne Hodinka had had tight penmanship, and the glare on the case made it impossible to read.

Closer to the front door, a pedestaled display case stood against one wall, holding a plain, white urn. A bronze plaque on the case read *Isaiah Michael (Erdmann) Schwertner*, with his birth and death dates printed below.

Crowding the wall behind the case—pinned, taped, and tacked—notes, drawings, letters, poems, and prayer cards fought for space. Some were written in spidery cursive, others in the large, awkward crayon lettering of elementary schoolers. There were drawings of the museum, of a dark-haired man with glasses, a white-haired man with a bow tie, and some drawings of all three together, at varying levels of sophistication.

The groundskeeper studied the urn. He felt himself studied back.

"So it's you, is it?" he murmured. "Been told you haunt the place."

The ghost was delighted that fame preceded him. The groundskeeper examined a crayon drawing of a simplistic, square boarding house, complete with historical marker. A waistcoated man waved from the door; a bespectacled man smiled out an upper window.

"Don't reckon it's you I been looking for," the groundskeeper said, "but I'm pleased to make your acquaintance anyhow."

The air flared mintily.

The groundskeeper's brow furrowed. "The cemetery, sure, I work there. What're you—?"

Footsteps approached. He stepped away from the urn.

"Peter." David's smile was smaller than usual. "I thought that was you."

The groundskeeper's breath caught. The spirit had twisted up in a burst of sun-bright love; David glowed in it as brightly as an angel.

An angel with odd fashion sense. Today, he wore a soft orange bow tie and a waistcoat chevroned in white and sky blue.

The ghost loved this building, but he hadn't stayed for it.

He'd stayed for David.

The groundskeeper swallowed a twinge of jealousy. It was different. David didn't know Isaiah was there.

If Jack had stayed, the groundskeeper would have sensed him every moment.

He buried everything he was feeling, nodding at the wall's chaos. "What're these?"

David gave a quiet laugh. The air twisted lovingly.

"Isaiah's sort of become our mascot." He adjusted his bow tie, though it didn't need it. "At first it was letters from people who knew him—writing to say they missed him, offering prayers, things like that. And then I had this group of kids in, must've been the first field trip I'd had since he died, and they took an interest, wanted to know about him, and...well, I didn't know what to say. He'd been gone two months, and I was reeling. So I told them how he grew up here—right in this building, in fact, the great-aunt who raised him was the last Kopczyk—and how much he loved the place, and a couple of them asked if they could add to the wall. And I guess they told the other kids at school, because the next group wanted to know about him, too, and so did the next, and the one after that, and now they tell ghost stories about him and draw him pictures and such."

He touched a pen-and-ink sketch more detailed than most of the others: a portrait of a dark-haired, crooked-nosed young man with glasses, smiling shyly.

"Is it a good likeness?"

"Mmm?" Every line of David's body drooped like a fading flower. "Yes. Surprisingly so. Or, well, not that surprising, actually, his photograph's right there."

The photo hung opposite the case, a black-and-white portrait of an old man with that same shy smile and crooked nose. The groundskeeper did not point out the age gap between the man in the photograph and the one in the young artist's sketch.

David's hand dropped to his side. "What are you doing here, anyway?"

The groundskeeper blushed, remembering his lunch-hour panic. He cleared his throat. "Said I could come by. For research."

"Right. Ghosts." David turned away from Isaiah's photo. "Come on back."

They entered the dining room, most of which was taken up by a traditional dining room table surrounded by an eclectic collection of antique dining chairs. Photos hung on the walls: unsmiling portraits from the 1860s and 1870s; the boarding house throughout its history; traffic on Main Street early in the twentieth century—cars, horses, carriages, pedestrians, the odd bicycle all sharing the street; various Kopczyks and Hodinkas through the mid-twentieth century, some in color. A large, sepia-toned portrait of Anne Hodinka and her daughter Nina, then eight years old, hung in the back of the room beside the entrance to the kitchen. They had the same pert nose, the same round chin, but Anne had dark hair, while her daughter was fair. The picture washed Nina's eyes—blue or gray in life—to a pale, ghostly honey color. She seemed to watch the two men as they passed.

The kitchen was fitted up to look as it had in 1836, except for the wood block counter in its center. The counter was stained with food coloring and candle wax from two decades of field trips and day camps. At the back of the room, the old pantry had been split in half to create two tiny offices, each crammed with a desk, chair, and filing cabinet.

David's office was fastidiously tidy: the chair was tucked into the desk; each filing cabinet drawer was neatly labeled; the books on the shelves above were organized by topic and author. David's backpack hung on a hook on the door. The only things out of place were a file folder and three books, but David said, "Sorry about the mess, one second—"

He filed the folder and returned the books to their shelves. On one shelf was a photo of David and Isaiah, twenty years younger, laughing together on a park bench. It was placed so as not to be visible from the desk or reflected in the computer monitor.

David gave a strained smile. "That's better. Come on in."

The desk, chair, and filing cabinet filled the space, but the groundskeeper shuffled forward an inch. Isaiah shivered with laughter.

"So. Ghosts." David dropped into his chair. "I admit I'm not sure how I can help. I'm a historian, not a what's-it—paranormal investigator or whatever they call themselves. You might be better off asking one of them."

"I don't want a paranormal investigator," the groundskeeper said. "I want you."

David's ears pinkened. "What do you want to know? You understand that, as a historian, I'm concerned with facts."

"Interpretation."

"Interpretation based on *evidence*. Records. Objects. Tangible things that tell me something about who people were in the past and how they lived. Ghosts are…"

The groundskeeper's mouth twitched. "Must have some interest in legends. There's a seed of truth planted in 'em somewhere, oftener'n not. And if not, well, a good tall tale'll tell you 'bout the people who told it, same's the things they left behind."

David scratched his forehead. "That's what Isaiah used to say. Local legends were his passion."

"So?" the groundskeeper insisted. "This is your home. You must know some good ghost stories."

David slumped in his chair. "It hasn't felt like home, since Isaiah died."

He ran his hands back and forth through his hair, mussing it up. He looked small and crumpled. Peter wanted to gather him up and smooth the lines in his forehead, but he locked the want away.

"I'm from Pennsylvania," David said. "From a town even smaller than this and a whole lot less accepting of people like us. Escaped as soon as I could, made my way to New York…met Isaiah there, working in one of the museums. We came back here so he could look after Aunt Margaret when she took sick, and we stayed on to convert this place into a museum like she wanted. I've lived here almost thirty years, and I've loved every minute of it. But…"

He let out a long breath. He looked so wilted today, so sad, so *old*.

"With Isaiah gone," he said, "it's like he's the only reason I belonged here."

The air twisted bitterly. Isaiah hadn't followed them into the office; he seemed to want to give them some privacy. But his spirit permeated the whole building, and he couldn't help overhearing.

David rubbed his face. "It's silly. No one's said anything. No one treats me any differently. For heaven's sakes, Nevaeh's family keeps inviting me to Sunday dinner. I know it's all in my head. But I feel so…"

"Out of place," Peter said. "Loss'll do that to you."

He'd felt the same in Melbourne after Jack's death. Never mind that he'd arrived in Australia long before Jack had. Hard to belong in a place anymore when your whole way of existing there had changed.

David gave another strained smile.

"Guess so." He sighed shakily. "Forgive me. I don't mean to be… It's our anniversary today. Would've been."

He hunched over his desk, his chin propped on his fists. Peter touched his shoulder. Isaiah spiraled about as if fluttering his nonexistent hands, but *someone* comforting David in a tangible way, like he could not, mollified him.

David squeezed his eyes shut. When he opened them again, he looked less shrunken. "Thanks."

The groundskeeper squeezed his shoulder once, awkwardly, and shoved his hands in his pockets before he could be so impulsive again.

David dragged a hand over his face. "Ghost stories. I'm sure I've heard some, but nothing comes to mind." He laughed wetly. The air was rosy with Isaiah's love. "Maybe I could find Isaiah's notes. He used to collect this stuff. Thought he'd write a book one day. I can poke around his office if you want."

The groundskeeper's eyes roved over David's face. "I'd be much obliged."

"Will do, then."

David glanced up. The groundskeeper blushed to be caught gazing at him.

"Lunch." David laughed ruefully. "You're here because I missed lunch. I didn't realize how late it was. That's it, isn't it?"

Peter nodded.

David looked away. "I'm sorry I didn't call. I meant to come out again today, but I'm... I don't know that I'd be good company. I think I'd better stay here."

Peter was unexpectedly disappointed, but he was ready to say, *all right, then*, and skedaddle—until the spirit whispered to him. David would wander through the museum alone, picking things up and putting them down at random. Trying to work but mostly wallowing in self-pity. He needed to leave the museum awhile, the spirit insisted.

Peter twisted his cap. "Don't reckon you need to be good company. I ain't so companionable myself."

David chuckled. Peter's spirits rose.

"The point's to sit with someone," he went on, "instead of by your lonesome, and that's all, aye? That's what you told me."

"I suppose I did." David smoothed his hair. "You're sure you don't mind?"

"Not at all," Peter said, and added, without thinking about it, "I like having lunch with you."

David's face relaxed into a smile, a real one. "There's a sandwich shop up the street we could walk to."

Peter liked being the reason David smiled. "Sounds great."

XXII

The groundskeeper returned to the museum a day later, partway through his usual lunch hour. David hadn't been by the cemetery today; he had a field trip to prepare for early this afternoon, so he'd be too busy for lunch together.

That's just what the groundskeeper was banking on. He wanted time alone with Isaiah, to ask him directly about his research into Harrington's ghost stories.

It was bright and sunny today, and Isaiah's golden presence permeating the entire museum made it that much brighter. The groundskeeper greeted the spirit as he mounted the porch steps, thinking he could chat with Isaiah out here, but the door flew open a moment later. David, holding a tent sign and looking frazzled.

Today's waistcoat was patterned with vintage postage stamps. It was buttoned wrong.

David pulled up short at the sight of the groundskeeper. "Peter, what—I'm so sorry—I have a field trip due in this afternoon, didn't I say?"

The groundskeeper scratched his head. "So you did. I plumb forgot."

"I'm sorry." David dashed down the stairs, plopped the tent sign (CLOSED FOR FIELD TRIP) at the bottom, and dashed back up again. "I'd have lunch with you if I had time, I just—blast it," he said, as they entered the museum, "where are those paint mixers, I swear I had them all ready to go—"

Isaiah stroked his cheek gently. He didn't feel it, of course, so it did nothing to calm him.

"Need help?" the groundskeeper asked.

David lunged toward a plastic tub sitting on the hall tree. The tub was filled with old paint mixers, each tied with a string. "There they are. Sorry. I'm not normally so unprepared with kids coming in, but I locked myself out of the house first thing this morning, and I had to wait forever for the locksmith—"

Could've called Samira al-Masri, the groundskeeper thought, but it didn't seem like a good idea to say so just now.

"—and that was *after* I went next door in my pajamas to borrow their phone, don't know that I'll ever be able to look my neighbors in the face again—and it's all been downhill from there. I should really give Nevaeh the spare key now that she's back in town."

In the kitchen, the butcher's block was covered with a plastic tablecloth. A double boiler filled with wax sat on the stove. David switched on a burner and set the paint mixers on the counter.

"By the time I got off the phone with a donor twenty minutes ago," he said, "I'd forgotten all about the field trip, and I've been running around like a chicken with my head cut off ever since I remembered."

He poked at the wax in the double boiler with a ladle. Isaiah wrapped around him as if in a hug.

"This is so much easier when Mari is on break," David muttered, then remembered he had company and added for the groundskeeper's benefit, "Our intern. She's worth a million dollars, started here back when she was in high school. But now that she's in college, she's only here on breaks. Keeps me on schedule. She's much better about tracking the time than I am. I don't know how I would've managed the past year without her."

Isaiah turned faintly blue with regret, wishing his husband hadn't been so alone the past year. If David had thought about the meaning of his own words, however, he didn't show it. He ran a hand through his hair, looking marginally calmer now that the kitchen setup was complete and he'd vented about his morning.

"Your buttons are wrong," the groundskeeper said helpfully.

Glancing down at his waistcoat, David laughed ruefully. "Jesus. It's a good thing you're here. I would've gone around all afternoon like this."

To the groundskeeper's chagrin, David started unbuttoning his waistcoat right there in the kitchen. Of course he was wearing a shirt underneath, so it didn't matter—not really—yet the groundskeeper's neck prickled. He looked away, hot with embarrassment.

"Anyway," David said, "thank you for offering to help, but I think I'm—"

The bell over the front door tinkled. David hastily fixed his last button.

"Fuck *me*," he muttered, and immediately looked guilty: they could hear children gathering in the entryway.

The groundskeeper raised an eyebrow. Isaiah vibrated with laughter.

"Don't tell anyone I said that. Coming!" David called, but he turned back to the groundskeeper. "I'm so sorry, I have to—"

"You go on. I'll just take a gander, if you don't mind."

"Yes, of course, whatever you want." David hurried back through the dining room and into the entryway. There was a chorus of hellos and then David saying, "Hey, kids! Who's ready to learn about nineteenth-century Northwest Ohio?"

He said it like it was the most exciting thing ever. The children responded in kind, shouting, "I do!" and "Me too!" and "Yeah!" until the adults hushed them. If the groundskeeper hadn't seen him rush out of the kitchen, he wouldn't have guessed the kind of day David had had. Isaiah glowed gently golden with fondness for both his husband and the children.

"Need to talk to you," the groundskeeper murmured. "Preferably somewhere they ain't."

Isaiah flared mintily, bombarding him with questions, but the groundskeeper shook his head.

"Get us somewhere private first."

Still curious, Isaiah pointed the groundskeeper to the narrow back stairs around behind the office. They met the main stairs at a second-floor landing before twisting to the right and continuing upward into darkness. Isaiah nudged the groundskeeper farther into the second floor.

Four bedrooms—two on the left, for the family, and two on the right, for boarders—clustered around a central sitting area. The bedrooms were restored to look as they might have between the 1830s and the 1890s, each mirroring a different decade. Velvet rope barriers barred museum visitors from disturbing the contents or layout.

The groundskeeper paused by the first bedroom, feeling wrong-footed by the sight of it. Except for its size and the bassinet in the corner, the fancier upholstery, and the larger windows, it looked much like the room he'd shared with Jack for so many years: double bed against the wall, a wardrobe in one corner, a mirror in the other, two chairs for a sitting area near the door.

His brow furrowed. If the room had been smaller, the furniture cheaper, if the walls had been whitewashed planks instead of patterned paper... He could picture Jack sitting on the side of the bed, his braces down around his hips, removing his boots after a long day's work.

Isaiah was minty, prodding. The groundskeeper shook his head to clear it of the image.

"Nothing," he said gruffly. "Thinking, is all. Where're these notes of yours?"

He was going to have to be more specific. Isaiah had had many notes, on any number of historical topics.

The groundskeeper sighed. "The ones David's trying to find for me. Local legends. Ghost stories."

Isaiah exploded with an overpowering smell of licorice—a new one for the groundskeeper, and so overwhelming that he stumbled back. He braced himself against the window, trying to sort through the things Isaiah was communicating to him all at once.

Ghost stories, he realized. Isaiah was trying to share everything he knew about Harrington's ghost stories. In his excitement to be asked about them, they came so fast the groundskeeper could hardly make heads or tails of them. Confused images of old books, letters, photographs, portraits, houses, headstones, and more tumbled before his eyes at top speed.

"Slow down," he said. "Can't understand a word you're saying."

Isaiah reined it in, but it was hardly better.

"One at a time!" the groundskeeper said. "Be easier if you tell me where your notes are."

The licorice stuttered. Isaiah didn't know where the notes were, but he was fairly certain they'd last been at the house.

"What d'you mean, you don't know where they are?"

Isaiah had had *many notes*, he reminded the groundskeeper. *Many* notes. That could not be overstated. And what was more, Isaiah had had ADHD, and it hadn't gone away just because he was dead now. He didn't know where those particular notes were, and that was that.

The groundskeeper sighed and dug out his notepad. "All right. Here's hoping David finds it, then. Go on, tell me about them, but one thing at a time or I can't keep up with you."

The information still came faster than he could take notes, but he managed, more or less. Isaiah started with the Morrow

Road ghost: Harrington's most famous spirit and the one most likely to attract bored teenagers looking for excitement.

Although the ghost had no name in the legends, Isaiah believed the story had been inspired by the disappearance of Claude Delacour in 1893. The Delacour property had fronted Morrow Road, and Claude's was the only known disappearance in that area. His mother had apparently never moved past his death—to her detriment, as her husband later left when it became clear that he would get no further children from her. The gossip of the time had attributed the lack of additional children to her refusal to any longer perform her wifely duties, but of course (Isaiah said) that couldn't be confirmed and didn't matter anyway. The point was, Isaiah was certain the Delacour tragedy had inspired the stories of the Morrow Road ghost.

As they often did, said stories conflicted. Everyone agreed that a child had vanished somewhere on Morrow Road, but they disagreed about the ghost's identity. Some said it was the lost child himself, a little boy who appeared to ask if one had seen his mother, only to vanish when one tried to take a closer look. Others said it was the mother, a woman in white searching for her son to this day. Sometimes, a keening wail could be heard on Morrow Road after dark. Here, too, the stories differed, with some attributing the wail to the mother mourning her lost son and others, confusingly, attributing it to an unseen infant.

"Nothing else about an infant in the story, eh?" the groundskeeper murmured as he added to his notes on Marie-Louise Delacour and Morrow Road. "No matter. Mother seems more likely, less'n the ween died bad. I don't suppose they ever found out what happened to him?"

They had not, but never mind that. Isaiah wanted to know what he meant by "more likely."

The groundskeeper hesitated, but it didn't matter if he told Isaiah about ghosts, did it? Isaiah was a ghost.

"Didn't come to town for nothing," he admitted. "Heard tell

of a powerful spirit scaring folks. Turns out," he added, "it was likely you. Some kid down in Savannah said he'd seen a ghost and been chased off the property."

Isaiah giggled, a swift vibration of green and gold. He *did* like scaring the kids sometimes. Not that he was any scarier now than he had been in life, but the kids loved catching glimpses of him. He'd appear so swiftly that only a few managed to do so, which made them objects of admiration and envy amongst their classmates. Like this...

The groundskeeper whipped around, but Isaiah looked just as he always did, as most spirits always did—a colorful haze. Below, however, where the field trippers had gathered in the back garden, several children were now pointing, open-mouthed, at the window. The groundskeeper hastily backed away so they wouldn't see him, but their excited cries floated up from the garden, muffled through the glass.

"I saw him!"

"Me, too!"

"I wanna see him!"

David's voice came, too, patient and even more muffled since he wasn't shouting. "I'm sure you just saw my friend who's visiting today. Now pay attention..."

Isaiah's giggles bubbled up like fizz. The groundskeeper shook his head.

"No more tomfoolery," he said. "It's a right good bet you're the ghost that kid was talking about, but there's something bad out in the cemetery. I'm sure of that. Less'n I can find it and figure out what's keeping it here, it'll go on getting stronger 'til it hurts someone."

Isaiah shifted into a pale greenish orange like unripe nightshade berries, alarmed. The groundskeeper shook his head.

"Don't you worry about that. I got ways to keep David safe. But that's why I need you to tell me everything you know—and to get my hands on your notes, if I can. The more I know about the local legends, the more likely it is I can find out who's so angry back there and what they might want and where they're buried. A mother who died grieving the loss of her child, not even knowing what happened to him, that's someone likely to leave behind a powerful spirit."

The alarm changed so suddenly into curiosity that the groundskeeper's eyes stung with its mintiness. Isaiah's questions tripped over each other in his haste to ask them all.

"No, not everyone leaves a spirit. No, I don't rightly know why. Best I can figure, the ones who don't are at peace when they go." The groundskeeper gagged; the scent and taste of mint was thick in his throat. "Slow down! I'd hope you know at least as much about ghosts as I do, seeing as how you are one."

The mintiness faded. Not completely, but enough that the groundskeeper could breathe without choking on it. Isaiah knew nothing about ghosts except what he'd experienced being one. The slow waking to consciousness—if one could call it that, when one was dead—a week or more after death. The strange sense of having no body, the shocking amount of energy it took to take form or even speak. The sudden ability to sense the feelings of the living in a way he couldn't when he was alive himself: their emotions wafted from them in faint haloes of color.

That was particularly terrible. Not when the children were screaming with excitement because they'd spotted him, or when other visitors were looking around with interest (or, occasionally, faint boredom). But he was always terribly, terribly aware of how much his husband was grieving, no matter how cheerful David acted when other people were around.

The groundskeeper hesitated, not sure how to say what he wanted to. He'd never had quite this kind of conversation with a ghost.

"You let the weens see you often enough," he said. "Ain't you shown yourself to him? It wouldn't be the same, I don't pretend it would be, but you could talk to him a piece, if you wanted. Let him know you're all right, far as that goes."

He almost added *let him know he ain't alone*, but he couldn't bring himself to say it.

At his words, Isaiah faded to a sad, wintry blue. Sure, he could show himself to David. David, who did not believe in impossible things like ghosts. The only time Isaiah had seen David doggedly, desperately faithful was when Isaiah was in the hospital—and that had not so much been belief that his husband would live as insistent denial that he wouldn't die. He'd been so determined not to talk about what would happen after Isaiah's death. Isaiah hadn't even been able to tell him about wanting to be cremated; he'd written funeral arrangements into his will instead.

Isaiah couldn't reveal himself. David would come up with a million and one rational explanations. It would be something he ate. A sudden fever. Something wrong with the medication he took to help with his arthritis.

"Ah." The groundskeeper rubbed his neck. "That why you don't follow him around? Could, you know. It's certain you're strong enough to follow him off-property, if you wanted."

Isaiah went bluer still. He did *try* to give David some privacy. Besides, keeping that close to David would be counterproductive. As much as it hurt, Isaiah wanted his husband to move on. To be happy again, instead of merely pretending to be happy so no one would realize how melancholy he was.

Before the groundskeeper could respond, David himself came creaking up the narrow back stairs. Isaiah brightened again, butter yellow with affection.

"Done already?" the groundskeeper asked.

David chuckled. "No, no, not by a long shot. They're outside playing some games. I tell them a little about the history, of course, but mostly it's to let them burn off energy before they come back in for candle-making. Much harder in winter, which is why I try to schedule as many field trips as possible in spring.

THE KEEPER OF LONELY SPIRITS 143

I just thought I'd pop in and check on you. Did you hear them out there? They caught a glimpse of you and were convinced you were a ghost."

The groundskeeper's eyes flickered toward Isaiah, but all he said was, "Did they, now?"

"Oh, before I forget," David said. "I'll want your help again in a couple of days, if you have the time. I thought I'd take rubbings of some of the headstones I mapped."

"No trouble," the groundskeeper said. "Let me know when."

Outside, the children cheered. David smiled, but it was strained.

"Well, back to work."

"All right?" the groundskeeper grunted.

"Oh, you know." David ran a hand through his hair. "I do love hosting field trips, but...well...it's been a long couple of days." He laughed. "Today especially. I'm never grabbing the paper without my keys again."

Isaiah twisted around him.

"Anyway." David started back down the stairs but paused partway down and said, without looking back, "I'm really glad you're here, Peter."

Then he was gone, downstairs and outside, shepherding the kids back in so cheerfully it was like he'd never had a hard day in his life. The groundskeeper was left stammering over a response he had no chance to give.

XXIII

The air weighed on the groundskeeper as he and David took rubbings of stones in the back lot a few days later. His muscles ached, but the crimson weight hadn't stymied the May growth. Phlox carpeted the forest like blue snow. Trillium scattered white among the trees. Pale green-and-yellow flowers laded the surrounding tulip poplars.

Despite the verdure, the forest was uneasy. The green, garland-like flowers of mulberries and walnuts hung tighter and shorter than they should've, afraid to venture too far from the branch. Wild roses rattled thorns in warning like massasaugas.

Still, David didn't notice. It might've comforted the groundskeeper—that the anger he felt so strongly was not yet strong enough to attract the living's notice—if he didn't suspect David was unaffected only because he was so deeply focused and because of the protective flowers in his waistcoat (paisley today).

Isaiah had provided more information before David's field trippers had left the other day, but it had merely confirmed and fleshed out what the groundskeeper had found in his own research. Aside from the Morrow Road ghost, there were three ghost stories that had either traveled to Harrington from somewhere else or appeared to have no basis in any historical figure whatever. The story of the ghost the town blamed for its troubles was too murky to be of much use: most stories left off its identity completely, focusing instead on the woes it caused and including only the detail that it was a man whose family had died of cholera. That was hardly surprising, given the angry pall that hung over the cholera graves back here, but so many folks had died or lost family in three separate epidemics that Isaiah had never even begun to figure out on whom the legend of this particular ghost might be based.

Now, David held a chalk rubbing to the light. "Still hard to make out—the first name might be Jane. I'm not sure about the last name. Can you read it?"

He handed the rubbing over. The groundskeeper opened his messenger bag idly, comforted by the candles, iron, salt, flowers, and herbs inside. He twisted the rubbing to and fro, one eye on the surrounding poplars. The air simmered.

An acorn bounced off his bag. He chucked it back, glaring in its direction. Roses rattled.

The groundskeeper returned to the rubbing, straining for any out-of-place sound as he studied the letters.

"Looks like *M-A-R-R*—no, sorry, that second *R* is a *K—O—*" He held the paper higher to catch more light. David waited, his notes app at the ready. "Might be an *N*—no, a *V—A*. What's that?"

David reviewed his notes. "Markova. That's a real name, anyway. The date should be 1852, that's clear enough on the stone."

"1852," the groundskeeper confirmed.

David rose from his crouch, groaning. He wobbled, reached for the headstone, thought better of it, and clung to the groundskeeper's arm instead. His hand was firm, steady, and calming in the forest's disquiet.

"One more. Then we're done for the day."

Relief rolled over the groundskeeper. Better for David to be here with him than alone, but best for him not to be here at all.

The last headstone was upright and hardly sunken, but moss enshrouded the inscription. The groundskeeper scraped it away, as he'd done several times earlier this afternoon, and brushed dirt from the inscription. He stroked the leaves of some phlox seeking reassurance against the forest's unease.

David knelt and took a rubbing.

"Oh, this one's good." Leaf-filtered sunlight dappled his face green and gold. "Look at that. Easy to read, even caught this little detail in the carving above the name. Beautiful. I might frame this one and put it up at the museum."

He rolled up the rubbing, taped its end, and slipped it into his backpack with the half dozen they'd taken previously. He stood, rolling his shoulders.

The groundskeeper ran a hand over his face. The phlox fretted.

David chuckled. "Do you want a handkerchief? You've got something—" he gestured at the groundskeeper's face "—everywhere."

The groundskeeper searched himself for tissues, came up empty, and swiped his face with the back of his hand, by far the cleanest part of him. After scraping moss and lichen from several headstones, he had dirt lodged under his fingernails, creased into his palms, smudged halfway up his wrist. "I get it?"

David laughed.

"You made it worse. Here." He plucked a handkerchief from his pocket. "Can I—?"

He cupped Peter's face in his hand.

Peter sat very, very still.

David's hand was soft and warm. Peter's heart thrummed. His eyes roved over David's face: the thick golden lashes, the square chin. The crease between his brows as he wiped dirt from Peter's forehead and jaw. The play of sunlight and shadows on his nose and cheekbones.

David glanced up. His eyes shocked Peter like electricity. Peter shivered. He was used to shivers, from the spirits, but nothing like this.

David's hand trailed down his neck, to the hollow of his throat. His eyes flickered over Peter's face, down to his lips, up to his eyes, and Peter came dangerously close to wanting something he could not let himself name. No one had looked at him like that in almost a century.

David scrunched his fingers against Peter's skin. He crumpled his handkerchief, giving a small smile.

"There. Much better."

Peter's chest heaved. Maybe he should have said *thank you*, but David was standing too close. Vines tangled in his brain.

The tulip poplars rustled despite the still air. The pale green-and-yellow flowers opened and closed like polyps. Peter's eyes slid toward them. The anger, the anger he'd forgotten for a moment, twisted as if curling its lip.

Anger simmered throughout the back lot, vibrating, buzzing, weighting the very air, and he was wasting time mooning over this historian with his bow ties and his waistcoats and his electric gray eyes.

He stepped back, tugging on his cap. "Should get going."

He avoided David's gaze.

"Okay," David said.

They trudged over the bridge. Last year's leaves hushed underfoot. The anger buzzed like hornets. The groundskeeper was lost in thought.

Some hundred years ago, he had decided to stop wanting. Anything he might want was fleeting, he eternal. Anything, anyone he wanted would be stolen away sooner or later. It would tear him apart as Jack's death had. And it would go on like that, an eagle eternally picking at his liver, because it couldn't kill him. Because nothing could.

But death itself couldn't stop a person from wanting. Every spirit he'd ever seen wanted something. Justice. Revenge. Assurance their loved ones were all right.

If even the dead wanted, how could the living hope not to?

Yet the groundskeeper had managed. He'd withdrawn from his Melbourne friends. Closed himself off from the people he'd met in the many places he'd lived since—helped them, but held them at arm's length. Whenever he'd started caring too much, he'd left. All he wanted, all he'd allowed himself to want, for more than a century, was death.

Now he wanted something else, badly.

He touched the hollow of his throat like he might yet find David's fingers there. He glanced over his shoulder.

His mouth went dry. The trees stretched off in every direction, gray and green without that paisley splash of color that had been at his side all afternoon.

He was alone.

He whipped around. "David?"

A pewee called back uneasily.

The trees' rustling crashed over him. The air pressed on him like a stone.

He hurtled back through the undergrowth. "David!"

"Found them!"

The groundskeeper's heart pounded, but he slowed—moving fast, letting his long legs carry him quickly, but walking now. "Found what?"

"My flowers, of course. Didn't you hear me say I'd lost them?"

He had not. He had hardly been aware of David as they'd walked, had been thinking of David standing too close by that last headstone.

He breathed deep. A walnut's leaves fluttered, the more nervous for his own panic. He had to calm down; his worry was affecting the forest same as the unknown spirit's anger.

A shout, wordless. Surprised and panicked.

A crash. A splash.

The groundskeeper froze. The trees held their breath.

Silence.

"Peter," David called hoarsely.

He sprinted to the creek and skidded to a halt.

The bridge was empty; its side had collapsed. The remaining stones huddled together.

In the creek below, David struggled to sit up. Water rushed

halfway up his waist. Jagged stones jumbled around his legs. His face twisted, but he held his backpack—and the rubbings—out of the water.

The air seethed.

The groundskeeper splashed into the creek and yanked stones away. Sunlight lanced across the water. An oak on the far bank stretched its branches, spreading shade over the two men. Solid and protective.

The groundskeeper's hands shook. "What happened?"

"I don't know." David's chest heaved. "Grabbed my flowers, but I got dizzy when I straightened up, and I stumbled into the side of the bridge, and—I don't know, it collapsed."

"Did something push you?"

"Push—? There's no one here. What do you—?"

"Did something push you?"

"No. I don't know. I don't think so."

David's arms trembled. The groundskeeper hurled his backpack toward the creek bank.

"Careful! The rubbings."

"They're less liable to harm than you, you ass." The groundskeeper's nostrils flared. David's left leg was at an odd angle. "The rubbing's'll be fine. Your leg's broke."

The groundskeeper squeezed his calf to assess the break. David closed his eyes, breathing raggedly. "Will you get the truck? I don't think an ambulance will make it back here."

"I will not."

"I need to go to urgent care."

"I ain't leaving you here alone."

David gave a smile more like a grimace. "I'm not going anywhere."

The groundskeeper didn't move. The oak groaned. He ignored it.

David sighed. "Okay, then call Nevaeh. My phone's in the front pocket of the backpack you so unceremoniously threw in the dirt."

The groundskeeper found it and dialed the office with shaking fingers. Nevaeh told him to sit tight and hung up before he'd finished explaining.

He splashed back into the creek, plunging to his knees at David's side. Digging through his bag, he slung a garland of rue and lavender around David's neck.

"Peter—what are you—what *are* these?"

"Don't take 'em off."

"But—"

The groundskeeper met his gaze, one hand cradling David's nape. "Don't take 'em off."

David's eyes flickered over him. "All right."

The groundskeeper got to his feet. His wet jeans chafed.

Except for rushing water and rustling leaves, the forest was silent. The oak had stopped groaning. Spirits from farther back in the woods approached the bank, vibrating crimsonly. The groundskeeper splashed back and forth like a hound on a fox's scent, clenching an iron cross and a garland of flowers, daring the spirits to come closer.

They shouldn't have been able to. Spirits couldn't cross moving water.

But the anger infecting them had spread across the water.

Its lip was still curled at him.

"Help me out of this wet," David said.

"No."

"Peter—"

"No."

David would get a soaking, but he'd be safest in the swift-flowing creek.

"But why—?"

"No," the groundskeeper snarled. David fell silent.

The anger simmered with smug satisfaction. The spirits buzzed. The groundskeeper curled his fists.

"Peter?"

He was at David's side instantly. The spirits' vibrations intensified, but they came no closer.

David leaned back on his elbows, eyes shut. "Do me a favor."

"Anything."

"Go home."

The air left the groundskeeper's lungs. He recovered enough to say, "I'm staying right here."

"Look." David pushed himself upright, face tightening. The groundskeeper's hand hovered at his back. "I'm in a lot of pain. You panicking isn't helping."

"Ain't panicking."

David snorted. "You, my friend, are many things, but I'm starting to think 'good in an emergency' isn't one of them. Nevaeh will be here soon. I'll be fine until then."

"I'm staying," the groundskeeper said stubbornly.

David's eyes fixed on his. "Without jumping at every little noise?"

The groundskeeper nodded.

"Without snarling at me?"

The groundskeeper flushed, but he nodded again.

David closed his eyes. "All right."

Peter's eyes never left the trees, but he shortened his bag's strap to keep it out of the water, settled behind David, and held him. David leaned into him wearily.

The anger sneered at them.

A vehicle rumbled through the forest. Peter exhaled sharply.

The engine cut, a door creaked open, and Nevaeh called, "Guys?"

"Over here."

Elijah had followed, drifting after the truck as it rumbled through the forest, but the groundskeeper didn't even think to warn him he ought to have stayed out of the back lot. His fingers trembled as he and Nevaeh maneuvered David into the passenger seat. He didn't relax until they were closed inside.

In the truck, they were safe. He'd warded it when he'd warded the cottage, office, and storage shed, belly-crawling beneath it to paint sigils on the insides of the tires, the undersides of the cab and bed, scratching minuscule Marian symbols under each door handle. Hence Elijah following the truck until they left the cemetery, rather than riding along inside. The groundskeeper never took chances with ghosts and motorized vehicles.

In the urgent care waiting area, David gripped his hand, squeezing tight when pain flared, until a nurse collected him. Children bickered over a yellowed toy chest in the corner. Vinyl chairs squeaked as people stood, sat, shifted. The groundskeeper hardly noticed.

Under the stuttering fluorescents, surrounded by clinical white walls sharp-scented with cleaners, it was harder to fear the things that had scared him in the cemetery.

Something was back there. He knew that. But in this no-nonsense room, he wondered whether a ghost *had* been involved in David's fall.

David had lost his protective flowers, yes—but hadn't he found them before the side of the bridge collapsed?

The bridge was two centuries old. Crumbling. Precarious. Nevaeh had worried about its stability only last week. The spirits had thrown pebbles, hidden birders' belongings, but no worse. And Samira had been in the back lot alone at least once—still sensed ghosts, too, he was reasonably sure, given her age and her simple certainty that Isaiah haunted the museum—but nothing had happened to her. She'd even wanted to return. Surely whatever angry spirit lurked among the trees, just beyond his ken, had not progressed to actually hurting people, or she would've been more fearful.

David had lost his balance, steadied himself on a frail old bridge, fallen into the creek, broken his leg.

No need for a ghost to be involved. Could've been an accident, plain and simple. Yet the groundskeeper had lost his head when he lost sight of David. He'd been in a useless panic until they escaped the cemetery.

Now, in the waiting room, Nevaeh touched his arm. "He'll be fine."

"I know," he said, though he knew no such thing.

She smiled thinly, adjusting her hair wrap. "Okay. You look... I thought you needed to hear that."

He looked her over. She was curled in on herself, taking up the least amount of space possible. One leg crossed over the other. Foot jiggling.

"Looks like you need to hear it more'n I do."

Her smile tightened. "I don't like hospitals."

"This ain't a hospital. It's an urgent care."

Nevaeh rolled her eyes, punching his shoulder gently. "You know what I mean."

He rubbed his shoulder. "Don't much like 'em myself. Spent too much time in 'em."

Nevaeh's fingers tightened on her arms.

"So did Dad. Only we didn't know it." She gazed at the wall. "He'd been diagnosed with some condition I can't even pronounce, and he didn't tell us. Granny says he didn't want to worry us."

She laughed bitterly.

"Didn't want to *worry* us. Can you believe that? So he went around like nothing was wrong. The coroner thinks he blacked out because of this condition we didn't even know he had, and that's how he lost control of the tractor."

Her nostrils flared. She turned away.

The groundskeeper's fingers twitched. He turned away, too.

The door to the back opened; a nurse stood aside. David stumped through on crutches. The groundskeeper was on his feet instantly but lingered by his chair.

Nevaeh met David at the receptionist's desk. If the groundskeeper hadn't seen her so small and closed off, he wouldn't have known she was upset a moment ago. She stood straight and tall, nostrils no longer flaring, expression unreadable except for the tension in her jaw.

"You don't look half bad," she said to David. She sounded almost normal. "How are the crutches?"

"They'll take some getting used to, but I can walk."

"He was lucky," the nurse told Nevaeh. "Clean break, didn't break the skin, didn't damage any arteries. He'll need that cast for at least six weeks, though."

David made a face.

The nurse shrugged. "If you want to aggravate your injury, go ahead. Let me know how that works out for you."

"Six weeks," Nevaeh said. "Got it."

The door closed on the nurse. David sighed.

"There goes my exercise for the next month and a half. Thank goodness Marisol's exams are this week. I'm going to need her." He ran a hand through his hair. "Getting around a nineteenth-century building on crutches is going to be terrible. I won't be able to get into my office, that's certain. If this cast isn't off by SummerFest, I might need a second intern to help with tours. It's our busiest time."

They joined the groundskeeper at his chair. David smiled.

"I see your panic has deserted you. Perhaps I'll revise my opinion of how you handle emergencies." He nudged Nevaeh. "You should've seen him."

The groundskeeper's cheeks warmed, but he didn't comment.

Nevaeh bit her lip. "I'll pull the truck around."

"Thanks."

Rubbing his cast absently, David waited with the grounds-keeper. "I'm fine."

The groundskeeper nodded without looking at him.

David tugged at the flowers. "What are these for?"

The groundskeeper said nothing.

"The doctor thought they were to ward off ghosts." David scratched his forehead. "She said her grandmother used to make her and her brothers wear them on Midsummer Eve. Hung them from the doors and windows until Midsummer was over."

The groundskeeper twitched, but he was silent.

The corner of David's mouth turned up. "I thought you were interested in ghost *stories*, not ghosts."

The groundskeeper blushed deeper.

David's expression softened. "I'm not going to make fun of you if you think a ghost broke my leg. I don't think that's what happened, but I won't make fun of you."

"I don't think a ghost broke your leg." The groundskeeper's next words were almost inaudible, like they wouldn't mean too much as long as no one heard them. "Glad you're all right."

Nevaeh drove them the four miles back to Harrington, parking in front of David's house on Second Street. It was a slate-blue Craftsman-style house with white trim, a picture window on the right, and a deep porch with a wicker furniture set on the left. The garden was small but pleasantly overgrown; pink, violet, and gold flowers bloomed every which way.

David's ears pinkened when he caught the groundskeeper gazing at it.

"That was Isaiah." He vacated the truck with difficulty. "I bought him this computer program one Christmas, a landscaping system, but he treated it like a computer game. He'd design gardens and save the designs and design new gardens, but none of it ever translated into our actual landscaping."

Nevaeh snorted, helping him onto the porch. "Sounds like him. I remember the azalea he showed me. It was hideous."

David struggled with the lock, then handed her his key instead. The words were complaints, or something like them, but the tone was wistful. It pricked at the groundskeeper's insides, for reasons he didn't care to examine.

"That was a clearance buy, I recall," David said. "He'd buy a plant because he liked it, or because I did, or because it was a store markdown he had to rescue so it didn't end up in a dumpster because it was sloughing leaves."

The groundskeeper rubbed his neck. "I come by most of mine the same way."

David shook his head with a smile. "I bet. I've seen your collection."

He gazed into the empty house, his smile fading. The groundskeeper resisted the urge to touch his shoulder.

"I do miss him," David said. Nevaeh squeezed him in a one-armed hug. "Old Eli, too."

A muscle ticked in her jaw.

The groundskeeper shoved his hands in his pockets. It wasn't his job to comfort her. Either of them.

"See you tomorrow," David said to the groundskeeper, then laughed and added, "I hope. If you'll be kind enough to come to the museum. I suppose I ought to stay off my leg."

The groundskeeper tarried on the porch as Nevaeh helped David inside. When she returned, they drove to the cemetery in silence. Her hands clenched the steering wheel.

The groundskeeper drummed his fingers on his knee. He almost asked if she was all right.

Almost.

The sun didn't set so much as fizzle out. In the cemetery, the season's first fireflies blinked intermittently. The spirits wavered. The air was sour.

Nevaeh cut the engine but made no move to get out. Her whole body was clenched, now.

He couldn't help himself. "All right?"

"I'm fine."

"Nevaeh."

She blinked rapidly. He covered her hand with his own. She clung to him, tears slipping down her cheeks.

His insides tightened. He hadn't expected tears.

She pulled away, wiped her eyes on her arm, and blinked up at the ceiling until she stopped crying. Tears glistened on her lashes. The groundskeeper didn't reach for her again.

She got out, shoulders hunched. Closed off, like she'd been before they'd hung signs together. "I have to go."

She grabbed her bike, but he didn't call after her. Just watched until she'd made it past the gate. Then he tugged his cap down and turned the other way.

She wasn't his problem. None of them were.

Elijah flared up mucky with rot as he passed. The other spirits jittered.

"What's got you in a tizzy?" the groundskeeper snapped, but he trudged toward the cottage without awaiting an answer.

Someone was already there.

"There you are," Samira singsonged, skipping out of the garden to hug him.

Their bicycles leaned against the garden wall. Sayid worried the Saint-John's-wort around his neck. The groundskeeper shook Samira off, irritated because he'd wanted to smile at them.

"Shove off," he grunted. "I'm busy."

Oxeye daisies bobbed in the garden. Samira latched on to his hand, swinging his arm.

"You're grumpy."

"It's busy I am." He tried to extricate his hand from hers. "And I told you to go."

"I asked this time. Promise. Mama and Baba are at the movies. They said we could come. Where were you?"

Sayid rubbed his arms. "Maybe we should go. Mama wants us home by nine."

"We've been waiting forever," Samira said. "I want to read more poetry."

That the groundskeeper wanted her to read him more poetry stabbed through him like a shard of glass. He wrenched his hand from her grasp. The daisies shied away. "Go home."

"Just for a little while," Samira insisted. "Why are you so mad today?"

"Because I'm not a babysitter!" the groundskeeper snapped. "It's late, I told you I'm busy—why must you cling to me so?"

She stepped back, fingers curling into her palms. Wood sorrel and black medick stretched toward her protectively. "I—"

"I told you to shove off, so shove off. I don't want you here."

She looked as stunned as if he'd slapped her.

Her face crumpled. She leaped onto her bike and sped away. Fireflies on-and-offed calm and green in her wake.

Sayid's eyes snapped to the groundskeeper.

"Why would you say that?" His voice trembled, whisper-soft with horrified confusion. "She's *eight*."

The groundskeeper's irritation left him as if he'd been winded. He stretched a hand out, trying to snatch his own words back.

"Sayid," he said hoarsely, but the boy biked after his sister with a shout. The spirits wavered. One raced after the children, remembering riding its own bicycle long ago, but they left it behind.

The groundskeeper slumped against the cottage. The plants curled away, muttering about his behavior. His chest heaved.

It was a fair bet the children wouldn't be back.

He pulled his cap over his eyes.

"Good," he whispered to himself. "Good."

It was, after all, what he'd wanted.

XXIV

He wanted to be done with this place. Harrington clawed at him, digging him open and scraping out his insides. The children's faces loomed like apparitions. His stomach twisted, but he shoved the images aside.

He wasn't in too deep. Not yet. Not like that diner in Brooklyn.

So instead of throwing his belongings into his trunk and bolting, he stormed through the cottage to refresh his bag's stock, thinking through the spirits that might be responsible for the back lot's unease. John Kowalczyk wasn't strong enough to affect other ghosts, nor to cast such a pall. The ghost the town blamed its woes on was nameless, and the groundskeeper had no leads on its identity, if indeed it existed.

But there was one ghost he could investigate. Marie-Louise Delacour had a name and a story and a presence near the cemetery's southern end. Separated from the back lot by a cornfield, yes, but if she was strong enough to affect other spirits, she was surely strong enough for her influence to stretch all the way from Morrow Road.

The greenlings whispered as the groundskeeper stomped through the kitchen for a fresh flower garland.

"Shut your yawping," he snapped, and felt ashamed of himself. Would he not stop shouting at soft little things that didn't deserve it?

The greenlings' whispering faltered. He paused in the doorway.

"M'after a ghost, is all," he mumbled. "Won't be but a tick. If she's the one, we'll be leaving soon enough."

He slunk out to the pickup. Antonia, the ghost of the Italian grandmother, nosed at him, fretting over his mood and his bean-pole build, but she flinched. The flowers, salt, and iron in his bag stung her. She whirled back to her grave, pus yellow, and sank into her headstone.

The groundskeeper ignored her. He had a more important spirit to worry about.

The twilight smelled dark and earthy. Scattered stars winked into existence one at a time overhead. Morrow Road stretched between a sprouting cornfield on one side and a stand of cotton-woods on the other, dirt and gravel, ghostly gray.

A stormy blue mass hung over a ditch. The ghost, in the last spot she'd seen her son.

A black minivan idled in the road.

The groundskeeper pulled over. The minivan's side window rolled down. The driver's pimpled face peered out.

"I don't see anything," the face whined, and withdrew.

Teenagers after some excitement. The passenger's-side window rolled down; the rear door slid open. More teenagers peered uneasily around from the minivan's safety, but they couldn't see the air's stormy color. If Marie-Louise Delacour left them alone, like as not they'd leave believing nothing about her.

"Where is he?" one of them asked.

He? Perhaps they thought the ghost was the Delacour boy. Isaiah had told him multiple versions of the Morrow Road legend existed—as was usually the case, in the groundskeeper's experience.

He'd been focused on the mother from the beginning, though. Sayid had sounded certain of its being her.

The groundskeeper tugged his cap over his eyes. No point, thinking about Sayid.

The spirit juddered. *Where is he?*

Her eternal question. *The* question. Her reason for remaining. Grieving because she'd never found her son. Angry because the authorities had barely looked. Regretful because she'd let him wander off.

She spiraled through the air, a midnight blue tornado only the groundskeeper could see.

He sucked in his cheeks, leaping from the pickup. She nosed at the van, at each window. So many children, surely one was her son—

She remembered Claude so powerfully that he materialized. No blurred photo, this. The groundskeeper's steps faltered as if the little boy were really in his way, curly-haired and brown-skinned and brown-eyed, in a gray jacket and trousers. Dressed like some of the more well-to-do children he and Jack had known back in Melbourne.

The spirit's investigation yielded nothing but unknown teenagers. Panicked, she vibrated until the van quaked.

"Do you guys feel that?"

The groundskeeper shook his head to clear it of the vision of Claude Delacour. He jogged toward the van. "Hey, you kids!"

They were arguing. A wind picked up, rustling the cottonwoods and the sprouting corn. The good, earthy smells rotted into decay.

"The van's *rocking!*"

"It is not."

"It's the wind—"

Her son wasn't there. The van swayed. The metal groaned.

"Maybe we should go."

The spirit bridled, suspended over the van like a wave.

The groundskeeper's mouth went dry. "Hey!"

The wave crashed.

The windows shattered. The teenagers screamed, scrambling away from showering glass. The car alarm blared.

"My dad's gonna kill me," the driver moaned.

"*That* wasn't the wind!" another kid said.

They squealed into Drive, kicking up pebbles. The van disappeared in a cloud of dust.

The spirit writhed. Something flickered within that stormy blue, person-shaped, fuzzing in and out like an image on a dial television.

The groundskeeper turned toward it, his heart in his throat. At least the teenagers had had the sense to get the hell out of here.

"Marie-Louise Delacour."

She flickered faster and faster.

"Marie-Louise Delacour."

The flickering stilled. Solidified.

There she was.

No smell or impression or color, but a translucent human form in the road. Marie-Louise Delacour.

She was tall and slender, with medium-brown skin and black hair smoothed into a bun, except for the curls frizzing over her forehead. She wore a long, drab skirt and a blouse with the high collar and long sleeves of the 1890s. Looking as she had when her son disappeared, rather than at her death in 1922. Her loss had frozen her in time.

Her dark, liquid eyes mirrored the darkening sky. Her voice echoed. "How do you know that name?"

The groundskeeper exhaled, praising Mam for teaching him the power of names and grateful Marie-Louise Delacour wasn't too far gone to remember hers.

He thumbed up the brim of his cap. "Never mind that. I know your son's name, too."

"Claude." She fizzled, clenching her fists. Without moving, she was right in front of him. "You know where he is?"

He shivered. "No, ma'am. Hey, now—"

She was vibrating again, her form jumping around him. "Claude—"

"Marie-Louise Delacour."

Her eyes snapped toward him.

"Marie-Louise..." He paused, reluctant to tell her, though surely she knew. "Mrs. Delacour, Claude's dead."

Her vibrations intensified. She appeared behind him, beside him, before him. Her fingernails dug into her fists. Dust devils danced down the road. The cornlings quivered.

"Mrs. Delacour, please. I don't know what happened to your little boy. I don't know when he died. But he vanished a hundred and thirty years ago. Whatever happened to him, he's long dead. Like you."

She wailed. The wind howled with her. The cornlings shrieked. The cottonwoods merely grumbled.

"Mrs. Delacour," the groundskeeper shouted over the wind, "you can see Claude again, but—"

The wind died. She was inches from him.

He stepped back this time. His heart pounded.

Her eyes shone. "How?"

Trees creaked and groaned.

"You can move on."

Her frizzy bangs drifted around her face. "Move on where?"

"Don't rightly know," he said wistfully. "I ain't dead. Whatever comes next, you focus on your son, instead of how it hurt you losing him, and you'll end up there."

The trees quieted. Her form blurred and shifted at the edges.

An image of Claude Delacour materialized once more, chubby-cheeked and brown-eyed. She'd spent a century hurting, but it hadn't sapped her memory as it could have. Clinging to her grief hadn't made her forget its object.

She reached for her son but drew back without touching him. Good. She realized it was a memory, a projection. She was clear-headed enough for that.

"And I'll see Claude," she said quietly.

"I hope so."

She closed her eyes. He said nothing. Just waited, in case she needed help.

She breathed deeply, or would have, if she'd had need of air. As she did so, she became more translucent. Shimmery as mist.

Claude vanished.

She opened her eyes. They were darker and more liquid than ever.

"My darling boy," she whispered.

She went fainter and fainter, shimmerier and shimmerier.

Then she was gone.

The night was clear and earthy. The weight of her grief lifted. Dust rose, then settled. The cornlings heaved a breath.

Morrow Road was empty. The cottonwood trees sighed in a flurry of cottony seeds.

XXV

Stars hung thick in the blue-black sky by the time the grounds-keeper returned to the cemetery. The spirits jittered, but he hunched his shoulders and ignored them. The fireflies had flickered out; the cemetery was darker than ever.

He tossed his messenger bag on the love seat. The greenlings whispered questions.

"She's gone. Went peaceful. If there's any justice in this world, that'll be the end of it and we can be on our way."

The whispers died away to a rustle. Hushed and persistent, secretive.

After a meager supper, the groundskeeper tidied the cottage and went to bed. He couldn't sleep. He lay in bed for well over an hour, tossing and turning. At last he stalked to the love seat and read poetry.

In the kitchen, after midnight, the telephone rang.

The groundskeeper started. The phone was an ancient, corded model. Nevaeh was the only one who'd ever called, twice, when she'd been in the office after hours and had questions.

The phone rang again.

Out the window, the office was dark. The air shimmered with the dead.

The phone rang a third time.

He answered. "Hello?"

Silence. A half-suppressed sob.

The groundskeeper cradled the phone to his ear. "Nevaeh?"

A shaky breath.

"Yeah. It's me." Her voice was ragged. "I need you to come get me."

"What happened?"

"Just come. Please."

"On my way. Where are you?"

"A field off Route 2." Her voice cracked. "I don't know how I got here."

His heart sank.

"Are you there?" Nevaeh whispered.

His fingers tightened on the phone. "I'm here. Sit tight. I'll be there in two shakes."

She gave him the name of the nearest intersection and hung up. He snatched his bag, checked his pocket for his watch, and slouched back out into the cemetery.

The sky was dark and moonless. The groundskeeper scrunched his nose. The air was sourer than before, wavering like the whole place was underwater.

Though the anger had only reached his back garden, the ghosts on the knoll were agitated. Adeline, the little girl found dead in a cornfield in the 1950s, convulsed at her grave.

The groundskeeper left the cemetery once more.

Harrington slept. Houses stood black against the blue-black sky. Silver maples rustled. The string lights over Main Street swayed.

West of Ashmead Creek, big-box stores shone pale and fluorescent. Scant traffic idled in a fast-food drive-through. Floodlights washed out empty parking lots, leaving them colorless and stupefied.

The groundskeeper drove until the stores gave way to rolling fields rustling with young corn and soy, silvery in the night. Stars gleamed brighter the farther he drove.

Ten miles from town, he pulled over.

The field before him rolled off into the darkness, cresting so high the horizon was lost. Unlike its neighbors, this one wasn't planted. The dirt was furrowed, but only thistle and prairie dock grew. A for-sale sign with SOLD slapped over it stood at the field's edge.

The groundskeeper strode up the hill, clutching his bag. The stars shone brilliantly.

"Nevaeh?"

She was curled in the dirt on the rise's far side. She rocked back and forth, clutching her head.

She wasn't alone.

Her father's spirit hovered at her side, sour with rot.

The groundskeeper sucked in his cheeks. He should've realized. Elijah had followed Nevaeh into the back lot earlier, but the groundskeeper had been so worried about David he'd hardly noticed.

He knelt beside Nevaeh.

"Thank god," she said, and she leaned against him and sobbed.

When her sobs petered out, he pulled back, brushing her tears away with his thumbs. "You all right? You hurt?"

"Twisted my ankle." She dashed a wrist across her eyes. Her hair wrap was askew. "It hurt. That's when..."

She rested her chin on her knees. Elijah shivered. The groundskeeper kept half an eye on him.

"That's when you come to?"

She nodded. Tears rolled down her cheeks. She buried her face in her knees.

Peter's heart twisted. He pulled her close. She gulped in heaving breaths.

Elijah was the only spirit in the field. He oozed rot, but he had not—never would have—possessed Nevaeh on his own.

It had been the anger's influence.

It had affected Elijah so much he'd possessed his own daughter. The very person he'd stayed for. This went beyond some pelted nuts, a slammed door, a draft.

Marie-Louise Delacour was gone, but the anger was still here.
There was another ghost to find.

Nevaeh hiccupped. The groundskeeper offered her a hand-kerchief.

"Where are we?"

She scrunched the handkerchief. "It's ours. Used to be."

"Ah," the groundskeeper said softly.

"Yeah."

A pang of regret, sharp and sudden. The groundskeeper understood the unsaid things in her tone. The Shaughnessys had lost their farm, after he'd left. Evicted, Jack told him. His brother had only been fourteen when the groundskeeper had fled. His mother had turned elderly overnight, at the loss of her oldest and youngest at once, and they couldn't make rent without him.

But this wasn't merely a parcel of cropland, part of the Key-Flores farm. Elijah's tractor had flipped on him here. He'd died here.

Fragmented images shuttered through the groundskeeper's mind at top speed, like someone was snapping through a slide-show. The sun overhead, glaring on dirt. The sky so bright it was white. Elijah's hands on the tractor's wheel. A flash of dizziness, blackness, confused images of the earth tumbling end over end, crumpled metal groaning, then nothing but pain, pain.

Elijah was reliving his death.

The rot festered, decaying the groundskeeper's body like an infected root.

"Hsst," he murmured. Elijah latched on to his voice, but the pain of nine months ago plagued the body he no longer had.

The groundskeeper slipped a flower garland around Nevaeh's neck.

She laughed wetly. "What is it with you and these flowers today?"

"Humor me."

"They smell nice." She fiddled with them. "You see why I

had to call you. Ma can barely drive past the cemetery without bursting into tears. If she knew I was here… Granny probably could've handled it, but she can't drive anymore."

She straightened her wrap. Her eyes roved the field, darkening. "I can't remember how I got here."

"What's the last thing you do remember?"

She wiped her nose on her arm before remembering the handkerchief.

"I was halfway home when I realized I'd left my wallet, so I went back for it. I don't think I ever grabbed it." She frowned. "I remember feeling…funny, once I unlocked the gate. Dizzy. I hadn't eaten since lunch."

"And then?"

She toyed with the handkerchief.

"And then…nothing. There's nothing else until I twisted my ankle." Her eyes squeezed shut. "Maybe I should go to the hospital."

"For a twisted ankle?"

"For dissociating that bad." She sighed shakily. "It's been a long time since I…"

The groundskeeper hesitated. Whatever her history with mental health, she hadn't been dissociating tonight. How could he explain she'd lost time to the spirit of her own father?

"Think you can walk?" he asked instead. She grimaced. "Don't need to do much. If you put your weight on me, I figure we'll make it to the truck easy enough."

She winced as he pulled her to her feet. They limped to the truck together.

Elijah didn't follow. The groundskeeper sighed.

He settled Nevaeh into her seat. "D'you mind waiting a minute? Think I dropped my pocket watch back there."

Nevaeh's brow furrowed. "I'm pretty sure this is, like, the start of a horror movie. You wander off alone 'for a minute' to find something, and when you come back there's a creepy message keyed into the side of the truck and I'm dead inside."

He chuckled despite himself.

"If there's anything frightening lurking about, guarantee you it's on the other side of that hill." He leaned on her door. "You keep those flowers on. Keep 'em on and stay in the truck with the doors closed, and you'll be all right."

"Okay, that makes it worse," Nevaeh said, but he slouched back up the rise.

On its other side, he produced his watch and flipped it open. The darkness effaced its Marian symbols. He squatted down where he'd found Nevaeh and set the watch in the dirt.

Elijah writhed, caught in a death loop. An isolated wind kicked up dirt. Images from Elijah's death flashed through the grounds-keeper's mind again and again, but he'd expected it this time. It didn't overwhelm him, though he again felt like a decaying root. He concentrated on Elijah.

"Elijah Key-Flores."

The images flashed faster and faster. Bright sun. White sky. Tractor. Blackness. Pain. Bright sun. White sky. Tractor. Blackness. Pain.

"Elijah," the groundskeeper repeated. "Elijah, it's all right. That's over now."

The spirit whirled around. The whisper of a face materialized. It might've been nothing more than a trick of the whirling dust: a fat, wrinkled face with wide eyes like Nevaeh's and high cheekbones.

The groundskeeper waved slowly. The eyes followed the trail of his fingers.

"There you are. There now, see? Nay, stay with me—" The spirit shuddered, the death images swirling. "Stay with me, Elijah. It's all right. Look here. The faster you calm down, the faster I can get Nevaeh home."

A note of mint permeated the images, the rot. Elijah clung to Nevaeh's name. The dust storm dwindled.

"She's in the truck this minute. If you'll hop into this watch, I'll take you to her."

The whispery face puckered.

"Don't fret about that. It wasn't you what done it. Not really. You know's well as I do you never would've done it. She's safe. Promise."

Elijah shifted. He was scared of possessing Nevaeh again, but she had distracted him from his death. His face grew fainter; his fear was fading, his energy along with it.

The groundskeeper nudged the watch toward him. "Here. See that symbol scratched in there? Keeps ghosts out. Keeps 'em in, too. If you hop inside and I close it up, there'll be no getting out 'til I open it. You won't be able to grab hold of her again."

The rot receded. The groundskeeper breathed deep, taking in the good, clean smell of turned soil. His body felt like a body again.

The ghostly face vanished. The spirit twisted in a subdued manner.

"Cross my heart and hope to die."

A moment of suspicion. The groundskeeper snorted.

"Course I'll let you out. Think I want to carry you around in my pocket for the rest of time?"

The spirit settled into the watch. Mint flared as Elijah poked around the cogs and gears.

"Don't break nothin'. S'all I got left of my own pa."

The groundskeeper closed the watch and headed back over the rise.

Nevaeh relaxed as he slid into the truck.

"Sorry that took s'long."

Her voice was accusing. "You said it'd just be a minute."

"Aye, and now I'm saying sorry it was longer."

Nevaeh watched him buckle in. "Can I see the pocket watch that almost made me a murder victim?"

He handed it to her. "Don't open it."

She turned it over, rubbing dirt off it with her fingers, and handed it back. He slipped it into his pocket.

"It's beautiful," she said. He pulled a U-turn, heading back toward Harrington. "Where'd you get it?"

"It was my pa's. Only thing I have of his."

The night was clear and quiet. The stars receded as they drove back through Harrington's shopping district. Nevaeh leaned against the window, her reflected eyes glistening in the glass.

The groundskeeper drummed his fingers on the steering wheel. "I'll take you to the hospital if you want. But what happened tonight, it was nothing to do with you."

"It's happened before."

"I believe you. But whatever you're dealing with normally, this ain't that."

Nevaeh swiped her face with an arm. Her eyes gleamed in the starlight, wide and brown like her father's. "You're sure about that, huh?"

"I am."

She leaned back in her seat. "What makes you so certain?"

He didn't take his eyes off the road.

"Do you believe in ghosts?"

XXVI

"Why can't anyone else sense ghosts?"

Nevaeh sat in a cushy purple armchair in her studio apartment, wearing sleep shorts and a tank top and wrapped in a blanket. Her ankle was elevated on a pile of pillows on a footstool. A floor lamp cast warm yellow light over the room, not bright but welcoming. Cardboard boxes were scattered everywhere; she'd never finished unpacking when she moved home. The place felt like a cutting that hadn't rooted.

The groundskeeper was in the kitchenette tucked away by the front door. Aside from the kitchenette, there was the chair, a sagging love seat, the door to a tiny bathroom, and a bed and side table squeezed into the back corner.

He rummaged in her freezer.

"Most people can." Something cavern-like had opened inside him as he settled her into her armchair. He couldn't remember the last time he'd been in someone's home—even if Nevaeh's felt temporary. "Leastways when they're children. But they grow out of it. No ice pack. How 'bout these peas?"

"Okay. They're probably expired anyway."

The groundskeeper wrapped the peas in a towel and brought them to her.

She held them to her ankle. It was swollen and discolored, but less so than when they'd returned. "Do you think my granny can sense ghosts?"

He hadn't told her who was possessing her, but he'd told her a ghost, not a dissociative episode, was responsible for her lost time. She hadn't said she believed him, but she hadn't stopped asking questions, either. He'd never heard her talk so much.

Then again, he rarely talked so much, either.

He wasn't used to telling people what he knew, but she wasn't scared anymore. So it was worth it, maybe.

He perched on the sagging love seat with his cap beside him. His knees bumped the footstool, which did not match the chair, which did not match the love seat. "I don't know your granny. You reckon she can?"

"She talks to Pops like he's still around." She hugged a throw pillow. "Not the way people do at the cemetery, like they're praying or something. She talks to him like he's right there having a whole conversation with her."

"Does she, now?"

"It's like he's following her around the house." She picked at the blanket. "Like, this is weird, I guess. But sometimes when she comes in from somewhere she'll say something like, *Cherry pie. Hank's in a good mood.* And you'll tell her you haven't made cherry pie, there's no cherry pie anywhere in the house, and she'll say she can see that, but she *smells* cherry pie."

"Hmm," the groundskeeper said.

Nevaeh threw the pillow at him. "Sure, share your secret ghost knowledge with me but *don't* tell me whether my granny can see ghosts."

He tossed the pillow back. "Most folks go their whole lives not *seeing* a ghost."

She threw the pillow again, harder.

"Yeah, yeah, yeah. No corporeal form. You know what I mean. Do you think Pops is still here? And Granny can sense him?"

"Does sound that way," the groundskeeper admitted. "Y'don't

usually see or hear 'em like people think. It's impressions, mostly. Colors. Smells. A taste or feeling."

"Like cherry pie?"

"That'd be a new one for me, but sure, if cherry pie made your granddad happy, it might smell like cherry pie when he feels uncommon good."

"Huh." Nevaeh pulled off her hair wrap, tossed it at her bed, missed, made a face, and started braiding her hair for the night. "Dad always worried that she was deep in denial or her memory was going. Like, Pops died fifteen years ago, and she was real sad for a couple weeks—*real* sad, I mean. Like I'd be helping her in the kitchen, and she'd stop what she was doing, and I'd realize she was crying, and I never saw her cry my whole life 'til then. And she started staying in bed real late, and I'd never seen her sleep in, either, not even on weekends. But then, I don't know, she went back to how she'd been before. Only more peaceful. Like she'd been meditating or something and, bam, she'd achieved inner peace. Do you think she can sense all ghosts, or just him?"

The groundskeeper put her hair wrap on the bedside table. The table wobbled; one of its legs was missing a foot.

"Hard to say without walking around a cemetery with her." He resumed his seat. "Precious few folks grow up without losing the sight, but sometimes folks can sense a ghost if it attaches itself to 'em. Could be what your granddad done. You thirsty? I'll make us tea if you got any."

"Tea would be great."

He returned to the kitchenette. It took up one wall, a line of countertop broken up by a sink and stove, ending in a fridge, with a row of cabinets above and below and a dishwasher too small to matter.

"The cupboard over the sink," Nevaeh said. "Mugs are in the one next to it."

"Kettle?"

"I don't have one."

The groundskeeper cocked an eyebrow. "How d'you make your tea, then?"

"I microwave water in a mug like a normal person?"

"Saints preserve us."

The groundskeeper rummaged through the cabinets for a pot. Nevaeh adjusted the peas. "Why do they stay? Why don't they... move on, or...pass through the veil, go into the light, whatever it is they say on TV? Scratch that. Where do they *go* when they move on?"

She sounded casual, but the groundskeeper understood her real question. *Where do we go when we die?*

He filled the pot at the sink and set it on the stove. "That, I can't tell you."

Nevaeh sighed. "Of course you can't."

"I've never died."

"Duh."

"Duh," the groundskeeper repeated under his breath. "The ghosts don't know, either, y'know. If they knew, it'd be because they were there instead of here. But they ain't."

"So it could be anything."

"Or nothing."

Nevaeh twisted around to look at him. "You don't believe that."

"No," he agreed. "Not sure what I believe these days, but ghosts is something after death. Hard to believe the ones who don't stay go straight on through to nothing."

The stovetop heated sluggishly. The groundskeeper flicked on the kitchen light, but its stuttering white light barely stretched beyond the sink. He flicked it off again, preferring the floor lamp's warm glow.

Nevaeh finished braiding her hair and shifted in her seat. "Why do they stay?"

"Fear, mostly. Anger. Sometimes love."

Nevaeh propped her chin on her fist. "Mostly fear and anger. That's comforting."

The groundskeeper wiped nonexistent crumbs from the counter. "Easier for most people to hold on to despair than hope."

"You don't need to tell me. I have depression."

"That ain't what I mean. Depression, anxiety, things like that, those're different." The water in the pot bubbled. "It's like this. How often're you having a day that's fine, good, even, and you're driving along, feeling peachy, enjoying yourself, and then someone cuts you off in traffic and you get real angry, angrier'n there's reason to be, and it ruins your whole day?"

Nevaeh's lips quirked. "Okay, that does happen a lot, considering how little I drive."

"Then y'take my meaning. When's the last time some small thing pestered you bad enough to turn you ratty the rest of the day? And when's the last time some small blessing lifted you up enough to turn your whole day back around good again? I don't say the second one don't happen, but the first one's far commoner."

The water boiled. The groundskeeper removed the pot from the heat.

Nevaeh leaned against the back of the armchair. "The peas have thawed."

"Just as well." The groundskeeper put tea bags in two mugs and filled the mugs with water. "Ought to let your ankle rest a spell. They can freeze up again in the meantime, be ready if you need 'em tomorrow."

He set one mug on the bedside table for the moment and traded the other for the peas.

"People aren't one way or the other." Nevaeh wrapped her fingers around her mug. "It's not like you're a hundred percent angry and afraid all the time or a hundred percent loving all the time. People are both. Maybe to different degrees, but people are both."

"People are both," the groundskeeper said. "Ghosts ain't."

She sipped her tea as he returned the peas to the kitchen. "Which one are you? A despairer or a hoper?"

He didn't answer.

"I mean," she said, "if you were a ghost, why would you stay?"

He paused with his hand on the freezer door. The faces of everyone he'd lost swam before him, clearer and far more painful than the spirits everywhere he went.

"I wouldn't stay."

He opened the freezer and put the peas away.

"You sound awfully sure of that."

"Ain't nothing left to keep me."

He collected his mug from the bedside table and settled on the love seat. He drank his tea, avoiding her gaze.

Nevaeh considered him over the edge of her mug. "What's keeping my dad here?"

He choked on his tea. She smiled.

"If everything you've told me is true," she said, "if what happened tonight went down like you said... I don't know who else would have a reason to go where you found me. It was him, wasn't it?"

He gulped down tea. Of course she'd figure it out.

He set his mug on an unopened moving box. "He's here for you."

Her fingers tightened on her mug.

"He wants you to talk to your therapist." The groundskeeper scratched his forehead. "About him, I mean."

She curled in on herself, as she so often did. Her hands shook; her tea sloshed. The groundskeeper set her mug gently on the moving box beside his.

"About his death," he continued. "About how you feel about it."

"I can't." Her voice was a whisper. "I can't, I can't, I can't."

"He wants to know you're dealing with it. That you're not facing it alone."

"I don't want to face it at all."

"That's what's troubling him."

Her jaw clenched. "Has he told you why he's so worried?" A challenge rang in her voice.

"You've told me enough yourself. But aye, he has."

She slumped in the chair, crossing her arms. "Unbelievable." She sniffed angrily and wiped her eyes. Her cheeks were wet.

"You're angry he told me," the groundskeeper said.

"No."

"I would be."

"Well, I'm not," Nevaeh snapped.

He leaned forward with his hands on his knees, shins bumping the footstool. She looked away.

"S'all right to be angry. It weren't none of my business. You don't have to pretend he never vexed you because he's dead now."

"I don't want to be angry with him." Tears slipped down her face. She burrowed into her blanket. "He was my daddy. And I love him. And he's gone. I don't want to be angry with him."

She buried her face in her knees. Peter shifted cushions off the footstool, sat on it and touched her knee. She leaned into him.

"Sure miss him, huh?"

She nodded, hiccupping. Her braids tickled his chin.

"He loves you more'n anything."

She inhaled shakily. She straightened, pressing the heels of her hands to her eyes, and stretched her leg over the arm of the chair to flex her foot. The swelling had subsided, though her ankle was still bruised a shade lighter than the upholstery.

"Can we talk about literally anything else?"

"As you wish."

But when she spoke again, she said, "I don't understand. If he's worried about me, why would he..."

Peter shook his head.

"It weren't him."

She snorted.

"Nay, I'm not denying your daddy brung you out there. But…"

She worked in the cemetery most every day. He didn't want to scare her.

But it'd be nice to have someone on alert for once. One person he could be honest with, one person who'd take his warnings seriously.

"He's not that kind of spirit, your pa. Sometimes, a powerful spirit, a spirit that's angry enough, its anger can infect other spirits, you might say. Make 'em angry or scared, even if that's not mostly how they are. The trouble it's causing comes from other ghosts who get a good whiff of its anger."

Nevaeh tightened the blanket around herself. "Are you saying there's a powerful, pissed-off spirit in my cemetery?"

He dragged a hand through his hair. "Don't know. Near certain there is, but I can't find it."

"But you can sense ghosts. Whatever it is, can't you just… feel it?"

He chuckled ruefully, handing her tea back to her. "A ways. I feel the anger. But it ain't that simple. It's muddled up with the griefs of other spirits. And its anger ain't bound to one place. Y'know when you're young, and there's times you can tell your mam is right pissed soon's you set foot in the house, whether she's there in the room or no? It's like that. This anger, I can feel it halfway across the cemetery. It's coming from that back lot—"

"Of course it is."

"—but I ain't found anything what might be the source. How's your ankle?"

"Still sore. How do we find it? The ghost."

"You want another ice pack? Saw some broccoli in your freezer with those peas."

"I'm fine. How do we find it?"

"Won't be put off, I ken," the groundskeeper said with a faint smile. "Research. Cross-reference. Fill in what gaps I can on the graves in back—names where there are only initials, dates where there ain't any. See if any of the folks in back fit the local legends."

"Like the boy on Morrow Road?"

He shifted to the love seat, slipping his notepad and pencil from his bag. Isaiah had given him plenty to work with, but it wouldn't hurt to ask Nevaeh what she knew. "It wasn't the boy. It was his mam, like I been told. Saw her myself this evening."

"You *saw*—"

"Never mind about her. She's gone. Moved on."

Nevaeh chewed on the inside of her cheek. "Who told you it was the mom? I always heard it was the kid. He's supposed to ask people for help finding his mom."

He chuckled, but his laughter died when he thought of the al-Masri children. "Sayid said it was the mother looking for her little boy."

She gave a small smile. "Is that what Sayid and Samira were doing visiting you after school last week? Telling you the local ghost stories?"

The groundskeeper flushed. "No."

Nevaeh sipped her tea. "Ugh, cold. I was glad to see them having a good time with you, to be honest. Yafa and I went to school together back in the day, but I've only gotten to know the kids since coming home. I've been away most of their lives, you know? Yafa and I sort of reconnected when I got into town, but it's been… We've been going through a tough time since we lost Dad, and they've been having a hard time, too. Her dad's been going downhill fast, and her brother-in-law died back in December. That's actually how I met Sayid the first time."

The groundskeeper glanced at her, couldn't help asking, "How?"

"He came in with his dad and grandparents to make funeral arrangements—I guess ideally Qasim would've been buried in a Muslim cemetery, but Harrington doesn't have one. Anyway,

Sayid was uncomfortable with all the funeral talk. He asked me all these questions about the cemetery's landscaping, though, when he said anything. He's a shy kid, but he really loves plants. If he wants a summer job working the grounds with you when he's older, I'll hire him in a heartbeat."

He wouldn't be here when Sayid was older. He'd be gone by Midsummer.

"Anyway," Nevaeh said, "everyone's been trying to help them out the last few months, like Leslie Wu organized a meal train not long after Yafa's dad went into palliative care. But—I don't know—it seems like you've been good for the kids."

His face was hot with shame. He cleared his throat. "Tell me about this other ghost. The one everyone blames their troubles on."

She raised an eyebrow at his change of subject but didn't comment on it. Her fingers drummed on her mug. "They say his family died of cholera. So he brings trouble on the town in revenge."

"Revenge for what? Cholera is cholera."

"I don't know. Isn't that just how ghost stories go?"

The groundskeeper's lips pushed in and out as he added to his notes. Isaiah hadn't mentioned anything about revenge, although perhaps that was because it made no sense. Then again, spirits weren't known for their grasp of logic.

"Don't think Isaiah mentioned how he died," he murmured, looking over his notes. "Don't suppose you've ever heard?"

Nevaeh's brow creased. "Isaiah like… Uncle Dave's dead husband, Isaiah?"

"Ah." The groundskeeper had been thinking out loud, hadn't meant to mention Isaiah to her. "Forgot you wouldn't know. He haunts the museum, old Isaiah does."

Nevaeh blinked at him. He chuckled at her expression.

"Jesus," she said. "Does Uncle Dave know?"

"The kids've told him. But he don't believe it. Thought it

was me they'd seen, when I was there the other day." His laughter faded. "Isaiah could show him, if he wanted. He's powerful enough. Takes form, sometimes. That's how the kids're so sure he's there, even the older ones. But he's bothered about how David would react."

"I can imagine. Uncle Dave's a total skeptic."

"So I gather." The groundskeeper scratched pointedly in his notebook. "This ghost. How's he s'posed to have died?"

"If you believe one version, he was murdered. I guess he'd be avenging his death, in that case. But most people say he died of cholera, too, after his wife and kids went. So make of that what you will."

"Cholera would place him in the back lot, like as not," the groundskeeper said slowly. "How long've folks been blaming their ill luck on him? I'm guessing he died mid-nineteenth century, if the latter story's right and he died of cholera like his kin. If you know when the stories began, it might narrow down his date of death. Not as good as a name, but it's a start."

Nevaeh took another sip of tea and grimaced; she'd forgotten it had gone cold. She set it on the footstool.

"I'm not sure. Everyone blamed the recession on him, even though, you know, it was everywhere. But they blamed him anyway. Granny says it was the same during the Great Depression and both world wars. I think it goes at least as far back as the Civil War, but I don't know. Didn't Isaiah say?"

The groundskeeper flipped his notepad closed. "He knows how far back the written records go, but that's turn of the century. Bound to have been told in stories before it was written down."

He ran a hand over his face. The moving boxes scattered through the dim apartment looked like headstones.

"Feels like I'm missing something. Got so many pieces, but I don't see how they fit together."

Nevaeh gave a small smile. "This is what you do, huh? Hunt ghosts?"

He swallowed his remaining tea. Talking about ghosts was one thing. Talking about himself was quite another.

"What do we do when we find it?" Nevaeh asked. "How do we get rid of it?"

His brows contracted. "*We* don't do anything. I'll handle that."

She cocked an eyebrow at his tone but said, "Aye aye, sir."

He set his empty mug on the moving box, fiddled with his flat cap.

"Thanks for coming to get me," Nevaeh said.

He fidgeted. "Don't mention it."

She leaned toward him. "Are you *blushing*?"

"No," he said, blushing deeper.

"You are!" She laughed. "Okay, wow, remind me never to thank you for anything. Hey, um—"

She laughed again, awkwardly.

"Okay, this is going to sound…ridiculous. Like, really ridiculous. But around the time you were making tea, I realized I have no idea what your name is."

Whatever he'd expected her to say, it wasn't that. His skin prickled.

What was it with these people?

"We've been working together for how long? And now, I mean, *this*." She gestured at the warm yellow light, the moving boxes, the pillows now piled on the floor instead of the footstool. "You're literally in my apartment. You drove me home in the middle of the night. You made me tea. And I don't know your name."

So many people already knew his name. With each person who learned it, he lost a little more power over his own destiny.

But she was right. How much had they shared already? Far more than he'd shared with anyone since Jack's death. Not one person in Savannah had known his name, let alone anything else about him.

Maybe names held more power over the dead than they did the living. Maybe other things held power over the living. A pot of soup shared at lunch. A walk to the sandwich shop. A cup of tea.

"Peter Shaughnessy," he said. "My name's Peter Shaughnessy."

She stuck out a hand. He shook it, feeling foolish.

"Nice to meet you, Peter Shaughnessy."

"Likewise," he said gruffly.

She smiled, but a yawn swallowed it. He was on his feet in an instant, bag over his shoulder and cap in hand. "I ought to go. It's getting late."

"It's been late." Another yawn shuddered through her. "My call probably woke you up."

"It didn't."

"Liar." She put as little weight as possible on her ankle as she stood. He reached for her. "I'm okay. It doesn't hurt much now."

"You'll put those peas on it again tomorrow?"

"Yeah."

"You'll stay home a few days?"

Her nose scrunched.

"Heal faster if you stay off it."

"I know. I just have so much to do."

Peter rubbed his neck. "If you're set on coming in, let me drive you in the truck the next couple days. Biking'll only make it worse."

Nevaeh rolled her eyes, but she grinned. It was the first real smile she'd given him, and he smiled back. "Okay, *Grandpa*."

She was teasing, but something bloomed inside him. He jammed his cap on his head, blushing again.

She limped to her bed. He hovered nearby.

"Would you stop looking at me like that? It's just a twisted ankle." She sank onto the bed and stretched her leg, flexing her foot. "See? Made it the whole three feet from my chair to my bed."

"I see," Peter said. "Good night."

She was gazing at her foot and didn't answer. He was halfway across the apartment when she said, "I have another question."

He turned. She rubbed her arms.

"If there's something...bad, in the cemetery...then, when I'm at work..."

"You're safe," Peter said at once. "Warded your office the first night I was there. You wear those flowers I gave you, and any iron you have, and stay in your office much as possible, and don't stay past sunset, you'll be all right."

She removed the flower garland and put it on her bedside table. "Okay. Thanks. Good night."

He nodded and turned away.

"Peter?"

He waited, his heart stuttering as usual at his own name.

Nevaeh was silent for a long moment.

"Can you say good-night to Daddy for me?"

XXVII

Samira couldn't sleep.

She'd biked home, let herself in, locked Sayid out—unsuccessfully, as he had his own key—and gone straight to bed. Her room was a mishmash of the princess-themed walls and bedspread from her princess phase and the spy paraphernalia, books, and posters from her current obsession. She burrowed into her pink comforter, her head ringing with Peter's words.

Why must you cling to me so? I don't want you here.

She was used to people's anger. Mama's and Baba's, tinged with confusion and sadness; Sayid's, more exasperated; her teachers' and principal's, straightforward, the easiest to handle.

But Peter had been so gentle. Like Jeddo. He hadn't been angry that first night, though she'd been somewhere she shouldn't have been, nor when she invited herself back later. She thought he'd liked spending time together at the library.

Maybe she'd been wrong.

I don't want you here.

She buried her head under the pillow. No one wanted her. She heard them, sometimes. Her teachers lamented having such a troublemaker in class. Only Mrs. Albright never said such things.

A knock at her door. Sayid's voice, muffled through the wood.

"Samira? Mama and Baba are home. Do you want to say good-night?"

The door scraped open. A sliver of light fell across her bed. She pretended to be asleep.

Sayid sighed and shut the door.

Samira listened to everyone get ready for bed. Her parents murmured as they closed blinds and locked doors downstairs. The tap ran in the bathroom. The stairs creaked.

Another knock. The door opening. Soft footsteps on the carpet, pausing as her mother stopped to pick up toys and books and put them on her desk or bookshelf.

"Asleep already?" Khalid asked from the doorway.

"Shhh, yes."

Bedsprings squeaking, her mother's weight beside her. A hand on her back, rubbing in circles. Samira wanted to cry.

"She must've been exhausted."

Yafa sighed, didn't answer. She kissed Samira's hair, rose and tiptoed from the room.

"I wish it could always be like this." She pulled the door shut, muting their voices as they headed for their bedroom.

Samira's stomach clenched. She squeezed her eyes tighter, but tears seeped out. No doubt it'd be easier for everyone if she were always as untroublesome as when she slept.

Her mind churned. The anger and exasperation of the adults in her life whirled through her like a tornado.

She wiped her eyes on her arm, listening.

Silence. Only the house settling.

She slipped into the hallway, where family pictures taunted her. A black-and-white picture of Jeddo as a boy, grinning from a streetside window in the Palestinian city after which he'd named their mother. Formal portraits of him and their grandmother, and their grandparents on Khalid's side. Photos of Sayid and Samira; their parents; Uncle Qasim; Auntie Maryam. Snapshots of a time when Baba had been home more and Mama had smiled more and Samira had gotten in less trouble.

Her lip trembled. She snuck downstairs to the foyer to retrieve her sneakers, then to the back door because it opened more quietly than the front. She didn't put her sneakers on until she was outside.

The cool night air rushed in her face as she biked to the cemetery. Her lungs and legs hurt, but it was better than spiraling in bed.

Now she was moving so fast the hurt couldn't catch up. That was all she wanted, when she ran off. To outrun her hurt, to hide from it for a while.

The cemetery gate was unlocked, though it was well past closing time. Samira didn't know what to make of that.

She hid her bicycle in the shadows of the lilacs. Spirits wheeled and shifted as she passed, nervous. The air smelled sour, and Samira's nose wrinkled as she slouched down the knoll.

The cemetery pulsed with anger, but she wasn't afraid. This anger wasn't for her. She wasn't sure who it was for. She didn't care. It was nice, anger not directed at her.

In the woods, something rustled in the underbrush. Samira walked on. Despite the simmering anger, she felt better here than she had at home.

The weight in the air lifted as she neared the back wall. Something butter yellow slipped into it, making her comfortable here like she rarely was elsewhere anymore. Faint but *there*, threading ribbonlike through his anger.

Her friend. The ghost.

She slipped through the pine grove and the break in the wall. The low, rounded shapes of weathered headstones hunkered amidst gleaming stalks of grass. The breeze smelled sweetly of clover. Samira followed the wall westward, picking her way through headstones and overgrown bluestem and beardtongue.

A ring of yew trees greeted her. Even older stones lay crumbled around it, overgrown with moss and ivy. The remains of the cemetery's original back wall.

Samira wriggled through the gap left by a dead yew that had

been uprooted by an early–April thunderstorm. It had flooded so much that school had closed for two days. She'd loved it.

Between the yews, clover and creeping phlox had gone untrod by any feet but hers for well over a century. A headstone stood at their center, unadorned except for a symbol carved roughly into the top and a date and initials engraved in its face.

O.S.

1851

Samira plopped down, plucking at phlox. The air, always a dark, bloody crimson here, twisted mintily. Asking what was wrong.

"Nothing," she said. "I just had to get away from everyone for a while."

The sensation of someone stroking her face. She lay on her side, pressing her cheek into the grass. The headstone blurred through the silvery-black stalks and heads of clover.

The air twisted again, prodding.

"It's different with you. You're not exactly here. And you don't get mad at me."

The air shivered with laughter. The corner of Samira's mouth turned up. The ghost didn't feel much besides anger. And she didn't make people happy much.

But sometimes she could make him laugh. And it made her feel better.

A little.

Samira squeezed her eyes shut. Peter's words sounded in her head.

"Can you tell me another story?" she whispered.

The yellow intensified, tinged a little blue. The ghost, of course, didn't tell her stories. He never spoke. None of the cemetery's ghosts were like the ones in the movies. No pale, translucent forms took shape, no voices whispered spookily through the trees.

But he shared memories with her. Often, the memories were of his mother, darning clothes by the fire and telling stories of wisps and selkies and other fey creatures with no name but *them folk*.

Tonight, the memory was different.

A girl her own age, with golden hair and an old-timey dress from a later period than his mother's. The girl sat in a hard-backed chair in a tiny attic bedroom, practicing needlepoint by candlelight. She talked as she sewed, enumerating the frightening and fey creatures *her* mother had told her about. Rusalka. Ovinnik, domovoi. Kikimora and zmey and vily.

Samira calmed as she listened. "Thanks."

A phantom hand rubbed her back like Mama had earlier. Like Mama had done far more often when she'd had time and energy to sit with her children at bedtime.

Samira staggered to her feet, touching three fingers to the symbol carved roughly into the top of the headstone. Two *V*s forming a triangle where they overlapped. The same symbol carved into Peter's windowsills.

The ghost asked a question, one he'd asked before and which Samira had answered the same way.

"I can't." She pulled away, hugging herself. "It's a grave. I can't destroy a grave. Do you know how much trouble I'd be in?"

The ghost's response was tart as cranberry juice. Samira scuffed the grass. The clover bobbed, sweet-smelling and silver in the darkness.

"I'm not scared," she mumbled. "But it's a *grave*. I'm sorry you're stuck in there, but—"

The ghost reined in his sarcasm and asked, patiently, whether she wouldn't like it if he were free. If he could accompany her everywhere, a secret friend at her shoulder, even when people were angry with her, even if no one knew.

She hugged herself tighter. "Of course I'd like that. Can't I scribble it out with a marker or something?"

But an image of the double *V* split and broken appeared in her head as it had on her previous visits. Samira didn't love the idea of vandalizing a headstone with a marker, but marker could be scrubbed off.

Cracking the stone was different.

She wished he could accompany her everywhere. Wished she didn't have to sneak off to visit him. But she couldn't destroy a grave to have a friend.

"I can't." She took a step back. "I'm sorry."

She fled through the gap in the yews, emerging scratched and dirty. The anger rippled as she sprinted away, like the ghost was angry with *her.* She shivered, nervous for the first time since she'd found his headstone. She slunk from tree to tree, preferring to keep their bulk and solidity between her and the ghost.

The anger evened out. Samira swallowed. She must've imagined that ripple.

"Samira!"

Her brother's voice, distant and trembling. She sighed, slowing as she slipped back through the pine grove. Her heart hammered from her run.

"Coming," she said dully, but he called her name repeatedly.

She found him rubbing his arms in the middle of the creek. The Saint-John's-wort was around his neck, like the ta'weedh their grandmother had always worn, except that it had grown. The oblong leaves and yellow flowers were thicker than ever.

"There you are," he said in relief. "Come on, let's get back before Mama and Baba wake up."

She stumbled over a root and fell. Dirt scraped her palms and knees.

She glanced around, but he was alone. "Where's Peter?"

Sayid's brow furrowed. "What do you want him for?"

She waded into the creek, shivering in the knee-deep water. "I thought he'd come find me. Like he did that first night."

Her brother's expression softened.

"He probably would have, but he wasn't home. I checked." His fingers tightened on his arms. "I did *not* want to come back here alone."

Samira's chest caved.

"Sorry," she mumbled.

Then she decided she wasn't sorry. Feeling bad was stupid.

She jerked her chin. "You didn't have to come. I was coming home eventually."

They splashed out of the creek. Sayid worried his Saint-John's-wort, which bristled importantly.

"Why'd you run off, anyway?"

She didn't answer. He wouldn't believe her. And the ghost had asked her not to tell anyone about him. He didn't like people, the ghost. Didn't want anyone to know about him but her. It made her feel special.

If she was unwilling to free him, surely she could keep him a secret.

A whistled *whip-poor-will, whip-poor-will* chorused their way through the woods. Sayid grabbed Samira's hand, but she shook him off. She wasn't scared; she didn't need to hold hands.

It didn't occur to her that he did.

He sighed. "Mama and Baba really worry about you."

Her stomach clenched. "No, they don't."

"Yes, they do. They're dealing with a lot right now. Can't you understand that?"

Vaguely, she could. Jeddo in the hospital, after the last months at home in which his health and memory had worsened in tandem. Bills—whenever Baba was home, her parents worried well into the evening together about money.

But Samira was eight. She'd been born after the years of long hours and tight wallets; she didn't fully grasp the money problems. Jeddo had gone to the hospital six months ago, and she hadn't seen him once. Mama visited him almost every day, but she wouldn't take Samira, no matter how often she asked.

Her skin prickled. Jeddo used to sit her on his knee and sneak her sweets when Mama and Baba weren't looking. He used to read to her and Sayid in Arabic. She'd understood few of the words, none of the writing when she'd peered over his shoulder to follow along, but she'd liked how he illustrated the stories with his gnarled hands, the rise and fall of his voice as he read.

She wasn't sure she remembered his voice anymore.

When Sayid reached for her hand again, she clung to him. He squeezed her fingers each time they passed a spirit, though he always insisted they didn't exist. Fireflies flickered among the headstones.

The weight in the air lightened. A tendril of buttery yellow reached for her clear from the back lot, like the ghost wanted to comfort her.

Even though he'd been mad at her, for once.

Even though she kept refusing him the one thing he asked.

Maybe she could free him. It must be boring, stuck at his grave. Samira had once been confined to her room for a week with the flu, and it had been the worst thing ever.

Not that she knew how to free him. She was an eight-year-old with no notable skills but sneaking out and lock picking. His headstone was a hunk of rock that had withstood over a century of rainstorms and snowstorms and high spring winds and sweltering summer suns.

Smashing up a headstone made her queasy anyhow.

Sayid relaxed as they biked away, but Samira couldn't resist looking back. The air within the cemetery walls was heavy with the ghost's anger. The other spirits jittered, nervous and upset. Sayid had been anxious the whole way through the woods, past the empty cottage, and up the knoll.

But full of death and spirits as the cemetery was, it was the place Samira had been happiest lately, until Peter yelled at her. Thanks to the ghost, it was the one place she still had a friend.

Sayid paused several yards ahead. "Come on, Samira. We gotta get home."

She pedaled sluggishly after him.

He gripped his handlebars. "Are you okay?"

Her eyes stung. She cycled past him, pedaling hard, and didn't stop until she'd beaten him home.

XXVIII

Elijah would not return to his grave.

The groundskeeper opened his pocket watch once he entered the cemetery, but Elijah wouldn't leave it.

"C'mon. Out. You can't live in my pa's watch forever."

Elijah twisted in the gears. He couldn't live anywhere anymore.

"Think you're right funny, do you? Y'take my meaning, so piss off."

Elijah didn't budge.

The groundskeeper pinched the bridge of his nose, flipped the watch closed, and trudged to his cottage. The spirits shuddered. He slipped an iron band and a flower garland from his bag and put the band on his wrist, with some difficulty, and the garland around his neck.

Adeline ripped up daffodils by her grave. They were past season, leaves browning, but he shivered as she destroyed the flowers she'd liked so much.

"Adeline," he said, "all right there?"

She flashed up in his face, red with rage and rotty with fear. His heart jumped. He stepped back, but with his iron and flowers she couldn't touch him.

"S'all right," he said, more calmly than he felt. "S'all right, Addy."

She receded. Let him pass.

When he glanced back, she'd returned to terrorizing the daffodils.

He shook his head. They were agitated, all of them.

He shut his garden gate with a sigh. The anger stretching from the back, the unease of the spirits, none of it could touch him within his garden, thanks to his warding.

He hung his cap on its peg, set his watch on the kitchen table, flipped it open, and went out back to check on the pullets. They clucked softly in their sleep. He gave a tired smile, wished briefly he were a chicken, and went back inside.

The greenlings rustled. The bulbs grumbled as he dropped into the chair beside them.

"It weren't her. We're staying. For now."

Elijah ventured from the watch. Shut safely in the cottage, he was calmer than he'd been, but minty and a little sour.

"You stayed for someone," the groundskeeper said wearily. "Don't expect you understand leaving. I'm staying anyhow. No need to fret about that."

Elijah fretted anyway. Who would protect his little girl if the groundskeeper left?

"Ain't that why you're here?" the groundskeeper snapped, or would've snapped, if he'd had the energy. It was so late.

Elijah moped back into the watch.

The groundskeeper sighed. "Nay, I know you can't. Know it's more powerful than you, whatever it is. Wish I could find it."

Elijah poked out of the watch again, glaring around it.

"Told you I'm staying, didn't I? So leave off. Just now I'm more worried about you anyhow. You're scared to stay out there anymore, frighten her again, fine. But you're not staying in here."

Elijah huffed.

The groundskeeper snorted. "Because I ain't fixing to have a spirit in my own home, watching everything I do. Bad enough, all of you peering over my shoulder all the time anyway. This is the one place I get any peace."

He dragged a hand through his hair, mulling over the night's events.

"Nevaeh's gran," he said. "Your wife's mam, or yours?"

XXIX

At ten the next morning, he was on the porch of the Key-Floreses' farmhouse outside town, cap in hand and watch in pocket. The house's paint was white and peeling, but the porch ceiling was blue. Despite the gray sky, the garden spilled color halfway to the road: false indigo, columbine, penstemon, geranium, lupine, daylilies. Trees crowded the house, a redbud, two crabapples, a flowering dogwood, lilacs blooming up against the porch. Bees drifted through the foliage, humming.

The groundskeeper knocked. He tried and failed to make his hair lie flat as he waited; it'd had a mind of its own since going gray, hence the cap.

Sigils were scratched into the porch railing and beneath the doorknob. He raised his eyebrows. The work of Nevaeh's granny, maybe, or someone before.

He knocked again. The driveway was empty. Perhaps no one was home, but Elijah had insisted his mother only left home on Thursdays for her evening bingo game. She had her programs to watch and her baking to do. She couldn't drive anymore, so she had to wait for her daughter-in-law to return from her shift at the hospital to go anywhere anyway.

A face appeared in the sidelight, a blurred shape in the frosted glass. "What you want?"

"To talk to you," the groundskeeper said, "if you're Marguerite Key-Flores."

Her voice was suspicious. "I ain't expecting company. What's your name?"

He scratched his forehead.

"Peter Shaughnessy." Strange that it wasn't strange, giving his name to yet another person. "I'm the groundskeeper over at Harrington Public Cemetery."

The dead bolt clunked, the door unlatched, and Nevaeh's granny stepped outside. While Nevaeh had an inch on him, her grandmother stood barely five feet. She was heavily wrinkled, in her eighties, wearing a housedress and a floury apron and the rubber-soled slippers popular in nursing homes. Silver braids wrapped around her head and up into a bun. She had the same wide, dark eyes as her son and granddaughter.

"Something happen to Nae-Nae?"

"No, ma'am," but that wasn't quite true. "Yes, I mean. But she's all right. She's at the office. Last night—that's why I'm here."

She gave him a once-over. "Then quit yammering and come in."

He followed her inside, wringing his cap. "Awful lot of sigils carved into that porch."

She raised one thin eyebrow at him.

"The symbols," he said. "To keep the spirits out."

"Did 'em up myself. The ceiling, too."

A spirit crowded her, warm and golden with affection. Nevaeh's grandfather.

"What about the ceiling?"

She snorted as they entered the kitchen. A picture of Nevaeh hung on the wall. She was around five years old, grinning from beneath a colander she'd put on her head like a helmet. One of her front teeth was missing.

"You know sigils but you don't know to paint the house blue? Ain't just the ceiling, neither."

Marguerite gestured him toward the worn wooden table and returned to the dough she'd been kneading. Flour rose around her, hazy in the light of her husband's spirit. A clock ticked in the other room.

She nodded at the kitchen window. "Did the doorframes and windowsills and shutters, soon as I moved in. My son thought my mind was going, but spirits won't cross it. Looks too much like water."

"But it ain't water."

She shrugged. Her elbows were pale and powdery with flour like the Formica countertop.

"Does it work?" the groundskeeper asked.

"Course it works. Otherwise I wouldn't've done it."

"How'd your husband get in, then?"

She paused in her kneading. "Nae-Nae told you about that."

"She did, but she didn't have to. I can see him here same as you can."

She sprinkled flour on the counter and resumed kneading. "He come with me when they moved me in. I don't exactly see him."

"I know it," the groundskeeper said. "Colors. Smells. Feelings."

He dimpled at the ghost, who twisted toward him in a haze of mint. Hank had never been seen by anyone but his wife.

"Cherry pie, Nevaeh says," the groundskeeper added.

And the kitchen did smell of cherry pie as Hank laughed fondly at his granddaughter's name.

Marguerite took a deep whiff, relaxing into a smile.

"Cherry pie always was his favorite." Her smile faded. She patted flour from her hands. "Nae-Nae and her mama don't see him. How come you can?"

"Ain't just him. I see all of 'em."

She finished kneading, put the dough in a proofing basket, and covered it with a towel. Hank flowed around her. Jealousy

twinged within the groundskeeper as it had at the museum, but
he buried it.

Marguerite poured two glasses of lemonade and sat across
from him. The kitchen was warm; the lemonade sweated, leaving rings of water on the table.

"Guessing you only see one spirit." The groundskeeper set
his watch on the table. "Hoping it might be two. You ever seen
your son when you been to the cemetery?"

"Ain't been to the cemetery since the funeral," Marguerite said
softly. "Nae-Nae and her mama won't take me. Why you ask?"

He flipped the watch open. "Well—"

In his home for the first time since death, Elijah burst from
the watch in a joyful yellow spiral. Hank spun up to meet him.
Marguerite pressed floury fingers to her mouth.

"My baby," she whispered. "Oh, my baby."

She laughed wetly as he enfolded her in a ghostly hug. His
father smelled more strongly of cherry pie than ever. The whole
kitchen was bright and golden and sweet-tart with cherries.
Marguerite all but disappeared in the love of her husband and
son, shining so brightly the groundskeeper shielded his eyes.

Her cheeks were wet, but she was smiling the biggest smile
he'd ever seen.

His heart twisted. He couldn't imagine feeling half the joy
on her face.

That wasn't what he was here for anyway.

"Can he stay with you a spell?" he asked, ignoring the twisting of his own heart. "There's something in the cemetery been
upsetting him. I'm trying to find it, but until I do he won't go
back. He's scared Nevaeh twice now."

The warm light grayed. Elijah fretted over last night's incident.

"S'all right, Elijah. I know you never would've done it if you
could help it. Y'see how scared he is," the groundskeeper said
to Marguerite, "of its happening again."

She steepled her fingers. "Where'd you learn so much about spirits?"

"Picked up plenty over the years. Learned some from Mam's stories back home."

"Where's home?"

He raked a hand through his hair. "Ireland. I ain't been back in an age."

She nodded. "South Carolina, for me. I sure do miss it. But when Nevaeh's granddaddy asked me to come back north with him, I said yes, even though it meant a snowy winter. Ain't that right, Hank?"

Hank glowed. Marguerite smiled. The groundskeeper clenched his hands together in his lap.

"Course my baby can stay." Marguerite went to the sink to wash dishes. "He's my child. He can stay forever if he wants."

Elijah hovered around her. She swatted soap bubbles at him, which he dodged as if they wouldn't pass right through him. He'd spent so long yearning for Nevaeh, looking after her without her knowing he was there. Now he basked in his mother's awareness of him. Except for the fact that two of them were dead and had no corporeal form, they were the picture of a happy family.

The groundskeeper looked away. If his brother or mother or sister were yet lingering—increasingly unlikely—he couldn't be with them this way. Eoin buried god-knew-where. Mam and Catherine back in Ballygar. Him with no way to get there, thanks to the curse, even if he wanted their spirits with him. Even if they hadn't yet turned to wisps. Even if they'd stayed in the first place.

Even if Catherine's spirit wouldn't have been terribly, terribly angry with him.

He shut the thought away. "You know it won't be forever. Only until he gets what he's here for."

A dish squeaked in the suds.

"Your husband, he's waiting on you," the groundskeeper said.

"That's clear enough. Moment you pass yourself, he's ready to go with you. But Elijah, he's worried about your granddaughter. She comes to terms with his passing, he's gone."

With a sigh, Marguerite put a dish in the drying rack. "Won't never happen. I love that girl, but she takes after her mama. Don't neither of 'em know how to sit with grief."

"Don't mean no harm. I just want you to understand."

She turned to him, wiping her hands on her apron. "I'm eighty-four. Bet I understand more'n you, youngster."

He did not correct her regarding their relative ages.

"I'll take every extra minute I can get with him," she said, "never mind how few they are. He can stay as long as he needs. As long as he's here."

She wiped flour off the counter. The groundskeeper stood, pulling his cap on. Something strangely like grief panged through him at leaving Elijah.

"You enjoy yourself, Elijah," he said. "'Bout time you relaxed a bit."

A touch at his shoulder, though no one was there. And of course, ever present, the sense of Elijah's concern for his daughter.

"Nothing'll happen to her. Not on my watch." The groundskeeper tipped his cap at Marguerite, though she had returned to her dishes and wasn't looking. "Thanks for the lemonade."

"You say hi to Nae-Nae for me. Tell her I'll see her Sunday."

He paused in the doorway. Looked at her washing dishes with her husband and son swirling around her. The clock in the other room ticked on.

Something tugged at him. "Is it worth it?"

"What you mean?"

The words stuck in his throat. "Knowing your husband's here even though he ain't *here* anymore... Does it make it easier? Is it worth having his spirit with you when you could've moved on by now?"

With a soapy hand, Marguerite stroked Hank's face, though there was no face to stroke. She glanced at the groundskeeper.

"Why you want to know?"

"Just wondering."

"Hmm." She turned back to the sink. "Don't expect I got much time left in this world. Having him here with me until I go, it's a comfort. It ain't the same as him being alive, but I don't have to hurt like I did at first."

He pulled his cap over his eyes, unconvinced. He had plenty time left. All of it, as far as he knew. He'd begun to suspect, by the time Jack died. He'd stopped aging a decade before; more than one accident over the years ought to have killed him but hadn't.

"Thanks," he said anyway.

He was nearly out the door when she called, "It's always worth it, having your folk with you."

XXX

It was drizzling when the groundskeeper returned to the cemetery. The spirits grumbled, their thoughts noisier and memories sourer than usual. Nevaeh hobbled outside, but she stuck by the office door, rubbing her arms.

She relaxed at the sight of him. "Hey, would you mind giving me a ride? I ordered a dress for this wedding I'm going to, and it finally came in. I won't be on my feet long, promise," she added, as his brow furrowed. "Just long enough to try it on. And then, um, there's a sandwich shop not far from there, if you want to get lunch?"

He thumbed up the brim of his cap. "Ain't having lunch with that Benji today?"

She flushed. "They're actually why I'm going to a wedding. I'm their plus-one."

"I see."

"It doesn't mean anything. We're going as friends."

He raised an eyebrow at her. Her flush deepened.

"Peter."

"Didn't say nothing."

"It's the way you didn't say it," Nevaeh said. "Will you take me or not?"

He opened the passenger door for her. "You tell me how to

get to this dress place, I'll find the sandwich shop. Been there before."

She locked the office, and they were off. The Victorians lining the east side of Thompson were less run-down than the buildings on Washington at the other end of town. Fresh paint dried on their trim; scaffolding had been set up for roof reshingling. But the tall, thin houses squeezed together as if shivering in the drizzle, and the memories wafting from several gave them a ghostly glow. The sky was iron. To the west, beyond a small, grassy park, Ashmead Creek burbled sluggishly, the same iron hue as the sky.

"It's owned by these sisters who went to school with me," Nevaeh was saying. "It used to be a CVS. My first job was there, actually. But it closed during the recession, and the building was empty for a while. I mean, you know, it wasn't just the CVS. A lot of mom-and-pop shops closed, too, and some families lost their farms. Dad sold off some of ours to save the rest. The whole town was hit pretty hard."

The groundskeeper drummed his fingers on the steering wheel. "People blamed the ghost, I s'pose."

Nevaeh laughed. "Yeah. Anyway, the good part was, it was on the market for so long that Margo and Cailey got it for next to nothing, and they've had the boutique open for, like, six years now. It's incredible. They restored it back to how it looked when it was a general store."

He pulled onto Main. The string lights overhead sparkled in the rain. The silver maples were a haze of silvery green. The brick storefronts huddled together, cold and tired, shimmering with memories.

"A general store?"

"Yeah—I guess you wouldn't know. It's one of the oldest buildings in town. But the last owner didn't have anyone to take over when he died, so it got sold off. Why?"

He parked on the street. The closest building's empty windows gaped like dead eyes.

Nevaeh leaned over the center console, lowering her voice. "Is it something to do with the ghost?"

"Could be. One of Sayid's schoolmates thinks he haunts the place."

His voice caught on Sayid's name. It had been only last night when he'd run them off, but it felt like weeks. Rain pattered on the truck.

"I don't think he can," Nevaeh said.

He looked at her in surprise. She pointed at the storefronts. The rusting remains of ancient horseshoes flaked into nothingness over their shabby doorways.

"Iron, right?"

He dimpled at her. "Aye, but I don't figure they'd do much in that state. Near rusted away."

"Just wait." Nevaeh unbuckled herself. "The one over the boutique's in mint condition. It's a tradition to take care of it. CVS didn't care, obviously. They got rid of the old one, I'm pretty sure, but Margo put a new one up as soon as she bought the place."

She slid out into the rain. The groundskeeper hurried around to share his umbrella, clucking over her like a hen. She shook her head but let him do it. Memories and the odd spirit wafted from the buildings, but they kept their distance.

Unlike most of the street, the general store gleamed with fresh paint, clean windows, and window boxes bursting with tulips. As Nevaeh had said, a whole, shining horseshoe was nailed over the entrance. The groundskeeper held the door open for her. Ambient lighting and racks of fashionable clothing greeted him as he followed her across the threshold.

Then emotions crashed over him.

A confusing but potent crush of memories not his own ripped through him. A woman laughing behind a register long since replaced by a string of ever-more modern models. A toddler standing on tiptoe, reaching into a pickle barrel no longer there. The echoes of a meal in the apartment above.

A yellow rag hanging from the stoop railing. The stench of a sickroom.

A crush of joy and love and sorrow and anger and mourning, so powerful the groundskeeper was drowning in it. He gasped and shuddered, reaching for the wall as the room reeled.

Nevaeh's voice echoed in his ears, asking if he was okay. Other faces crowded beside hers, but he wasn't sure how many were present and how many were echoes of the past.

"Can you say anything?" someone asked distantly. "Do you need anything?"

"Get him a glass of water."

"On it."

Heels scrabbled on the floor and clicked away.

The memories weighed on him, compressing his lungs. "Marker."

"Shhh! He said something."

Nevaeh leaned close. "What did you say?"

"Marker." The groundskeeper flinched. Someone else's sorrow pierced him, lodged inside him like a shard of glass amidst all the shards of his own griefs. "Get me a marker."

Nevaeh's brow creased. "Are you sure you don't want water? Or—"

He grasped her hand. Distant voices babbled in his ears. "A marker, lass, please. I beg you."

The heels clicked back. "Here's that water."

The groundskeeper's fingers tightened on Nevaeh's.

"Do you have a Sharpie or something?" she asked.

The heels clicked away and back again. The groundskeeper took the proffered marker and inched back the cuff of his left sleeve. With an effort, he drew a complicated symbol on the inside of his wrist. The faces and voices crowded him.

When the last loop of the symbol closed, the memories cut out as quickly as they had come. The voices quieted. The faces vanished, except those of Nevaeh and two other women crouching before him.

He gulped down air. The wall was cool and hard behind him.

Nevaeh gripped his shoulders. "Are you okay?"

He rubbed the mark on his wrist. The echoes of the onslaught faded. "Fine. I'm fine."

Nevaeh's fingers dug into him. "Don't lie to me."

One of the other women touched her back.

"S'all right," the groundskeeper said. "It's passed. Promise you I'm all right."

"See?" the woman said. "He says he's fine."

"I can call 911 if you're still worried?" the other woman said, phone in hand.

"Sure, there's no need for that. But I'll take that water, if it's no trouble."

The woman glanced at Nevaeh, handed the water to the groundskeeper, and went to ring out a customer who had watched the ordeal with wide eyes.

The other woman squeezed Nevaeh's shoulder. "I'll get your dress from the back. I'll put it in a changing room for you if you want to try it on?"

Nevaeh's eyes didn't leave the groundskeeper's face. "That would be great."

The woman left them. Nevaeh sucked in a long breath and released the groundskeeper's shoulders. He sipped his water.

Fashionable modern clothes and recessed lighting aside, the store looked as it had in the nineteenth century: broad wooden floorboards; narrow, floor-to-ceiling shelves, once filled with dry goods, now filled with shoes and historic photos of Harrington; a wooden counter running along one side of the room, the mechanical registers replaced with computerized models.

"What happened?" Nevaeh lowered her voice. "Was it a ghost?"

Breathing came hard, but he smiled faintly. "Sure, you think everything's ghosts now you know they're real."

"Was it?"

"Might've been, once. Hard to say." He rubbed his face, exhausted from the weight of the memories. "Plenty buildings hold memories. Don't have to be haunted to do it, but it's a fact the folks who leave the strongest memories are the likeliest to leave spirits. All that's here now are memories."

She sat beside him with a wince, stretching her leg. "You can feel those, too?"

"Tune 'em out, mostly. But if someone left real powerful memories behind, it can hit me like that."

She took his hand and turned it over. "So this symbol helps you shut them out?"

He pulled his hand away, but she yanked it closer, pushing his sleeve up.

She stared at the three long, jagged scars running from his inner wrist to his inner elbow.

"What are these?"

He wouldn't meet her eyes, but he wouldn't look at the scars, either. They reminded him of a time he'd rather forget. Shamed him for her to see them.

But he regretted their not working, too.

"They're old."

She looked at him. He gazed at his lap.

"Should I be worried about you?"

"They're old," he repeated. "Very old."

He gently extricated his wrist from her grasp. Rolled his sleeve back over the scars, tugging the cuff past his wrist and the symbol he'd inked there.

"It was long ago."

Nevaeh bit her lip. "And you've gotten help since then?"

"I've learned since then," the groundskeeper said, "it won't do no good."

She rose without comment. Maybe she wouldn't have, if she'd understood him. It did no good because it was doomed to failure.

He remembered sitting in his chair for hours, waiting. To this day, he didn't know whether his blood had replenished itself or his body had learned to function without it.

It had been the last time he'd tried. After that, he'd given up.

Nevaeh pulled him to his feet. She hugged herself.

"If you ever want to talk about it… I mean, I'm not great at talking about it. Obviously," she added, with an attempt at a smile. "I just. You know. I've been through this kind of thing, too, so if you ever…"

His eyes prickled, because of her or some remainder of the overwhelming memories. He touched her arm.

"Thanks." He shoved his hands in his pockets. "You got David's phone number?"

Her smile relaxed at his embarrassment. "Duh. Home or office?"

He blushed. "Why would I need his home number?"

Nevaeh raised an eyebrow. "I don't know. You're the one asking."

"It's about the ghost," he said pointedly, blushing deeper.

She snorted. "I told you, Uncle Dave's a total skeptic. He doesn't believe in ghosts." But she dialed the museum and handed him her cell. "I'll be by the dressing rooms when you're done."

She wound her way through racks of colorful shirts and dresses. He remained by the door with the phone ringing. It rang for so long that he chewed his lip, worried. The building's memories ate at him.

David's voice was in his ear. "Hey, Nea, what can I do for you?"

The groundskeeper's heart fluttered. "It's me."

"Peter, hi," David said in delight, and his heart fluttered harder. "Sorry, I recognized the number. Is Nevaeh all right?"

"Aye, trying a dress on."

David laughed. The groundskeeper's heart was a bird. This man was going to kill him.

"And she brought you along to be her fashion consultant, did she?"

The groundskeeper cleared his throat. "Be serious."

"Sorry. What can I do for you?"

"D'you have records of who owned the general store?"

"Some of them, sure. What years?"

"Don't rightly know. Mid-nineteenth century, I'm guessing."

A pause. "You want to know who owned the store, but you don't know when you want to know who owned the store?"

"Yep," the groundskeeper said.

"I'll see what I can find. You are an enigma, you know that?"

"Reckon I'd know it if I knew what 'enigma' meant."

David chuckled. "You're very mysterious, is what you are."

The groundskeeper wasn't sure how to respond to that, but he liked how David said it. The bell over the door tinkled. The groundskeeper stood aside as a customer entered.

"Hey," David said, "while I've got you on the phone—I have something for you." Papers rustled. "I found this notebook— not the one on local legends, still haven't found where Isaiah kept that, he was the most disorganized man you ever saw—"

The groundskeeper believed it. Even Isaiah couldn't say where he'd left those particular notes. "Thought you were supposed to be staying off that leg."

"Wow," David said, laughing. "I see the thanks I'll get for trying to help you. I'll have you know Marisol's taking a look for me. She got back into town earlier than expected. Do you want to know about this notebook or not?"

"Course I do."

"Then hush. Okay, so we've got the diary of the woman

who originally ran the boarding house with her husband. She was the daughter of the man the town's named for. Fascinating stuff, but it's tricky reading—an antique, of course, and some of the pages are faded or torn, and that's on top of the fact that she's got tight handwriting—and she doesn't name anyone but her family. Everyone else is only identified by initials. It's hard to know who she's talking about unless you've cross-referenced the initials with other records of Harrington's residents at the time and have enough context from the diary to make a comparison. We digitized it years ago—I can get you a copy if you want it, but this notebook—Isaiah loved a puzzle, so he was working through the whole diary. You know, taking notes and formulating questions and trying to match initials to names."

Paper rustled like he was flipping through the notebook in question.

"He couldn't definitively decipher all of them, of course, but he sure tried." David laughed fondly. The groundskeeper prickled with jealousy. "You should've seen him—there's this one, O.S., and Isaiah couldn't find a shred of information on him anywhere but the diary. He lived at the boarding house for something like a year, he *died* there, but there's nothing about him anywhere else. Isaiah drove himself up the wall trying to discover who this man was."

The groundskeeper swallowed against the prickling. Pointless, jealousy.

"Anyway," David said, like he'd remembered he was on the phone, "I wasn't sure whether you'd want a look, but maybe Anne Hodinka has something to say about the ghost stories they were telling back in her day."

"I'd be much obliged."

"Come by tomorrow, and you can have it. You can even have your flowers back."

The groundskeeper choked on air. He covered with a cough, but David laughed.

"Sorry, couldn't resist. Was that doctor right? The flowers were for ghosts?"

The groundskeeper tugged at his cap. "Don't see how it matters. You don't believe in 'em."

"Well, no. They're a way to explain the unexplainable. Like monsters. Or luck. Or curses."

The groundskeeper said nothing.

"People don't like mysteries," David continued. "Not really. That's why we try so hard to solve them. It bothers us when we can't explain things. So if there's no explanation, we make one up."

"Part of it's made up, oftener'n not," the groundskeeper conceded. "That don't mean the whole thing's made up. All ghost stories start somewhere. Usually a kernel of truth in 'em."

A pause. "You must think me an awful skeptic."

"Why's that?"

"It's obvious enough you believe in ghosts."

The groundskeeper huffed a laugh. "Don't need to believe in 'em. I see 'em. Everywhere I go."

Silence, as expected. He'd known David wouldn't believe him, which was why he'd told him. He kept so much of himself buried away. It relieved him to release pieces of it on occasion. Little truths no one would believe, mattering to no one but him.

It had been a far greater relief than expected to tell Nevaeh—not everything, not by a long shot, but a sight more than he'd told anyone else this last century.

She was showing her new dress off to the store owners back by the dressing rooms. It was bright red, knee-length, and off one shoulder. Nevaeh's expression was sheepish as the owners exclaimed over her.

"Benji's going to *love* it!" one of them cried.

Nevaeh caught Peter's eye and hastily looked away again. "Okay, whatever, it fits. Can I put my normal-people clothes back on now?"

The store owners hustled her back into the dressing room, still exclaiming.

Peter's mouth twitched. "Should get going. Looks like Nevaeh's about done."

"Okay," David said, but he didn't hang up.

Peter didn't, either.

"Question for you," David said at last.

"All right," Peter said, but David stayed silent.

Peter gazed absently at the racks of clothes. Bright colors and patterns, like David's many waistcoats.

"I was wondering…"

A long pause. David laughed ruefully at himself. Peter's heart contracted.

"Wow, this is tough. It's been a long time since I…" David's breath whooshed into the phone. "Would you like to have dinner sometime? With me. As a…as a date."

Whatever Peter had expected him to ask, it wasn't that. His breath caught.

For a moment, he felt like a dandelion clock: light and airy. Full of wishes and possibilities, ready to float away at the lightest breath of wind. Like he was nineteen again. Like he'd felt that bright May morning two hundred years ago, angling on the banks of the Suck, when Jack had sauntered down the path and given him a crooked smile and said *Pe-ter Shaughnessy* in that way he used to, right before they kissed for the first time.

For a moment, Peter believed he and David could have dinner together. That they'd enjoy themselves so much that they'd do it again sometime, and again after that, and again, and again. That eventually dinner would give way to other things.

That he could have a future—not one stretching before him bleak and endless, but one where someone's fingers intertwined with his.

The feeling faded, leaving him tired and gray like fields after a drought.

He squeezed his eyes shut. "I can't."

Silence, for a fraction of a second too long.

"Oh. Okay."

"I'm sorry."

David laughed again, but his heart wasn't in it. The laugh stung. "Oh—no, don't be sorry. I just, I thought I'd ask."

"If I could—"

"You don't have to say—"

"Hard to explain why—"

"You don't have to explain anything."

"It ain't that I don't like—"

"Peter, don't." David expelled a long breath. "Don't say—you don't have to say that. Really. I don't need—"

The groundskeeper tucked himself into the safety of a dim corner. He listened to David breathe into the phone.

"I'll have that notebook for you," David said, attempting to sound cheerful. "And a list of everyone who owned the general store in the nineteenth century. Come by anytime."

"All right," the groundskeeper said softly.

The phone disconnected.

He stood in his corner, gazing at the darkened phone screen.

It was for the best. Bad enough he'd spent so much time with Nevaeh, told her so much of the truth. Comforted her. Teased her. Made her tea.

If he was to finish this ghost hunt, he had to draw a line somewhere. He wasn't sure quite where. But accepting a romantic invitation from David was certainly across it.

He tugged his cap low and joined Nevaeh by the registers. His eyes stung; the store was awfully dusty.

XXXI

The groundskeeper drove down the street in silence, but Nevaeh attributed it to the lingering effects of the memories and didn't bother him. She'd thought it silly to drive such a short distance, but he'd insisted she stay off her ankle. The drizzle lightened to a mist, dampening their faces and curling their hair as they slipped from the truck. The silver maples trembled.

They ducked into the sandwich shop. Nevaeh frowned. People crowded by the plateglass windows or stood by the walls to eat. Three of the five tables were crowded with diners, the other two with trash. The line at the counter wasn't moving. Three workers rushed about, getting in each other's way and wearing the same harried expression.

"I've never seen this place so slammed," Nevaeh said as they waited in line.

The groundskeeper's mind was on David, and he didn't answer.

A couple ahead of them in line consulted the time, shook their heads, and left. A few minutes later, a kid wearing earbuds did the same.

They didn't reach the front of the line for another twenty minutes. The manager taking orders had a scruffy jaw and baggy eyes, thrown into harsh relief by the fluorescents.

"Hey, Nea," he said wearily. "What can I get you?"

Nevaeh leaned over the counter. "What's going on?"

The manager scrubbed his face with a hand. "Understaffed. Robbie never showed up. I don't know where the hell he is. I've called three times." He sighed harshly. "What can I get you?"

Nevaeh's brow puckered. She ordered, rubbing her arms. The fluorescents had been plenty bright when the groundskeeper had come here with David, but now they couldn't chase away the shadows in the corners.

The groundskeeper asked about the absent Robbie's last known location, but the manager said, "I don't know," then actually looked at him. "Are you his grandpa or something?"

The next customer was tapping her foot, so the groundskeeper joined Nevaeh in the corner she'd chosen for their lunch.

The tables had not yet been vacated or cleaned, but a chair had been shoved aside and forgotten, so at least Nevaeh could sit. She unwrapped her sandwich, glancing around.

The groundskeeper sucked in his cheeks. "You know this Robbie?"

She shook her head. "Not really. He's a college kid, only works here on his breaks. Mike speaks pretty highly of him, though. Why?"

He didn't answer. He glared like he could scare any ghosts into revealing themselves. Not that any ghosts were about. The symbol on his wrist might've hampered their lingering memories, but no symbol could keep him from sensing the spirits themselves.

It was probably nothing. A kid who didn't feel like coming in.

But Nevaeh's possession was on the groundskeeper's mind for the rest of the afternoon.

XXXII

Benji picked Nevaeh up from her office for lunch the next day. She avoided the groundskeeper's gaze as Benji helped her into the car, perhaps because she'd put an awful lot of thought into her looks for lunch with someone she was so terribly insistent was nothing more than a friend. Her curls were vibrant, her lips plum-colored, her blouse more colorful than usual and paired with jeans instead of slacks. But the groundskeeper bid them goodbye vaguely, his mind on the sandwich shop. He took the pickup there alone for news of the missing college kid.

The rain had dried. The sun shone white and hazy, looking tired. An August sort of sun, though it was May.

The shop buzzed with gossip. Robbie, a scrawny nineteen-year-old with blond peach fuzz, was back at work, but the diners speculated about his absence the day before. The groundskeeper eavesdropped as he ordered.

The whispers varied in content, but everyone agreed Robbie had called the manager for a ride home hours after his shift should've ended, panicking because he couldn't remember how he'd gotten wherever he was. Here, the whispers differed. He had called from a church, or a park, or a gas station so long abandoned that its faded sign advertised gas for $1.09.

No matter. The important point was clear. Robbie had had

the same sort of spectral experience as Nevaeh. The grounds-keeper paid and slunk from the shop.

It was worse than he'd thought. The spirit's influence had spread beyond the cemetery. He was sure Robbie hadn't been there, and none of the spirits had gone missing. Robbie had been possessed by a spirit elsewhere in town.

As May slipped into June, Harrington was on edge. Rumors abounded everywhere the groundskeeper went. As the birders had weeks ago, folks complained of cold spots and vanished items. Another handful of people turned up in odd places with no idea how they'd gotten there. On the swing set at the elementary school. In the museum's root cellar, which had been boarded up for decades. Knee-deep in the shallows of the creek, off the small park on the west side of Thompson.

The groundskeeper was on edge, too. Things had gone further than he should've let them, and he was no closer to finding the ghost. Midsummer loomed only weeks away—Midsummer, when the spirits would be at their strongest.

June always put him on edge anyway. Midsummer was when he'd been cursed.

His best lead was the general store. He was sure David had a list of owners by now, but he hadn't been to the museum since before their call. Still in a cast, David hadn't come by the cemetery, either. And Nevaeh's lunches with Benji had gone from frequent to daily, though she usually stopped by to tell him she was going.

Lunchtime had gotten awfully lonely.

It was fine. It was what he wanted. Like he'd wanted the children to leave him alone, and they had. They hadn't been back.

Perhaps he ought to have tried harder not to spend time with Nevaeh, but he worked with her. Avoiding her was pointless.

That was what he told himself.

He rubbed his eyes. He was on a library computer again this evening. It was quieter than it had been during the birders' visit but filled with uneasy whispers like everywhere else in town. A freak storm had flared up south of Harrington, ravaging a pig farm. Several pigs had died, the rest had run off, and a barn roof had collapsed. The whisperers blamed the ghost, more rightly than they guessed.

His research yielded nothing. Aside from John Kowalczyk, whom he'd already dismissed, the groundskeeper had found only one of the general store's owners. The McLaughlins owned the place from 1855 until well into the twentieth century. Preceding them was a ten-year gap in which the store might've had one owner or a dozen.

Nothing the groundskeeper found on the McLaughlins fit either Nevaeh's story about the ghost or the memories at the store. They'd started the tradition of keeping a horseshoe over the door; most likely, they'd been the first to repel the ghost—not its origin.

The groundskeeper leaned back in his chair. His back ached.

He'd have to return to the museum.

He logged off, stood up, and stretched.

When he turned, he was face-to-face with Sayid al-Masri.

They stared at each other. Sayid wore his circlet of Saint-John's-wort. It rustled at the groundskeeper, proudly showing off its new growth, but its owner's brow furrowed. The groundskeeper tried to smile but couldn't manage it.

Sayid hurried past him.

The groundskeeper's skin prickled. "Sayid."

The boy squared his shoulders and stammered, without turning around, "Samira really likes you, you know."

Despite Sayid's stammer, the groundskeeper flinched as if struck. "I know."

"She didn't do anything wrong."

"I know," the groundskeeper said. "I'm sorry."

Sayid's voice trembled, but he pressed on, his words tumbling out in a rush. "She won't say so, but it's really bothering her that

Mama's home late every evening and Baba's gone all the time. And then we met you," he said scathingly, if in a voice pitched higher than usual, "and things were better for a while, and then you yelled at her. And now she thinks she did something wrong, only she doesn't know what. So she's back to getting into trouble. Because that's what she does when she's hurt." His fists clenched. "I have to keep sneaking out at night to find her, because she keeps running off after Mama and Baba fall asleep."

The groundskeeper hadn't meant to hurt her. He'd only meant to preserve himself. But it had amounted to the same thing. "Is she here?"

Sayid's anger ebbed away. His hands fisted in his T-shirt. "Over there."

She was hunched over a table, her head drooped on her arms. Yafa sat across from her. Her nose was buried in a mystery novel, but her eyes kept flickering toward her daughter.

The groundskeeper's skin prickled. "Has she been like that since I…?"

Sayid glanced back at his sister. The Saint-John's-wort curled around him. "Mama finally took us to see Jeddo. Samira's been begging to go, but I don't think she understood there's a reason he lives at the hospital now, even though Mama keeps explaining."

Yafa's eyes were back on her book, but they weren't moving. Her brow creased.

"Your pa's out of town again?"

Sayid shook his head. "He's signing Samira up for this program they have where little kids can practice reading out loud to dogs. He thought it might cheer her up."

His family's situation had exhausted his hard-won fight; he no longer looked angry. But Peter wouldn't have blamed him for protecting his sister. He pulled his cap from his head, twisting it.

"Can I say hello?"

Sayid pursed his lips. "Without yelling at her?"

Peter blanched but said evenly, "It's a library. Don't reckon they'd like it much if I yelled."

Sayid frowned.

"Joking," Peter said hastily, twisting his cap tighter. Sayid considered him.

"You might want to work on that. Her sense of humor isn't *that* weak." He hesitated. "Okay, I guess. If she wants to talk to you."

"Understood." Peter hesitated. "'M sorry I yelled at you, too. You're a good lad. A good brother. You didn't deserve that."

Sayid's ears pinkened. "Well, you didn't really yell at me, anyway."

Setting her book aside, Yafa smiled as Peter approached; the children appeared not to have told her about their falling-out. He tamped down his gratitude.

"It's nice to see you again." Yafa touched her daughter's hand. "Samira, look who it is."

Samira did not look. She merely withdrew her hands, tucking them under her chin. Peter's insides clenched at her form drooping like a wilted flower.

Yafa's face sagged, but her smile was back in place by the time she looked up. "Khalid is around here somewhere."

"So I hear. Must be nice, his being back."

Samira turned her head toward him but didn't look at him.

"Hello, child," he said.

She turned away again. His stomach tightened.

"It's wonderful," Yafa said, as if there'd been no interruption, but her brow puckered. "Sayid, would you take your sister to check out her books?"

A small stack of books lay untouched beside Samira. Peter had a feeling Yafa had picked them out herself.

Sayid scooped up the books, tugging Samira's arm. She hid her face in his shirt, but not before Peter glimpsed the tears rolling silently down her face. His heart twisted.

Yafa slumped in her chair. Peter sat gingerly across from her.

A nearby group of middle-aged women, who were supposed to be a book club, whispered about the wrecked pig farm instead of their latest read. But Peter's concerns about the ghost paled in comparison to his concern for Samira.

Yafa pinched the bridge of her nose.

"Sorry about that. It wasn't you. We visited my father today. He lived with us until about six months ago, but when it got to the point where we couldn't safely care for him…" She let out a harsh breath. "I knew I shouldn't've let her come."

He was certain it was at least partially him, no matter what Samira's mother or brother said, but he didn't say so. "Sayid said she's been asking. You wouldn't've had a moment's peace until you let her go."

Yafa laughed hollowly. "I'm not sure a moment's peace was worth this."

"Might've been harder on her to wind up at his funeral down the road without seeing him first."

"Maybe." Yafa bookmarked her mystery novel. "She's always been…lively. But ever since we put him into palliative care…"

"Sure, that's hard."

"I don't know what to do." Yafa picked lint from her shirt. "I'm a therapist, and I can't get my own daughter to talk to me."

Her husband appeared, polishing his glasses on his polo shirt. "Sayid's getting Samira into the car. And she's signed up for that read-aloud thing— Oh, hello," he said, noticing Peter. "You're the fellow who brought the kids home a few weeks ago, aren't you? I'm so sorry, I'm blanking on your name."

Yafa's voice brightened at her husband's presence. "Peter Shaughnessy," she said with a smile.

"Right, Peter."

As always, Peter's heart stuttered at his own name, but he pulled himself together and shook Khalid's hand.

"Thanks again," Khalid said. "And for introducing Samira to

that poet. You should've heard her. She called to tell me about E. E. Cummings."

Peter's skin prickled hot with fresh shame.

Yafa's eyes softened. "She couldn't get over the fact that someone had published a book without following the rules she's learned in class."

Khalid chuckled. "That might come back to haunt us in the future."

"And she kept repeating that line—what was it?"

"I can't remember. Something about bells."

"'Up so floating many bells down,'" Peter said.

"That's the one," Yafa said. "'Up so floating many bells down.' She said it over and over. At one point she was almost singing it." She laughed. "Sayid was so annoyed."

"We found her one of E. E. Cummings's books today," Khalid said. "But I don't know if she'll read it now."

Their energy died away. Peter fidgeted.

"I'm sure she'll bounce back," he said, sure of no such thing.

Khalid rubbed his chin. Stubble covered his jaw; dark crescents ringed his eyes as they did his wife's. They were no older than Nevaeh, but their worry aged them.

"You're probably right," Khalid said. "Sayid seems okay, and I thought he'd have a harder time with it." He rubbed his chin again, giving a wan smile. "Man, I need a shave. Yafa, do you want me to call in to that Indian place? If I call it in now, by the time we get there—"

"Sounds perfect. The usual?"

"That's what I was thinking."

Yafa smiled, touching the back of Khalid's hand. He wrapped his arms around her and leaned over her shoulder.

"Would you like to join us?" she asked Peter. "There's always plenty."

His breath caught, his heart puffy and floaty as it had been on the phone with David.

This time, he reined his hopes in before they could run loose and trample him.

"I can't," he said. "I'm sorry."

"What are you sorry for?" Yafa gave a small smile. "It's all right. Next time."

"More food for me this time," Khalid said.

His wife elbowed him. He kissed her head.

The groundskeeper ached. As often as Khalid was gone, they were so easy with each other. He barely remembered that feeling.

He sat there for half an hour after they'd gone, drumming his fingers on the table. The library emptied, whispers fading away with the uneasy townspeople. Yafa had forgotten her novel, neatly bookmarked.

He ought to return to his research. The library was open another hour yet. He could dig deeper into the McLaughlins, for all the good it would do.

Samira's form swam before him, slumped on the table.

He thumbed through the forgotten novel. Yafa's bookmark had a picture of horses galloping along a beach at sunset.

He could return to his research.

Or he could bring her book to her.

He slipped the book into his messenger bag and walked the three blocks to the al-Masris' house.

The first stars glimmered in the royal blue expanse overhead. The horizon was a thin slice of yellow like a lemon rind. Fireflies drifted over lawns, blinking in boxwoods and hydrangeas. Robins peeped sharply, hopping along garden beds and drip lines with faint anxiety as darkness fell.

The al-Masris' two cars were in the driveway. Samira's bike lay on the front lawn. Light spilled yellow and warm from each window. Even the porch light was on, as if they'd been waiting for him—which they hadn't, of course.

He tripped over a box of chalk on the porch steps. Drawings

of flowers, stars, and bees covered the porch, with secret messages thrown in for good measure.

Voices drifted through the storm door; the front door was open to let in the evening air. Samira's querulous voice cut through the others.

"—*my* samosa, Sayid!"

His spirits lifted. She was peevish but ready to argue. Livelier than she'd been earlier.

"There's more than enough for both of you." Khalid's voice turned mischievous. "But *this* one's mine, actually."

"Hey—"

"Baba—"

Samira broke into a brief, if unwilling, peal of laughter. The groundskeeper rapped on the storm door.

A brief argument ensued over which child should answer. Neither wanted to leave the samosas unprotected from the other.

Footsteps. Samira appeared. Her brows contracted at the sight of him.

He fiddled with the strap of his bag, skin prickling again.

She gazed at the doorframe. "What are you doing here?"

Everything left his head except what he'd done. He twisted the strap of his bag tight.

"I'm sorry," he blurted. "I'm so sorry."

She said nothing. His throat closed up.

"I didn't mean what I said," he said hoarsely. "Not a word of it. That's no excuse. I shouldn't've said it. I just want you to know."

Samira ran a finger along the door, tracing the outline of the screen. "You said you didn't want me."

"I know. I know I did."

"No one wants me." She said it matter-of-factly. "I'm a troublemaker. That's what everyone says."

He hesitated. "I don't think you're a troublemaker. I think you been going through things, same's I've been. Only I took mine out on you. And I shouldn't've. And I'm sorry."

She stopped tracing the screen and slipped onto the porch. She stood against the door, gazing at her toes. He could've touched her, but he didn't move.

"So you don't hate me?" she asked softly.

A huff that was half a laugh and half a sob escaped him. "Of course not. I—"

She flung herself forward and threw her arms around his waist.

His breath hitched. He wrapped her in a hug. It was more than he deserved. A prayer of thanks half slipped from his lips before he'd thought about it.

She sniffled. He brushed her hair back, wiping her tears away with his thumbs.

"Samira, who is it?" Yafa's footsteps approached. "If you don't hurry up, your father and brother are going to eat all the samosas."

Samira wiped her nose on her arm. "It's Peter, Mama."

Yafa smiled through the storm door. "Did your plans fall through?"

He fumbled in his bag for her novel. "I brung your book. You left it on the table, there."

"Thanks." She opened the door. "Do you want to come in? Star of India was having a special. We've got lots extra."

He ought to turn around and go straight home. Alone.

He twisted the strap of his bag. "I'd like that very much."

Yafa held the door open. Samira slipped a hand into his and led him inside.

XXXIII

When the groundskeeper finally returned to the museum, David was working on the porch, in a wicker chair with his crutches propped behind him. A matching wicker chair and mismatched water-stained glass table kept him company. A ceiling fan creaked overhead. Papers scattered across the table, weighted with books, coffee mugs, pens, his phone, and his key fob.

He whistled as he frowned at his laptop. Perhaps because of the frown, the whistling had a grumpy quality.

The groundskeeper stopped at the property line. He'd expected to see David when he returned, but not outside. He'd thought he'd have time to prepare himself first.

The walk here ought to have done it, but he was too inside his own head. Too aware of his failure to find the ghost, of the anger weighing on him within the cemetery and Harrington's unease weighing on him without.

Of Midsummer rushing toward him.

He hadn't cut a hunt this close in decades. He spent his Junes holed up in solitude. Far from spirits. Far from the living. Somewhere to panic in safety and silence, to lose his head without anyone suffering for it.

He headed up the museum drive. Gravel crunched underfoot.

The groundskeeper calmed as he approached the building. With Isaiah's love spread over the grounds, Harrington's anxiety faded, unable to withstand the light of that love. Even the lawn was greener than elsewhere in town. Dandelions dotted the yard, bickering good-naturedly with their neighbors. Red clover bobbed in the groundskeeper's direction. The air was sweet with blooming things.

Yet somehow—warm and bright as it all was—it seemed less bright than usual. Perhaps it was the groundskeeper's own anxiety bleeding into everything he saw and felt. He made a mental note to check on Isaiah anyway when he got the chance. Just in case.

The groundskeeper dimpled as David's whistling crescendoed, still grumpy. David glanced over, and the dimple vanished.

David faltered, then fixed a smile into place. "Hey, Peter."

The groundskeeper attempted to smile back and failed. He didn't know if it was better or worse, David greeting him nearly like normal. Isaiah flared up warm and yellow at his entrance, though perhaps with a little less enthusiasm than usual.

"Marisol found this furniture in the shed and brought it up here for me," David said, his cheer sounding forced.

Worse. Definitely worse.

David fiddled with the cuff of his sleeve. "She thought as long as the weather cooperated, I could work outside. You should've seen me trying to squeeze into my office on crutches."

His waistcoat was pink, patterned with gold pineapples. His bow tie, white with a larger, more haphazard pineapple pattern, lay furled on the table. The top button of his shirt was undone.

The groundskeeper tore his eyes from David's throat. "Maybe she wants your office for herself."

David huffed a laugh. The groundskeeper couldn't help looking at him, the tightness in his chest loosening hopefully.

"She's welcome to it. It's much nicer out here."

The ceiling fan creaked and hummed.

"How's Nevaeh?" David asked, after far too long a silence. "She told me she twisted her ankle?"

"Doing all right. Recovering." The groundskeeper gripped the strap of his bag. "I come for that notebook."

David's smile slipped, but he recovered and sent a text.

"Mari's a godsend. She'd make a great museum director, but she'd have to move somewhere bigger if she wanted to make real money at it." His phone buzzed. He glanced at it. "She'll have that notebook for us when she's finished in the kitchen. She's taking inventory for me."

Papers rustled in the waft of the ceiling fan. Isaiah lurked in the entryway, intent on giving them privacy.

It only made the groundskeeper feel worse.

Discomfort swelled between them until it burst. They both broke the silence at once.

"Sorry if I—"

"I didn't mean to—"

Their words collided and failed. David laughed awkwardly, running a hand through his hair. The groundskeeper blushed and tugged his cap down. He longed to run his own hands through David's hair, but he quashed that want as he had the other desires that had sprouted through the cracks in his heart since his arrival in Harrington.

"Go ahead," he said gruffly.

He gazed at the table. He'd either forgotten or never fully appreciated how gray David's eyes were.

David scratched his forehead. "Can we forget about the other day? I value your friendship more than I can say. I'd hate to lose it because I asked for something different."

The groundskeeper wouldn't forget if he lived a thousand years.

"It's forgotten."

He glanced at David. Mistake. David caught his eye and smiled. The groundskeeper's heart sang.

"Thanks," David said.

The groundskeeper sat, pulling off his cap.

"Tell me about this diary," he said, anxious that David should believe it well and truly forgotten. Someone valuing his friendship was an alien idea—though if he examined it, he'd realize the others valued him, too. Nevaeh. The al-Masris.

He chose not to examine it.

David thumbed through some papers.

"What do you want to know? It covers a good three years, mid-1849 to late 1852." He shifted papers. "I have copies printed here somewhere. We're pretty sure Anne kept a diary her whole life—this one starts off like she's continuing her journaling and ends with her husband promising to bring a new one back from Detroit—but this is the only volume we have. Her daughter saved it."

His enthusiasm for history animated the forced quality from his voice.

"She mention anything odd?" the groundskeeper asked.

David's smile faded. The groundskeeper clenched his hands, not sure what he'd said wrong.

"Odd like the...incidences lately?"

The groundskeeper nodded. "Like that."

David bit his lip. "You know Mike, at the sandwich shop?"

The groundskeeper's notepad was ready. "Know of him. What about him?"

"Disappeared two days ago. So his staff says." David's brow furrowed. "I've never seen anything like this. Not in my lifetime. Even historically... A pretty well-publicized disappearance in the 1890s turned out to be a murder. A little boy vanished in 1893, never found. And some people vanished in the thirties, but that was the Depression, most of them popped up years later, further west or in some big city somewhere. And then a little girl in the 1950s, but she turned up later, too. Dead, I'm afraid. They never did find who did it. But this..."

David laughed uneasily. The groundskeeper's fingers twitched, but he didn't touch him. Isaiah sidled onto the porch, drawn by the fear in his husband's voice.

"Harrington has always felt so safe," David said. "But with all these people experiencing... I don't know, what would you call it? Blackouts? An actual disappearance? I don't understand what's happening."

Isaiah's love encircled him like a shield, so thick it was as if David were behind stained glass. Perhaps the groundskeeper had been imagining his faded quality after all; now, protecting David this way, he seemed strong as ever.

"You ain't got a thing to worry about," the groundskeeper said. "It won't happen to you. Promise."

A phantom finger touching his cheek, so gently he could've cried. Isaiah, grateful for someone giving David his messages, though David never would've believed they'd come from him.

A college kid with glasses and long, dark hair slung into a ponytail poked her head outside. "David? I have that notebook."

David took it from her. "Excellent, thank you."

"We'll need more candle wax. And dried corn if you plan on doing cornhusk dolls again."

"I don't think so. The last group wasn't as interested as I'd hoped. Thanks, Mari."

She withdrew. David traced Isaiah's handwriting on the front of the notebook. Jealousy pricked at the groundskeeper like thorns, but he buried it. Silly to feel jealous of a ghost. Particularly when he wasn't going to do anything to put himself in competition with said ghost.

He cleared his throat. David glanced up as if he'd forgotten his company. He smiled and slid the notebook across the table, shifting books and mugs aside.

"Sorry. Keep it as long as you like."

"Much obliged." The groundskeeper fiddled with his cap. "So? Anything odd?"

David shook his head with a chuckle. "Still on about ghosts, are you?"

"Still skeptical, are you? It was you what said ghosts are an explanation for the unexplainable."

"This isn't unexplainable." David sounded uneasy again. Isaiah's warmth soured at his husband's anxiety. "It could be—I don't know. Heat stroke. Drugs. Something in the water."

"Then why should it worry you?" the groundskeeper asked, as if he weren't worried himself. But it was his worry to carry. Not David's.

David snorted. "Just because something can be explained doesn't mean it's not something to worry about. It doesn't have to be ghosts to worry me."

"What if it is ghosts?"

"You're incorrigible."

The corner of the groundskeeper's mouth turned up. "Reckon I would be, if I knew what it meant."

"Absolutely impossible." David's mouth twitched.

It felt almost like it had before. Before David had broken a leg or asked him out or made him want things he hadn't wanted in so long.

"If you're such a skeptic," he said, "what do you believe in?"

David drummed his fingers on the table.

"People," he said. "Despite all the evidence that says I shouldn't."

He shifted a stack of papers needlessly, as if embarrassed. The groundskeeper couldn't see why. He wished he believed in people.

He slipped Isaiah's notebook into his bag and stood, jamming his cap back on his head. The ceiling fan ruffled his shirt.

David's brow puckered. "Leaving already?"

The groundskeeper fiddled with his bag. "Don't want to overstay my welcome."

"You just got here."

The groundskeeper rocked on his heels, gripping the back of

his chair. He ought to go. He had the notebook. That was all he'd come for.

"Stay," David said.

He sat back down. David let out a small breath. Peter's heart stuttered.

"Are you hungry?" David asked. "Mari's ordering pizza for lunch."

"Starving," Peter said.

XXXIV

"Unexplainable phenomena," David said, once the pizza had been ordered (supreme for Marisol, half pepperoni/half cheese for the old men). Marisol had gone inside for paper plates and napkins. "Okay. The general store had a fire sometime late in 1851 or early 1852. That was common enough at the time, all those wooden buildings, fires used for cooking and bathing and heating the home—there are over half a dozen fires in this diary, and Anne Hodinka mentions every one of them in passing except this one."

The groundskeeper flipped his notepad to a fresh page. "What was different about this one?"

David traced the water stain on the tabletop. "It was odd. The owner almost died of smoke inhalation, but the building was fine except for a few scorch marks."

"Promising. What else?"

"I don't know if this'll interest you as much," David said, "but the cholera epidemic in 1852? She runs out of pages toward the end of that year, but before that she mentions how lucky they are that cholera hasn't touched the boarding house this time."

"This time?"

"Yes, in 1849 two tenants fell ill, and so did Anne's little girl, Nina. She recovered, but the tenants died, and more tenants moved out. Left town, too. They weren't the only ones. Harrington had a population of five hundred at the start of 1848, but by the end of 1849 less than three hundred people were left. The folks who didn't die of cholera fled. But anyway, sorry, too much information—"

The groundskeeper dimpled despite himself. "Not at all."

"—the point is, the first outbreak hit the boarding house like the rest of town, but the second outbreak passed it over. Well, I mean, it could've hit after the diary's end, but as far as I can tell from this, and the records we have of the Hodinkas' tenants around that time..."

"No one at the boarding house got sick."

"Exactly."

The pizza arrived. David paid the driver; Marisol shifted things off the table so they could eat. The groundskeeper made a note about the diary, the boarding house, and the cholera outbreaks.

There might've been something to these stories. The episode with the general store supported the idea that the spirit might've had ties to it. Spirits couldn't bless and curse the way *them folk* could, but they could protect and destroy. The museum, with Isaiah's love permeating every board, was protected now. Judging by the cholera story, it might've been protected by someone else long before.

The general store—the building itself—might have been protected, too. Its owners, on the other hand... Ghosts were not above protecting a building while destroying its inhabitants. Particularly if they viewed its inhabitants as intruders.

Marisol joined them at the table with a metal folding chair. David resumed his seat with a soft groan.

"My cast comes off in two weeks, if I'm lucky."

The groundskeeper wasn't listening, his mind stuck on his notes. "Who owned the general store after the fella in the fire?"

"Mmm." David swallowed some pizza and dabbed his mouth

with a napkin. "That reminds me. Mari, where'd we put that list?"

"The people who owned the general store?"

"That's the one."

She went inside, returning with a slip of paper. She handed it to David and plopped in her chair with her phone. David smoothed the paper. Isaiah joined them on the porch, peering over his shoulder at it.

"This is everyone we know of who owned the store in the nineteenth century," David said. "Mari checked my work. She's a whiz at research."

Marisol pinkened, but she was scrolling Instagram and eating pizza and didn't respond. Isaiah's laughter rippled across the lawn, ruffling the dandelions and clover.

"Anyway," David said, "we've got John Kowalczyk, of course, he built the place, owned it up to 1845 or so. We know that from his family's letters—we don't have a bill of sale, but his kids had gone West and he was getting on in years. Then there's a possible gap in the records until 1851. There's a bill of sale to Martin Grüber for that year, but the seller is a bank, not sure whether the bank bought it off Kowalczyk in 1845 or if someone else bought it and the bank foreclosed on them."

"The latter seems most likely," Marisol said, without looking up from her phone.

David chuckled, nodding in approval. His pizza lay forgotten beside him. "Yes, 1845, that's only a few years after the Panic. And the canals were being finished up, so plenty of folks were looking for new opportunities… Many went farther west, but one of them could've bought the general store. If they didn't have the money or business acumen to make it work, well, it wouldn't have been the first foreclosure in Harrington, nor the last one on that building. So, yes, the working hypothesis is, Kowalczyk sells the store in 1845, the new owner is foreclosed on between 1845 and 1851—I imagine closer to 1851, I don't think the building would've sat on the market that long—and Martin Grüber buys it from the bank holding the mortgage. Grüber, he was the one in the fire."

The groundskeeper scribbled in his notepad. "When did he sell?"

"Pizza's getting cold," Marisol commented.

David took a pointed bite of pizza. Isaiah shivered with laughter; Marisol used to prod him to eat this same way, and he was glad she was there to look out for David, too.

"You should set an alarm on your phone when you eat at work," Marisol said. "Then I wouldn't have to remind you."

David chuckled but tucked a napkin into his collar and worked on his pizza more diligently as he kept talking.

"Grüber sold not long after the fire and took his family back East. 1852. The next family had the place about a year before they sold, too—not sure why, but it sold fast and for less than it was worth. The family after that was foreclosed on in nine months. The next owner, he didn't even try to sell, skipped town late in 1854…middle of a third cholera outbreak. Probably got scared. We don't see a mass exodus during the second and third epidemics like we do during the first, but people still fled. Anyway, the folks who took over lasted about three months before selling to the McLaughlins in 1855."

The groundskeeper's fingers shook with excitement. "Awful lot of owners for such a short time."

"People said it was haunted," Marisol said.

"Did they, now?"

David groaned. "Don't encourage him, Mari."

The air shivered with Isaiah's laughter. Peter grinned.

Marisol grinned back. "That's why the McLaughlins put a horseshoe over the door. Isaiah said—"

She broke off, glancing at David, but he was eating more pizza.

"Well…he said they thought horseshoes warded off ghosts,"

she finished quietly. "Iron, I mean. Not horseshoes specifically. That's just what they put up."

He knew. He'd been meant to put up horseshoes himself, over the doors and windows of the Shaughnessys' farm on a Midsummer Eve two hundred years ago. Horseshoes and flower garlands and holy water.

But he hadn't.

He hunched over his notepad, burying memories of that disastrous Midsummer. "Did it work?"

David rolled his eyes.

Marisol swallowed a laugh. "Must've. The McLaughlins had the place for decades."

David sighed. Marisol raised an eyebrow at him.

"That part's true," he admitted begrudgingly.

The phone rang. Marisol wiped her hands on her jeans and went to answer. Her folding chair scraped on the floorboards. The groundskeeper flinched.

He dropped his pencil and dragged a hand through his hair. It wasn't Midsummer yet. It wasn't Midsummer yet, and it wasn't *that* Midsummer.

The shakiness persisted. Isaiah nosed at him, questioning. He shook his head. A sensation like a hand on his shoulder, then Isaiah drew back. The groundskeeper leaned toward David.

"We need to fill the gap in the records," he said in a low voice. "I need to know who owned the general store between 1845 and 1851. And if there's the slightest chance of it, I need to know where they're buried."

David rubbed his eyes with the heels of his hands. "Peter—"

"I know you think I'm off my rocker." He gripped David's hands compulsively. "I know you think it's codswallop, all this ghost talk."

"I don't—"

"David, please."

David fell silent.

"You don't need to believe it," Peter said. "Just trust me. And help me. Please."

David gazed at their linked hands. His thumb brushed across Peter's knuckles. "Okay."

Marisol poked her head out the door. The groundskeeper yanked his hands away from David's, blushing.

"Call for you, David."

David's fingers curled as if looking for Peter's, but he grabbed his crutches and headed inside with her. "Be back in a minute."

The moment the door had closed behind them, the groundskeeper murmured, "Isaiah?"

The air on the porch grayed, as if Isaiah were letting his true feelings show now that David wasn't there to see them, though David couldn't see them in the first place. To the groundskeeper's astonishment, a faint whisper echoed in his ears.

Help me.

"Ain't imagining it, then. What's ailing you?"

Isaiah twisted around him, tired and worried. He'd felt the same anger and unease the groundskeeper had been feeling, now that it had spread around town. As strong as Isaiah was, it still took an effort for him to fend it off.

The groundskeeper rubbed his neck. "Could help you some, but you might not like how."

It didn't matter how. Isaiah was worried. He'd never felt like this as a ghost. If he couldn't keep up his strength, maybe he couldn't protect David. He'd take any help he could get.

"If I ward the property," the groundskeeper said, "you won't have to work to keep it off. But," he added, as Isaiah brightened, pleased with such a simple solution, "you won't be able to leave, even if you want to. The wards'll work on you, same as they'll work on whatever spirit's so angry."

Do it. Please.

Before the groundskeeper could respond, David was back.

"Sorry about that," he said. "Where were we?"

It was late afternoon by the time David headed back inside to finish his work: his laptop had died. Marisol helped him squeeze into his office, cleared the lunch things away, and went home.

After saying goodbye to David, the groundskeeper glanced around to make sure he was alone—except for Isaiah—and went prowling along the boundaries of the property.

With buildings or rooms, he warded entryways like doors or windows (both, when he could manage it). With a whole property, depending on its shape, the corners were usually best, unless there was a clear entryway like a gate.

"Here to the outer edge of the parking lot, aye?" he said to Isaiah. "And the other way to that fence?"

Isaiah confirmed the property line as he went. Washington and Main Streets bounded the western and southern edges of the property; the neighboring property's fence bounded the east. Those were clear enough. The northern edge was harder, as the museum's back lawn and gardens bumped up against other unfenced yards. Isaiah pointed the way past the gardens, crammed with picnic tables where their field trippers ate lunch, and the bit of lawn where they played tug-of-war and other games. He led the groundskeeper along in a straight line until they reached the fence on the eastern edge of the property.

The groundskeeper thumbed up his flat cap. "Square. Good. Corners'll do. You'll want to keep back."

Isaiah did not keep back. He was immensely interested in the groundskeeper's search for something to mark in each corner.

"Any old object won't do it," the groundskeeper said. "Leastways not a good idea. Could mark any pebble of gravel from the parking lot, but if it ain't something that'll stay put then it won't do much good."

Isaiah wanted to know if warding the house wouldn't be easier.

"Sure, but then you'd be bound inside the house. Figured you might want more space than that."

The neighbor's fence worked for the northeast and southeast corners. It had been freshly repaired and painted and seemed unlikely to be replaced anytime soon. The groundskeeper carved Marian symbols low on the corner fence posts and moved on to the other side of the property.

The northwest corner was similarly easy, if unpleasant. An old sycamore twisted from the corner of the parking lot, providing the only shade. The groundskeeper asked its permission before carving into it, murmuring soothingly as he made his mark. Isaiah was interested in that, too, but the groundskeeper was too busy looking after the tree's well-being to explain to him about the plants.

The southwest corner was the most difficult. The parking lot extended down to the corner, but it was all gravel, with no parking bumpers. Nothing grew in this corner. The roadside curb was in disrepair, so cracked and crumbling the groundskeeper worried any mark he made in it would be instantly destroyed.

"What's under this lot?" he asked.

Isaiah couldn't remember the name of it, but he remembered what it looked like, and that was enough. Permeable plastic grid pavers, nearly visible in some spots where the gravel had worn away until the parking lot was bald.

Not quite so, right there in the corner, but the groundskeeper could see black plastic showing through a spot nearby. With a penknife, he dug a line through the gravel from where the pavers showed until he reached the corner, then dug down until he found the pavers there.

"David's not coming, is he?" he asked. "Don't think he'd appreciate me busting up his parking lot, however little."

Isaiah confirmed David was still in his office. Helpful, the groundskeeper thought, having a ghost along like this. Maybe he'd make use of it more often in the future, assuming he ever met an equally friendly yet powerful spirit again.

It took a lot longer, scratching into underground plastic with his penknife, but at last the property's southwest corner had been warded.

The effect was instant. Isaiah flinched, jolting back from the marked paver.

The groundskeeper sighed and worked to replace, as best he could, the gravel he'd dug up. "Said you'd want to stay back, didn't I?"

When Isaiah calmed down, the air on the property was brighter than ever. Isaiah spiraled slowly from one corner to the other, examining the wards without getting too close.

"That better?"

Isaiah's sigh ruffled the grass and dandelions. Dandelion clocks broke, sending seeds drifting through the air. The groundskeeer stood, stretched, and brushed gravel dust from his knees.

"Thanks for your help," he said. "Might be back for more, once I read your notes."

He left Isaiah still nosing at the wards.

The evening was warm and quiet. He sat out in his garden to read poetry, enjoying the lighter air of his cottage and the companionable clucking of the pullets before they decided it was too dark and stalked into their coop for the night.

He glanced up at the woods, red-hued in the twilight, from the sunset or the anger or both. His finger paused on the page as he considered the back lot. David was safer now—when he was at the museum, at any rate—and Isaiah could keep up his strength. Elijah was out of harm's way. Nevaeh at least knew the groundskeeper's concerns and would likely be cautious as she worked in the cemetery.

Still, the red air of the woods, the increasing anger in the cemetery, the growing unease all across town—his brow puckered. He'd let things go too far. By this time in Savannah, he'd already sent one ghost packing and been on the trail of another. The ghost he'd sent on here hadn't done anything worse, as far as he knew, than bust a van's windows and scare some teenagers.

"Peter!"

"Back here, lass."

Nevaeh came around the side of the cottage with a cordless phone in her hand, her expression pinched. He was on his feet at the first sight of her.

"What's wrong?"

"Yafa just called," she said. "Have you seen the children in the last couple of hours?"

His mouth went dry. "Why?"

Nevaeh fidgeted with the phone.

"They're missing," she said.

XXXV

Nevaeh hurried through the trees with him despite his warnings. He'd hoped she'd be more cautious, now that she knew about ghosts, but it hadn't stopped her from joining his search for the children. The cemetery was her responsibility. She knew the family. And she wasn't letting him go in the back lot alone with night falling, no matter how scared she was to go there herself.

This last touched him more than he cared to admit, but he'd still tried, fruitlessly, to convince her to stay in her office.

"How's your ankle?" he said now, pointedly, as she stumbled over a sunken headstone.

"Shit." She righted herself, gripping his arm. "I told you, my ankle's fine. I saw the doctor and everything. It's completely healed." A sudden branch loomed from the darkness at the height of her face. She ducked. "God, I can't see anything back here."

The sun hadn't quite set, but the woods were thick with June foliage, darker than his cottage garden and the knoll. Nevaeh had brought a pair of flashlights whose thin white beams flashed across leaves and trunks. It was that twilit time that was too light for flashlights to be much use but too dark for their eyes to make things out without help. The trees seemed close and far-off all at once.

Spirits whirled all around, red and jittery, too close for comfort despite the flowers he'd made them both wear, the iron cross he'd given Nevaeh to hold on to. After David's accident the other week, with the children missing, he was far more worried for her than himself. He'd snapped at her when she'd suggested they split up, swallowing it back only because she'd raised an eyebrow at him and said she was scared, too.

Leaves rustled. A great horned owl hooted distantly. Peter gripped the strap of his messenger bag.

A whispery voice echoed from the darkness.

Stole.

Nevaeh halted. "Did you hear that?"

Peter sucked in his cheeks. The voice spoke again before he could respond.

Stole! He stole from me...

"C'mon," he said, and tugged her along.

She clung closer than ever.

"Was that—did I just hear—" She swallowed. "I thought they couldn't talk."

"Most of 'em can't." A twig snapped underfoot. He flinched. "Told you. Whatever's back here, it's affecting the rest of 'em. They're more powerful than they should be."

Nevaeh shivered. "I really hope the kids aren't back here."

He said nothing. If the children weren't back here, he didn't know where they were. No one did. Yafa had told Nevaeh over the phone that they were supposed to have been home by four. She'd taken a personal day from work, visited her father in the hospital early in the day, and planned to surprise the children with an evening at the movies together. Instead, she'd come home to an empty house. She'd called, but Sayid's phone had gone straight to voicemail. Repeatedly. It never went straight to voicemail; he never turned it off.

More spirits whispered intermittently. Peter shut out their voices as best he could. They jumbled in his head, tangling up with his own panic.

"Shit!"

Nevaeh tripped over something bigger this time, went down and took Peter with her.

He breathed hard through his nose. "You all right?"

"I think so." She reached for him. "You?"

"Fine."

They helped each other back up, then shone their flashlights on the ground to see what the hell they'd tripped over.

The beams fell on a person. A middle-aged white woman with a honey-colored bob and pantsuit in disarray, face down in the dirt.

With a yelp, Nevaeh scrambled away from her. Peter's heart stuttered, but he bent to check the woman's pulse.

Nevaeh's voice quivered. "Is she dead?"

The woman's pulse was weak, but it was there. He let out a breath.

"Knocked out, is all."

"What do you think she was doing here?"

A spirit hovered over her, pulsing angrily. Not one he'd seen before, this spirit.

"Didn't come under her own steam, I reckon." Peter lifted the woman gently, just enough to slip a flower garland around her neck. Her eyelids fluttered. The spirit flinched and spiraled away. "Help me get her out of here."

"I could get the truck."

He shook his head. "I'll not have you walking back alone. We'll take her ourselves."

The woman woke as they lifted her. She was groggy and confused, had no idea what she was doing in a rapidly darkening forest, but she could walk. Her name was Laura. She wanted to go to the hospital. She didn't remember seeing any children.

Peter had been planning to go straight back into the woods once Nevaeh and Laura made it safely into the pickup, but Nevaeh grabbed his wrist.

"You are *not* going back there alone."

"The weens," he said anxiously, but Nevaeh shook her head.

"Not alone. Jesus, Peter, are you kidding me?" Her grip tightened. "I know you're worried about the kids, okay, I know that, but—" she lowered her voice, although Laura was dazed and already shut inside the truck anyway "—I could *hear* the ghosts. Please. Don't go back there alone. Let me drop you off at Yafa's, okay? Maybe the kids are back by now, and if they're not," she said, raising her voice as he tried to object, "you and Yafa can come up with a plan *together* that doesn't involve you running around a deeply haunted forest alone. Okay?"

She wasn't going to let go of him until he agreed, so he did. He tried to remind himself, as they turned out of the cemetery, that Sayid always wore his Saint-John's-wort. That would protect him.

But his mother had said his phone was never off, and now it was. Maybe he hadn't worn the Saint-John's-wort. Even if he had, Samira had nothing to keep her safe. And she was so determined to throw herself headlong into danger, so fearless no matter how much there was to be afraid of.

Peter leaned his forehead against the back of Nevaeh's seat and panicked all the way to the al-Masris' house.

XXXVI

Yafa's eyes were red. She clutched a tissue.

"You didn't have to come," she croaked, letting Peter in.

Peter trailed into the kitchen with her. The room that had been so cheerful when he'd come for supper now seemed lost. The kitchen table, a long rectangle of shiny dark wood, seemed sad and dull. It huddled near the laminate counters, which shrank against walls that were colorless and low and too close. Peter tugged at his collar.

Leslie Wu sat at the head of the table on her phone, with a phone tree bound and printed in front of her. A small army of townsfolk clustered around her, in chairs, standing, or cross-legged on the floor, each flipping through a different phone tree. Their babble assaulted Peter's ears. He gripped the strap of his bag, overwhelmed by sound.

"Everyone?" Yafa said. They all looked up, half of them still on the phone. "This is Peter Shaughnessy, a family friend. He's come to help."

His skin prickled at being introduced to so many people at once after a century of being introduced to no one at all, but the introduction passed with minimal acknowledgment. Several folks put their hands over the mouthpieces of their phones to mouth *hello* at him; others waved. Leslie Wu nodded in recognition, and he nodded back. That was it. The phone calls were more important than his name, but he couldn't relax, too aware of the situation that had necessitated them.

Another woman, who looked like Yafa but younger, in a suit instead of Yafa's jeans and tunic, was at the stove, setting a kettle to boil.

"You're Peter?" she said. He nodded. "I'm Yafa's sister. Maryam Mansour."

He shifted from one foot to the other; he was too unsettled to sit. "You've not heard anything?"

Yafa collapsed into a chair beside Leslie. She'd shrunk alongside her kitchen. Leslie patted her hand without missing a beat in her next call. One of the other townspeople offered her a package of Fig Newtons; in addition to their phones, they seemed to have brought enough snacks to feed a small country. Yafa gave them all a watery smile but shook her head.

"I called them." Her voice was tight, barely audible over the clamor of phone calls. "I tried Sayid's cell and the landline before I left the hospital, and then his cell again I don't know how many times when I got home, and I called all our friends and neighbors and the library, but nobody's seen them."

"Then she called me." Maryam joined the crowd at the table. "And no sooner had I gotten here than she calmed down because she realized she hadn't called the cemetery yet."

Yafa moaned. "I was sure, I was so sure they were with you—"

Her sister touched her back. Peter twisted the strap of his bag, grounding himself against the encroaching walls.

"—everything that's been happening lately, I don't know what to think."

"I called the library again," Maryam said, "and the school, just in case, and a couple other places, and asked them to keep an eye out. And Leslie came straight over to get a call tree going. I called the police, too, but—" she made air quotes with her fingers, her nose wrinkling "—'they're probably blowing off steam.'"

Yafa buried her head in her arms.

Leslie briefly lowered her phone in the midst of a call.

"We'll find them," she said firmly. "Someone has to have seen them."

Her nearest neighbors nodded emphatically.

Maryam kicked her chair back and stood, putting a firm hand on her sister's shoulder. "Come on. You need rest."

Yafa raised a tearstained face, her expression so fierce she looked exactly like her daughter. "I don't need rest. I need to find my children. If you'd let me look for them myself—"

"You're in no condition for that. Besides, in case they're out somewhere having fun—"

Yafa snorted wetly. Peter fished a handkerchief from his pocket and handed it to her with shaking fingers. Maryam continued as if there'd been no interruption.

"—if they *are* just hanging out somewhere, you need to be here when they come home. Go wash your face."

"No." Yafa wiped her eyes on her sleeve. "My face is fine."

Maryam flicked her shoulder. "Go. Wash. Your face."

Yafa shoved away from the table, nostrils flaring, and stalked from the kitchen. A bathroom door slammed. The kettle hissed on the stove. The phone calls started winding down.

Maryam dropped into her chair, sighing. She propped her chin on a hand. "You see where Samira gets it."

Leslie set down her phone, flipping her phone tree closed. "That's all my contacts."

She looked inquiringly around at the others, some of whom were still finishing up their own calls. The rest shook their heads.

Leslie grimaced. "Well, at least people know to be on the lookout now."

Maryam nodded. With Yafa out of the room, she looked glum, like her firm, no-nonsense expression had been for her sister's benefit only.

She glanced at Peter. "Yafa says the kids have been spending a lot of time at the cemetery lately?"

"Samira loves the place." A wet chuckle escaped him. "Sayid don't like it much."

His heart squeezed, his chest tight and hot. He steadied himself on the table. He wouldn't have worried, would've been sure Samira had merely run off again, sure Sayid had gone looking for her—except for the lost time, the disappearances. What if Samira had been snatched by whatever spirit lurked in the back lot, spreading its anger all over town, or another that had been affected by its anger? If that happened, no matter how scared Sayid was, Peter knew, he'd go after her.

His voice wobbled. "He don't like it, but if he thought she went back there, he'd go, too."

"Go where?" Yafa reentered the kitchen with a clean face and a worn expression, her fight gone. There was a flurry of movement as neighbors rushed to offer her snacks, but she waved their offerings aside.

"Cemetery." Peter headed for the foyer with Yafa, Maryam, and Leslie trailing him. Nevaeh wouldn't like it, but she wouldn't know he'd gone back alone until he returned. "I'm going back for a better look. If—"

The latch clicked; the front door opened.

"—gonna get in so much trouble, you gotta stop running off—"

"You gotta stop worrying about getting in trouble," Samira said, clomping inside with Sayid at her heels.

They froze at the sight of the adults.

Silence.

The tightness in Peter's chest released. The house sighed back to its normal proportions.

They were all right.

Yafa's face crumpled. She pushed past him and pulled her children into a bone-crushing hug, crying, "Alhamdulillah, alhamdulillah." The neighbors appeared in the kitchen doorway, their expressions relaxing at the sight of the children.

Sayid reddened, but he mumbled, "Hi, Mama," and returned her hug, patting her back awkwardly.

Samira stood stiffly in her mother's arms, but Yafa pressed a kiss to her head. "Where have you been? We've been calling all over town trying to find you."

Sayid avoided Samira's gaze. "Sorry, Mama. My battery died."

She kissed him, too, and he ducked in embarrassment. "I know, habibi. I know. You never turn off your phone. Where were you?"

"Out."

Maryam and Leslie raised their eyebrows. He was clearly trying to spare Samira, but Yafa was so relieved to have them back that she didn't notice his vague answers or Samira's stiffness.

"I know it's boring here all day." She wiped her eyes. "With Baba in Maryland and school out...but I need you to be home when I say, okay? I need to know where you are, all these people disappearing—"

Sayid shivered. "I know, Mama."

Samira's nostrils flared.

"—if you really want to go somewhere, promise me you'll call Mrs. Holloway next door, or Mr. David, or Peter. Please, promise me you won't leave the house again without an adult."

Samira flung her arm away, scowling.

"We're *here* all day without an adult. What's the difference?"

Yafa looked as if she'd been slapped. Sayid's arms tightened around her.

"Samira," he said softly, but his sister ignored him.

In the kitchen, the kettle whistled, but no one went to get it. Leslie started surreptitiously nudging the neighbors toward the back door with murmured instructions to call everyone back and let them know the children had been found.

"You're never home anymore." Samira's fists clenched and unclenched. "You *or* Baba. What difference does it make whether I am?"

"Young lady," Maryam said sharply, but Samira wrenched away and stomped up the stairs. The kettle's whistling built to a scream. "Hey—"

"Don't," Yafa whispered. "Don't, Maryam."

Her sister faltered, eyes flickering between the staircase and Yafa. "Do you want me to... Should I call Khalid for you?"

Yafa nodded. Maryam disappeared into the kitchen. The kettle's screaming died.

"Don't tell him," Yafa called after her. "What she said. Don't tell him. Please."

Leslie all but shoved the last few stragglers out the door. She stood in the entryway awkwardly, wringing her hands.

"Yafa," she said softly, "if you need me to stay—"

Yafa shook her head. "We're all right," she said, sounding anything but.

Leslie hesitated, then nodded and slipped out. Without her army of callers, the house was suddenly quiet.

Sayid met Peter's gaze, his eyes dark and sad. "It's okay, Mama."

Yafa squeezed her eyes shut. "Samira's right. I'm never home."

"You have to take care of Jeddo. And you have to work more. And Baba does, too. It's okay."

She shrank in on herself. "I'm such a bad mother."

"No you're not," Sayid said firmly, but his eyes were sadder than ever. His brow creased. "You're doing your best."

She whispered something to him in Arabic and stopped hugging him long enough to press the heels of her palms to her eyes.

Peter shifted from one foot to the other. He wanted to wrap them up safe and tight, hold them until their difficulties passed. But it was impossible. Dangerous to want anyway.

Yafa wandered dazedly into the kitchen. Peter tugged on his cap and asked Sayid quietly, "What d'you normally get from that Indian place?"

Sayid rattled off the al-Masris' usual order and added, "You might want to call it in before you go. It takes a while." He lowered his voice. "And maybe you could bring baklava from the bakery next door? That's what Baba does when she's having a bad day."

XXXVII

Samira refused to come out. Yafa called up the stairs but retreated when Samira shouted that she wasn't hungry. Maryam spent a quarter hour in the upstairs hallway, arguing through the door, to no avail. Sayid picked at his food, glancing toward the staircase as if he wanted to give it a try but couldn't bring himself to do so.

"You should eat, Mama," he said.

They were in the kitchen, sober and quiet but busy with food. The scents of garlic and garam masala wafted through the room. Yafa fussed over a bowl for Samira. She hadn't sat down once.

She piled rice and chicken tikka masala in the bowl. "She must be starving."

"*You* must be starving," Maryam said. "Listen to your son and eat. Samira will come down when she's hungry."

"You don't know how stubborn my daughter can be."

"I know how stubborn *you* can be," Maryam muttered. "If you're so worried about dinner, bring it upstairs. She can eat in her room."

Yafa paused by the naan at the end of the table. "She won't open the door. She doesn't want to talk to me."

Maryam shrugged. "I'll do it."

Yafa snorted.

Her sister sighed. "I promise not to yell at her. I won't even argue with her."

Yafa wrapped some naan in a napkin. Peter handed her the samosas.

She took three. "Would you do it? She might open the door for you."

He abandoned his supper. Yafa handed him the bowl and napkin.

"Second door on the right." She hesitated. "Thank you."

He traipsed up the stairs. The al-Masris had invited him to watch a movie with them after supper last time, but he'd declined, already pushing things. He'd only been in their kitchen.

Now he was terribly aware of the private rooms at the top of the stairs and the little time he'd spent in anyone's home but his own in the last century, with the recent exception of Nevaeh's apartment.

The upstairs had worn wooden floors and seafoam walls hung with photos. Yafa and Khalid on their wedding day. Khalid with an arm slung around the shoulders of a man so like him it could only have been his brother. A monochrome photo that must have been either Yafa's or Khalid's father, in his youth some fifty years ago. Sayid as a baby; as a toddler, clumsily lobbing water balloons at a toddler Chloe; as a little boy holding an infant Samira, frowning quizzically. Sayid maybe ten or eleven, in a group of boys in polo shirts, shorter than the others but grinning like the rest as he held up a science trophy. Samira feeding a giraffe at the zoo, riding her bike, waiting in line with her brother for the Ferris wheel. Waving so wildly from a playground that her hand blurred. And one family portrait: the four of them with Maryam and an older couple who must've been Yafa's parents. The grandparents sat on a stiff little love seat with the others around them, staring seriously into the camera like they'd taken the picture in the 1880s rather than five years ago. Samira, then a chubby toddler in Khalid's arms, glared like it was the only way she could manage not to smile instead.

Peter's mouth twitched. He moved on.

The second door on the right had a whiteboard on it covered in doodles of djinn, flowers, and spies. Numbers were written in the center, with (KEEP OUT) smaller beneath them.

Peter shifted the food to one arm and knocked.

"Go away."

"It's me, child."

Silence.

"I got your supper."

More silence.

"I got samosas."

Bedsprings creaked. "I guess you can come in."

He entered.

Her bedroom was small and pink, with a border of white crowns printed along the top of the walls. But instead of gowns and palaces, spy paraphernalia crowded the room. A *Spy Kids* poster took up most of one wall. Books featuring ten-year-old spies and secret organizations crammed into the small Disney-princess bookshelf alongside battered copies of *Encyclopedia Brown*. Unbent paper clips and a padlock lay atop the bookshelf. A black hoodie was thrown across the tiny pink desk chair, having been (unsuccessfully) attacked with scissors in an attempt to transform it into a stealth outfit. On top of the desk was a book on code breaking, a cut-up lemon, a notebook scribbled with encoded messages, and loose papers smelling of lemon where Samira had tried and failed to make her own invisible ink.

Samira lay on her stomach on the rumpled pink comforter, arms around her pillow, facing the wall. Peter set her food on the desk, pulled the tiny pink desk chair up next to the bed, and folded himself onto the chair with difficulty. She didn't move.

Peter scratched his forehead with a thumb. "Do you want to talk about it?"

"No. No one cares anyway."

"They do."

Samira snorted.

"I do," Peter added.

Silence. A sniffle.

Samira buried her face in her pillow, body quaking.

Peter shifted from the chair to the bed and touched her shoulder. She flung herself into his arms, sniffling into his neck. He held her and rocked her and said over and over, "There now, child. S'all right. It's not s'bad as all that."

He squeezed his eyes shut, remembering in her arms around his neck his baby sister. Catherine had been thirteen years his junior, born eight months after his pa's death; Mam hadn't known she was in the family way when they'd buried him. Catherine had been Peter's darling. All of them had loved and doted on her—him, Mam, Eoin, the whole of Ballygar—but when she'd been in a mood, not a one of them but Peter could calm her.

She'd been the curse's first victim. Only six years old. The reason he'd fled.

She'd been sprawled on the ground, leaves and twigs in her golden hair. Her nightdress rumpled and dirty.

Dead, not a mark on her.

So he'd thought until Jack, near two decades later, had told him everyone else had seen a bullet hole and blood, clear as day. *Them folk's* trickery, to chase him from home.

He buried his face in Samira's hair, raised it again, and forced his eyes open. The pink room with its spy books and paper clips and lemons chased away the dark midnight forest of memory.

He relaxed, bouncing Samira on his lap. Her tears subsided. Her breath hitched and stuttered, hot and damp on his neck.

"She's never home. And Baba's never home."

Peter bounced her again. "She's home now."

Samira's hands fisted in his shirt.

"You miss her," he said. "Is that it?"

She wiped her eyes on her arm.

"She used to take us to the zoo every week," she said. "And we went to the reptile house to see the crocodile, Mama and me. His name's Baru. He's my favorite animal. Sayid doesn't like snakes, so he doesn't come with us." She hiccupped. "And Baba used to take me to the museum every time he came home from a business trip."

She pushed hair out of her face, but a strand stuck to her cheek. Peter tucked it behind her ear.

"Now she's always at work." Samira gazed at his shirt. "And then she visits Jeddo. And when she's home, she sleeps. And Baba's always away. And when he's home..."

She gave a long, shuddering sigh. She was light and frail as a newly hatched bird. Exhaustion radiated off her.

"They must be plumb wore out," Peter said, "trying to do so much. Bet they miss each other when your pa's away, same as you miss them."

Samira shook her head. "Nuh-uh. They text all the time."

"That's enough, you figure? If your pa texted you all day, that'd make up for never seeing him?"

"I guess not."

She toyed with the placket of his shirt. He bounced her until a huff of laughter escaped her.

"That's better," he said. "You know they miss you, too, don't you?"

Her small smile vanished. "No they don't."

"Of course they do."

She leaned into him. "They don't. They think I'm bad. Like everyone else does."

"I've never heard them say you're bad," Peter said firmly. "Not once. They've said you're having a hard time, and they've said they're worried about you. And today, when we didn't know where you and your brother were, you should've seen how your mam cried, she was so scared she'd lost you both. She never once said you were bad."

Samira sighed softly but said nothing.

"Samosas're probably cold," Peter said. "But if we go down-stairs, I bet your mam'd reheat 'em for you."

She kept fiddling with his shirt. At last she said, "Okay."

They traipsed downstairs hand in hand. Peter held the bowl of rice and chicken tikka masala; Samira clutched the naan and samosas.

The chatter in the kitchen was livelier now, but it cut off as they entered. Peter set the bowl at an empty chair and resumed his seat. Sayid finished his dal, took his dishes to the sink, and washed them loudly.

Yafa smiled tentatively at her daughter. "Are you hungry, habibti?"

Samira nodded. Yafa busied herself preparing another bowl like she'd forgotten the one Peter had brought down.

Samira rocked on her heels, her eyes following her mother through the kitchen. She darted forward and threw her arms around Yafa's waist.

Yafa froze, then hugged Samira. She whispered in her daughter's ear. Samira whispered back. She sat at the table, her mother set the new bowl down, and it was like nothing had happened, except that Samira was so much quieter than usual and Yafa kept blinking.

"Can we call Baba?" Samira asked.

The evening improved. No one forgot what had been said, but Sayid was relieved the fighting had stopped. Maryam told stories that made even Samira smile. Khalid spent an hour on speakerphone with them—joking with Maryam, asking Sayid about his latest book, threatening to eat all Samira's samosas next time he was home—and spoke privately with Yafa for half an hour more.

Peter was quietly pleased, yet he observed it with a pang. Having once thought of Catherine and Eoin and Mam, he couldn't stop. The bickering they'd get up to, how it'd flare up from nothing and resolve the same way. The suppers they'd eaten. The tales Mam told as she darned shirts by the fire, tales of wisps and selkies and *them folk* and all the ancient heroes of Ireland.

Before he left, he reached into his bag for a thin iron band. He gave it to Samira as they said goodbye in the foyer. She slipped it onto her wrist, examining it with interest.

"This is a weird bracelet."

"I know. But do me a favor and wear it next time you leave the house by your lonesome."

"Mama said not to leave without a grown-up."

He chuckled. "I know you better'n that. When you leave the house alone again, as you'll surely do, you wear that iron. Can you do that for me?"

"Okay."

"Good lass."

He couldn't keep her from running off any more than her mother could. Probably less. But he trusted her to wear the wristlet. As long as she wore it, she'd be safe.

XXXVIII

"We have a problem," Nevaeh said. "Specifically, a funeral. Saturday."

The Wednesday sky was steely and oppressive above like the spirit's anger was in the cemetery below. Nevaeh sat in Peter's kitchen, picking at her sundress nervously. She was always nervous now. The anger had grown so strong that the living felt it, though most didn't recognize it for what it was. The cottage air wasn't as heavy as the air outside, thanks to Peter's warding, but the kitchen was dimmer than it had been a month ago, even when the sun shone. Gray light filtered through the window and the Dutch door. Muggy June heat followed. Nevaeh's hair was tugged into a curly bun to keep it off her neck.

Peter thumbed through Isaiah's notebook. He'd eaten quickly, desperate to return to his research in the hopes of finding something, anything, that might help him discover the identity and location of the ghost. Saturday was a week from Midsummer Eve.

"I don't know what to do." Nevaeh speared shepherd's pie on her fork but let it drop again uneaten. "I can't tell them they can't have their funeral, but with everything going on, I don't want people in the cemetery."

Two more people had gone missing; several had shown up in odd places. Tales spread of mysterious noises and accidents narrowly avoided, even of apparitions, spoken of in hushed tones and scoffed at with insincere skepticism. A herd of dairy cows escaped when a barn door was left unlatched overnight, and the farmer swore the ghost had unlatched it.

The only topic relieving talk of the ghost was talk of SummerFest, Harrington's annual street fair. But Peter was as jittery at that as he was anything else these days: it started two days before Midsummer.

"If I could find the damn thing, it'd be plenty safe. But I don't know where it is." He paged through the notebook restlessly. "Been through this thing a thousand times and I'm no closer. Got David looking into some things, too, but that's come to naught yet."

Nevaeh scooched closer. The tabletop herbs drew their leaves aside to give her a better view. "What is that?"

"Some of Isaiah's research. Notes on Anne Hodinka's diary."

"Anne Hodinka." Nevaeh frowned. "The original owner of the boarding house?"

"Mmm. Isaiah was figuring out who everyone was, on account of Anne only gives initials."

Peter stopped at a spread where Isaiah had tried to identify someone with the initials O.S. Three of Anne's diary entries had been printed and taped to the page. The first was from December 1850.

John is dubious of our new tenant. He doubts O.S.'s ability to keep up with the rent and moreover considers him a bad influence, especially on Nina, who is quite fascinated by him. I admit I do not understand myself why he should be of such interest to her; he is curt and grim and on the whole very unpleasant. But he did carve her a wooden horse as a Christmas gift, and he never tells her off for staring at him, which she does near constantly. I reminded John that the poor man lost his family to cholera, and doubtless Nina reminds him of his own child; so we must be kind, no matter how unpleasant he is, and we shall not worry about his financial state until it adversely affects our own.

The second was from August 1851.

O.S. has been late with the rent twice now, and John's patience wears thin. It has become impossible to make peace between them. But for better or worse, O.S. has taken it upon himself to hide away in his room at all times, so there are fewer arguments now than there were last month. I am glad for the sake not only of ourselves and our other tenants, but for Nina. John has forbidden her from speaking to her friend, but still I find her sneaking off to see him whenever he emerges from his room. I admit I do not have the heart to forbid her myself, nor to tell her father. I think she may be O.S.'s only friend.

The third was from November that same year and a great deal shorter.

O.S. died today. Nina is inconsolable.

In the margins, Isaiah had written name after name and excised each one. The marks and handwriting betrayed increasing frustration, until the last name on the page, Orville Schuster, was written nearly illegibly and crossed out with a single, angry slash.

"This man, O.S.," Peter said, "Isaiah drove himself to distraction trying to find him. I figure he's the best bet because there's the least to say about him."

Nevaeh snorted. "Is that normally how you decide who a ghost is?"

"Not in the slightest." Peter scratched the back of his neck. "But I can't find head nor tail of it, so someone we know nothing about may well be it. And there's this."

He shoved the notebook toward her, flipping to a different page. He'd been over it obsessively and had the diary entry memorized.

John has finally agreed to pay for a headstone for O.S. I am sorry it's neither a better stone nor a better site, but I count myself lucky he will not go to the potter's field. I should not have won John over had not Nina burst in upon our argument with a ring O.S. had given her that belonged to his dear wife. Nina says he gave it to her to pass onto us, no doubt as back payment for his rent, but the poor child kept it as a memento of her friend until she realized her father would not pay to bury him. It is to be a simple stone, and John paid a song for a lot back by the souls lost to cholera. I comfort myself that the poor man will be buried nearer his wife and daughter that way.

Isaiah had drawn a map of the cemetery on the page opposite, but his notes were illegible, a chaos of scribblings and crossings-out and question marks. Isaiah had had no better idea where O.S. was buried than who O.S. was.

"He lost his family to cholera," Nevaeh said slowly, "like in the stories."

"Right," Peter said. "Anne don't say whether he had any ties to the general store, but he fits the legends well enough. But Isaiah never figured out who he was. I been asking."

Nevaeh let out a huff of laughter. "Poor Isaiah. I can't believe you're making him relive his greatest research fail after death."

He chuckled, lighter and looser than he'd felt in days. The herbs stretched toward him, pleased with his mood. "He don't seem to mind. Think he likes having someone to talk to."

Nevaeh's laughter faded. "It's too bad he can't talk to Uncle Dave."

"Sure he'd love to, if he thought David would handle it all right."

Peter ran a hand through his hair, avoiding Nevaeh's gaze. Jealousy stabbed at him, jealousy and the uncomfortable sense that, if he examined his feelings too closely, he might find he was glad that Isaiah was unwilling to reveal himself to David.

Nearby lemon balm murmured comfortingly, its citrus scent softer than usual.

"Anyway, this funeral." Peter cleared his throat. "If you know where you're setting up, I'll make sure it's safe. Safe enough for an hour or so. Getting everyone in and out'll be the tricky bit, but I'll do what I can. And I'll keep watch 'til it's over."

For the next three days, he put protections into place. He planted Saint-John's-wort, rue and lemon verbena, lavender and rosemary and mallow around the area Nevaeh had marked. He spent an evening in the storage shed, scratching Marian symbols into the underside of every folding chair they had until well after nightfall. He pounded iron nails into the ground amongst the plants and raked grass over them and told Nevaeh not to mow.

The last problem was Adeline.

Her grave was within the bounds he'd erected. Unable to escape, she swooped back and forth, kicking up tiny windstorms and tearing up grass because she couldn't touch the new plants. Her daffodils were long gone.

Friday evening, after Nevaeh left, he stepped inside the site with his watch in hand. The sky was molten with sunset. Adeline was in his face in an instant, red and jittery, but he'd expected it.

"Hey, Addy. Don't much like it in here, I'm guessing."

She writhed, trying to break through the barriers, but the iron burned her. The flowers watched stoically, perfuming the air.

He held out the watch. "Come on, Addy. You hop inside this watch and I'll get you out of here."

She twisted away, sour with suspicion.

"All right. Stay here, then."

She didn't like that. She zipped into the watch as he walked away.

He snapped it shut, sucking in his cheeks, and headed to his cottage.

The twilight sizzled with anger. Clover curled in on itself, quivering. The trees dotting the front of the cemetery hung heavy and quiet. The knoll's spirits jittered far too close, but he was wearing his flowers and iron, and they couldn't touch him. They turned away.

He brought the pullets inside and released Adeline in his back garden. She rocketed out of the watch, drifting confusedly past the hydrangeas, the coop, the little stone well long dried up. Safely within the warding, outside the anger's influence, her color softened from crimson to grapefruit to faded peach. Her constant anger in the last weeks had exhausted her.

"There you are," Peter said. "Better?"

She sank into the hydrangeas, vaguely minty with dull curiosity.

"Won't be able to leave until I let you. Won't be able to get into the house, neither. But that anger can't touch you long as you're in the garden. All right?"

The hydrangeas rustled.

He still had to worry about tomorrow's mourners entering and exiting the cemetery—would worry for the hour they were within its walls, despite his protective measures—but at least an angry spirit wouldn't be hurtling around their seats.

By 11 a.m. Saturday, he was itchy and uncomfortable in his suit. It was dark and woolen, totally unsuited to the June heat, too obviously old-fashioned, but he didn't have another. He stood behind the rows of folding chairs, sweating and tugging at his collar.

Nevaeh looked more comfortable in a blouse and trousers, her hair in the same curly bun she'd been wearing all week to combat the heat, but also more anxious. She glanced around like she expected a ghost to pop up and shout, "BOO!"

Mourners settled in their seats.

"S'all right," Peter murmured. "S'long as they sit here, they should be fine."

Nevaeh tucked an errant curl behind her ear. "'Should' isn't as comforting as you think it is."

He elbowed her. "Hush. We're at a funeral."

She swallowed a reluctant giggle.

"Hush," he whispered again. "What will people think?"

She elbowed him back. "You started it."

A priest stood to say some words. Nevaeh sidled away, but Peter hardly noticed. He was thinking of all the funerals he hadn't been to.

He'd fled Ireland the night of Catherine's death and never gone back. He hadn't learned of Mam's death until two years after the fact, when Jack had found him in that Melbourne pub. That had been the last he'd heard of his brother, too, alive as far as Jack had known but having ill luck finding work after emigrating. He hoped his brother had lived to a ripe old age. His father and sister had died far too young; his mother hardly less so, only in her fifties.

He could've gone to Jack's funeral, but he hadn't been able to bear it.

Sometimes he regretted missing it. Jack might've been there, a lingering spirit. Waiting for him. Disappointed when he didn't come.

Funny: he hadn't gone, in part, for fear Jack's spirit wouldn't be there.

His eyes prickled. He sucked in his cheeks, burying the memories and regrets with more difficulty than usual. Since Harrington had brought them out, he'd found them harder to ignore.

The mourners mopped their faces, sweating in their black clothes. The priest droned on, but a wind picked up and muted him. Cottonwood seeds whirled through the cemetery like snow. Two small children chased them. Peter started, but their guardians grabbed them before they broke free of the protective barriers.

The mourners scooched forward, but the wind persisted. The priest's words were lost, as were those of the deceased's siblings and niece afterward. The grass ruffled. The flowers Peter had planted bent. The spirits beyond them wavered, buzzing like yellowjackets, but whenever they came too close, they veered away again, muttering about flowers and iron. Some of them actually muttered, their voices a sibilant hiss that was nearly words.

Nevaeh sidled back over, jaw tense. "Is this...?"

"Don't know. Might be."

Someone's hat blew off. Peter darted after it and returned it to its owner, an elderly woman who probably wouldn't have chased it anyway. He stayed close, ready to catch anything else so the mourners wouldn't leave the protective square. They huddled together, wringing their hands. The wind howled.

The dead man was lowered into his grave with indecent haste, and the funeral was over. No one lingered at the grave; no one stayed to chat; no one stopped by the graves of relatives previously buried. The mourners hurried away in tight groups, clutching their jackets and children.

Peter sweated through his suit, hovering until the last mourner left.

His relief was short-lived. Nevaeh darted around, collecting chairs. The remaining chairs rattled in the wind; one tumbled toward her.

"Nevaeh," Peter said, but she dodged the chair. Her face was strained. "Leave 'em."

"I have to put them away," she said, but her eyes were wide as another chair tumbled across the shivering grass.

"Not right now, you don't." He dragged her through the gate. "You got a bag or anything in your office?"

"No. My keys and phone are in my pocket."

An errant chair crashed into the wall. Peter slammed the gate shut. "You need to leave. Go on home and don't come back until it's safe."

"What about work?"

"Never mind about work. You can't be here. That thing'll only get stronger 'til Midsummer."

More metal crumpled, more chairs crashing into the wall. The moss furring the wall thickened, as if to save the stones from the impact.

Nevaeh flinched. "I thought you warded those."

He had. But a spirit wasn't throwing them; a spirit was whipping up a wind. The wind didn't care about warding and sigils, flowers and iron.

Peter gripped her hand. "Nevaeh."

She wrenched her eyes from the gate. "I…"

"Stay away. Promise me. Until it's safe."

She swallowed. "I guess I have some PTO I could use."

He let out a breath. They were safe from flying chairs here, but the air outside the cemetery was sour and weightful.

Nevaeh's brow puckered. "What about you? You *live* here. You could crash on my couch if you want? Or…there's a spare room at my parents' house? Or—"

His eyes prickled. She looked so worried.

"This ain't my first go-round." He attempted a smile. "I'll be fine. Need to keep looking for this ghost anyhow. I'll bring some things by your place later, all right? Flowers'n'things you can put up for extra protection."

"All right."

He retrieved her bicycle and watched her pedal off until she rounded a corner. His chest was tight and hot, his hands cold and shaky, but she was safely away. Her apartment door was warded already, as was the door of the building. He'd do her windows, too, when he went back, and he'd give her flowers and iron and salt and holy water. Somehow, he'd make sure David and the al-Masris were equally safe in their homes.

One way or another, he'd find the spirit before Midsummer.

XXXIX

Nevaeh had been home five minutes when she left again. Her apartment was too quiet, her thoughts too loud. She had a therapy appointment in less than three hours, and she itched to cancel again, especially with a ghost terrorizing her workplace.

She couldn't stop thinking about Peter. His face pale as he told her to leave, while he remained like he wasn't in just as much danger.

She biked to Benji's apartment, a utilitarian building on Washington whose severe exterior didn't suit them. She pounded on the door of their second-floor unit, embarrassed when Benji's thirteen-year-old cousin Chloe answered instead.

If Chloe was bothered by the pounding, she didn't show it. She gave Nevaeh a once-over, opening the door wider on a burst of color; Benji had hung scarves and pride flags everywhere. "Benji! Your girlfriend's here!"

Nevaeh's face warmed. Inside, Benji said, "Shut *up*, I told you to stop saying that—"

Approaching, they broke off. In spite of everything, Nevaeh's heart sang at the sight of them: their beautiful dark brown skin, their high cheekbones, their dark eyes and inky lashes, their endlessly stylish array of jeans and jackets that made her feel basic by comparison. Especially today, when she'd dressed so conservatively for the funeral. She picked at her blouse self-consciously.

"Hey, Nea." Their eyes raked over her outfit. "What's the occasion?"

"G i r l f r i e n d," Chloe whispered, drawing the word out.

Benji shoved Chloe out of sight behind the door.

"Stuck babysitting," they said. "Auntie's on a cruise 'til after SummerFest. So?"

"A work thing," Nevaeh said, because funerals were work things now. "Not important. Can you take me to Ma's?"

Benji's eyes went over her again, their brow furrowing at her strained face and tense posture. "Let me grab my keys."

Chloe came with them, even though Benji insisted they wouldn't be gone long. Fortunately, she said nothing about girlfriends from the back seat of Benji's beat-up Neon.

They drove through farmland in silence. Corn and soy gleamed green in the June sun. The Neon kicked up a trail of dust as they went farther from town. Benji kept glancing at Nevaeh, but they didn't say anything.

She liked that about Benji: they never pushed. They gave her space until she was ready to talk about what was wrong, *if* she wanted to talk about it.

Her therapy appointment loomed closer. She hadn't canceled yet.

She still wanted to.

Fields rushed past the window. Benji pulled into her mom's driveway and put the Neon in Park, cut the engine.

"Do you need me to come with you?"

Chloe sighed. Benji ignored her.

The corner of Nevaeh's mouth turned up. "I'm good. Really. I just… I need to talk to Granny about something."

Benji took her hand. Nevaeh chewed the inside of her cheek, trying not to act like she was screaming internally, which she absolutely was not.

Benji squeezed her hand and let go. "Lunch next week sometime?"

She confirmed it, said goodbye to Chloe, and got out. She resisted the urge to watch them drive off.

The porch was sweet with the scent of lilacs, but the acrid smell of fresh paint lingered. The window frames, lintel, and ceiling had been touched up, their blue bright and unchipped. Nevaeh paused with her hand on the doorknob, then went inside.

Marguerite was in her rocking chair in the living room, knitting baby socks for a family at her church. Nevaeh held her breath at the sight. The living room looked exactly as it had when she was growing up. Cream-colored carpet, floral-print couch, rickety side table, her dad's worn leather armchair and her granny's rocking chair.

Before her dad died, stepping into this room had always comforted her—the one place in Harrington that never changed. Now, conspicuously empty, the leather armchair reminded her that even the unchanging old farmhouse was different than it once had been, no matter how *same* it looked. Elijah would never again walk through the front door after a long day of farming. He'd never sit in that chair working on his crossword puzzle. He'd never take Nevaeh to the diner for breakfast, no matter how often she was home.

Nevaeh's fingernails dug into her arms. His loss was a physical thing inside her, like she'd had an organ removed.

She missed him. She missed her daddy.

But Marguerite worked away placidly, humming an old spiritual to herself, as calm a presence as she'd been throughout Nevaeh's life. The clock behind her ticked quietly.

"Granny?"

Marguerite's wrinkled face broke into a smile.

"What you doing here, Nae-Nae?" She rose stiffly to hug

her granddaughter, drew back when Nevaeh hugged her back mechanically. "Everything all right?"

"Can you see ghosts?"

Marguerite pursed her lips. "You been talking to that grounds-keeper of yours."

Air punched from Nevaeh's lungs. "You can, can't you?"

Marguerite sat back down, glancing at Elijah's armchair. At nothing.

"Some ghosts," she said softly.

Nevaeh sank onto the couch. Years thinking her grandmother was a little eccentric. Years of her dad worrying that his mother was losing her grip, her mom saying that people coped with loss differently and that as long as she was functioning it was fine.

Her eyes stung. "Pops?"

"Mmm. Your granddaddy's one of 'em. And your daddy…"

Nevaeh's chest tightened. It wasn't fair.

"I wish," she said, then stopped, because she couldn't admit it.

Her grandmother leaned forward and took Nevaeh's hand. Marguerite's hands were soft and wrinkled like worn leather, but strong and firm, too. She smelled like baby powder, a scent Nevaeh found comforting.

Marguerite rubbed the back of her granddaughter's hand with a thumb. "Wish you could see 'em, too, hmm?"

Nevaeh nodded. "How come you can?"

She cringed at her own words. She sounded like a kid, not a grown woman.

Marguerite squeezed her hand.

"Don't know, Nae-Nae. Ain't seen any others since I was a little girl." She sat back, rocking, and resumed knitting. "They're here, y'know. Both of 'em. That Shaughnessy man, he brung your daddy to me a while back."

Nevaeh's throat closed up. Her fists clenched.

Peter hadn't told her *that*.

"He's here?" she croaked. "Last Sunday—was he here when I came for dinner? Is he here now?"

Marguerite didn't look up from her knitting.

"Yes, yes, and yes." She paused. "Sorry I didn't tell you sooner, babygirl. Figured you wouldn't believe me anyhow. I know you used to shake your head at me same as your daddy when I talked about Hank. Didn't figure you'd ever come round wanting to know about ghosts."

Nevaeh put her head in her hands. Peter should've known she'd believe it. If she hadn't been so worried about him alone in the cemetery with an angry spirit, she would've been furious.

Never mind about him.

Her dad was here. Now.

Her fingers dug into her skull.

Her dad was *here*.

She lifted her head. "Can I talk to him?"

"Your daddy?" Marguerite said gently. "You don't need my say-so, Nae-Nae. You go on and say anything you like. He's right here with us."

Nevaeh didn't speak for a long time.

No one was there. She and her grandmother, that was it. Her mom was at work. The rocking chair creaked as her grandmother knitted. Her dad's armchair was empty. The clock ticked on.

What was she supposed to do, talk at the air?

This was ridiculous.

She was ridiculous.

"Dad?"

No one answered, of course.

Jesus Christ.

Nevaeh closed her eyes and pushed on. "Dad, I'm mad at you." She stopped.

That wasn't what she'd meant to say.

"I miss you, I mean." She squeezed her eyes tighter. Her fists curled in her lap. "But I am mad. Why didn't you tell us something was wrong?"

Marguerite's hands stilled on her knitting, but she said nothing.

Nevaeh's voice quivered. "You left us and we weren't ready. We didn't even know anything was wrong."

Her eyes stung worse, but she blinked back her tears. Her heartbeat pulsed in her ears.

Marguerite stirred. "Hush now, honey. Let her say what she needs to say."

Nevaeh blinked faster. She couldn't meet her grandmother's eyes. She looked at the stripy cream-and-beige wallpaper instead. It was older than she was, faded by time. "Did he say something?"

Marguerite picked lint from her dress.

"Granny?"

"He's sorry, babygirl." Marguerite smiled, but her eyes drooped like a hound's. "If he'd known how fast he was gonna go…"

Nevaeh clenched her fists; her nails dug into her palms. The physical discomfort distracted her from the ache inside.

Marguerite's voice was steadier when she spoke again, her eyes brighter. "Nae-Nae, baby, he wants you to go to therapy."

"I know."

Marguerite's eyebrows crept upward. "You do?"

"Yeah. Peter told me." Nevaeh could still cancel. If she wanted to. "I have an appointment in two hours."

If she didn't go, her dad might stay forever.

Not that she could see him. Or feel him. Or whatever.

Marguerite resumed knitting. "Your mama'll be home in half an hour if you need a ride."

The clock ticked her appointment closer. She wouldn't have to find a ride, if she waited for her mom. Her dad wanted this.

She drew her legs up onto the couch, resting her chin on her knees.

She couldn't talk about it. She'd gone to one appointment,

over two months ago, after a gentle recommendation and referral from Yafa. She'd wanted to leave after thirty seconds.

The therapist had invited her to sit. He'd asked what was on her mind.

There was so much on Nevaeh's mind. Always was, always had been, and she'd never in her life been able to talk about it.

This time, with her father's death so fresh, her throat had closed up. She managed to garble something about moving back home, about how much home had changed. She stumbled her way through the next hour and only mentioned in passing, as the appointment ended, her father's death.

"Granny?"

"Mmm?"

Nevaeh hugged her legs tight. "If I go, will you come with me?"

Marguerite leaned forward again and patted her knee. "Of course I will, babygirl. Of course."

Nevaeh didn't cancel.

Half an hour later, her mother came home. An hour after that, they drove to the therapist's office.

The waiting room was generically friendly and nonthreatening, with abstract art prints giving it the illusion of personality. Nevaeh sat on a hard little chair between her mother and grandmother, clinging to Marguerite's hand until her therapist invited her in back, alone.

Nevaeh perched on the edge of the considerably more comfortable chair in his slightly less generic office.

This time, she didn't wait for him to ask what was on her mind.

She clenched her jaw and told him her dad was dead. That she was struggling. That she needed help and didn't know how to ask for it. That she didn't know what kind of help to ask *for*.

When her hour was up, Marguerite was there in the waiting room.

"Your mama's pulling the car around. You all right?"

"I have another appointment in two weeks," Nevaeh said shakily. She felt like a newborn colt, wobbly and weak, working new legs.

Her grandmother hugged her. "I'll come with you, Nae-Nae. Anytime you want."

XL

Anger hung heavy and sour over the cemetery. The sun glared the sky into white. The lawn gasped and shriveled, thirsting for rain no matter how the groundskeeper cared for it. The spirits ripped up flowers, kicked up dust devils, tore down tree branches, pelted the office and cottage with pebbles. The wind howled day and night.

The groundskeeper spent as much time away as he dared. Running errands. Supper with Nevaeh or the al-Masris (or both). Lunch with David at the museum, where Isaiah's love enveloped them until anger was a distant memory.

But he had to find the spirit. So he spent most of his time in the cemetery, alone.

Without Nevaeh there to distract him, he fixated on Midsummer: the one hurtling toward him, and the one he'd been cursed.

He was nineteen years old, and he and Jack were courting in secret. Stealing moments alone whenever they could. On the banks of the Suck, when their mams sent them angling and none of the other boys were around. In the alleyway behind the smithy on market day.

Peter, ever the more anxious of the two, constantly worried they'd be seen.

He liked their stolen moments, to be sure. How Jack pushed him up against the wall of the smithy. How he'd lie back on the riverbank and grab the collar of Peter's shirt, pull him in and kiss him. Peter had never kissed anyone before. He'd worried time and again over his disinterest in courting any of Ballygar's many pretty girls, the way his eyes lingered on the other boys at their work.

Jack made him feel it was all right. Like nothing was wrong with him because he was attracted to other lads instead of lasses.

Jack made him feel attractive himself, which was a feat. He'd always been tall and gawky, thin and angular, too pale, his nose too large and crooked, his hands too big. Jack, in contrast, had beautiful dark curly hair and the loveliest blue eyes and a nose like a French aristocrat and fine fingers like a pianist, though his hands were calloused because he worked in the smithy. When he kissed Peter, it made Peter want things he'd never wanted.

While Peter had hardly dared look at anyone before, Jack had experience with courting, had even tumbled about on occasion with lads as well as lasses. He was as discreet about his occasional couplings as he could be about anything (not very), but all Ballygar knew, in their way, that he was different. His father had beaten him more than once, though perhaps this had nothing to do with it; his father had beaten his mother and the other children, too, before drinking himself to death. A gang a couple years older than them, who liked to harass most everyone in the village, beat him often enough as well. Jack was a pet target of theirs.

He acted like he didn't care. He'd appear on the riverbank with a black eye, a split lip, bruised ribs. But when Peter cried and fussed over him and made him a poultice, he'd give that crooked smile and say, "There now, I've got you tending my wounds."

Like he'd done it on purpose so Peter would touch him.

Peter, however, lived in terror of anyone learning about them. Of people he'd known all his life looking at him differently, of being targeted by such violence as Jack was.

It shamed him: he was a terrible coward. If Jack could take it, surely he could.

But he didn't want to.

Still, the stolen kisses, that crooked smile, Jack's casual attitude as if nothing could ruffle him—everything about Jack made Peter's blood quicken, made him spend every moment they were apart waiting until they were together.

Midsummer Eve was their first and best opportunity for some unbroken solitude. All Ballygar bustled about the town square. Adults quit work early; children begged donations for the bonfire; friends gossiped in the market. People built a bonfire and braided flowers into garlands, hung horseshoes and stopped by the chapel for a blessing and some holy water.

In their alleyway, Jack kissed his jaw and breathed in his ear, "Meet me in the barn. An hour before sunset."

He slipped away to his work, leaving Peter panting against the smithy wall.

That evening, as his mother took his siblings to town to visit with friends before the night's festivities, Peter walked the half mile back to the Shaughnessys' farm alone, with a basket of garlands, horseshoes, holy water, and salt, and Mam's instructions in his ears to protect the barn and house and garden and join them when he was done.

Instead, he dropped the basket outside the barn door. Smashing, unknowingly, the offering Mam had left for the fey creature she swore up and down lived on the property they tenanted.

He thought nothing of it. Thought of nothing but Jack, how much he wanted Jack, as he entered the darkening barn with his heart pounding, palms itching.

"Jack?" he whispered hoarsely. Scared. Elated.

The cow lowed. The sheep bleated sleepily. The barn was sweet with hay.

Jack emerged from a straw pile. Met him in the middle of the barn, ran his fingers through Peter's hair. Kissed him long and slow and deep.

Something dropped low in Peter's stomach.

"I've never," he whispered.

"I know," Jack said, and kissed him again, slower still.

The bonfire was blazing by the time they returned to town, flushed and grinning and inserting themselves in different parts of the crowd so no one would notice they'd come together. Mam touched Peter's cheek, thanked him for putting up the Midsummer protections.

"Sure, you've earned a bit o' fun," she said. "Should've sent Eoin back to help you. I didn't reckon it'd keep you s'long."

He blushed. "S'all right, Mam."

With their neighbors singing and laughing, with Jack grinning across the fire at him and the phantom touch of Jack's lips and fingers tingling all over him, he decided not to worry, for once. He could sneak home early and put up the Midsummer protections before Mam returned with the weens.

Couples danced to whistles and fiddles, pipes and drums. Children tossed firebrands as high as they could and ran screaming when their missiles rained back down. People jumped through the fire for luck: farmers leaping high for tall crops and a good harvest; newlyweds hopping along for fertile marriages and easy pregnancies; merchants vaulting through the flames for luck in new business ventures. Elders taunted the jumpers, divining past wrongdoings and future fortunes in the flickering flames. Young unmarried couples held hands and leaped through together, merely flirting, but if they weren't known to be courting beforehand, they were assumed to be courting afterward.

Jack jumped through the fire alone, landing before Peter with a grin, to the cheers of neighbors who thought he was jumping for fortune. It was almost as good as jumping through the fire together or dancing like the other couples.

As night wore on, Peter worked up the courage to jump through the fire himself. He bit his lip, dimpling at Jack, and leaped through the flames. Their neighbors cheered.

His trouser leg caught fire.

The cheers hushed.

He beat the flames out, his breathing harsh, too loud in the silence. Musicians had frozen midnote, dancers midtwirl. Mam's fingers pressed to her mouth; Jack's brow furrowed. All around were silent, stony faces.

The fire crackled and popped, unaware of the bad omen it had gifted him.

A baby squalled, a child threw a firebrand into the air, and the noise took up again. The musicians started first, then the singers and storytellers. The couples returned to dancing. The elders huddled together to gossip. Jack touched Peter's shoulder, forgetful of the crowd, and asked if he was all right. Mam rambled about him needing new trousers anyhow. Catherine and Eoin had already forgotten their brother's mishap.

No one else jumped through the fire that night.

Peter hurried home alone with a torch, the flames unable to ward off the night. He jumped at every noise, shying from shadows he'd been walking past since he was a ween. Spooked. Trying to convince himself it didn't mean anything, the fire, but feeling deep in his bones as if something were watching him.

Something was.

One of *them folk*. The fey creature Mam left offerings for, angry at the destruction of its Midsummer meal.

It was no higher than his knee, but its eyes glowed like embers and its voice was an ancient tree creaking. He stumbled back, his torch throwing wild shadows. Apologies tumbled from his mouth like stones skittering off a cliff—for destroying the offering, for disturbing it in the night, for everything and nothing at all, anything that might spare him the wrath of this creature.

Too late. The fey thing pronounced a curse upon him: to wander eternally far from home.

His one comfort was that the curse could not come true. He could not wander eternally far from home when he *was* home.

Leave Ballygar? Unthinkable. If he never left, surely the rest of the curse could not come true, either.

It didn't stop him tossing and turning.

Midsummer dawned dark and stormy. Ballygar shied at the unseasonable weather, remembering the incident of the previous night. Mass was said hastily and with extra, fervent prayers muttered as the parishioners left. Farmers grimly sprinkled ashes from the bonfire on their fields and pastures. Children squabbled; babies fussed. A pall hung over the Shaughnessys' household: Peter anxious, Mam worried, Eoin snappish, Catherine tense. They went to bed that night gratefully.

Peter had barely fallen asleep when he jolted awake. Something was snarling in the woods behind the barn.

He sat up, listening. He dressed silently and hastily in the dim, reddish light of the hearth, reaching for his father's old gun.

He'd been worried for the sheep. If the Shaughnessys lost the sheep, they lost everything.

Hair rose on the back of his neck as he followed the sound. Trees twisted out of the darkness, beech and ash, the odd pine, hoary and dark. Branches creaked. The thing's snarling cut through them.

Peter's breath was tight and shaky, goosebumps erupting on his arms, but his hands were steady when he aimed at the snarling beast he couldn't see.

He took the shot. The snarling cut off.

He lowered the gun, exhaled. Broke through the undergrowth.

No wolf or bear or monster greeted him.

Just his own darling Catherine, dead on the ground.

Desiccated leaves on her nightgown, in her hair. Her tiny face pale but unmarked, unbloodied—to his eyes alone. So serene she could've been sleeping, except she wasn't.

Mam and Eoin found him first. Then their nearest neighbors.

Then all of Ballygar. With him holding a gun over her small body, the neighbors turned on him.

He dropped the gun and ran.

He hid in bracken and brush until he reached town, barely ahead of them. Tapped at Jack's window, sweaty and feverish, asked for the O'Neills' horse. Rode the old nag clear to Galway, sent it back alone, and bartered for passage on the first ship leaving port. He'd sailed away with nothing of home but his pa's old watch in his pocket and the ghost of Jack's last kiss on his lips.

He'd never been back.

XLI

It had been two hundred years since that terrible Midsummer. Yet every June, no matter where he was or what he was doing, he grew anxious.

This year, in Harrington—unable to find the ghost he was hunting, memories loosed he'd kept tightly caged for so long—it was worse than ever.

He'd be rereading Isaiah's notes or searching for the headstone he'd somehow missed, and he'd come over cold and shaky. Mouth dry, heart pounding, chest tight, skin prickling. Lightheaded and dizzy, like the world was a rug yanked out from under him.

He'd hunker on the ground, clutching his head in his hands, and count blades of grass, or identify birdcalls, or focus on the damp earth beneath his trousers and the breeze on his skin. But he never quite calmed, because the anger hung thick and dark, inescapable while he was in the cemetery. The warding on his garden wall and cottage offered some relief, but beyond the anger roiled like a storm.

Sometimes, mid-panic, he'd shut his eyes. Mistake.

When he shut his eyes, he saw the fire.

His neighbors staring at him in shock.

The woods. Catherine sprawled on the ground.

The image would loom over him, surround him, crash down on him, until he was terrified to open his eyes, because if he did he might find he was back there, back then, and nothing had changed, and he had two hundred lonely, miserable years ahead of him.

He was cleaning up on the misty Tuesday evening after the funeral when it hit him again.

He clutched at the countertop, gasping. His eyes squeezed shut. The dark forest sprouted into being. The edge of the countertop was smooth and rounded, no countertop but his father's gun. The countertop was a gun, the water gushing from the faucet was leaves in the wind, the snarling he remembered had died away, and now he would find—he would find—

The phone rang.

It cut through his memories, jangling, discordant. His eyes jolted open. He glanced around wildly, gulping down air, the forest receding in the warm light of the cottage kitchen.

The counter was a counter. The water was water. He was in Harrington.

He shut off the faucet. His chest heaved.

He wiped his hands on a kitchen towel, to chase away the phantom feeling of his father's gun, and answered the phone.

"Peter!" David was breathless with excitement. The groundskeeper latched on to his voice. "It's amazing, you have to see it—this room, I found a *room*, it's walled up—we thought it was a fire wall, there's a matching wall at the other end of the attic—but anyway I think it's a bedroom—"

"What're you on about?"

David gushed about the museum attic, used for storage, about hammering through the drywall at one end until he'd found wooden slats, about tearing the slats away until he'd glimpsed a long-forgotten room on the other side. He went on and on, talking in circles, forgetting what he'd already said in his eagerness to say it.

The groundskeeper listened in confusion, his brain clinging

to David's voice, trying to figure out how it related to the wood and the gun and the leaves in the wind.

It didn't. It was here and now; the wood and gun and leaves were two centuries behind him. *He* was here and now, in the warm, bright kitchen of his cottage in Harrington. His heartbeat calmed.

A room. David had found a boarded-up room at the museum.

The groundskeeper pulled himself together. "What were you doing going into the attic on that leg of yours?"

"Oh, I—" David faltered. "Well, er... I thought I..."

His voice trailed into a mumble.

"What was that?"

David cleared his throat. "I said... I thought I heard something. In the attic."

Isaiah, no doubt. The corner of the groundskeeper's mouth turned up despite himself. He hadn't thought to have Isaiah explore the house for clues; his whole focus on Isaiah had been the research Isaiah had done in life.

"What was it?"

"I don't know." David sounded embarrassed. "Nothing. My imagination."

He would say that. The groundskeeper almost asked, *A ghost, p'rhaps?* But his impulse to needle David came from a need to make himself feel better after his panic attack. His voice was hoarse, his breathing ragged like he'd been sprinting. He slumped against the wall, running a hand over his face.

"Never mind. When can I see it?"

"As soon as you want. Tomorrow. If you promise to stay for lunch." A pause. David's excitement reined itself in. "Are you all right?"

The groundskeeper clutched the phone tight. Resisted the urge to close his eyes again.

"Course," he said quietly. "I'm fine. Peachy, even."

"Are you sure? You sound..."

The groundskeeper opened his mouth, his whole history caught in his throat. He'd never told anyone a word of it. He'd never had anyone to tell. No one would believe it.

He'd never wanted to tell anyone anyway. He didn't like so much as thinking about it; he couldn't possibly speak about it.

"Peter? Are you sure you're all right?"

A long breath whistled through his nose. "No."

Another pause. "Do you want to talk about it?"

The groundskeeper gazed at the pot of bulbs in their chair.

"No," he whispered.

They were silent. He might've felt awkward, sitting on the phone in silence. Instead, it comforted him.

"Do you want to come over?" David asked.

XLII

Droplets beaded on the groundskeeper's skin as he walked to David's house. Damp seeped into his clothes. He could've taken the truck, but he needed to move, to shake off his anxiety. The houses huddled together, black and silent.

David's porch light was on. The mist diffused the golden rays of light; the house looked brighter, warmer, than the rest of the street.

The groundskeeper scratched a minuscule Marian symbol beneath the doorknob. With Midsummer approaching, he was taking no chances; he'd scratched one into the al-Masris' door after leaving supper last night.

The door opened. David was in a tartan dressing gown, his hair damp. Rain pattered on the roof.

"Do you want to come in?" David smiled at him. "Or did you want more time to enjoy the scenery?"

The groundskeeper blushed; he was enjoying the scenery now. His eyes traced the path of a droplet down David's neck, trailing from his hair into his collar. It glistened in the golden light.

David laughed, a little awkwardly. "Sorry. I thought I'd have more time to shower before you got here. I was—well, trust me when I say, if you'd seen what I looked like coming out of that attic, you would've taken one look at me and run the other way. It was awfully dusty."

"S'all right," the groundskeeper said, without being quite sure what was all right. A sliver of David's chest was visible where the gown closed.

"Anyway, come on in. I thought we could watch a movie. They're playing *My Fair Lady* on TCM tonight."

The groundskeeper lingered in the entryway. A Christmas cactus with stems drooping halfway to the hardwood floor sat on a stool in the corner. It stretched toward him curiously.

David paused ahead of him. "Are you coming?"

The groundskeeper flushed. The house was warm and dim, softly lit with lamps and sconces, and David was standing there in his dressing gown with his hair damp and the odd droplet trickling down his neck, and the groundskeeper wasn't entirely sure he should have come, but he didn't want to leave, either.

He ran a finger along the cactus's leaves, more comfortable for the green thing there with him. "Admiring your Christmas cactus, is all."

David's mouth twitched. "Admire it while you can. I have the most terrific black thumb. Isaiah's Aunt Margaret left it to him when she died, and I'm terrified of killing it off."

"You should be. Herbicide is a serious business. The legal fees and paperwork for one dead sprout is a mile long."

"I'm serious!" David said, but he was grinning. "Well, this way."

The groundskeeper waited until he'd disappeared into the living room.

"I know it ain't season," he murmured to the cactus, "but you might put out a bloom or two for him. You do that, I'll see he moves you somewhere with better light, aye?"

The cactus patted his arm with a toothed leaf. The groundskeeper stuffed his hands in his pockets and ventured farther back.

David poked his head out of the living room. "This way!"

It was comfortably crammed with a couch and side table. A television was mounted on the wall, already on, with the host of

Turner Classic Movies giving background on the filming of *My Fair Lady*. Photographs hung on either side, but the glare of the television in their glass frames made them impossible to distinguish. A rug with a geometric pattern in turquoise and white hid the floorboards.

David made popcorn. They sat on the couch, leaving an empty spot between them as if saving a seat for one of Harrington's ghosts. The groundskeeper scrunched his cap in his lap. David tapped his fingers on the arm of the couch in time to the musical numbers. The groundskeeper spent more time watching him than the film.

Outside, a car took a corner too fast, its tires screeching like an unseen beast. The groundskeeper's skin crawled.

The living room closed in on him. His knee bounced. His breath burst from him. His fingers shook.

He crushed his cap and focused on his breathing. The film. The rug's pattern.

Nothing helped. The glare of the television in the picture frames blazed like fire—

"Peter?" David scooched closer, touched his clenched fists. "Are you all right?"

The groundskeeper shook his head.

David bit his lip. "Do you need to be left alone?"

A violent shake of his head. It had been worse earlier, alone.

"Then I'll stay right here."

The groundskeeper exhaled shakily. David put an arm around him.

Peter leaned into him. David held him tight, humming along with the reprise of "On the Street Where You Live."

Peter's breathing steadied. He released his cap, unclenched his hands, flexed his aching fingers. He curled against David with a weary sigh. David's hair had dried and stuck out at odd angles.

The movie ended. The host appeared to announce the next

picture, *An American in Paris*. Peter sat up and dragged a hand over his face.

"Better now?" David asked.

"Aye." Peter hesitated. "Thanks."

"Anytime."

David ran a hand through his hair. Peter itched to do the same. To know what it felt like.

Instead of clenching his fingers into fists, keeping that itch buried, he smoothed a lock of hair into place behind David's ear.

His hair was thick and soft. Peter cradled the back of his head with a hand.

David angled toward him. His hand found Peter's face; his thumb brushed across his cheek. He'd never changed after making popcorn, and that sliver of chest was still visible at the closure of his dressing gown. Peter wanted to touch it so badly he ached, but he couldn't bring himself to do it. He touched David's neck instead, tentatively.

David exhaled sharply, pulled Peter so close he felt David's breath on his skin. The whisper of David's mouth on his.

"Peter," David breathed against his lips.

A shiver ran through him. He wanted. He *wanted*.

He jerked away as if scalded. Grabbed his cap, leaped to his feet.

"I have to go."

David's fingers clutched at air. "What?"

The groundskeeper turned away from the hurt confusion on David's face.

"I have to go."

He strode toward the door. The Christmas cactus fluttered with questions.

"Peter—"

He wrenched the door open. David grabbed his wrist.

"Peter, wait. Can't we—"

"I have to go," the groundskeeper said, more forcefully. "Unhand me."

David let go but blocked the door. The groundskeeper wheeled in the entryway like a spooked horse.

"You can't leave like this, you can't just—" David dragged his hands through his hair, looking like he wanted to tear it out. "I don't understand you. I was fine being your friend, I meant it when I said I value your friendship, I *do*, and then you go and— one minute you're practically kissing me, and the next—"

The groundskeeper pulled his cap low over his eyes.

"I have to go."

David's eyes flickered over him. He stood aside.

The groundskeeper fled into the drizzly night.

The door slammed shut behind him.

XLIII

Someone knocked on the groundskeeper's door not long after he got home. He rubbed his eyes, staggering up from the kitchen table. It was barely nine but felt later. The cottage was dim, hushed, the light faintly blue. The greenlings whispered amongst themselves in a subdued manner. The rain had subsided, but the smell of wet grass and damp earth persisted.

Yafa was on his doorstep with the children, her face strained. The groundskeeper stood aside to let her in, peering into the cemetery. Water dripped from the cottage's eaves. The spirits wavered redly.

"You shouldn't've come—" he said, but she cut him off.

"I'm sorry, I know it's late—can you watch the children for me?" Her voice wobbled. The children staggered inside. "I have to go to the hospital, my father's nurse called…"

She squeezed her eyes shut. The groundskeeper's heart clenched. The plants murmured comfortingly.

"Khalid's not back until Thursday, and Mrs. Holloway's gone to Florida, her granddaughter's having a baby, and Maryam's meeting me at the hospital. They're not sure—" She faltered. "They're not sure he'll make it through the night."

Sayid and Samira huddled on the floral-print love seat.

"Usually I'd leave them home, but today's been—"

Yafa's eyes slid toward her daughter. Samira scuffed the floor.

She caught the groundskeeper's eye, then looked away. Her eyes were red, even in the dim light. He squeezed her shoulder briefly.

"You go," he said to Yafa. "I'll watch 'em."

"I don't know how late I'll be."

"Don't fret about that. They're fine here."

Yafa exhaled harshly. "Thank you."

She pressed kisses to her children's foreheads. "Bed by eleven. I'll call when I'm on my way back. Be good for Peter."

"Yes, Mama," Sayid mumbled.

Samira hugged her mother tight but said nothing. Yafa pulled away and was gone.

The groundskeeper frowned faintly. "Wasn't that gate locked?"

He'd been in a state when he'd returned, but he was sure he'd locked up.

Sayid blushed. "Mama asked Samira to unlock it so we could get in. She meant to call, but she couldn't find your number."

He fiddled with the Saint-John's-wort around his neck. The groundskeeper's heart swelled with affection. Sayid had worn the circlet religiously since that first night. It had grown thick with oblong greenery and bright yellow flowers.

"You hungry?" the groundskeeper asked.

The children picked at their food. Dark crescents ringed Samira's eyes like she hadn't been sleeping. She sat closer to her brother than she normally would have, shrinking against him on the love seat after supper. Sayid looked more rested but more anxious, hands tangled in the Saint-John's-wort. He whispered to it, and it whispered back.

The groundskeeper's eyebrows shot up. He'd have to talk to the boy about that; he hadn't met anyone with his knack for plants in decades. When this ghost hunt was over—

He caught himself. When this hunt was over, he was leaving. That was the whole point.

Sayid crashed around ten, sprawled across the bed with his

mouth hanging open. He started to snore. Samira wrinkled her nose.

The groundskeeper chuckled, repositioning Sayid so there'd be room for Samira. He pulled the Saint-John's-wort over Sayid's head and laid it on the crate beside the bed. It stretched toward the boy's pillow, anxious at the separation. The groundskeeper stroked its leaves.

Samira clambered into bed not long afterward, curling up tight. The groundskeeper turned out the lights and sat on the love seat with Sayid's phone. Moonlight slid through the room as the clouds outside dissipated, turning the floorboards white.

The groundskeeper nodded off, exhausted from June's anxiety and the day's multiple panic attacks. The love seat was cushy; the greenlings smelled of soil and flowers. The children's soft breathing was more of a comfort than he cared to admit.

At midnight, a creaking floorboard jerked him awake.

He blinked. The moonlight had traveled farther into the room. The greenlings grumbled sleepily. Sayid was no longer snoring, his breathing deep and even.

Samira had slunk out of bed to retrieve her sneakers.

The groundskeeper had expected it. Samira might have been quiet, but she'd had her paper clips on her when her mother asked her to unlock the cemetery gate. And the shadows crescenting her eyes suggested her nocturnal wanderings hadn't ceased.

She picked up her sneakers, didn't put them on. Turned the doorknob slowly, pausing when it squeaked. She cracked the door enough for a skinny eight-year-old to slip through.

"Going somewhere?"

She flinched, turning to face him. "I thought you were asleep."

"Nearly." He stretched and stood. "Fancied a moonlight stroll, did you?"

"I wasn't going anywhere."

"Sure, I reckon that's why you grabbed your shoes and were halfway out the door."

She said nothing.

"Sleepwalking, maybe. There's no accounting for yourself when you sleepwalk, so I hear tell. Well, let's go."

Her brow furrowed. "Go?"

"I could tell you to get back to bed, but I figure you'll sneak out again the moment I nod off. We might as well take a turn about the garden first. I could stand to stretch my legs."

Her frown deepened.

"If you don't mind the company," he added, though he had no intention of letting her wander off alone.

"Okay."

He scrawled a note to Sayid, in case the boy woke up and found them gone. Samira insisted on adding her own note—in code, of course.

Wispy remains of clouds drifted past the quarter moon in shreds. The stars shone brilliantly where they broke through. Fireflies blinked along the knoll, brighter but fewer at the edge of the woods. The cemetery shimmered with spirits. The garden was cool and clear, but the knoll was faintly red with anger, and the woods were a dark, bloody crimson.

The groundskeeper glanced at Samira's wrist. "Going without your iron, I see."

"It's in my pocket."

He relaxed but led her around back instead of out the garden gate. The moon glinted on the chicken coop's roof. The pullets clucked softly in their sleep; he'd brought them back outside once Adeline was sufficiently calmed. "Do you better on your wrist."

"They don't like it."

He looked at her. "The ghosts, I'm guessing you mean."

"You see them, too?"

"Everywhere I go."

Her mouth twisted. She pointed at the hydrangeas, where

Adeline was nosing through the flowers. She'd taken a liking to the hydrangeas. "Do you see that one?"

"Sure, Adeline likes daffodils."

"Why's she in your garden?"

Samira seemed unaware of the anger hanging over the cottage like a cloud. He couldn't make heads or tails of it. The anger weighed on him every time he left his garden, yet she didn't seem to notice it. He might've asked whether she felt it, too, but he didn't want to scare her.

"She's having a tough time of things, Addy is."

Adeline drifted from the hydrangeas, curious. Samira's gaze followed her.

"Huh." Samira's mouth curled into a tired smile. The spirit nosed at her. "I thought grown-ups couldn't see ghosts. Baba and Mr. David never notice Mr. Isaiah. Have you seen him?"

"Aye, we're well acquainted." The groundskeeper held his mind in place on Isaiah and his notes so it wouldn't wander off to David and his living room and his dressing gown and his breath hot against the groundskeeper's lips. "Most grown folk can't see 'em."

"How come you can?"

He faltered. "Because of the curse."

Samira's brow furrowed. She kicked at the dirt as they walked through the back garden and the front garden and back again. Adeline followed them. Plants rustled sleepily.

"There's no such thing as curses."

"There's no such thing as ghosts, neither, your mam and pa would probably say."

"You don't *look* cursed."

He huffed a laugh. "What would someone been cursed look like, you reckon?"

Samira rolled her eyes. "Don't you watch movies? If you were cursed, you'd be a beast. Or a frog. Or an ogre. Or you'd be asleep in a castle surrounded by thorns or something."

"I see," the groundskeeper said seriously. "And how would I go about breaking such a curse?"

Samira trailed her fingers along the coop.

"I'm pretty sure you'd have to get Mr. David to kiss you."

He choked on air. Samira pounded his back with a tiny fist. The pullets awoke, peeping at the disturbance.

"Why," he gasped, "would I need to do that?"

Samira shrugged.

"True love's kiss breaks the spell. That's what the movies say. He definitely likes you. He talks about you all the time." She fussed with her ponytail. "I know what that means. Sayid never shuts up about Chloe, either."

The groundskeeper sucked in his cheeks. "Well, I am cursed. And I don't reckon true love's kiss would do the trick."

"Have you *tried* it?"

He blushed. He'd kissed Jack plenty, but clearly that hadn't done it—even if he'd considered this a possibility at the time, which he most certainly had not. "No."

"Then you don't know. It could work. But you don't look cursed."

He didn't respond. The conversation had gotten out of hand.

They walked circles about the garden. Adeline drifted alongside them. Butterfly bush and bleeding hearts shone white in the moonlight.

Samira slipped her hand into his. He held it like he was afraid of breaking her.

Distant fireflies blinked out. The moon slipped below the horizon. The cemetery glimmered dark and red, but the garden was clear and silvery and light, sweet with flowers.

Samira shivered. Peter slipped an arm around her.

"You ready for bed yet, missy?"

She yawned so hard she stumbled. He carried her into the cottage, less anxious than he'd been all week with her arms over his shoulders and her face snuggled into his neck. He tucked her in beside Sayid, chuckling to himself at the way her brother's face was buried in his pillow.

Such a wave of affection welled up in him that he wanted to cry.

He loved them.

He loved these children. As if they were his own.

He sat on the love seat and buried his face in his hands.

At three in the morning, Sayid's phone vibrated. Peter jolted upright. He'd been nodding off again but had never quite fallen asleep, his mind too full. He fumbled with the phone.

Yafa sounded exhausted. "I'm leaving the hospital."

"How's your pa?"

She let out a breath. "Alive. Stable, for now. He—he knew us. Maryam and me. He remembered us. For a minute. He knew it was us."

A sob escaped her.

"Sorry," she whispered.

"S'all right." He pressed the phone closer to his ear. "S'all right, lass."

She cried into the phone. He wished she were here, so he could offer her a handkerchief.

Her tears abated. She sniffled.

"Sorry," she repeated. "He…he's hardly known me in months. Or Maryam. Or Khalid. Or the children. And tonight, he looked right at me, and he said my name and called me amirati like he used to, and he asked why I was crying, and I—"

She sighed shakily.

"I was so happy," she whispered. "But it was terrible, too."

"Sure," Peter said softly. "I know how that is."

"Thanks for watching the children tonight. I'm sorry it's so late, I didn't think—"

"There's no need for that."

"Sorry." She laughed wetly. "I don't mean to keep saying

sorry. I mean...thank you. It was very kind of you. Like you were my own ammo. My uncle, I mean."

His skin prickled, but she lowered her voice and continued before he could say anything.

"They think of you like a grandfather. The children. I was nearly out of my mind trying to think who could watch them tonight, and they asked to stay with you. You're really part of the—"

His heart twisted. "You don't have to say it."

He rubbed the back of his neck. Samira rolled over in bed, snuggling against her brother with a sigh.

"They're like my own wee ones."

They were silent. His eyes stung.

"I'm on my way," Yafa said. "Should be... I don't know... half an hour or so."

"You head on home. They can stay. I'll bring 'em home in the morning."

"I can't ask you to do that."

"Don't need to."

She laughed again, less wetly.

"You all right to drive? Don't want you falling asleep at the wheel."

"I'm fine," Yafa said automatically. "I've been up this long. It won't kill me to be up a little longer."

"Hmm."

She chuckled. "You're sure you don't mind them staying?"

"Certain. You go on home, get some rest. And call me when you get there, all right?"

He heard her smile through the phone. "Okay, ammo."

XLIV

He had to get out of here.

It beat a refrain in his head, over and over. He had to get out of here. He had to get out of here. While he'd been worrying over how much he liked David, bothering about how much time he'd spent with Nevaeh, the children had slipped in and stolen his heart.

He had to prune Harrington from his heart like a rotting stem. He had to get out of here.

He had to leave. Ghost or no ghost. They'd be fine.

He paused in the midst of throwing things into his steamer trunk, remembering Nevaeh crying into his chest in a field of furrowed dirt.

He dumped an armful of books in the trunk. He couldn't stay. Not this time. It was him or them.

He caged the fears he might've had about what would happen to them if the ghost, wherever it was, should get loose. He tore back and forth, collecting his belongings: flannel shirts shoved deep inside the trunk, dressing gown ripped off his bedpost, coffee mug yanked from its cabinet and stuffed with old socks. He'd never left a place in broad daylight, but he couldn't wait another minute. He'd dropped the children off late in the morning, after calling their mother to make sure she was sufficiently awake to receive them. She'd made him stay for lunch.

Samira had given him several more drawings. Sayid had shown him a sprig of Saint-John's-wort he'd stuck in a pot and talked into sprouting.

It had been wonderful, and terrible, and the groundskeeper had driven home too fast and started throwing things into his trunk.

The phone rang. He ignored it.

The phone rang repeatedly. He ignored it repeatedly.

Distressed by his frantic packing, the greenlings fussed at the noise. He ignored them, too.

The phone rang again and again. He launched to his feet, lurched into the kitchen, and, with a snarl, ripped the phone from its hook. It dangled against the wall. He kept packing.

Ten minutes later, someone pounded at the front door, or rather its lintel, because he'd never closed it when he'd returned.

Nevaeh peered inside. "Okay, you *are* here."

"Where else should I be?"

"I don't know. Uncle Dave said he's been trying to call and can't get through. I was worried."

"Shouldn't've come. I told you to stay away."

She frowned. He'd stripped the room of everything but plants. "What's going on?"

He closed the trunk. "Nothing."

"Why is your stuff packed up?"

He creaked to his feet and smoothed the bedclothes.

Nevaeh sighed. "Okay, whatever. Call Uncle Dave. He said he found O.S."

Vague curiosity pricked at the groundskeeper, but he buried it. He didn't care about O.S. or anyone else.

He finished fussing with the bedspread. Nevaeh followed him into the kitchen.

"You're going to call, right? You said O.S. might be the ghost."

He wished he hadn't told her about that. About any of it.

She stopped at the sight of the phone dangling from its cord. "Is this why his calls aren't getting through?"

He cleaned up the breakfast dishes. He hadn't planned on cleaning up, but he wasn't about to leave with her glowering at him. He didn't like giving anyone the chance to stop him going.

Samira's drawings hung on the icebox. He hadn't bothered packing them.

Nevaeh grabbed the phone. "You're leaving, aren't you?"

He scraped bits of egg off a plate.

Nevaeh pointed the phone at him. "You can't leave. There's a ghost. You said so."

He paused, gazing at the suds on his hands. His chest prickled, but he breathed through his nose and focused on the suds and the plate and his hands and nothing else.

He resumed washing dishes.

"Is there or is there not an angry ghost in this cemetery?"

"There is. Somewhere."

Nevaeh hugged the phone to her chest. "Then you can't leave. You can't. All the shit that's been happening? The funeral? How are we supposed to stop it if you leave?"

"You'll be fine."

"Yeah, at home. Anywhere you've warded. What about everywhere else? Everyone else? What about my mom? My granny? My friends?"

"Your granny knows her stuff."

"You said it was dangerous." Her voice grew louder, her eyes scared, and he kept his gaze pointed firmly away because if he looked he'd only want to comfort her. "You won't even let me come to work. But I'm supposed to believe it'll be fine because my granny 'knows her stuff'?"

He scrubbed a bowl that was already clean.

"You have to help us." Nevaeh's voice shook. "Please. You can't leave."

"You're leaving." His fingers were getting pruny. "Ain't that been your plan from the start? Never even finished unpacking."

Nevaeh flushed, her hands curling into fists. "Maybe I've changed my mind. You have to stay. You *have* to."

The bowl splashed into the sink. He leaned on the counter, wiping sudsy water from his face.

"I can't."

Her nostrils flared. She slammed the phone into the receiver and dialed on her cell instead. "Uncle Dave? Hi—yeah, I've got him here."

She held out her phone, but the groundskeeper shut off the water and sat without taking it. She sighed loudly, said, "Hold on," put the phone on speaker, slammed it onto the table, and stalked from the room.

"Peter?"

The speaker crackled. David's voice shivered through him. The groundskeeper held his head in his hands.

"Peter, you have to get over here." David was breathless with excitement, like whatever he'd found had driven the previous night from his head. "Mari's been upstairs all morning with Noah Rosten's sister's kid—they're in construction, agreed to come demolish that wall for me. They got into that room I found—there's this little box, you should see it, it's amazing. I was going to wait to open it until you got here, but..." He faltered. "You weren't answering your phone, and I thought you might not..."

The groundskeeper laid his head on the table. After everything, David's first inclination had been to share the discovery with him.

David cleared his throat. "Anyway, sorry, rambling again. The point is, I got overexcited and couldn't wait, so Mari opened it, and, Peter, there's a bill of sale in there for the general store—the gap in the records, it was him, O.S. Or I guess it's really E.S.? There are a couple different spellings on these documents, pretty

typical at the time, officials weren't terribly concerned about—
I'm rambling again. The *point* is, he bought it, must've lost it to
the bank, and that's why he moved into the boarding house."

He sucked in a breath.

"Sorry, I just—Isaiah spent years, *years*, trying to discover this
man's identity, and this box, there's so much in here. I mean, not
a *lot*, it's a small box, but, my god, compared to what we knew
about him before—"

The groundskeeper dragged his fingers through his hair.
David sounded so excited, and the groundskeeper loved him
for it. He didn't want to love him for it; he wanted to leave.

Preferably before David could say something to convince
him to stay.

"Anyway, his name," David said. "Kind of neat, I thought,
he was a Shaughnessy, too."

The groundskeeper bolted upright.

"Owen," David continued. "*O-w-e-n* on the bill of sale where
it's printed, but he signed *E-o-i-n*, so I guess that's the right spell-
ing. That would still be pronounced the same way, right? Eoin
Shaughnessy?"

The kitchen tilted.

"Yes," the groundskeeper whispered.

"Eoin, okay, thank you. Eoin Shaughnessy. *Eoin Shaughnessy.*
Oh, my god, I can't believe I know his name, after all this
time—do you want to come by? There's so much to see—the
doctor's awfully mad I went upstairs on my crutches yesterday,
but Mari and Ty can show you—"

"I'll be right there."

But when David hung up, the groundskeeper clutched his
head in his hands, chest heaving. The room spun. The sunlight
thinned away to nothing, the walls dark and close and suffocating.

He was trapped in that night. Catherine dead on the ground.
Ash and beech looming, twisted and black. Mam staring, too

shocked and confused to hurt yet, clinging to Eoin like she'd never let go. Eoin, so much like a stockier, darker-haired version of his older brother. Eoin, who'd been a mere boy of fourteen when their lives were destroyed.

When Jack found him in that pub in Melbourne in 1847, Peter's first questions had been after his family. Mam had died sick and starved in the Great Hunger. And Eoin—after they'd lost the farm, Eoin had emigrated to the States, hoping to bring Mam over later. It had never happened. Last Jack knew, Eoin had been heading West to find work when Mam died.

"Are you okay?"

His head snapped up. Nevaeh frowned at him from the kitchen doorway, arms folded, but the sight of her grounded him in the present. His hands shook.

"I need to get to the museum," he croaked. "Can you take me?"

He was wobbly, ready to melt. He didn't feel equal either to walking or driving.

She stuck her phone in her back pocket. "I guess. If you need me to. What—?"

"The ghost."

She hugged herself and lowered her voice, forgetting to frown. "Uncle Dave found him? The ghost? Who is he?"

"My brother," the groundskeeper said.

XLV

The sun blazed, bleaching the colors from the Victorians on Washington. The apartment building glared in its parking lot. The dog park was empty, its grass parched. The church's windows glinted like eyes.

His hands squeezed together, shaking. Nevaeh's brow creased, but she wasn't as skeptical as she might've been. She peppered him with questions as they drove to the museum.

"I thought you were looking for a nineteenth-century ghost."

"I was. He is."

"O-*kay*, but if he's your brother—"

"I'm older'n I look."

She opened her mouth, closed it again. He leaned his forehead against the window. The glass was cool.

"Yeah, that doesn't clear things up."

His laugh was half a sob. "Don't make me explain. Not now. Please, lass. Wouldn't believe me anyway."

She drummed her fingers on the steering wheel. Turned the radio on, flipped through several stations, turned it off again.

"You know," she said, "if you'd told me about ghosts two months ago, I probably would've thought—I don't know what I would've thought. I definitely wouldn't have been all, *Yeah, okay, ghosts, that's totally a thing that exists*."

Neither of them said anything more. They pulled into the museum, gravel crunching under their tires.

They didn't get out.

"Should I drop you here, or—?"

"Come with me." A strangled whisper. "Please."

She put the truck in Park. He unclasped his seat belt with trembling fingers, then leaped from the truck, heart pounding.

David was working on the porch again, in the same wicker chair, at the same water-stained table, surrounded by the same mess of papers and mugs and books. He looked up with an uncertain smile, but it faded at the groundskeeper's expression.

"Are you all right?"

"Fine and dandy," the groundskeeper said, without knowing what he'd been asked.

David glanced at Nevaeh. She shook her head. He bit his lip and grabbed his crutches.

"Through here. Upstairs."

The groundskeeper bounded up the main stairs.

David gazed after him. "Careful."

Nevaeh patted his arm and followed.

The steps twisting from the second floor up to the attic were narrower, dimmer, and less regular than the main stairs, but the groundskeeper took them two at a time. In the attic, shelving, boxes, moldy books, filing cabinets, and holiday decor crowded together. Someone had tarped things up and shoved them aside to clear a path. Splintery gray slats lay piled by the wall. One was painted with a sigil—useless now, cracked in half by the demolition. A narrow doorway was outlined jaggedly in the drywall.

Marisol stood in the corner, talking to a person a little older than she was. Their T-shirt, jeans, and safety glasses were coated in a fine film. Dust clung to their eyebrows.

"Oh, hey, you must be Peter Shaughnessy." They extended a calloused hand. "Ty Greenburg. Davey said you were coming to have a look. Anyway—"

They grabbed a portable floodlight, clicked it on, and led him into the room.

It was an attic bedroom, windowless and cramped. Water dripped through a crack in the ceiling as it had, unknown, for months. A water ring stained the floor.

A rusty bed frame huddled in the corner. Beside it, a chair rotted on its side. A bureau with a cracked mirror squatted against the opposite wall. The lumpy stub of a candle that had melted in the attic heat and resolidified countless times stuck to the top of the bureau.

Ty angled the floodlight at the ceiling. It washed the room in pale, silvery light. Nevaeh had followed, but she hung back, worrying her lower lip with her teeth.

"It's not wired for electricity in here." Ty stuck their thumbs through their belt loops. "Davey figures it was boarded up before the Kopczyks had electric lights installed, around the turn of the century, he said, or maybe earlier, but we're stumped as to why. Best guess right now is contagion. I had a poke around after getting that wall down, and you can see everything pretty well with this flood. I have a couple flashlights, too, if you want one."

The groundskeeper didn't answer. The dim gray room had sucked the breath from his lungs. He gazed into it, chest heaving, fists clenching and unclenching.

Ty scratched their hairline with a thumb. "You okay?"

"Fine," the groundskeeper whispered.

Ty glanced at Nevaeh. She nodded, still worrying her lip.

"Well, okay." Ty jerked a thumb toward the outer room. "Give a yell if you need anything."

They waited, but the groundskeeper said nothing. He hadn't heard. Hadn't noticed Nevaeh following him, though he'd asked her to come.

Dust motes swirled. A ray of sunlight sliced whitely through the crack in the shingles, illuminating an inch of floorboard.

He moved into the room as if in a trance. Though he'd never been in this room, it felt familiar. Full of tragedy beneath Isaiah's

love for this building, painted with rage and despair that made
him heartsick for his brother's unknown life, but familiar, too.

Like Harrington. Like home.

A hoarse chuckle escaped him. *E.S.* was carved into the wall
beside the bed, thinner and shakier but just as Eoin had carved
it over his bed back in Ballygar. Peter ran his fingers over the
letters, eyes stinging.

He sat on the bed with his hands clenched in his lap. A cavity gaped in the floor; the box had been found beneath a loose
floorboard beside the bed.

He gulped down air, preparing himself.

He closed his eyes.

At first, he felt Isaiah's love for this place. Isaiah had never
been in this room in life, but his love for the boarding house
permeated this room as it did every other. It covered over the
room's memories like wallpaper, memories Peter knew were
there. Traces of them lingered under Isaiah's sunburst of love.

He let himself bask in that love briefly, unwilling to feel what
lay beneath it. But whatever he could glean of his brother's life
from this room, he had to know.

He pushed deeper.

The same room. The floorboards gleaming in candlelight,
the ceiling whole and white. A knitted blanket on the bed—a
blanket Peter recognized because his mother had made it.

His lungs seized, but he kept pushing, digging for more memories.

He broke through.

As they had at the general store, they slammed into him.

A woman's voice at the door, soft and musical; she'd made
supper if Eoin wanted it. Her footsteps on the stairs when he
failed, again, to respond.

A roll of bills in that cavity in the floor, growing thinner and
thinner. Fingers scrabbling at the cavity, coming away empty
because the roll had thinned away to nothing. The money gone.

A man pounding on the door, demanding to speak to him

about his rent. Low-pitched voices arguing through the wall, two floors below, out in the garden, everywhere, always arguing about him. John Hodinka wanted to evict him—he was so unpleasant, wasn't paying his rent—but Anne Hodinka insisted it was their Christian duty to help him whether they liked him or not, and think how he must be hurting, poor man, his wife and child dead little more than a year ago...

Peter gasped for air, but the memories kept coming. Eoin's emotions consumed him like they were his own. Shame because he no longer had any way to pay his rent, because Anne was so unerringly kind no matter how cantankerous he got. Hatred for her pity, for her talk of his family, like she had any idea what he was feeling. The desolation of the attic as the other tenants avoided him, and John did, too; Anne wouldn't let him hassle Eoin anymore.

A fog of pain and sickness. A child seated in the chair by the bed, telling him stories as she bent over her needlework, though John had told her to stay away from the man in the attic.

Constant sleep. A rag doll tucked into his arms. Hers, Nina Hodinka's. She'd snuck it to him when her father wasn't looking, because she always slept with it when she took sick.

The wall opposite the bed, at eye level if you were lying down, spiderwebbed with cracks. Eoin had stopped getting up; it was all he saw anymore.

"Peter." Hands gripped his shoulders. "Peter. Hey."

Peter shot upright. The hands jerked away.

He was sitting on the floor with that slice of sunlight stabbing into his eyes. He pulled back, blinking. His cheeks were wet.

Nevaeh knelt before him, her hands on her thighs. Behind her, Ty scuffed the floor. The stairs creaked with footsteps and crutches, and David asked frantically what had happened, and Marisol said she didn't know.

Nevaeh looked shaken, but she touched Peter's shoulder. "Are you okay?"

His face puckered. He dropped his head to his knees and

clutched his skull like he could shield himself from the memories he'd taken in. The bed frame pressed into his back.

Nevaeh squeezed in beside him and put her arm around his shoulder. He wept.

He barely noticed when David and Marisol entered, or when Marisol and Ty, uncomfortable with the situation, went downstairs for lunch. He didn't hear David ask, "Is he all right?" or Nevaeh say, "I think he had a panic attack," or David say, "Another one?"

He leaned into Nevaeh, wiping his eyes. She squeezed him, wrapped her arms around her legs, and rested her chin on her knees.

David sat on the bed, propping his crutches against the wall. "Are you all right?"

If only they'd stop asking. He was very much not all right, but he couldn't bring himself to say so.

He picked at his jeans. The inch of sunlight wavered on the floorboards. "Shouldn't've come upstairs. Your leg'll heal faster the less you're on it."

David sighed.

"Yes, yes. My doctor already gave me an eloquent lecture on the subject, so you'll pardon me if I prefer not to hear another." He ran a hand through his hair. "Mari came running to say you'd collapsed. I was worried."

He patted the bed. The ticking coughed dust.

"Awfully dusty up here, isn't it?" A pause. "That box is in my office."

Nevaeh unfolded herself and stretched. "I'll get it. You should rest your leg before you tackle the stairs again."

David grimaced. "It's on my desk. Little wooden box."

Peter rested his cheek on his knees as she left, wrapped his arms around his legs the way she'd been sitting. David's brow creased. The room was grayer than ever after the onslaught of memories.

"Shouldn't've worried about me," Peter whispered.

The crease in David's brow deepened, but he said nothing.

Peter joined him shakily on the bed, gripping its edges. A splinter dug into his thumb. "I'm sorry. You been nothing but kind to me since the moment I laid eyes on you, and I—"

He swallowed. The memories weighed on him, an anchor in his stomach.

"Even now," he croaked. "I hurt you running off like that last night—nay, I know I did," he said, as David opened his mouth. "I know I did. And you still called today to tell me what you found. You still come running when you heard I was poorly."

He dragged a hand over his face.

"I wish you wouldn't." His voice was bitter. "I don't deserve it."

David's fingers twitched, but he folded his hands in his lap. "Peter—"

"Anyway, I'm sorry." Peter expelled a long breath. "That's all I wanted to say."

David touched Peter's knee briefly, lightly, like he couldn't help it, and withdrew.

"It did sting," he admitted. "But there's— It's clear you're going through something. I mean," he said, attempting to sound playful, "almost kissing me probably isn't the best way to deal with it, whatever it is—"

Peter blushed. "I didn't—"

"I was there," David said, smiling faintly, "and you did so. I just mean…it's okay. But don't do it again unless you mean it."

Peter started to say, *I did mean it*, but caught himself. "Right."

They listened to Nevaeh's footsteps on the stairs. David glanced at him, like he wanted to ask, again, whether he was all right, but said nothing.

Nevaeh returned with the box in hand. "It was *not* on your desk. It was on your bookshelf."

"Right," David said. "Sorry, I'd forgotten I moved it."

"Forgotten." Nevaeh arched an eyebrow at them. "Sure."

David took the box, opened it, and offered it to Peter.

It was three inches wide and seven inches long, two inches

deep, with a slide-off lid like that of a cigar box. It had once been a shiny mahogany but was now faded, with a dark stain on one corner. Brittle papers poked out of it.

Peter's chest tightened. The box trembled in his hands. Nevaeh sat beside him, peering over his shoulder.

First, three wedding rings. Two Peter recognized, together on a chain. Pa's and Mam's, clinking together as he removed them. The third was smaller, polished lovingly, wrapped in a yellowed handkerchief. Eoin's wife's. A sister-in-law Peter had never known.

In the same handkerchief, a sterling silver rattle with a rose and tiny bells at the end. Peter clutched it tight. The bells tinkled. He'd been an uncle briefly without knowing it.

Next came a small leather case, the spine pale and worn like it had been opened and closed many, many times. Inside was a daguerreotype of a woman in a high-backed chair, holding a toddler. Eoin stood with a hand on the back of the chair, staring unsmilingly into the camera like his wife.

"Oh," Nevaeh said. "Is that him?"

"Best I can figure." David leaned in. "We know he had a wife and daughter." He frowned. "Huh. He looks a little like you, Peter. I didn't notice before."

Peter's eyes fixed on his brother's softly blurred face. No longer the round, boyish face he remembered, but hard and angular. The face of a working man who had lived a hard life.

Judging by the daguerreotype and its case, the sterling silver rattle, the clothes worn in the portrait, Eoin had achieved some measure of fortune. But the room's memories lingered on the periphery of Peter's mind. The despair. The loneliness. The exhaustion, the pain, the illness.

The roll of bills growing smaller and smaller until it ran out.

Whatever happiness Eoin had found, it had been snatched away too soon. He'd been shy of thirty-six when he'd died.

Peter threw the daguerreotype down so quickly that David squawked, "Careful!" and snatched it up, closing its case gently.

Nevaeh slipped an arm around Peter's waist. He slumped against her, reaching mechanically for the papers in the box.

A bill of sale for the general store, folded and tied with a string. Signed the way Mam had taught her children to sign their names, clear and careful.

A letter from Eoin's wife early in 1845, before they wed, agreeing to marry him when she came to Ohio. Her name had been Kathleen.

A letter from an old Ballygar neighbor the same year, expressing condolences: Mam had passed. Enclosed with their letter was the last Mam had ever written, completed but unsent before her death.

Tears pooled in Peter's eyes. His gaze traced every letter of his mother's handwriting, each one carefully formed but a little awkward. She'd grown up illiterate but had worked to learn her letters after marrying so she might teach her children. As she had.

It was short, as all her letters were because they took so much time and labor.

Dearest Son,
I can scarse express the joy I feel that you have found success at last. Pray the ill luck that has plaged us since my darling Peter left may be over. I await your next letter egerly, that I may join you in the States and meet my new dawter.
I am,
Your loving mother,
S.S.

His eyes traced the lines and loops of his own name.

My darling Peter, his mother had written. *My darling Peter.*

He read it over and over. *My darling Peter,* more than fifteen years after he'd left.

My darling Peter, though she'd had nary a word from him all that time because every letter he'd written home had gone astray.

Like the curse, not content with his exile, refused to let so much as a piece of paper he'd touched return to Ireland.

Something painful boiled in his stomach, spread to his chest and arms. His neck. His face. He crushed the letter in his hands.

"Careful!" David squawked again, but Nevaeh intervened.

"Go downstairs. I'll handle this."

"Handle—? What do you mean 'handle'? This letter is over a hundred and seventy years old, he'll damage it."

"Look at him. He's having another panic attack."

Their words meant nothing. He was shaking, the crumpled letter rattling in his hands. His skin prickled like a million pins were stabbing him from inside. His skull pounded.

"Peter?"

Nevaeh crouched before him. She uncurled his fists, slipped the letter from his grasp, and set it on the bed. David had vacated the room. Peter's eyes burned.

Nevaeh put her hands on his arms. "Hey. Look at me. I'm right here."

He met her gaze with difficulty. Her brown eyes were warm and concerned.

His throat closed up. The burning in his eyes spilled over into tears.

"My mam," he croaked, and his words retreated into his throat, and he pitched forward into Nevaeh's arms and sobbed into her shoulder.

She shifted onto the bed and held him. Rocking him like he was a child, she whispered over and over, "It's all right," and cried herself because her mom had broken down like this after her dad's funeral and Nevaeh had held her this same way.

They were a damp, snotty, headachy mess by the time they'd quieted. The stab of sunlight faded as clouds wisped across the sky outside, but the floodlight shone brighter for it. Isaiah curled into the room, brightening it from gray to buttery yellow.

Nevaeh giggled wetly. Peter tucked a curl behind her ear.

"Didn't mean for you to cry," he said anxiously, handing her a handkerchief.

She pushed damp hair back from her forehead. "S'okay. I needed a good cry. Ugh. I'm so...puffy."

She leaned against him. The bed creaked.

"Tell me about the letter," she said. "And don't say I won't believe you. I don't understand what's happening, but...he's a Shaughnessy. You're a Shaughnessy. He looks like you. And I guess you wouldn't be doing so bad if you didn't legit have some sort of connection to this guy."

She handed his handkerchief back.

"Let's say he is your brother. How... I mean, you know how old this stuff is, right? How does that...work?"

He'd never told anyone. Never. Unless you counted his brief attempt to tell Samira, who hadn't believed him. A *child* hadn't believed him.

He heaved a sigh. Felt lighter.

Isaiah hovered around them, his concern cocooning Peter like a blanket. The room that had been so grim and empty in the year in which his brother had inhabited it had been filled with his friends for the last half hour. Friends who cared about him. Who worried about him.

Who loved him even when he didn't deserve it.

"It's the curse," he said.

XLVI

Talking to someone about his curse was a comfort. He'd never thought it might be.

In the earliest days after Jack's death, as he'd begun to understand the truth of the curse, people had looked on him suspiciously. As the old friends he'd withdrawn from died one by one, those left muttered about unnaturalness. Peter looked as he had the day Jack died. As he had ten years before.

He used to carve toys for Melbourne's children, but now parents kept their children away. They crossed themselves and crossed the street when he approached. At Mass, he sat in back, alone, with the sign of peace and kind words from no one but the priest, who'd known him since his arrival in Australia almost seventy years prior.

When old Father Cooney died, the new priest listened to the muttering, met him on the steps of the church that first Sunday, and told him he was no longer welcome.

He'd left for Europe, but he didn't stay long. He was within spitting distance of home but unable to set foot there. As it had when he'd tried leaving Melbourne decades ago, something went wrong every time he tried to return to Ireland. Transportation was canceled or broken down, disaster struck, his ticket was lost, stolen, declared invalid, or he was denied entry at some border along the way for any number of reasons.

Once, in desperation, he'd flung himself into the North Channel and started swimming. The chop battered him for hours before the sea spat him out near Portpatrick. He coughed up lungfuls of water and fell to his knees on the rocky shore, screaming at the hazy outline of the distant Irish coast until he was out of air.

Easier to be an ocean away, where going home didn't feel so horribly, hopefully *possible*.

As time wore on and the world believed less in ghosts and *them folk* and curses, the few people who noticed him chalked his unchanging looks up to good genes, a good diet, or good skin care. So it was pointless telling anyone he was cursed, even if he wanted to. No one would believe him.

Now, in this tiny, dark, attic room, Nevaeh knew. And she did believe him.

Unfortunately, she also had many, many questions. He couldn't answer most of them.

"How does it work?"

Isaiah was positively bursting with mintiness, as fascinated by the curse as she was.

Peter explained, in as few words as possible, about his failed attempts to go home, the times he ought to have died but hadn't.

But she picked at a splinter in the bed frame and said, "No, I mean… How are you, you know…alive, when you shouldn't be? Like what's keeping you alive? How does it *work*?"

Well, he didn't know how it worked. It was magic. None of the stories about *them folk* explained the mechanics of their magic, only its effects. The mint sharpened as Isaiah bombarded him with questions about said stories, which he ignored.

"But if you don't know how it works," Nevaeh said, "how are you supposed to break the curse?"

He laughed bitterly. "You figure that out, you let me know."

"Oh."

He stared at the water-stained ceiling, the slice of sunlight. It had brightened again, the sunlight. The room was warmer.

"Used to think the right ghost would do it. Never saw ghosts before I was cursed, then suddenly I could. Thought if I sent the right one packing, or enough of 'em… Now I figure it's another way for the curse to needle me."

"Do you think—"

"What, lass?"

She leaned back with him, bumping the toes of her shoes together. Their shapes blurred in the bureau's cracked mirror.

"I was thinking…this is a ghost you have a connection to, so maybe this time…"

"I've thought on it," he said softly. "But I don't dare hope."

She threaded her fingers through his. He liked it more than he ought to.

But he couldn't leave. Not now he was looking for Eoin. That being the case, it'd do little enough harm to enjoy himself. Just this once. With rules in place for his own well-being.

What rules, he wasn't yet sure. But comfortably, platonically holding hands with someone seemed all right.

"For what it's worth…" Nevaeh hesitated. "Okay. Uh. I don't want this to come out wrong. So let me preface this by saying I'm not glad you're cursed. It sounds like it sucks."

He chuckled despite himself.

"But if you hadn't been cursed, you would've died, what, like, a hundred years ago? More? You wouldn't be here." She squeezed his hand. "I'm glad you're here."

Something blossomed in his chest. He felt dandelion-clock light again. He almost told her he was glad he was here, too.

But saying such things would violate his new rules.

He squeezed her hand back. Let that content him.

It was more than he'd had in a hundred years.

XLVII

That day and all the next, Peter hunted feverishly for his brother's grave. Only two days away was Midsummer. The day his brother's spirit would be stronger than ever. The day that had destroyed their lives.

He kept Isaiah's notebook in his bag, perused the notes over and over, read and reread everything Anne Hodinka had ever written about O.S. Her last entry indicated he'd been buried in back—where Peter had thought the ghost was all along—though Eoin had died not of cholera but some unknown malady.

But Peter had been over every stone in Harrington. Multiple times. By himself. With David. He hadn't found a stone with an Eoin, an Owen, or a Shaughnessy, or even an E.S. or O.S., which would've been the cheapest option. If the stone said anything else—*father, friend,* or merely *1851,* with no name—Peter would never find it. Thursday evening, as sunset bathed the depths of the forest in shadow, he found the remains of a stone washed away in a flood earlier this year and worried Eoin's stone, too, might simply be gone.

That night, unable to sleep, he stepped outside and called into the darkness, "Eoin? Eoin, please. It's me. It's Peter. Please."

The anger rippled, like it was a pond and his voice a cast stone.

But Eoin didn't respond.

Spirits were illogical, narrow-sighted. So eaten up with anger,

Eoin might not recognize his kin. Or he might rage as much at his brother as at the rest of the world. He might be nothing anymore *but* rage.

Peter should've expected it, but it upset him nonetheless. He slumped against the cottage wall.

He lay awake in bed for hours, turning over the forest's every leaf and twig in his mind. When he slept, he dreamed of *them folk* and gunshots and ghosts. He woke up sweating, kicked the bedclothes onto the floor, collapsed onto the bare bed, and awoke again far too early, exhausted.

As he spiraled deeper into despair and anxiety, Harrington perked up. To him, Friday was the day before Midsummer Eve. To Harrington, Friday was the first day of SummerFest.

It meant danger to him. The nights he most wanted everyone safe at home were the nights they'd be out and about.

"So come with us." Nevaeh on the phone, Friday at lunchtime. She'd insisted on checking in with him since his panic attacks on Wednesday. "I'm going with Benji and Uncle Dave and Uncle Noah and I think Noah's son and his fiancée. Okay," she said, like she'd seen him blanch, "I know you're on edge. I'm worried, too, believe me. But everyone's ready for some fun after this freaky summer we've had, and frankly I'm worried about you."

A breeze wafted through the Dutch door, ruffling the herbs, scattering their scent through the kitchen. He twisted the phone cord around his finger.

"Don't need to worry about me," he said quietly.

"You need to get out of your own head for a while. I know Midsummer's close, but Midsummer Eve isn't until tomorrow. It'll be safe tonight, right?"

"Safer'n tomorrow."

"Okay, so that's…something. And we can wear anything you want, okay, whatever flowers or weird iron jewelry."

Out the window, downhill from the cottage, the forest looked bloody in the red air.

"I don't know."

"Peter. Seriously. Come with us. You've done nothing but panic all week. You need to take your mind off it for a night. One night, okay? Not the whole night, just a few hours. I know how exhausting it is to panic nonstop, trust me."

It was exhausting. He was constantly tense, constantly worn from the tension yet unable to sleep.

He wasn't sure he wanted to go, but she was right. He needed a break. He'd spent two centuries locking away memories of his family, but Harrington had pried apart the bars. Now, the attic room, the box and its contents, his mother's letter—they had smashed the cage to bits. He couldn't fend the memories off anymore.

After so long spent burying them, he didn't know how to face them.

He accepted Nevaeh's invitation, hoping SummerFest might distract him from ghosts and family and Ireland and curses for one night.

XLVIII

Thanks to the Marian symbols on the doors of Nevaeh's apartment and the building itself, the air in the hallway outside her door was lighter than that outside. He breathed easier, composed himself. Just because Nevaeh had called to check on him didn't mean she needed to know how much he was struggling.

Nevaeh opened the door excitedly when he knocked, but her smile slipped. He pulled his cap off, wringing it.

"Am I too early?"

"Oh—no, you're good." She blushed. "I, um, I thought it was Benji. They said they were on their way."

He considered her. Her sequined halter top winked in the light. Her hair was tied back with a silk scarf, leaving her curls in a high crown atop her head. She'd tucked sprigs of rue into the scarf, he was pleased to see, but the protective measures had been an afterthought to the outfit.

He scratched his forehead. "Maybe it's best I don't tag along, if you're going courting."

She covered her face in her hands. "Oh, my god. No. We're not...*courting*."

"Sure about that, are you?"

"*Peter.*" Even her voice blushed. "Yes. No. I don't know."

He loitered in the kitchenette. The apartment seemed bigger than before; several moving boxes had vanished. Books were piled on the bedside table. Photographs hung on the wall by the door. Candids, mostly: Elijah smiling from the seat of a combine; Marguerite waving from the porch of the Key-Flores farmhouse; a woman with Nevaeh's sepia skin and rounded chin, her mother, tickling a much younger Nevaeh from behind while Nevaeh squealed with laughter.

"You unpacked," Peter said softly.

Nevaeh shrugged, but her eyes were bright. "Like I said. Maybe I changed my mind."

A knock at the door. She wrenched it open. Her face glowed with a smile.

Benji brushed her cheek with their lips, stretching to do it: they were shorter than she was. "Sorry I'm late. Had to drop Chloe off at a friend's house for the night."

"That's okay," Nevaeh said breathlessly, and Peter didn't blame her. Benji's dark eyes were fixed on her face with such intensity that he couldn't have been more embarrassed if he'd walked in on them kissing.

He cleared his throat, jamming his cap on. Nevaeh jumped.

"Right, sorry," she squeaked. "Benji, Peter. Peter, Benji. Um. So. Let's get going. Everyone else is meeting us there."

Benji drove them to the elementary school. Their teeth ached in the cinnamon-sugar air. Stands selling elephant ears, caramel apples, popcorn, ice cream, and pop funneled visitors toward a ticket booth. Food trucks lined the drop-off lane. Carnival games and rides flashed and blinked and zoomed and roared in the twilit parking lot in back. Children shrieked and laughed throughout the midway, their parents strolling after them, stopping to chat with friends and neighbors.

Everywhere, Peter was pleasantly surprised to see, yellow flowers were hung, planted, and bouqueted, like whoever was in charge of decorating knew the lore same as he did. Perhaps that was why everyone was so relaxed: the angry pall hanging over the town lifted here. The air was lighter, clearer.

He relaxed, too, as he wandered the crowded lot with Nevaeh and Benji. Carnivals comforted him; he'd spent a couple decades bouncing around various circuits. Immortality was easier in carnivals than it was in most places. Especially in those days, carnies hadn't asked many questions, all with their own hurts and horrors to hide. They didn't look at you twice because something was off about you, and they protected their own.

And it was magical, a carnival, in a way that had nothing to do with charming plants or sensing spirits (though every carnival had a smattering of ghosts). He'd always liked a carnival's liveliness, the excitement surrounding him, wrapping him up, thrumming through him until he felt *alive* in a way he often didn't. He felt a part of people without the danger of being a part of people, because one day the carnival would vanish. Those who had run through shrieking would be safely home, and he'd never see them again.

Nevaeh craned her neck as they neared the lot's far edge. A Ferris wheel reared into the sky, overlooking the soy fields stretching north beyond the school.

Their friends stood in its shadow. David, still on crutches, wore a waistcoat printed with silvery constellations that flashed in the midway lights. A little old man hunched over a walker, with thinning silver hair, thick glasses, and a knit sweater. A young couple chatted with him. And to Peter's surprise, all four al-Masris stood beside them, and Chloe and Jess with them.

As usual, Sayid wore his Saint-John's-wort. The plant was even bigger than it had been days ago. Samira held a plastic bag with water and a tiny orange fish in it, clinging to her mother with her other hand. She didn't throw herself at Peter as she normally would have; he resisted the urge to go to her instead.

Nevaeh kissed David's cheek. He hugged her with one arm. "I hope you don't mind the extra company. We ran into the al-Masris and invited them to join us."

Nevaeh smiled at Yafa. "Of course."

"The more the merrier." Benji fist-bumped Chloe. "Hey, cuz. Didn't realize your friends were bringing you out tonight. Sick of me yet?"

Introductions all around. The old man with the walker was David's friend Noah Rosten; the young couple Noah's son, Adam, and future daughter-in-law, Priya.

Noah leaned over his walker for a look at Peter.

"Oho, so this is Peter," and the way he said it made Peter blush. "It's good to meet you. 'Peter this' and 'Peter that,' it's all I hear." He jerked a thumb at David. "He's been talking my ear off, this one."

"Yes, thank you," David said loudly. Yafa, Khalid, and Nevaeh bit back laughter. "I'm sure he's flattered to learn I never shut up about him. If we're all here, let's go, shall we?"

Sayid, Chloe, and Jess dragged them around the carnival, to the carousel, to an elephant-ear stand, to the beanbag toss, back to the Ferris wheel, to various horrible spinning rides designed to make them throw up. Yafa and Khalid joined them for some rides but mostly walked a little apart from the others, holding hands and laughing together. They looked younger when they laughed, like their laughter had flung off their usual cares. Samira lagged, holding her fish tight. Benji and Nevaeh similarly walked apart, though they didn't hold hands. They stopped by the ring toss and let the group leave them behind.

Anxiety nipped at Peter, but Nevaeh had that rue in her hair, and yellow flowers hung everywhere.

Noah joined his son and future daughter-in-law on gentler rides while David and Peter waited by his walker. Between rides, he talked nonstop with Priya, who lived out of state and was meeting him for the first time. Adam walked beside them, beaming. David ambled after them contentedly. Peter plodded along at his side, hands in his pockets.

David paused by a photobooth tucked between a Skee-Ball

and a milk-bottle toss. "Noah, come take a photo with me. I haven't seen one of these in ages."

"You've seen my face." Noah cackled. "I'll break the camera!"

His son scoffed. "Untrue. Where do you think I got my good looks?"

Noah grabbed his face and pressed a loud kiss to his head. "From your other papa, of course. No dice, Davey. You want a picture of me, ask. I have a million and one of 'em at home. No need to torture myself and a perfectly good camera with more. Perhaps your quiet friend will oblige."

Peter blushed but stumped into the photobooth with David as the others headed for the Skee-Ball. Samira trailed into the booth after them.

Peter had never been in a photobooth. Jack had insisted on taking a handful of photographs of their life together in Melbourne; three were hidden in his steamer trunk. But he hadn't liked taking his picture toward the end. His failure to age past his seventies, while Jack looked older and older, had unsettled him. He'd avoided mirrors and cameras with equal vigor.

He didn't need to be immortalized in photographs, anyway.

But he let David pull him into the photobooth and wrung his cap as David studied the screen's many options. They could project different backgrounds, add stickers and special effects, correct red eye and color and brighten and add filters. Samira pressed quietly against him.

"There weren't this many options the last time I was in one of these," David murmured. "I think we'll skip all these effects. Is that all right with you?"

"As you wish."

"Excellent. Unless Samira wants to try working this thing?"

David smiled at her, but she shook her head. Peter picked her up. She laid her head on his shoulder. David's smile faded but fixed quickly back into place.

"Plain it is. Can I...?" He slipped an arm around Peter's shoulder. "Is this...all right?"

He was so hesitant, where before he'd been so forward. Guilt gnawed at Peter's insides.

"This is fine."

David relaxed. "Great. Okay, so have fun with it, and smile when the little light comes on."

Peter did not smile when the little light came on. It wasn't yet the usual practice to smile when he'd last been photographed. Jack had been so proud of their portrait, stern-faced like the subjects of old paintings. If any photos existed of Peter smiling, they were long-lost candids from picnics or barbecues.

So he stood stiff and unsmiling, Samira similarly unsmiling in his arms, as David made faces. Before the light flashed a final time, David pressed a kiss to Peter's cheek, long enough for the camera to capture it.

Long enough for Peter to think that if he turned his head, they'd be kissing.

The flash went off. David jerked away, his ears pink.

"Sorry—I didn't mean to—I was trying to think of fun poses—I wasn't—"

"S'all right," Peter said, squashing the desire to pull David back in to show him exactly how all right it was. *Don't, unless you mean it.* And Peter didn't mean it.

Rather, it didn't matter if he meant it. He was leaving. As soon as this was over—as soon as he found his brother's spirit and somehow, *somehow*, got him to stop terrorizing Harrington—he was leaving.

Samira's arms tightened around his neck, like she knew. His breath hitched. He carried her out of the photobooth.

David snatched their strip of photos from the print slot. He shook his head with a chuckle, whapping Peter on the shoulder.

"Look at you! You didn't smile in a single picture—wait,

no." He peered at the strip. "I take it back. You *nearly* smiled in the last one."

Four photos were in the strip, each with a grinning David, a Samira whose face was half-hidden in Peter's neck, and a grave Peter—except the last, in which Peter's mouth turned up at the corners as David kissed his cheek.

David tore the picture off. "Dibs on the rare smile. Do you want any of the others?"

Peter shifted Samira to one arm and tucked the entire strip into his breast pocket.

Just because he was leaving when this was over didn't mean he couldn't take something with him.

XLIX

The forecast called for rain, but Midsummer Eve dawned blue and bright. Cumulus scudded across the sky, twisted into fantastic shapes.

Harrington bustled with activity. Fly fishermen had lined the Ashmead since dawn, in one long, thigh-deep stretch of camo overalls, baseball caps, and fishing reels. Jewelers, artists, candlemakers, beekeepers, vendors of all sorts set up tents on Main Street and were in business by 9 a.m. People hurried to Creekside Park to claim a picnic table or some grass and a grill for the day's cookout. Children who usually slept late on lazy summer Saturdays raced through town all morning, descending on the midway like a flock of geese when it opened at noon. On the creek's west bank, where grass stretched for half an acre, firemen oversaw the construction of a public bonfire, to be lit that evening.

In the cemetery, Peter feverishly put up the Midsummer protections he'd failed to set two hundred years ago.

Rue, Saint-John's-wort, sage, rosemary, lavender, thyme, long fennel, and laburnum wreathed the front gates and every window on the property. Horseshoes gleamed over lintels. The spirits flinched away, keeping a respectful distance as Peter whirled through the cemetery with flowers and iron.

While everyone else headed to Creekside Park for the cookout or Main Street for the sales, Peter stole into the church on Washington for holy water. The heavy wooden doors scraped open reluctantly.

Inside, the church was expectant. Like a funeral parlor before a visitation. Watchful. Still. Humming with silence. The pews wavered in the stained-glass windows' blue-and-red light.

It felt like bad luck, stealing holy water. Never mind that the church was unlocked. Never mind that the baptismal font was full, as if for this purpose. He'd gone without for decades, but with his friends in danger he was taking no chances.

Peter crossed himself and crept toward the font, muttering half-remembered prayers. Each Midsummer back home, all Ballygar had traipsed to the chapel to beg holy water off the priest. Now, thievery was his only way to get some. He didn't like it.

He took the stolen holy water back to the cemetery, saved some in a vial, and sprinkled the rest on his garden.

With their extra protections, the cottage and garden breathed easier, but he had no time to enjoy the lighter air. He filled a crate with more iron, salt, and flowers and drove to Nevaeh's.

She answered the door in sleep shorts and a tank top, though it was gone noon.

"Oh, ah, hi." She tugged her hem lower over her belly. "You're not... I thought you were pizza."

He barely heard her. "Get to your gran's. If you—"

"Is that the pizza?" a voice said. "I'm starv— Oh, uh, hi. Peter, right?" Benji shuffled from one foot to the other, in a state of undress and embarrassment similar to Nevaeh's. "So, um, yeah, nice seeing you. Hey, Nea, I'm gonna shower before the food gets here, if that's all right."

"Okay." A small but brilliant smile cracked through Nevaeh's embarrassment. Her gaze trailed Benji through the apartment before she turned back to Peter. "Sorry. Uh. Things went really, really well after we dropped you off last night. So...yeah."

She bit her lip, but her eyes were still smiling. "What were you saying?"

"Get to your gran's," Peter repeated urgently. Her smile faded. "Until I can find where Eoin's buried, her house is the safest place for you. I told you, she knows her stuff. Bring Benji and tell your gran I said don't go out for nothing. She'll understand."

She swallowed. "Okay."

He gave a tight smile. "S'all right, lass. You stay inside, nothing'll happen to you. I won't let it. Promise."

The al-Masris weren't home, and he spiraled back into panic. He coped by hanging garlands over their windows and nailing a horseshoe over their door. He wrote a note in case they returned before he'd seen them, shoved a bowl of salt under the porch swing, and comforted himself with the thought that, wherever they were, Sayid was wearing his Saint-John's-wort, and surely Samira had her wristlet in her pocket, if not on her wrist.

David wasn't home, either. Peter secured his house, too, and went to the museum. His muscles ached from the air's weight. Harrington was faintly red, to no one's eyes but his.

Not the museum, however. Wrapped in Isaiah's love, with the extra protection of Peter's wards, its air was clear and light. Peter stepped from the truck with a sigh, muscles loosening.

Visitors trickled into the museum. Marisol was giving tours. David was working on the porch, chatting people up and answering questions from out-of-towners come for SummerFest.

Marisol led a family of five inside. David smiled as Peter dropped into his usual chair, calm for the first time all day.

"Doing good business today."

"Always do, this time of year," David said. "SummerFest, Halloween, and Christmas are our busy times. People love hearing about the Hodinkas' Christmas traditions. And Isaiah used to tell the kids local legends at Halloween. He loved that."

"I know," Peter said. Isaiah beamed goldenly.

"Are you staying? Can I get you a coffee?"

He needed to move. Find the al-Masris. Get them home somehow.

But he could *breathe* on the museum porch. The cottage felt like surfacing from a sea of anger. The museum felt like making it back to land.

"Coffee'd be lovely." He watched David grab his crutches. "Would you do something for me?"

"Other than the coffee, I suppose you mean?" David smiled. "Anything. What do you need?"

Peter met his gaze gravely. "Stay in today."

David laughed. "It's a little late for that. I'm already out, in case you hadn't noticed."

"I mean it. Stay here. Don't go out for lunch or nothing. Stay in today. Please."

David softened. He put a hand on Peter's shoulder.

"You're mysterious today," he said. "Look, we're open late for the festival. I'll be here until then. I can call in lunch."

"Straight home when you close."

David's mouth twitched. "Straight home when I close. You can even walk with me if it'll make you feel better. Carry my books and everything."

Peter didn't laugh. David squeezed his shoulder and went inside.

Peter waited for the next wave of visitors to make it off the porch. "Isaiah?"

Isaiah wrapped around him.

"You keep eyes on him this weekend."

Isaiah bristled. He always looked after David.

"Don't take on so. I didn't mean nothing by it. Listen."

He paused as a young couple mounted the steps. Spread his fingers on the table.

"You're the only spirit in town might be strong enough to stand up to my brother, if he gets loose," he continued, when the couple had gone in. "I been looking for him, but…"

The air twisted mintily, milder than usual.

Peter dragged a hand over his face.

"I've tried. He won't talk to me. I don't know why." He hunched over the table, fiddling with his cap. "He's not like you. He's so angry. Ate up with it. He had such a hard life."

Isaiah engulfed him again. Peter sank into it, wishing he could always feel this way. He ran a hand through his hair and tugged his cap back on.

"I wish…"

Isaiah prodded gently, minty again. Peter pulled the cap over his eyes.

"I wish," he whispered, "I'd been brave enough to see if Jack had stayed for me the way you stayed for him."

Comfort, the soft orange of a winter sunset.

Then Isaiah pointed out that if Peter had Jack, whoever that was, he might not be here for David this way.

He snapped upright. "What's that s'posed to mean?"

Isaiah shared images. Impressions. Faint smells and colors emanating from David, as they did the dead, whenever Peter was around. How happy David had been the last couple months, after a drawn-out year in which he'd been quiet and lonely despite his efforts to appear as cheerful as normal.

The hopes Isaiah had, though it hurt him to hope them.

Suddenly, Isaiah's comforting presence was a yoke.

"Just because he's what you're here for," he said in a trembling voice, "don't mean he's what I'm here for. No—" He jerked away as Isaiah tried to calm him. "I'm sorry you're stuck here because he's lonely and you're worried. But you've got the wrong man. It's not me. It's not meant to be me."

Isaiah went minty again, and a little sour. The groundskeeper stumbled toward the steps.

"No I don't," he lied through gritted teeth. "I ain't here for him, I ain't here for you. Soon's I find my brother, I'm leaving. Find someone else."

He jogged away from the boarding house, shuddering off Isaiah's grasping fingers. The cemetery pickup sat forgotten in the gravel drive.

David returned with a coffee mug. He looked around the empty porch in bewilderment.

"Where'd he go?" he asked no one.

L

The groundskeeper stumbled down Main Street, buffeting
people. He hadn't intended to return to the cemetery yet but
couldn't remember why. After the museum's respite, the air elsewhere weighed heavier on him than ever, the street tinted red.
The red dimmed and brightened as clouds staggered through
the sky.

He replayed the conversation with Isaiah, a fresh wave of anger
and despair washing over him. He wasn't here for them. Not for
David. Not as a fix for whatever was keeping their dead here.

At his core, where he'd spent over a century burying anything he might desire, he wanted what Isaiah wanted for him.
He could have it, if he'd reach for it.

But if he did, it would be snatched away again. Maybe not
now. Maybe in ten years. Twenty. A little longer, if he was lucky.

Regardless, it would be taken from him, in what seemed ages
to mortals but was a blip in his long and pointless life. Afterward,
time would stretch on until the memories of his brief happiness
eroded and mossed over like old headstones, forgotten.

He bumped into someone, mumbled an apology. They blocked
his path.

"Oh, hey." Sayid fiddled with his Saint-John's-wort, which
was bushy with leaves and yellow blooms. It rustled proudly.

"Mama's looking for you. She wanted to invite you to the cook-out."

The groundskeeper remembered why he hadn't returned to the cemetery.

He glanced down the street. White tents lined either side. Vendors sold necklaces, paintings, novelty clocks, local honey, soy candles and goat's-milk soap and gluten-free cookies. Chloe and Jess queued at an ice-cream cart nearby with Jess's older brother, but the al-Masris were absent.

Jess waved. He waved back vaguely.

"Where's your mam? And your pa, and Samira?"

"Baba took Samira to get a doughnut, and then they're going to the museum. Mama's holding our spot at the park with Auntie Maryam. They ran into some friends."

Peter put his hands on the boy's shoulders. "You need to get 'em home. And keep 'em there."

Sayid frowned. "But the festival…"

"You have to, lad. You must. Safest to stay in tonight."

Sayid bit his lip, toying with the hem of his T-shirt. Peter expected him to ask why; instead, he said softly, "Because of the ghosts?"

Peter's eyebrows disappeared into his cap. "Thought you didn't believe in ghosts."

Sayid twisted his T-shirt in his fists. Peter relented.

"You see 'em?" he asked in a gentler voice.

"Not exactly," Sayid mumbled. "It's hard to explain. I don't like it. It's easier pretending they don't exist."

That bore looking into, a boy of his age still sensing ghosts, but Peter had more pressing concerns.

"No matter. I sense 'em, too." He lowered his voice. "Then you've felt the anger all around town."

Sayid nodded. "That's why I started wearing the flowers everywhere."

"Good lad. I'm looking for the spirit causing all the trouble."

He sucked in his cheeks, his insides twisting. "Haven't found him yet, and he'll only be stronger over Midsummer, and the other spirits, too. Get your family home any way you can, and keep 'em there. Think you can do that?"

Sayid bit his lip. "Maybe. I could fake sick. Mama and Baba would take us home if they thought I was sick. But..." His voice dipped to a whisper. "What if the ghosts get in the house?"

Peter shook his head. "They won't. Already stopped by your house and secured the place. Your parents ask, you tell 'em it's an old Midsummer custom. That's true enough."

"Okay," Sayid said softly. "Okay. Will you be safe?"

"Course. This ain't my first go-round."

Sayid flung himself forward and wrapped his arms around Peter's waist as Samira so often did. Peter's throat closed up. He returned the boy's hug, patting his head gently.

"Go on, now."

Sayid darted back to his friends at the ice-cream cart.

Peter shielded his eyes. The sun hung in the west. True to the forecast, despite the morning's sunshine, dark cumulonimbus encroached on the fading blue of the western sky, threatening rain. The silver maples on Main flashed a warning with their leaves.

He headed home to hunker down for the weekend. With Midsummer Eve upon them, going after Eoin was too dangerous. He'd be more powerful than ever. So would his anger.

Peter would wait out the weekend while Eoin's rage beat against the garden wall like a storm. As long as his friends followed his instructions and stayed home, they'd be safe, too.

LI

Samira had been awaiting the cookout all weekend, but Sayid said he felt sick. Their parents took them home. The house darkened as clouds gathered in the west. Yafa turned on lights in the foyer, the kitchen, the living room, trying to chase away the darkness.

Khalid channel-surfed on the couch until he found a Marvel movie playing. Yafa sat cross-legged on the floor to work on the thousand-piece warbler puzzle covering the coffee table. Sayid curled under a blanket in the corner of the couch. Samira snuggled into her father's side, eyeballing her brother and resisting the temptation to (gently) kick him, but only because their parents were there.

He didn't look sick.

But he didn't like lying, and he did like the annual cookout.

She turned back to the movie her father had put on, which was more interesting than Sayid anyhow. She twisted the iron band around her wrist absently.

The phone rang.

Her parents exchanged a glance. Yafa scrambled to her feet, her eyes wide and dark. When she hung up, Khalid said, "Your father?"

Samira's head snapped in their direction.

Sayid sat up, tugging the blanket around him. "What is it, Mama?"

Yafa's voice was tight. "Jeddo is... He's not going to..."

Something inside Samira swelled like a balloon, stretching painfully.

Yafa squeezed her eyes shut. "I have to see him. Baba can stay here, if you don't—"

"I can watch Samira," Sayid said.

Yafa's face crumpled, but she didn't cry. She kissed his forehead. "Thank you, habibi."

She kissed Samira, too, but the balloon-like thing grew bigger. Stretched so thin it threatened to snap. Her parents hurried from the house.

Sayid abandoned his blanket. He swung his heels against the couch. "Do you want to watch *Spy Kids*?"

Samira stiffened. Sayid never offered to watch *Spy Kids* unless something truly terrible was happening. He didn't understand her obsession with a movie so much older than they were.

She didn't answer. Sayid put the movie on anyway and made a bowl of popcorn.

Samira perched numbly on the couch, small and drawn. Her hands clenched together, her feet dangling half an inch off the floor because every muscle in her body was pulled taut. She gazed at the TV blankly, not processing the movie. Not noticing how her brother kept glancing at her, leaning forward like he meant to say something but never doing so. They didn't eat any popcorn.

When the phone rang again, she snapped to attention.

Sayid jumped up to answer. "Hi, Mama."

Samira's eyes fixed on her brother's face.

His expression twisted. He turned away.

The balloon-like thing popped. Everything inside Samira collapsed as if that had been the only thing keeping it in place.

She already knew what had happened, but Sayid was going to tell her. Any moment, he would hang up, and he would tell her.

She didn't want to hear it. Maybe, if she never did, it wouldn't be real.

While his back was turned, she bolted from the living room on tiptoe, snatched her sneakers from the rug by the front door, and sprinted to the cemetery.

The clouds had thickened. The air was red with anger that weighed on Samira even though it wasn't for her. Her lungs burned and her legs ached; she'd run the whole way. Hadn't thought to grab her bicycle.

The darkening sky rattled her. The spirits followed her path at a distance, wary of the iron on her wrist. She shied away. She'd never been scared of the cemetery, but the things that scared her at home had followed her here.

She clenched her fists, squared her shoulders, and hurried into the forest's groaning depths. The spirits wheeled away.

She slipped through the pine grove and the gap in the back wall, jogged through the meadow, crashed through the yews, and threw herself down before the headstone.

The ghost hung back, prickly as a briar, which upset her more until she remembered the wristlet. Sayid had insisted she wear it that morning. She flung it into the grass.

"Sorry," she whispered, "I forgot," and then, to her horror, she burst into tears.

The ghost was more agitated than usual, his anger sharper, brighter. Wound tight like a snake, ready to strike. The clover hunkered low to the ground to escape it.

Samira's tears cracked it open. The ghost descended upon her, affection flickering warm and yellow in the midst of that sharp, bright anger.

"I can't tell you," Samira whispered. "I can't tell you or it'll be real."

Grief wafted from her small form, grief and anger and confusion tangled in a knot.

Eoin understood that.

As he had before, he shared memories with her. Different ones this time. Not his mam or Nina Hodinka telling stories, but Kathleen doing the washing. Dressing the baby.

Their faces were blurred; he no longer remembered what they looked like. He only remembered that he'd loved them, and they'd been taken from him.

The memories turned.

Kathleen pale and weak in their bed, eyes glazed. Their child crying weakly as she took sick, too. A fog of fear because he'd lost his wife, and he was going to lose his daughter, and he couldn't prevent it, and he'd had no time to grieve. The neighbors' doors locked against him as he paced the street with Kitty in his arms, begging for help from someone, anyone.

Samira shuddered. The memories weighed her down. They rolled over her faster and faster, flashing like images in a slide-show.

Two small, simple headstones reading only MOTHER and DAUGHTER and 1849 because he'd had no money for more. An eviction notice on the door of the general store as there'd been on the door of the Shaughnessys' farmhouse thirty-five hundred miles away and a decade earlier. Voices arguing out-side a dim attic room.

His panic as the townsfolk, under the instruction of an old woman recently immigrated, planted the yews and carved the symbol into his stone. The symbol that burned him even as it maddened him. His wife had prayed to the Virgin daily; now he was trapped by the Virgin's power.

His panic and anger, in memory and now, crashed through Samira until she couldn't breathe.

"Stop. Please." Her fingertips brushed against his headstone. *"Please."*

The memories swept out of her.

She rolled onto her back, panting up at the sky. Clouds hung thick and black overhead. Tears for a woman and child and fear she'd never known rolled down her cheeks. Her chest buzzed. Aching. Ready to shatter. His anger was her anger, his grief her grief.

She scrambled to her feet, breath bursting from her as she gazed at the Marian symbol. His panic over its creation roiled inside her, suffocating. Around her, his anger pulsed and heaved like a heart run ragged from being hunted.

Samira's nostrils flared. She lunged at a stone in the grass, a remnant of the wall. She clutched it to her chest.

Everything ballooned back up inside her, everything, everything. The phone's jangling. The look on Sayid's face when he answered. Baba's absence, Mama's absence. Her teachers angry at her, her parents angry at her, Peter angry at her.

Jeddo thin and sick in a hospital bed, mumbling and barely conscious. The last memory she'd ever have of him.

Her eyes stung. She smashed the rock into the headstone.

The collision rattled her teeth. She wiped her nose on her arm and smashed the headstone again.

Again.

Again, again, again. Over and over, putting her fear and grief and anger and confusion, compounded by his, into each strike, until her arms and shoulders and teeth ached.

LII

By six o'clock, the clouds had swallowed the sun, and a wind had picked up. The vendors on Main Street added rope, zip ties, and sandbags to their tents, then gave up and closed early. The bonfire was canceled, to much grumbling, which the fire department ignored. The cookout continued, but everyone was muted, tense without knowing why. People packed up their plasticware, leftovers, and picnic blankets as soon as they'd eaten. The fly fishermen had taken their day's catch of bluegill and smallmouth bass and gone. Shops and restaurants downtown twinkled with warm yellow light, but outside the maples flashed their warning. People turned up their collars and hurried home through the hastening darkness, heads bowed against the wind.

At seven thirty, someone pounded on the cottage door.

Peter looked up from the volume of poetry he'd been trying to read. Eoin couldn't possibly get into the cottage, yet he hadn't been able to focus. For hours, he'd jumped at every creak of the house settling, kept getting up to make sure the spirits were still outside the garden wall. The wind sighed.

The pounding continued. A familiarly anxious voice moaned, "Let me in! Come on, open the door, please—"

Peter jolted up and yanked the door open, his heart in his throat. Sayid fell in on him, babbling in a high-pitched voice, "You have to help me, she's gone—"

Peter guided him to the love seat. "Samira?"

Sayid drew his knees up to his chest. "I did like you said, I told Mama I had a stomachache, and she called Baba, and we went home, and everything was *fine*, and then the hospital called—"

"Your granddad?"

Sayid dashed an arm across his nose. "Mama called half an hour ago. He's gone."

His lip trembled. He buried his face in his knees, sobbing.

Peter's heart squeezed. Anxiety for Samira flooded every limb, but he fought it, digging his nails into his palms to stay present. He handed Sayid a handkerchief and hugged him until the boy stopped crying.

"Sorry." Sayid sniffled, scrunching the handkerchief in his fist. "Mama and Baba went to the hospital, but I said I could watch Samira. She's been so quiet the last few days, I thought— She was really upset, but I put on a movie and made her some popcorn and I thought it'd be fine, but then Mama called to say he was—he was gone, and they were on their way home, and when I hung up, Samira was *gone*, and I didn't know what to do. Things are getting real bad downtown—"

Peter was already on his feet. He rifled through his messenger bag, making sure he had everything he might need, and slung the bag over his shoulder. "I'll find her."

"I'm coming with you."

"No, lad. Not this time."

"Yes this time." Sayid fixed him with a watery glare that made him look very much like his sister. "You said it's dangerous. I gotta find her."

Peter's hand was on the doorknob. "Safer for you to stay here."

"I have my flowers. You said they'd protect me."

The Saint-John's-wort rustled, assuring Peter it would indeed protect the boy.

"I won't leave your side," Sayid said earnestly, though his voice quavered. "Promise. Please?"

Like as not he'd run after Peter anyway, as he had that first night.

"Fine. Here." Peter handed Sayid a canister of salt. "Hold on to this. If you see anything you think you shouldn't, chuck salt at it."

The sky was so deeply gray it was almost black, especially in the west. The wind whistled. The saplings on the knoll bent; the hoarier trees of the back lot roared like waves. Adeline twisted through the garden, shying away when Peter and Sayid appeared with their salt and iron.

The anger outside the garden gate punched Peter in the stomach. He bent double with a groan.

Sayid danced around him. "What is it? Are you okay?"

"M'all right." Peter's nostrils flared. "Hard to breathe, is all. Come on."

The grass flashed silvery-green, rolling in the wind like waves. Spirits shimmered crimsonly. Sayid gulped and drew closer. Peter grasped his hand tight, worming his other hand into his bag, ready to fling salt, iron, or holy water at any spirit that came too close.

The spirits glared but kept their distance. Images flickered in their midst, none strong enough to materialize fully but all strengthened by Midsummer. Sayid whimpered.

Under the thick June canopy, the forest was pitch-dark. Peter released Sayid's hand to light a sea-salt candle.

Sayid's voice was strangled. "Don't let go of me."

"Only a moment, lad. If you'll hold on to the candle, I'll hold on to you."

"Okay," Sayid whispered.

He was trembling, but he clutched the pink candle like a lifeline. Peter gripped his hand and led him through the woods, calling for Samira. The trees cracked and groaned. The ocean-like rush of leaves was deafening. Occasionally they glimpsed the storm-gray sky through the canopy, but the treetops always shrouded them again.

Beneath the creak of trunks and rush of leaves and their own breathing—Peter's quiet and even, Sayid's harsh and ragged—the forest was silent. The birds, frogs, and crickets that sang so cacophonously at dusk hid away, silent. No squirrel or chipmunk skirted through the underbrush. The wisps had vanished. The roar of leaves muffled the creek's burbling. A great horned owl watched the two humans progress through the forest with its head cocked but did not comment.

The pine grove enveloped them in the spicy scent of resin.

"Samira?" Peter called.

Sayid squeezed his hand.

No response but the wind in the trees.

Peter's heart clenched, but he moved deeper into the pines, expecting Samira to detach from a trunk as she had the night they'd met.

"Samira?"

Pine needles shifted underfoot. Sayid pointed past the crumbling remains of the back wall, where a small meadow broke the canopy open. Dim light shone grayly.

"What's that?"

A dull glint in the grass. Peter and Sayid crept through bluestem and beardtongue toward the glinting thing.

A pair of unbent paper clips.

"Those are Samira's," Sayid whispered.

Peter slipped them into his pocket.

"Samira," he called, but his voice fell short. The first few hesitant drops of rain dripped onto the meadow. "Let's snuff that candle 'til we need it again."

Sayid extinguished the candle. Peter held it loosely in one hand and hitched his bag up his shoulder. Moss and lichens mumbled along the wall's length.

Sayid stumbled.

"All right, lad?"

"Yeah. There was a rock or something." Sayid peered into the grass, rubbing his ankle. His voice crept upward. "Oh. No. It's a headstone."

Peter's stomach clenched. "What?"

He dropped to his knees and shoved grass and flowers aside, ignoring their mutters.

Slate flaked from the headstone. Only a date, 1849, was readable in its weathered face.

"What?" Peter repeated in a whisper.

He craned his neck. The dark curves of more headstones reared from the tall grasses. The candle slipped from his hand.

Another plot of graves. Graves he'd never seen. Graves walled off from the rest of the cemetery like they'd never existed.

He'd been so close—all along, he'd felt the spirit's anger without finding its grave site. Had he never found what he was looking for simply because he'd never stepped through a gap in the cemetery wall? He'd never had reason to do so.

He gripped the stone, something expanding painfully in his chest. Because he hadn't stepped through a gap in a wall. Because he hadn't stepped through a *gap* in a *wall*. Because he hadn't...

Sayid tugged his arm.

"Come on," he squeaked. "Come on, we have to find Samira."

"Samira." Her name rooted in Peter's mind. He shot to his feet. "Samira!"

They jogged through the meadow, eyes peeled for more headstones. Sandstone and slate, carved with angels of death and broken columns, sunken halfway into the ground. Engravings so weathered they were barely visible. Sayid skittered away from them.

At the meadow's far end was a ring of yew trees. Peter skidded to a halt.

Sayid shied like a spooked horse. "What is it?"

Clenching his fists, Peter approached the yews. Their glossy leaves trembled in the wind. One tree was uprooted, leaning like a sinking ship, its leaves brown and crumbling.

"Fuck," Peter whispered.

Sayid's eyebrows shot up, but he repeated, "What is it?"

"Something was back here. But it's a sure fact it ain't now. They must've planted these trees to keep it in. Walled this off from the rest of the cemetery so's no one'd disturb it." Peter rubbed a leaf between his thumb and forefinger. "Good plan, 'til it was me looking for it."

They picked their way past the dead yew. Rain pattered. Peter's heart hammered despite his calm voice. Two months of searching, frustration, confusion.

Now he was here.

Within the circle of yews, a headstone.

O.S.
1851

The painful expansion in his chest exploded. He gasped, couldn't get enough oxygen no matter how hard he sucked down air. To find his brother's headstone—the only grave he'd seen of any of his family—

"Samira," he gasped, because he couldn't break down, he couldn't—

"Peter."

His nails dug into his palms, leaving red crescents in his skin.

He took a long, shuddering breath, gripped the strap of his bag. Forced himself to focus on Sayid. The thin anxious face, the wide dark eyes. The hands twisting in the hem of his T-shirt.

"Look," Sayid said.

A Marian symbol was carved into the headstone, but a jagged crack ran through it, splitting it in two. Peter ran a finger over it, chest heaving.

A few feet away lay a thin iron band.

He lunged for it.

"No," he whispered.

"What?" Sayid's voice pitched higher than ever. "What is it?"

Peter's chest was on fire. The rain turned to a drizzle.

"The ghost is loose," he said, "and Samira freed him."

LIII

"They must be downtown." Sayid's voice shook. "It was—things were—" He swallowed, grasping Peter's hand so tightly it hurt. "When I crossed Main on the way, the wind—and the trees—the anger was so heavy—"

Peter's feet guided them downtown mechanically. "Must've been headed that way."

The drizzle plastered their hair to their foreheads, their shirts to their skin. It fell harder as they jogged toward Main Street. Thunder rumbled.

He should've known. The pine grove overlooked the gap in the wall. He should've guessed Samira had explored the other side, should've checked back there when he couldn't find the grave site.

He'd figured there was none. No headstone, anyway—unmarked, or eroded away to nothing.

It hadn't occurred to him the grave might be outside the cemetery. Or, as it turned out, within the cemetery—within its original bounds but walled off from the rest. Not one of the cemetery maps he'd seen had included that plot. It was as if it had never existed.

If only he'd asked Samira about the anger when it hadn't seemed to affect her. But he hadn't wanted to scare her. And now—

Sayid pinched his arm.

Busted hydrants flooded Main Street. Shattered glass glinted on sidewalks. Wind howled through broken windows. The buildings shifted and creaked as if in a hurricane.

People darted outside in spurts, fleeing down alleyways. Emergency vehicles' lights flashed in the west, sirens wailing. Lightning forked through the sky. The maples waved their silvery leaves in alarm.

"There she is," Sayid said in relief.

She was coming down the steps of the general store. Rain soaked her hair and clothes.

She glanced up. Found Peter's face through the rain.

Her lip curled.

His stomach twisted, his fingers curling into fists. A downed powerline sizzled.

"No," he whispered.

Sayid splashed in her direction, but Peter gripped his shoulder. "Don't, lad."

"I have to get her home, I have to—"

"That ain't her. Not right now."

"What do you—?"

He pulled Sayid along by the scruff of his neck. Samira strode toward them with a stormy glint in her eye. Streetlights burst in her wake. The downed powerline sparked, smoldered. Smoke hissed whitely through the rain.

"The ghost," Sayid whimpered. "The ghost has her, doesn't he? That's him."

Peter nodded, his mind racing. He had to get Sayid out of here, but where? In all the chaos, with broken glass, busted hydrants, downed powerlines, running home alone wouldn't be safe. Samira might go after him. And maybe—

His thoughts lost their footing as a Focus barreled past. He yanked Sayid from the road. The car hydroplaned, screeching to a stop up the street.

The doors banged open. Yafa and Khalid leaped out. Peter's stomach clenched.

Yafa grabbed Sayid with a cry.

Khalid's face was pinched. "Where's your sister?"

She was striding through the rain, her dark hair billowing. Khalid didn't relax, exactly, but he exhaled and put his thumb and forefinger to the corners of his eyes.

"Samira!" he called, but Sayid tugged his arm.

"Baba, don't."

"Don't—why—?"

Screams erupted up the street. Fire blazed from the downed powerline as Samira passed. Flames roared, racing up the pole, licking the side of a building. Power cables sparked and popped.

"Samira!"

Her parents darted forward, but Peter blocked their path.

"You need to get to the museum. Now."

"The museum?"

"Why?"

"I'll explain later."

"Later is right." Khalid shoved past. "I'm not going anywhere without my daughter."

Peter tried to herd him toward the car, to no avail. Car alarms blared up the street. The al-Masris' Focus honked and whooped along with them. Khalid ignored them all, his gaze fixed on Samira and the fire following in her wake.

Desperate, Peter grasped his wrist. "You stay here, you're in danger."

Khalid wrenched away and struck him in the jaw.

Peter swore. He grabbed Khalid around the waist and dragged him back toward the car. Khalid flailed in his arms, trying to break away or hit Peter again—anything to get to his daughter.

Peter's jaw radiated pain, but he'd had worse. "Sayid, get your mam and get in the car."

He threw Khalid in back, slammed the door, and leaped into

the driver's seat. Sayid shoved his mother inside and scrambled into the passenger's seat, hitting the child locks.

"Sorry," he said shakily. "It's for your own good."

"Sayid—"

"Peter—"

"What are you *doing*?"

"We're not leaving Samira!"

Peter ignored their protests: Yafa's pleading, Khalid's yelling. The Focus shrieked even as Peter pulled a U-turn and sped toward the boarding house. Sayid shrank into his seat with his fingers in his ears. The Saint-John's-wort curled around him protectively. The tires screeched. Khalid clambered halfway over the back seat and tried to wrestle the steering wheel from Peter's grasp.

Peter grunted, bending over the wheel so Khalid couldn't reach. "God almighty."

Sayid turned around, his expression scared. "Don't, Baba. Please."

Khalid's chest heaved as if he'd run a marathon. His eyes glistened with angry tears, but at the fear in his son's voice, he slowly sank back into his seat.

"Your sister," he rasped.

"It's all right." Sayid's voice pitched high. "It'll be all right. But you have to come with us right now."

The museum lights twinkled. The building creaked and moaned but was otherwise unbothered by the gusting rain.

Except for the forgotten cemetery pickup, David's car was alone in the parking lot. Peter threw the al-Masris' car into Park, pocketed the keys so they couldn't race right back downtown, and stumbled through the lot. The car alarm finally quieted.

Yafa begged to go back, to get her daughter, but Sayid dragged her toward the museum.

"It's all right, Mama," he said, over and over. "It's going to be all right."

Khalid was silent. He stumbled along in a daze, gripping his wife's hand.

The porch was deserted. The wicker chairs had blown over in the wind.

The front door flew open as they mounted the steps. David's brow was creased.

"What's going on? I've been hearing sirens—Nevaeh called this afternoon to tell me the same thing you did, to stay put, and Noah called twenty minutes ago, something about trouble downtown—"

Peter pushed past him.

"Isaiah!" he roared.

David's eyebrows shot into his hairline, but he turned to the al-Masris as they staggered inside. He fussed over their drawn faces and slumped shoulders. Sayid dragged the wicker chairs into the entryway; David made the couple sit.

His brow furrowed at the three of them. "Where's—?"

Khalid dropped his head into his hands with a moan. Yafa leaned into him. Sayid stood over them like he was their parent.

David stumped after Peter on his crutches. "What's going on? Where's Samira? What's happening downtown?"

Peter didn't respond. *"Isaiah!"*

"What are you yelling about? And why on earth are you—?"

The museum lights flickered and stabilized.

A figure materialized. A young man with dark hair and a crooked nose, taller than David, in trousers and an oversize sweater. Looking as he had the day they met, how David most often remembered him, rather than how he looked in the photo on the wall.

David stared, his face pale.

"Isaiah?" he whispered.

Isaiah smiled at him. David ran a hand over his face, squeezed his eyes shut, and opened them again. "What...?"

Khalid gazed at Isaiah dully. The stairs were visible through him, pale and wavery as if seen through old glass-block windows.

"I don't understand," Khalid mumbled. "I don't understand what's happening."

"He's a ghost, Baba," Sayid said. Yafa said nothing, her eyes fixed on Isaiah. "Mr. Isaiah. Like the one who took Samira."

"Took...?"

"Isaiah," Peter said.

Isaiah tore his gaze from David's face.

"He's on his way." Peter sucked in his cheeks, gripping the strap of his bag. "He's got Samira."

Isaiah's expression darkened. The lights flickered again and again stabilized. The letters and drawings on the wall behind his ashes fluttered and settled.

"I'll head him off if I can," Peter said. "But if he gets past me, if he gets past me, you keep him out of this building. However you can. Keep them safe."

Isaiah vanished. David slumped on his crutches, his eyes damp. Peter grasped his shoulders and kissed the creases from his forehead.

"Stay here," he said gently. "Isaiah'll look after you."

David's laugh was half a sob. "He always did."

Peter strode for the door. Yafa shot to her feet, grabbing his hand.

"Peter—"

"I'll bring her back. I'll get her. Somehow. Promise."

She released him. He leaped down the steps and headed back up the street to meet Samira—and his brother.

LIV

Lightning flashed. Smoke billowed. Broken windows gaped like mouths with jagged teeth. Rain stung Peter's face, his hands. He called for Samira as he jogged back downtown, blinking rain from his eyes.

She came to meet him.

Wind gusted. Ambulances rumbled back and forth. Fire trucks at the west end of the street wrestled with the fire now blackening the bricks of several buildings. People trickled from broken storefronts at the instruction of emergency services personnel.

"Brother," Samira called, in a voice that was not quite hers. "At last."

A paramedic jogged toward her. "Hey, kid!"

"Don't!" Peter shouted.

One moment, the paramedic had a hand on Samira's shoulder, asking where her parents were. The next, a shock wave blasted him through the air.

He smashed into a building and collapsed on the sidewalk. Blood trickled from his forehead.

Peter's heart hammered, but he focused on Samira. If he kept his brother's attention, no one else need get hurt.

She stopped barely six feet from him. It was Samira's face. Samira's dark eyes and hair. Samira's thin shoulders and tank top and shorts and sneakers drenched from the rain and the busted hydrants.

But her eyes flashed, and something in her stance was familiar from old, old, *old* memories. Something languid, despite the tension in her jaw, the anger in her eyes, in the air.

"Knew it was you," she breathed, in that voice that was not quite hers. "Felt it, when you come here. Harrington felt familiar in a way it never did before."

"Like home," Peter whispered.

Her fists clenched.

"Like home." The street flashed silver with maple leaves. "Even though it was you what ruined it."

Peter twisted the strap of his bag. "What're you on about?"

Every light in every building on the block went out.

Samira was inches from him, glaring at him with eyes so big they swallowed up her face. He shivered, suppressed the urge to step back. The storm overhead was suddenly far away.

"Sure, so guiltless, aren't you?" she whispered. "You've no idea what happened to us after you left, do you?"

"I have some idea," Peter said quietly.

Samira's eyes smoldered. Electricity crackled in the dark buildings.

"Our farm, gone. Our income. Mam's health. And no one'd give me more'n odd jobs because everyone knew my brother was a murderer."

Peter flinched. She plunged a hand to his chest, her fingers twisting in his shirt.

"Everyone. Every friend and neighbor we had. They all knew you done it."

"Samira," Peter said hoarsely. "Samira, I know you're in there, child, I know—"

"Everyone," she repeated more forcefully.

Her fingers clawed into him. He forgot about the fires and

flooding and emergency vehicles. Everything swept away in the wake of that night and the centuries after.

"Not everyone. Mam didn't. I know she didn't."

She released him. "No, Mam never did, lord knows why."

"Jack, neither," Peter whispered.

She huffed a disdainful laugh. "Him, neither. Broke his heart, it did, you leavin'."

"I know," Peter said, and knowing he and Jack had found each other again did nothing to comfort him.

"He *pined* for you. It was more'n you deserved."

"I know," Peter repeated miserably.

She pushed him. His boots caught on the pavement. She seemed to grow taller, her dark eyes huge in her face, her hair drifting around her, her anger—Eoin's anger—towering over him, suspended like a crimson tidal wave.

"Y'ruined us. Mam, me—Catherine dead at your own hand—"

"I didn't." She pushed him again, harder. He fell but didn't get up. The concrete scraped his elbows. "I swear it, Eoin, I swear to you I didn't. One o' *them folk* struck me a curse—"

She crouched before him, grabbed him by the collar. Thunder rumbled, distantly, muted. The towering anger swayed.

"I don't care," she said through gritted teeth. "Either way, our sister dead, you run off, my home gone—my income—my dignity—my *mam*, my *wife*, my *daughter*—"

The anger broke upon him, and so did the storm. The wind howled. Rain lashed his eyes. Thunder cracked. She didn't push him this time: she *threw* him.

He crashed into the pavement, rolled over and over. His left arm crumpled in a blaze of pain. The elbow of his other sleeve had torn. His arm oozed blood.

He clawed at his bag. The strap had twisted around itself, choking him. He struggled to open the bag, grasping for salt, holy water, anything he could lob at her to drive the spirit away without hurting her.

She reached him before he got the bag open. His broken arm dangled uselessly.

"Everything I had," she snarled, "gone because of you."

"Eoin—"

She threw him again. He slammed into a building with a yelp. His spine throbbed like a horse had kicked him. His whole body throbbed, no body at all but a mass of pain held together by nothing but his curse. The street fuzzed.

She kicked him, snatched his bag, flung it into the street. An ambulance rumbled over it.

Peter reached for the building at his back, focusing on the bricks' roughness, desperate for anything but pain, tried to think, *think*—

Her words bored into him. "Ill luck hounded me my whole life. Like I was cursed when you scarpered. And this town—*this town*—"

Her eyes crackled. Lightning sizzled. The whole block blazed with fire. A van skidded by, lost control, and slammed into a building. The driver fell out, clutching their head. The van's engine smoked.

Peter crawled away from Samira, but she flung out a hand, blasting him into the air. She threw him again and again, like it was nothing, like he was a rag doll she'd come to hate.

"This place was supposed to be mine," she roared. "Harrington promised me a future bright and glittering, gave me the first happiness I'd known in more'n a decade, only to snatch it away again."

She'd thrown Peter so far the boarding house was in sight, its lights twinkling as if unaware of the chaos.

Peter spat blood from his mouth. He staggered to his feet despite the screaming of every cell in his body, dragging a broken leg.

"I'm sorry," he said wearily. "I'm sorry I left. Wouldn't've, if I'd've had a choice."

She'd been striding closer, but suddenly she was in his face. Her fists clenched in his shirt. Her eyes flickered over him, stormier than ever.

"Not sorry enough. But you will be."

"Samira—child, please—"

Her grip tightened.

"I am going to kill you," she whispered, "avenge Catherine and Mam and the life you took from us. And then I will raze Harrington to the ground for all it took from me."

Peter's breath stabbed out of him like he'd punctured a lung. Perhaps he had.

"Guarantee you won't kill me," he said, "but you can try."

LV

Peter hit the boarding house's porch steps. The metallic tang of blood soured his mouth. His heart rabbited against his rib cage. He sat up, again, impossibly.

Isaiah pulsed crimson at his side, ready to attack. Peter shook his head. Sharp pains stabbed his neck.

Samira prowled before him. Her hair drifted eerily despite the wet.

"How are you still alive?" she snapped. "You should be dead ten times over."

She kicked him in the ribs, her words punctuating her kicks. "How—are you still—alive?"

The museum door banged open. She snarled up at the person framed in the doorway.

Khalid stared at them with wide, horrified eyes. Sayid was behind him, a hand clenched in his father's shirt. The house rumbled with thunder.

Peter froze.

"Samira?" Khalid whispered.

Sayid dragged him back inside. Peter held his breath.

Samira's lip curled. Her eyes darted over his face.

"I see," she said softly.

The hair on the back of his neck stood up. "Don't. Don't, Eoin, please, I beg you—"

She shoved him aside and leaped up the steps. He grabbed her ankle, but she kicked his hand away.

"No—" He dragged himself up the steps. "Isaiah!"

The lights in the boarding house dimmed and brightened. Isaiah materialized in the doorway.

He rushed at Samira. She tumbled down the stairs with a yelp. Though she was Eoin right now, Peter reached for her. Eoin was destroying downtown, breaking Peter's bones, threatening his friends, but Samira's body was paying the price.

She leaped to her feet, clawing hair from her eyes. Isaiah vanished and reappeared at the bottom of the steps, between her and Peter.

His voice echoed softly. "Go."

"Don't hurt her," Peter said hoarsely. "Get him away from her if you can."

Isaiah nodded. Samira threw herself at him with a snarl.

Peter scrambled up the steps. His body was tearing itself apart.

His friends assaulted him with questions as he burst inside, but he ignored them. The museum's usual calm had gone, sucked away as Isaiah used his power to fend off Eoin. Without him, the building was drab, weighted by anger like everywhere else in town. Thunder rolled; the building shook. Photographs trembled on the walls.

"Salt," Peter barked at David.

David's eyes raked over his body, his broken arm, his broken leg, his bloody nose, his cuts and bruises and torn shirt and the gravel and glass embedded in his skin. "Wh-what?"

Peter limped toward the kitchen. His broken leg dragged. He bumped into the dining table, flinching as pain jolted him.

"Salt. I need salt. And iron."

Nina and Anne Hodinka's sepia-toned eyes followed him from the wall.

David trailed after him. "You need—bandages. Casts. A hospital. Look at you, you're—"

"I'm fine."

"We have iron." Sayid had a fireplace poker in his shaking hands. His parents were similarly armed with tongs and a shovel. "I remembered. About the iron."

"Good lad. But we need salt, too. If he comes in here and we don't get him away from Samira, these'll be all but useless. David!"

David jumped, staring at him blankly.

"Salt," Peter repeated. "Where d'you keep it?"

"Over the sink."

Thunder crashed. David jumped again. The house creaked and moaned. Outside, Samira tussled with Isaiah, trying to get in.

Peter reached for the cupboard but recoiled, sagging against the counter. His broken limbs needled him.

"Sayid." He spat blood into the sink. "Be a good lad and get the salt for me."

He ached. He *ached*. But he had to hold together until Eoin was gone. Until they were safe.

Sayid retrieved several canisters of salt, herded David back into the dining room, and poured a circle of salt around his parents and David.

"I saw this on TV," he said solemnly.

It wouldn't do any good, with Eoin possessing Samira; she could easily step into the circle. But taking charge this way seemed to calm the boy, so Peter didn't correct him.

The three adults stood meekly inside the salt circle, holding their wrought-iron fire tools. Yafa's and Khalid's faces were wan, tear-streaked, but, like David, they had no idea what to do. So they did whatever Peter and Sayid told them.

The lights flickered and went out.

The front door banged open. Wind gusted papers and blew salt away. Sayid dumped out more.

Samira stepped inside, bringing a storm with her. Rain whipped into the entryway. A picture of Main Street in the 1920s rattled off the dining room wall and crashed to the floor.

Peter's mouth went dry. Yafa moaned, whispered something inaudible. Khalid gripped her hand.

David's voice trembled. "Isaiah?"

Smoothing damp hair back from her face, Samira sauntered into the dining room.

"'Fraid not," she said lazily, in that voice that was not quite hers, always carrying an undercurrent of tension. "He was strong. But I'm stronger."

David's face crumpled. "He's gone?"

"Wore out, is all. Can't take form," Peter said. Isaiah hung around them, a faded sunset color. "S'all right, Isaiah. *You* weren't hitching a ride with an eight-year-old."

Samira scowled. Yafa staggered forward, without leaving the salt circle because Sayid was holding on to her.

Samira cocked her head. "This is the girl's mother, I s'pose."

"The girl has a name," Yafa whispered.

Samira's eyes roved over her.

"Samira. Aye, she told me. Told me plenty about you, too." Her eyes flickered to Khalid. "All of you. 'Bout how alone you left her."

"We didn't—"

"You *left* her," Samira repeated forcefully, "like my dear brother left me."

Her eyes fixed back on Peter, and so did everyone else's. Sayid clutched the canister of salt. The room was dark with storm clouds.

"I don't understand," David said.

Peter didn't look at him, at any of them, didn't take his eyes off Samira. He wasn't far from the picture of Anne and Nina hanging beside the entrance to the kitchen. They gazed at him solemnly, their eyes like honey. If he could only get at it—if he could only remind Eoin of something, anything other than his anger.

Samira's hair whipped around her face. Papers rustled, scattering throughout the room. David shivered. Sayid thumbed the canister of salt open as Samira approached.

Her hands balled into fists. The salt blew inward, swirling around the al-Masris' ankles and David's. Khalid pulled his wife and son close.

"He left me," Samira said, "and my neighbors abandoned me. And now I will have recompense for all I lost."

She stepped into the circle.

Sayid flung salt in her face. She leaped back with a roar, shaking her head. She was smoking, her body unharmed but the spirit within her burning at the contact.

Sayid shoved his parents and David into the kitchen. David stumbled, his crutches snagging on carpet, but Yafa and Khalid dragged him along.

Peter snatched the Hodinkas' picture off the wall. He dove across the kitchen doorway before Samira could follow his friends.

The museum lights came up again. Papers blew around Peter's aching body and into his face. Samira snarled, sweeping salt from her eyes.

"Eoin Shaughnessy!" Peter roared.

Samira shuddered, brushing salt from her skin. Her hands smoked at the contact. She lunged at him, but he thrust the photograph toward her.

She barked a laugh. "What in god's name is that s'posed to do? All out of salt, are you?"

She wrenched the photo from his grasp.

She froze.

The wind died. Papers rustled to the floor.

Her eyes flickered over the photograph. "Nina?"

Peter let out a quiet breath. "Nina. Heartbroken when you died, I hear."

"What would you know about it?" Samira snapped, but she made no move to attack.

"Her mother's diary. November 12, 1851. 'O.S. died today. Nina is inconsolable.' That's you, ain't it?"

Samira ran her fingers over the photograph. "Didn't think anyone cared, when I died."

"She did," Peter said. "Her mam, too, it seems. Who was she to you?"

Nina Hodinka's serious sepia gaze reflected in Samira's eyes.

"The only kindness I knew, in the end," Samira said quietly. "Her pa didn't like me none. He'd've sent me packing once the rent money ran out, if not for her and her mam. We'd lost the store, no one'd give me work... Ballygar all over again."

Her lip trembled. Peter ached to pull her into a hug. If it had really been Samira's lip trembling, he would've.

If Eoin would've accepted his comfort, he would've.

"My worst fear," Samira whispered. "'Twas my worst fear, and it happened again. Everything I had, everything I scraped and clawed and saved for, gone, all gone. My home—my wife—my child—"

Her face twisted. Peter's fingers twitched, clutching for a canister of salt he was no longer holding because he'd put it down to grab the picture, because he only had one functional arm.

The wind picked back up. Dust devils swirled papers and salt through the room.

"I liked to imagine," Samira said, "that Nina was my own Kitty. How Kitty might've been in a few more years, if she'd lived. Used to bring me treats, Nina did, when her mam did the baking. She fair mothered me. Told me stories like Mam used to, tucked me in when I took cold...gave me her doll to sleep with one night. Heard me weepin', she did. Thought it might comfort me like it did her."

She dragged a hand over her face. "It was more'n I deserved. And I knew it. And I loved the little lass for it."

"She must've loved you, too," a quivering voice said from the kitchen.

David was at Peter's shoulder. Sayid thrust a canister of salt over David's shoulder like a gun. Yafa and Khalid pressed against them.

Samira glared at them. "What?"

Peter sucked in a breath, reached for David. David shifted closer and spoke again, like he couldn't help himself because it was history.

"Nina Hodinka?" he said. "She married Kasimir Kopczyk in the 1860s. Their youngest son was named Eoin. That's you—isn't it?" His brow furrowed. "Eoin Shaughnessy? She named her son after you."

Her expression softened, slowly. Went so hopeful it hurt.

"She never."

David's voice still quivered, but he shrugged. "She named him Eoin."

Samira stared at him. She licked her lips.

"Did she," she asked hoarsely, then faltered. She cleared her throat, clutching the photograph. "Did she live...? When she died, was she...?"

"She was in her nineties, as I recall," David said, his voice slightly less quivery, like reciting the Hodinka-Kopczyk family history soothed him.

Samira sighed quietly.

"I'm glad of it." Her shoulders sagged. "If my own little girl could've lived so long..."

Peter lurched forward. Lurching was the only way he could move now. The adrenaline that had sustained him through Eoin's rage was fading. Fog curled at the edges of his mind. Pain rushed in like a tide.

"Samira's someone's little girl, too." Behind him, Yafa and

Khalid clung to each other. "You'd take her from 'em like the cholera took your Kitty? Like one o' *them folk* took our Catherine?"

Yafa pressed a hand to her mouth. Samira glanced at her dolefully.

"S'pose not."

She crumpled. The Hodinkas' photograph clattered to the floor.

Yafa let out a sob. Khalid's grip on her tightened, his face taut. Isaiah fluttered helplessly. Sayid darted past David, but Peter had already caught her, sinking to his knees with a groan.

Mistake. Samira weighed on his broken body like an anchor. Pain streaked through his bones like fire.

Sayid took his sister from Peter, brushing hair from her face. Her eyelids fluttered.

"It's all right," David said shakily. "It's all right, she's alive…"

Yafa pushed past him and pulled her children close, crushing them against her. Khalid knelt slowly beside her, but his brow was furrowed.

Three feet in front of them, a translucent man took form. Tall but hunched, shoulders bowed. Peter's height, with the same nose and the same chin and the same blue eyes, but eyes fainter and sadder and, even now, angrier.

"Mam always said it was *them folk.*"

The fog in Peter's brain thickened, spread, but at his brother's voice, the voice of someone from home—so familiar, so different—his heart stuttered.

"Always insisted it wasn't you what done it. Took to blaming *them folk* for everything and anything, after you left… Thought she'd gone mad with grief." Eoin gazed at his brother. "Always did warn us 'bout *them folk*, didn't she."

Peter rasped a laugh, but he wanted to cry. "She was right, Mam was. She always warned us, and I didn't listen."

Eoin rubbed his chin, looking exhausted. "Spent so long

raging at you. But I guess if you hadn't've cleared off, I never would've come looking for work…never would've met Kathleen."

He shoved his hands in his see-through pockets.

"Don't hardly remember her." He shone blue with grief, the color hazing through him, softening his edges. "My Kathy. Kitty, neither. My whole world, they were, but I don't hardly remember their faces."

"Held too fast to your anger." Peter tasted blood. "Held too tight to the things you were afraid of, instead of holding on to how you loved 'em. David—" something stabbed at his lungs "—get me that picture. The one from the box."

David stumped into the office and back. He slipped the daguerreotype of Eoin and his family from its protective case.

Eoin eyed it hungrily, drifting closer.

Peter shivered—flinched; the shiver rattled his aching bones. He held out the daguerreotype. It trembled in his hand, shaking the gently blurred faces of Eoin's wife and child.

A sharp intake of nonbreath because Eoin didn't breathe. The spirit took the daguerreotype in his ghostly hands, skimmed translucent fingers over his wife's face.

"Kathy." Pearlescent tears rolled down his cheeks. "My Kathy."

"I'm sorry," Peter said.

Eoin dashed tears away with an arm. "Always thought I'd see 'em again, when I died."

"Still can."

The fog in Peter's head blackened. He wobbled on his knees, steadied himself on Sayid's shoulder.

"You let go of that hurt, that anger, you'll move on." He hesitated. "'Twasn't right, what happened to you. If I could've stayed—"

He squeezed his eyes shut. Another mistake. Stars burst behind his eyelids. He clamped down harder on Sayid's shoulder, forcing his eyes open. The whole room was translucent now.

"I wanted to stay," he said faintly. "I'm sorry I left you. You and Mam and the farm. I wish you'd lived better. Longer. Your wife and child, too. All I can do now is help you move on. If you want it."

Eoin drifted. "They'll be there? They'll be there waitin', if I go?"

"I don't know," Peter said wistfully. "I've never died. They ain't here anymore, that much is certain."

Eoin's mouth curved up. "One way to find out, eh?"

"Tell us about Kathy."

Eoin gazed at the daguerreotype as if he'd forgotten everyone staring at him.

"Met her back East," he said, "livin' in Brooklyn. She used to do seamstressing with her mam. Sang like a bird, she did. Used to hear her warbling away at her work in the tenement across the alley…fell in love with her voice before I ever met her."

He softened as he spoke. Not his expression, but his whole body: he became vague and shimmery like morning mist.

"Her pa didn't like me none, thought I was a good-for-nothing because I never had a job long. Had a hard time finding work, same's back home. She didn't care. First time I met her, 'twas a Christmas dinner party, and she looks me up and down and she says, 'I know who you are.' I used to grow a garden up there on the rooftop, see. And she'd seen it and loved it like I'd loved her singing."

His form grew fainter, shimmerier. The dining room gleamed, the edges of the table and chairs gilded softly silver.

"She stuck by me all the time I was looking for work, helped me save up for a train ticket when I wanted to try my luck out West. She was the light of my life, was Kathy…"

"Say hi to Mam for me," Peter whispered.

Eoin's voice faded, and so did he, in a gentle glow like the sun burning away fog.

The daguerreotype fluttered to the ground. A weight lifted from the boarding house, his anger evaporating with him. Isaiah twisted through the building like a sigh.

Peter let out a breath, in too much pain for more than a vague sense of relief, of loss.

Samira stirred in her mother's arms. "Mama?"

Peter's breath caught.

"Habibti!"

Yafa smothered Samira with tearful kisses, her forehead, her nose, her eyes, her cheeks. Khalid leaned into them, his own eyes damp and red, and suddenly the al-Masris were piled in a hug on the ground. Samira sobbed into her mother's chest, saying over and over, "I'm sorry, Mama. I'm sorry."

"Is—is he gone?" David asked. "Or...like Isaiah?"

"He's gone." Peter collapsed with a groan, a relief after holding himself together for so long. "Moved on. He won't be back."

David stumped closer. "Peter—are you—"

The room blurred. The al-Masris disentangled from one another. Peter glimpsed Samira's face, pale and panicked. He tried to tell her it was all right. Instead, he coughed blood.

"Call 911."

Yafa's voice echoed like his brother's. Khalid was already on the phone. Sayid crowded at Peter's side, his thin face anxious. Peter grasped his hand, let go again. His broken bones stabbed him from within, his skin burned, and the metallic tang in his mouth made him want to gag, but he couldn't gag because it hurt too much.

Not now. The world fuzzed and darkened. He'd wanted to die for so long, but not like this. Not without saying goodbye. Not afire with agony after all the agony of his life. Not with people he cared about there but unable to do anything. He thought of

Nevaeh with a pang; she wasn't even here, because she'd done as he'd asked and gone safely away.

Sirens blared. The rain pattered. Isaiah hung over him, lemon-yellow, bitter as dandelion greens.

The last thing he heard, as he lost consciousness, was Samira crying and David calling his name hoarsely, over and over.

LVI

Beeping. A faint electrical hum. Voices. Soft and indistinct, pleasantly blurred.

They suggested he was not, perhaps, dead.

He wasn't sure how he felt about that.

The voices coalesced into words.

"—said he's doing much better today."

"I'll believe it when he wakes up and not a second before."

Vinyl squeaking, someone shifting in their chair. "What if he doesn't wake up?"

"He will. He has to."

A pause. "David—"

"He will."

Right, he wanted to say. *Matter of fact, I already have.* But his mouth was cottony, his throat rusty. His tongue had forgotten how to form words.

A creaky groan escaped him.

The voices silenced. The beeping continued, rhythmic and gentle.

"Peter?"

Another groan loosened things up.

Scuffling. The creak of bedsprings, a dip in the mattress. Someone's weight at his side.

His eyes blinked open. Squinted against the harsh fluorescents.

He dimpled, a lump in his throat. David was sitting beside him. Nevaeh had a vinyl armchair scooched up to the foot of the bed. Yafa and Khalid stood by the door.

It looked like any other hospital room. White and clinical, smelling of cleaners. Full of machinery with glowing green screens, most hooked up to him: heart monitor, IV, blood-pressure cuff.

But with his friends there, the hospital room—like his cottage, like the cemetery, like Harrington—felt like home.

He glanced around. Panic gripped him—he tried to sit up, couldn't because David put a hand on his chest—

"Samira," he rasped.

Her mother smiled thinly. "Sayid took her to the cafeteria for lunch. They're both fine. Thanks to you."

He sank back on his pillow. He ached everywhere.

David smoothed his hair. Peter closed his eyes and let him do it.

"How are you feeling?" Nevaeh gripped the arms of her chair. "I was here when they brought you in. You looked..."

"It's amazing you're alive." Khalid leaned against the door-frame, arms folded. "You broke your neck. It looked like you broke your neck. But you're not even..."

Peter touched his neck but changed his mind because moving hurt. He wasn't wearing a neck brace, that much was sure. He was reasonably certain his neck, were it broken before, was not broken now.

"You're doing shockingly well, considering," Yafa said. "It's a miracle they were already able to remove your casts."

"Lucky duck." David's voice quivered. "Six weeks I had mine on, and when I went in to have it off, they told me I had to wait another week. I'm glad I'm finally rid of it."

He kept stroking Peter's hair.

"Been better," Peter said. Nevaeh laughed wetly. "Been worse, too."

"It's hard to imagine that." Khalid's arms tightened across his chest. "Everyone says you should've died."

Yafa elbowed him. "What a thing to say. It wasn't his time, alhamdulillah."

"Alhamdulillah," Khalid echoed, but his arms were crossed so tightly his muscles bulged. "I don't understand. That—ghost. David's been telling us about him. About who he was, I mean, showed us his room and his things and what Anne Hodinka wrote about him in her diary. But the things he said that night… He called you brother."

David put an arm around Peter and stroked his shoulder with a thumb. Peter couldn't remember ever being so content, never, certainly not in any of his many hospital stints over the last two centuries. He forgot how alien he was. Forgot the carefully built walls holding in his strangeness and secrets.

"That's because he is my brother. Was my brother."

The al-Masris glanced at each other. Nevaeh shifted in her seat. David's thumb stilled on Peter's shoulder, then continued its progress. The heart monitor beeped on, unconcerned.

"How is that possible?" David asked. "Eoin Shaughnessy died in 1851."

Peter closed his eyes. "You wouldn't believe me if I told you."

David rubbed the back of his neck.

"I know I told you I work in facts." He laughed ruefully. "But after everything that happened that night… I admit I might not believe it if everyone hadn't seen the same thing, but right now I'm feeling pretty open-minded."

Peter glanced at Nevaeh. Her fingers were tight on the vinyl armchair, but the corner of her mouth turned up. Affection for her washed over him. He dimpled at her despite his pain.

He said it to her, because telling someone who already knew was easier.

"I can't die." It sounded ridiculous, out loud. "Can't be killed.

Been around more'n two hundred years already, and no sign of stopping. As you see."

He gestured at himself, hoping they'd laugh. No one did.

David's thumb brushed hesitantly over the three long scars on Peter's inner arm, visible for once past the sleeves of his hospital gown.

"Is that why...these scars..."

"That was the last time." Peter gently withdrew his arm from David's grasp. "Jack..."

His voice caught. Jack's crooked smile shone behind his eyelids, seared into his memory. An image he'd carry if he found himself wandering the desolation alone at the world's end.

"1893 it was when he died." His voice wobbled. "Both of us in our eighties and me not looking a day older'n I do now, but I figured I'd follow him soon enough. So I waited. And waited. And waited. And my hundredth birthday came and went, and still I looked no older, and all our neighbors, they muttered about dark magic and crossed themselves when they saw me coming. And I began to understand."

David touched his cheek. Peter met his eyes and found them soft, concerned. Such wanting welled up in him that he could've cried. He hated the way this town, these people, made him want so much: it only gave the curse something more to take from him.

Khalid draped an arm around his wife, his expression wary.

"Understand?" Yafa whispered.

"The curse." The clinical white walls of the room wavered, shifting between hospital and forest. Peter rubbed his blanket between thumb and forefinger to ground himself. "To wander eternally far from home. I should've died many times over, but I haven't, and every time I've tried to go home, it's gone wrong. He never knew, Eoin. Thought I up and left 'em. He never knew about the curse."

He dragged a hand over his face.

"He was right about me," he whispered. "Everything that happened to 'em, Catherine, the eviction—the curse. My fault."

David dabbed Peter's cheeks with a handkerchief; tears had slipped down his face. His lungs seized. He saw himself dumping his basket as if it were happening this moment, but it wasn't. It was two centuries past, and he couldn't stop it.

"It destroyed us." His breath burst out of him. The heart monitor beeped faster and faster. "My baby sister, God rest her, and me chased clear out of Ireland, and the Hunger took Mam, and Eoin—"

His brother's life had been so brief and miserable the curse might've followed him across the Atlantic.

"If I'd only hung the garlands like Mam asked." A sob escaped him. The walls closed in on him. David rubbed his back in slow circles. "But I didn't, because Jack was waiting, and I wouldn't leave him a moment longer. All of 'em gone because I wanted—I wanted—"

Two hundred years of guilt and grief ripped through him, kept at bay for so long by walls Harrington had long since crumbled. It cracked him open and tore him apart and spilled his worst parts out everywhere.

David's arms around him were all that kept him anchored, and Nevaeh's, too, when she bolted from her chair to sit on his other side. Dry sobs racked his body.

At last he quieted. He hiccupped intermittently in their arms. The walls receded. The heart monitor's frantic beeping calmed.

"M'sorry," he mumbled.

David's arms tightened around him. Nevaeh wiped her eyes surreptitiously.

"What are you sorry for?" Yafa asked softly. Khalid's face was strained.

Peter wasn't sure what he was sorry for, so he snuggled into David's chest. For everything. For nothing. For wanting too much and attending to too little.

Nevaeh stood and stretched, sniffling. She blinked at the ceiling, smiled a few times, stretching her cheeks and lips until her smile looked natural.

"So, um, not that this hasn't been super fun," she said, "but I promised Granny I'd help with the baking today. Her church group's having a bake sale. If you're still okay to give me a ride?" she said to Khalid.

He pushed off the doorframe, brow still furrowed. "Sure thing. I could use a coffee anyhow."

"I'll walk you out." Yafa gave Peter a small smile, less thin. "The children will want to see you, if you have the energy."

Peter wiped his eyes on his wrist. "I'd like that."

Nevaeh hugged him. He sank into it, hugged her back. She smelled like coconut oil, and her arms were warm and tight around his neck.

"Granny says Dad misses you," she whispered. "You should come by the house for dinner sometime. You know. When you're out."

His heart contracted. He didn't plan to stay, once he was out. His arms sagged around her. "Right."

She trailed after Yafa and Khalid, leaving him alone with David.

David pulled him close and held him. Living forever would be no punishment, he thought, if he could stay here like this. David's heart beat steadily in his ear, keeping time with his own.

"I'm so glad you're all right," David whispered.

Peter wanted to tell him that he was glad, too. To thank him for being here. He almost opened his mouth to say it. The words stuck in his throat.

He listened to David's heartbeat, memorizing its rhythm for when it was no longer with him.

David moved away. He pulled the vinyl chair up alongside the bed, clearing his throat. Peter settled onto his pillow.

"So," David said. "What's next on the immortal ghost-hunter's agenda?"

Peter looked at him. "You believe me?"

David huffed a laugh. "It explains a lot."

He smoothed wrinkles from Peter's blanket.

"I don't know. It's impossible. But so are the things I saw that night." He propped his chin on his fists. "So? Really. What now?"

Peter didn't have to tell him. He never told anyone. He appeared one day and left another without anyone ever knowing where he'd come from or where he'd gone.

But they did know where he'd come from, now. Knew his name. Knew *him*.

David cocked his head, birdlike. Peter had a feeling he'd wait forever rather than push for an answer.

It made this so much harder. He spread his hands on the blanket and gazed at his fingers.

"I'm leaving. Soon's I'm out of hospital."

Silence. Then David said, "You're not serious?"

"It's what's best."

"For whom, exactly?"

Peter spoke to his fingers, quietly. "Everyone."

"Bullshit."

They fell silent.

David scratched the back of his neck. "Look at me."

Peter dragged his gaze away from his fingers, but his eyes only flickered over David's before settling on his mouth.

David leaned in. "Do you want to leave?"

He had never wanted anything so little. The thought of leaving Harrington put a weight in his stomach, made him ache in a way that had nothing to do with the stark room or the hard little bed or the beeping monitors.

"Yes," he whispered.

David's shoulders sagged. "Peter—"

"I can't," Peter said. "I can't. When Jack died—"

He rubbed his scars.

"I lost everyone who ever meant anything to me." A weight settled in his chest. "If I let myself stay, it'll be more of the same. I can't go through that again. I won't."

David snorted. Peter looked at him in surprise.

"So, what? You run off to protect yourself, and the rest of us get no say in the matter? What about our loss?" David gestured at the door. "These people care about you. *I* care about you. I—"

He ran a hand through his hair. Peter buried the part of himself that wanted to do the same, trying to forget how soft David's hair had been that night on the couch.

"I don't expect you to understand."

David laughed hollowly.

"You know," he said, drumming his fingers on the arm of the chair, "you're not the only one. I lost Isaiah. More than thirty years together, and it ended in a hospital room with him in so much pain he barely knew I was there." His voice shook, but he kept talking. "Isaiah's Aunt Margaret died long before. Nevaeh and her family, they lost Eli. The al-Masris buried Yafa's dad not two days after we got you to the hospital. And I don't suppose they told you, but Khalid's older brother died in a car crash late last year, before you came to town."

"David—"

"That's what life is." David sounded annoyed, almost angry. "You lose people you love and you love more people and you lose them, too, and you keep loving anyway because what's the point otherwise?"

"It ain't the same."

"Why not?"

All the two hundred years he'd lived pressed in on him at once.

"Because you'll die someday," he said. "And I won't."

David's anger ebbed away. His fingers stilled on the armchair. His gray eyes roved over Peter's face, soft and sad.

Then something shuttered in them.

Peter swallowed and tried not to care.

"Okay." David rubbed his thighs, stood up, and paced once around the room. "Okay."

"David," Peter said, but he slipped out and was gone. The door shut with a snap.

Peter's eyes stung. He buried his face in his hands. The room that had seemed so warm and homelike, despite the clinical walls, was now cold and gray.

Best this way, he reminded himself, as he had every time in the last hundred years he'd cared too much and vanished in the night before it could hurt him. *Best for you to forget them and them you.*

This time, he didn't quite believe it.

The door opened.

His head snapped up. A blur shaped more or less like an eight-year-old girl hurled itself onto his bed and tackled him with a strangled yell.

"Careful!" Sayid said, hurrying along behind her.

Their mother seated herself in David's vacated chair. "Gently, children. He's in the hospital for a reason."

Sayid deposited himself at Peter's side. Peter was buried in Samira's limbs and hair, but he pulled Sayid in, too. He closed his eyes and held them close. A fragile thing inside him splintered as they clung to him.

"I'm sorry," Samira said in his ear. "I'm sorry. I'm sorry. I'm sorry."

Maybe, if he kept his eyes closed, he could stay like this. Maybe, if he kept his eyes closed, he'd never have to leave, move on to the next town, the next cemetery, the next ghost, and forget Harrington.

Samira pulled away. Her thin face was worn, her eyes baggy and shadowed.

"Mama said you'd be happy to see me."

His breath hitched. "I am happy, child. I'm happy you two are safe."

She touched his cheek hesitantly, with one finger. "You're crying."

He'd tried so hard to hold it back when David walked out, but she'd knocked it loose when she bowled into him. Yafa's eyes were on him, but she said nothing. Sayid snuggled into him.

"You're not supposed to cry when you're happy," Samira said.

A chuckle slipped out. He swallowed hard.

"All right, then," he said hoarsely. "No more tears."

She slipped her arms back around his neck. He held her and her brother tight and wept silently into her hair.

LVII

David did not come back.

Peter did not stop waiting for him to walk through the door.

His only comfort was that David hadn't told the others. Yafa and the kids visited almost every day, and Nevaeh more often than not, but none of them betrayed any knowledge of his plans.

He hadn't told them himself. He'd regretted telling David the moment the door had closed behind him. He couldn't tell the others he was leaving, too.

It was for their own good. Each visit they had was more cheerful than the last. He didn't want to ruin it.

They had their uneasy moments; they couldn't forget what they'd gone through. But Yafa had put her entire family in therapy, which helped even if they couldn't tell their therapist about the ghosts, and Peter's indecently hasty recovery relaxed them.

Not so the hospital staff, who were flummoxed by his improvement, annoyed their gloomy prognoses hadn't held true, and vexed he refused to undergo a barrage of tests to decipher how he'd recuperated so fully from such extensive injuries in such little time. Needing to exert some modicum of control over his treatment, his doctors kept him in the hospital for days after it was clear he'd recovered. The recommended physical therapy lasted a single session. The physical therapist walked in, examined him, had him try some exercises, raised an eyebrow, and asked the doctor, "Why am I here?"

Yafa threw a party the day he was released in mid-July, declaring they needed a celebration after the last six months' gloom. There were pizza and baklava in abundance, mutabal and pita from Maryam, and balloons because Samira insisted, and a Marvel marathon on TV because Khalid insisted. He was more relaxed than Peter had ever seen him: he'd taken a marketing job in Toledo that paid less but required no farther travel than his daily commute.

Chloe and Jess were there, too, with Chloe's mother. Nevaeh had brought Benji, who looked awkward. Benji relaxed when Samira, eyeballing their bomber jacket like she'd like one of her own, dragged them upstairs to see her spy paraphernalia. Everyone crowded around a food-laden folding table that Khalid had set up in the front yard. They ate standing, with paper plates or napkins or no tableware at all.

David did not attend. Yafa said he had a prior engagement.

"I'm sure you'll see him soon enough." She passed Peter more pita. Sayid and Samira had fought over the mutabal as much as they fought over samosas, even though Maryam assured them, sternly, that she'd brought more than enough. "I had the impression he was planning to take you out for a private celebration."

Peter didn't correct her. He'd had a lump in his throat all afternoon. The children chased each other and Benji with water balloons; the al-Masri parents sat on the porch swing, talking to Nevaeh and Leslie. Not one of them knew they'd thrown him a going-away party.

The sun set long before the party ended. As stars brightened overhead, Maryam headed for her car. Leslie reluctantly put away the photos of birds she'd seen on her cruise, which she'd been showing to Yafa, and herded Chloe and Jess toward her own car. Sayid yawned his way inside and went to bed. Samira had already fallen asleep in Peter's lap. She gave one loud, grunting snore.

Yafa gave a small smile. "Bedtime, I think."

She reached for her daughter, but Peter said, "I'll take her."

Yafa's smile widened into a yawn. She settled back in the porch swing. Peter carried Samira inside. The Marvel movies still running on mute in the living room cast dim, silvery light over the entryway.

At the top of the stairs, Samira stirred. Her arms hung limply around Peter's neck, but they tightened as she snuggled into him.

"Peter?"

He shifted her in his arms. "Mmm?"

"Love you," she mumbled.

His chest caved. He didn't answer. She had already fallen back asleep.

Only once he'd laid her in bed, tucked her in, and turned on her night-light did he kiss her forehead and whisper, "I love you, too."

LVIII

Nevaeh and Benji offered to drive him home, but he declined. He trudged back alone, drinking in Harrington's Victorians and Craftsman-style homes. The boxwood and creeping juniper in their gardens. The singing of crickets, katydids, and grasshoppers, the strange mechanical buzzing of cicadas.

Free of Eoin's rage, the cemetery air was light and clear. The spirits dozed, worn from weeks of borrowed anger, but they wafted from their headstones as he passed. Faintly minty at first, they flared up warm and yellow when they recognized him.

His chest prickled. He patted each stone as he passed, letting the spirits twist over him, but didn't respond to their many questions.

In the cottage garden, he laid a hand on the wall. The stones radiated warmth like a living thing. Adeline nosed at him before returning to the hydrangeas. Out back, the pullets clucked softly in their sleep. His friends had cared for them during his hospital stay.

He went in but didn't pack his things. Lay in bed but didn't sleep. Linked his hands behind his head and listened to the frogs singing outside and the greenlings whispering inside. If he focused on listening, he almost forgot the cave-in in his chest, the pit in his stomach.

The sky was lightening when he dragged himself out of bed

and started packing things into his steamer trunk. Slowly, the way a casket was lowered into the ground. His books. His candles. His mug.

He paused, half hoping Nevaeh would find him packing and stop him again. But it was barely dawn, and she didn't.

He trailed into the kitchen to clear the icebox of expired food and Samira's pictures. Drawings of the cottage. The cemetery, complete with spirits depicted as scrawls of color. The chickens. Peter alone. Peter holding hands with Samira. Peter in the garden with her and Sayid.

He collected the drawings into a sheaf. The cave-in in his chest felt in danger of collapse, like a single remaining tunnel was about to give way.

Best this way, he told himself, trying to dull the ache in his breast. *Best this way.*

Best for whom? he heard David asking, and suddenly he pictured, for the first time in his life, what it would be like once he left. Not for him; for them. When they didn't see him. When their calls went unanswered. When they found the cottage empty, his things gone.

He added a final picture to the pile with trembling fingers. Peter and Samira in his kitchen, a book open between them.

She'd think he didn't want her.

His heart squeezed. He dropped into a chair and put his head in his hands. The bulbs, past blooming, sleepy now, murmured to him comfortingly from the other chair.

When he looked up again, his eye fell on the photo strip.

He'd hung it beside the handle so he'd see it every time he opened the icebox. Three photographs of him and Samira and David. He and Samira so solemn, while David pulled faces at their side.

He touched his cheek, remembering the feeling of David's lips pressed to it.

He pushed up from the table and walked out of the house.

Mist hung golden and pearly around the headstones, suspended over streets and between houses. Stars winked out in
the pinkish-gold sky. Robins peeped in lawns; blackbirds trilled
overhead. Peter walked until he reached David's house.

He stopped at the bottom of the porch. The overgrown garden
was a riot of color, pink-and-white rose mallow, purple phlox,
yellow and red coreopsis. Moths zigzagged through the plants.

He gazed at the door, swallowed. It should have been easy to
mount the steps and knock.

It should have been, but it was impossible.

A movement in the window caught his attention. David, un-
shaven, in his dressing gown. Peter hoped and dreaded David
might see him, but once David had thrown the curtains open
he turned away. He reappeared a moment later to set the table.

Peter watched him. The way the light gleaming on the table
reflected on his face as he bent over it. The way he set bowl,
plate, mug, silverware, and napkin just so. The path of his hand
through his hair. The sliver of chest where his dressing gown
closed.

He turned away again.

Peter sighed.

The front door opened.

"Peter."

David was half-bent in the doorway to grab the newspaper
on the mat. He straightened slowly and stepped onto the porch,
pulling the door closed.

Peter's heart contracted at the sight of him, at his voice, and
he was on the second step of the porch without realizing he'd
moved. So much want was in him it hurt. So much hope it
seemed impossible this could end any way other than how he
wanted.

Dangerous, he told it. Foolish. But it filled him until he felt
like a hot-air balloon straining against its tether. A mourning
dove called its lament.

"Thought you were leaving," David said flatly.

"I was." Peter took the third step gingerly, as if David were a skittish deer. "I meant to."

"It's what's best." Still flat. "That's what you said."

Peter nodded, his eyes stinging. "It is. Always is."

He was on the porch now, rocking on his heels too close to the steps. David shifted closer.

"Thing is," Peter blurted, "it's always been easy to leave. Find a ghost, send it on, move on myself, to the next place that calls me. It's how I've lived for a hundred years. More. But…"

He closed the distance between them. David's fingers twitched, but he didn't move. They were so close Peter felt the heat of him.

"It ain't what I want."

David's eyes flickered over him. "What do you want?"

Peter's heart thrummed. He cupped David's cheek in his hand. Skimmed that sliver of David's chest with a trembling finger, carefully, like it might break. David shivered. Peter bent until David's breath warmed his skin, until their lips barely brushed together.

"Peter?" David whispered.

The want swelled in Peter's chest until he thought he might shatter.

He kissed David softly on the mouth.

David inhaled sharply and yanked him closer until they fit together, chest to chest, stomach to stomach, thigh to thigh. Peter's fingers curled against his neck and fisted in his hair. He kissed him harder, frantically, and David laughed into his mouth and slipped his arms around Peter's neck and kissed him back. Around them, birds chorused the dawn.

Peter leaned his forehead against David's.

"I want to stay," he whispered. David's arms tightened on his neck. "I want to join Nevaeh for Sunday dinner. I want to show Sayid how to garden. To help Samira with her reading. I want to go to supper with you and take a walk afterward and lose track of time and get home far too late because the stars are so beautiful above us. I want to stay here with you."

His cheeks were wet.

Muscles moved in David's jaw and neck. At last he asked, "Have you eaten?"

Peter shook his head.

David gave him that crooked smile.

"Well, then," he said, "you'd better come in. I'll make us some breakfast."

Peter smiled so hard he wept, took David's outstretched hand, and followed him inside.

The front door closed behind them. The mist lying golden over Harrington burned away in the rising sun; two blocks away, a spirit did the same, leaving the old boarding house silent and empty.

THE END

★ ★ ★ ★ ★

ACKNOWLEDGMENTS

Wouldn't it be cool if acknowledgments in books scrolled like movie credits? They don't, but I hope you'll read them anyway. To (mis)quote Homer Simpson: A lot of people worked really hard on this book, and all they ask is that you memorize their names.

I won't say this book is the book of my heart, because every book I write is the book of my heart. However, *The Keeper of Lonely Spirits* is deeply personal to me in so many different ways, and I'm eternally grateful for the many, many people who helped bring it into the world.

First, my ~~gun rock star~~ agent, Keir Alekseii, whose favorite parts of the manuscript I queried were all my favorite parts and who saw an elderly main character in a fantasy book and went, "Yes, brilliant, we're gonna sell this." *Thank you* doesn't feel adequate, but thank you so much for your support, not only of this book but of my debut and my career. Publishing is an absolutely bonkers industry, but with you in my corner I feel like I can handle whatever it throws at me.

Next, my incredible editor, Dina Davis. From the moment of our first call, I knew you were the right editor for this book. I'm endlessly grateful for your advocacy, and also for the silly conversations we have in the comments of the manuscript.

Beyond agents and editors, so many people work behind the

scenes to bring a book to life. Thank you to all the people at MIRA Books who worked on *Keeper*: Nicole Brebner, Gina Macdonald, Margaret Marbury, Tamara Shifman, and Evan Yeong on the editorial team; Riffat Ali, Randy Chan, Daphne Guima, Puja Lad, Ciara Loader, Ana Luxton, Ashley MacDonald, Pamela Osti, Lindsey Reeder, and Brianna Wodabek in marketing; galleys/cover manager Denise Thomson; the subrights team, Nora Rawn, Reka Rubin, Fiona Smallman, and Christine Tsai; Kamille Carreras Pereira and Heather Connor in publicity; the leadership team, Amy Jones and Loriana Sacilotto; managing editorial, Stephanie Choo and Katie-Lynn Golakovich; audiobook producer Carly Katz; and the entire sales team who worked so hard to get this book on shelves. If I missed anyone in this long list of people, thanks to you, too. I can't say how much I appreciate everyone's hard work on *The Keeper of Lonely Spirits*.

Special thanks to: Gina Macedo, my copy editor, because I have strong opinions about grammar and usage and am convinced I'm hellish for any copy editor to work with; Tamieka Evans for your incredible typesetting work (seriously, I can't overstate how happy MOTHER and DAUGHTER made me); and Erin Craig, Sean Kapitain, and Xuan Loc Xuan for my gorgeous cover. Thanks also to my publicist, Justine Sha; my audiobook narrator, David Sweeney-Bear; and Jasmine Shea Townsend and Sheeba Arif for their thoughtful comments that added so much depth to the characters, their relationships, and the community of Harrington.

Thank you to CJ Connor for taking me on as a mentee during Author Mentor Match, Round 9, and helping me shape *Keeper* into the manuscript that got me an agent. Shout-out to my fellow AMM mentees and other mentors who supported and encouraged me, including fellow mentee Lúnasa Robinson and mentor Esme Symes-Smith.

Long before I had an agent—long before I even thought of applying to AMM—I had friends and fellow authors who kept me going through the writing and revising of this book and all the stories before it. I apologize in advance, because between the amount of time that has passed and the implosion of Twitter, I'm bound to miss some people. If you read an old draft of the book at some point for positivity and/or feedback, thank you.

(If you're named in these acknowledgments because I thought I vaguely remembered sending the book to you, but I remembered wrong or you never got around to reading it: I won't tell if you don't.)

Thank you to my friends and beta readers for this book: Ari, Rhianne Atkins, Monica Bee, Carly Bishop, Alliyah Blakeley, Emma Freylink, Mel Grebing, E.B. Gula, Charlotte Hayward, Michelle J., Tylor Kunkle, K.A. Mielke, Milo, Ceilidh Newbury, Molly O'Sullivan, Morgan Paine, Gates Palissery, Halley D. Roache, Robert, Amber Roberts, Becky Sabetta, Amani Salahudeen, Ysabelle Suarez, Amanda Tong, Ashley Van Elswyk, Petro van Niekerk, and Brittany M. Willows. Thank you to the entire Cool Kids Table.

Special thanks to Astra Crompton and Shayna Lambert for their fantastic fan art and to my friends Chelsea Abdullah, Victoria Alexis, Kamilah Cole, Arianna Emery, Abbey Francis-Williams (aka #1 Peter stan and infinite tear-shedder over all things *The Keeper of Lonely Spirits*), Shoshana Grauer, Ashley Varela, and SJ Whitby for their eternal support. I love you all.

Thank you to Mom, Dad, Lucy, Kate, Matt, and Henry for their love and support now and forever. So many writers can't share their writing with their parents, but my parents read everything I write. (This may make things a tad awkward if I ever publish anything with an on-the-page sex scene, but it's okay, guys, I already have a plan in the unlikely event that it should happen.) My niblings are still too young to have helped write a book in any tangible way, but hey! I like being a tia. And I continue to think it's cool for their names to be in a book, so: Eli, Nate, and Emmy, your names are in this book, too.